Immaculate Midnight

ALSO BY ELLEN HART

The Merchant of Venus
Slice and Dice
Hunting the Witch
Wicked Games
Murder in the Air
Robber's Wine
The Oldest Sin
Faint Praise
A Small Sacrifice
For Every Evil
This Little Piggy Went to Murder
A Killing Cure
Stage Fright
Vital Lies
Hallowed Murder

Immaculate Midnight

ELLEN HART

ST. MARTIN'S MINOTAUR NEW YORK

www.minotaurbooks.com

Library of Congress Cataloging-in-Publication Data

Hart, Ellen.
Immaculate midnight / Ellen Hart.—1st ed.
p. cm.
ISBN 0-312-26676-6
1. Lawless, Jane (Fictitious character)—Fiction. 2. Women detectives—Minnesota—Minneapolis—Fiction. 3. Suicide victims—Family relationships—Fiction. 4. Minneapolis (Minn.)—Fiction. 5. Serial murders—Fiction. 6. Restaurateurs—Fiction. 7. Restaurants—Fiction. 8. Revenge—Fiction. I. Title.

PS3558.A6775 I46 2002
813'.54—dc21

2002017147

First Edition: July 2002

10 9 8 7 6 5 4 3 2 1

For Avery, Dylan, and Mirabel,
with much love

Cast of Characters

Jane Lawless—Owner of the Lyme House Restaurant in Minneapolis. Daughter of Raymond. Sister of Peter.

Cordelia Thorn—Creative director for the Allen Grimby Repertory Theater in St. Paul.

Raymond Lawless—Jane's father. Defense attorney in St. Paul.

Peter Lawless—Cameraman at WTWN-TV in Minneapolis. Jane's brother. Raymond's son. Married to Sigrid.

Sigrid Lawless—Family counselor. Married to Peter.

Elizabeth Piper—Attorney. Works for Raymond Lawless.

Conrad Alto—Music director at Grace Episcopal Cathedral in St. Paul. Organist. Father of Bobby and Henry. Husband of Shirley.

Bobby Alto—Artist. Jeweler. Son of Shirley and Conrad. Brother of Henry.

Taylor Jensen—Bobby's girlfriend.

Dr. Henry Alto—Emergency-room doctor. Son of Shirley and Conrad. Brother of Bobby.

Dr. Shirley Alto—Professor of music. Wife of Conrad. Mother of Bobby and Henry.

Barrett Sweeny—Real estate agent. Friend of the Alto family. Bobby's best friend.

Joe Vasquez—Waiter at the Lyme House.

I have ceased to question stars and books;
I have begun to listen to the teachings my blood whispers to me.

—Herman Hesse,
Demian

"How about a little fire, Scarecrow?"

—The Wicked Witch
in
The Wizard of Oz

Immaculate Midnight

Prologue

Summer, 1996

He stood motionless in the woods behind the house and watched the flickering glow coming from the bedroom window. It was just after midnight. The witching hour. The time when laws blurred and rules shifted. Out in the boonies, this far from the main road, the nearest neighbor was a good half-mile away. He'd chosen the house because of its remoteness. His preparation was, as always, precise. He'd come to appreciate that fire was a necessary cleansing. The desire to surrender to its magic, to its chaos and gloriously destructive power, was a pure, primeval urge.

It had started as an accident. A bit of cigarette ash dropped carelessly on the bed sheets after sex. The cigarette was a cliché, of course. What happened next wasn't. He should have smothered the fire immediately, should have dragged his drunken partner to safety, but instead he just sat there, mesmerized by the tiny glowing specks as they crept slowly across the cotton blankets, smoldering at first, almost going out. When the pillow case finally caught, it was all over. Fireplay was edgeplay, he'd later read in a magazine. Injury or death could result.

He'd stayed too long that first night. Nearly got himself killed. He'd escaped the house choking on the smoke, gasping for air.

He should have felt guilty, or terrified, or both. He should have called 911 on his cell phone, but instead he got in his car and left. The next day, the desire to repeat the incident was so overwhelming that he found himself unable to concentrate on anything else. He went home that night and built a bonfire in his Webber grill. He stood in the dark, as he did now, and watched the glow turn to flame. But it was too controlled, too small. Nothing was at stake. In the end, he saw it as a lesson, a way to understand himself more fully. He would succumb to this new, illicit need. He had no choice.

That's when he took on a new persona, calling himself Hyde. It had started as a joke, but ended as an omen. He merely wanted to appropriate a name that sounded dangerous. Mr. Hyde. Lieutenant Hyde. Sometimes Pastor Hyde. It didn't matter, of course, because it was simply the cloak of anonymity he used when he needed it. People even poked fun at him. If he was Hyde, where was Dr. Jekyll? Next came the big belly laughs, the slaps on the back. Hyde was always polite. He laughed right along with them.

But he wasn't laughing now. Every cell in his body was enraptured by the sight of the burning house. The flames were rising, seducing, devouring, traveling up the walls, bursting through the roof vents, caressing the shingles with hungry, grasping fingers. The darkness had turned dangerous and bright. Even this far away, he could feel the growing inferno as it pressed hot and raw against his skin. The house creaked under the weight of falling beams. It was glorious. Purifying. A living, breathing, all-devouring beast that owed its life to *him.*

1
The Present

The last rays of cold February sunlight stretched across the concrete steps as Raymond Lawless entered the doors of Stillwater State Prison. Built in 1914, the institution was designed by a man noted for a lingering fondness for Gothic and Romanesque architecture. While impressive and innovative for its day, the sight of it never failed to depress him. Ray knew the stink of prisons well. He'd been a defense attorney in St. Paul for almost thirty years.

The massive wall surrounding the prison was in terrible shape. Parts of it were so severely decayed that chunks of masonry weighing as much as half a ton had broken off. To Ray, it felt like a boil waiting to burst. He'd overheard a prison guard once say that there were enough nicks in the wall that, if somebody athletic tried hard enough, he could probably scale it.

As the metal gate clanged shut behind him, Ray felt a wave of fatigue wash over him. He followed the guard down the long corridor to his client's cell, a young man named Bobby Alto. Ray had first met Conrad Alto, Bobby's father, the day before his son was to be arraigned on murder and arson charges. Earlier that day, Conrad had come to Ray's office and explained—in a confidential, earnest voice—that his son had been wrongfully accused. He wanted Ray to take the case. He made it clear that money was no object. His son's welfare was the only issue that mattered to him.

Just like everyone else in the Twin Cities, Ray had been reading about the Midnight Man homicides in the papers for months. Because of his personal contacts in the law-enforcement community, he was privy to certain details of the case that hadn't been made public. For one thing, he knew that the police were about to make an arrest. He had no idea, however, that the Midnight Man's defense would land in his lap.

After taking on the case, Ray learned that early in 1998, Bill Younger, a sergeant who worked arson for the Anoka police department, had begun to notice a pattern. That year, two women, one in Anoka and one in Champlin, had burned to death in their homes. Both deaths had been attributed to smoking in bed. In reviewing the fire investigator's reports, Younger observed several similarities. First, both fires started close to midnight. Both the women were single and lived alone. And they'd both been drinking. But one small item caught his attention. Both of the women had been wearing a round pendant, about the size of a quarter. After checking further, Younger discovered that the pendants were identical, the figure represented on them as bizarre as it was beautiful. It was a bird of prey—a hawk, or a falcon—struggling to free itself from an egg. All around it were stars and near the top of the circle, a crescent moon. Since the pendants appeared to be hand cast in platinum, they hadn't completely burned in the fires.

When Younger checked with the families of the victims he found that nobody had ever seen the women wearing the pendants before the fire, but no one could be positive that the women hadn't bought the pendants prior to their deaths. For Younger, the presence of the jewelry pointed to one thing and one thing only: serial homicide.

After several weeks of intense investigation, Younger was able to nail down two more house fires, both in the metro area, in which the victims—again, single women living alone—had died right around midnight with the same pendant around their necks. One of the deaths had occurred in 1996, the other in 1997. A significant pattern was beginning to emerge.

In the spring of 1999, the last house was torched. Again, all the markers were there. But this time, Younger saw his chance. He had the lab run a tox screen on the victim's blood and found that, in addition to alcohol, the woman had ingested a substance called Rohypnol, a drug similar to Valium, but many times stronger. While illegal in America, Rohypnol—or "roofies," as it was called on the street—was easily obtained in Mexico, Europe and South America. Rohypnol produced symptoms similar to intoxication. It was often called the date-rape drug because it also impaired judgment and caused a loss of inhibitions. Sedation usually occurred within twenty to thirty minutes. When the fire started, the women were probably out cold. Younger was positive now that he was looking for both a serial arsonist and a murderer.

The case against Bobby Alto was developed over the next seven months. Bobby owned an art gallery/jewelry shop in Frogtown, a down-and-out section of St. Paul just west of the Capitol. He made all of the jewelry himself. From the display cases, Younger saw that the young man liked to cast precious metals, often with religious or mystical themes. The similarity in design to the bird pendant was unmistakable.

After interviewing a possible witness to the 1999 fire, Younger began to put it all together. One thing led to another and he was eventually able to get a search warrant for Bobby's house. Under a floorboard in the bedroom, he found a red velvet bag that contained two platinum pendants, both identical to those found on the victims. Combining this with the other information he'd turned up—and the fact that Bobby had no alibi for the night in question—Younger felt he had his man.

When Ray took on the case, he thought they had a good chance to beat the charges. The evidence was all circumstantial, though some of it was tricky. He discussed a plea bargain with Bobby and his family right up front, but Bobby remained adamant. He had nothing to do with the murders. He was innocent. He expressed a childlike faith that the jury would see that and set him free.

Over the course of his career, Ray had been accused of trying too many cases—cases that some said he should have settled out of court. But that decision was his client's. And anyway, good trial lawyers didn't always make good negotiators. If Bobby had wanted to plea bargain, Ray would have given it to one of his associates. At sixty-four, he only took the cases that interested him. If the prosecution saw Raymond Lawless coming, they knew they were in for a fight.

Ray readily agreed that most of his clients were guilty. He also knew that there was no correlation between a client's guilt or innocence and whether that client did time or got off. He assumed that the general public, if they thought about it at all, considered a defense attorney's job innately sleazy. Sleaze defending sleaze. But Ray disagreed. He took each case as a challenge, as one of the most sacred obligations of his profession. Nobody liked a defense lawyer—until they needed one.

In the end, the jury had convicted Bobby Alto of the murders of Amber Larson in 1999 and Sharon Dehkes in 1998. He had received two life sentences to be served concurrently without the possibility of parole.

The appeal began in the fall of 2000. The year before, Ray had brought a new appellate lawyer into his practice. Elizabeth Piper would research and write the briefs for Bobby's appeal, and eventually do the oral argument before the state supreme court. Ray expected a verdict within the year, but the process had dragged on. The longest he'd ever seen the court take to render a decision was sixteen months. He felt the appeal Elizabeth had put together was one of the strongest he'd ever seen. But sixteen months had come and gone, and still no verdict. Not until late this afternoon.

Ray waited silently as the guard unlocked Bobby's cell.

Through the bars, he could see the young man lying on his bed. So much of Bobby had disappeared during his years of incarceration. His body had grown thin. His dark brown hair, once worn loose and shaggy, was shaved short. More significantly, his face had aged and his eyes had lost their innocence. They had "the fear" in them now. Eventually, all prisoners succumbed to that fear. The eyes were the hardest part for Ray. Human beings were soft fruit. Four years in prison had changed Bobby forever. But as Ray had grown older, he'd also grown more fatalistic. Deep in his soul, he believed Bobby was guilty. He had from the very beginning.

"What's up?" asked Bobby, rising to meet him. He looked expectant, anxious.

Ray nodded to the bed and they both sat down. "The Minnesota Supreme Court ruled on your case today."

"And?" There was still a glimmer of hope in his eyes.

"I'm sorry. I thought we had a chance, but they refused to overturn the lower court's decision."

Bobby's face froze. Lowering his head, he looked away.

Ray gave him a few seconds to absorb the news.

Finally, in a faint, toneless voice, Bobby said, "The end of the line, huh? Have you told my parents?"

"I drove out to your dad's house before I came here."

"How'd he take it?"

Ray didn't want to get into it. The fact was, Conrad Alto had spent the better part of an hour railing at the justice system, the judge, the jury, and finally at Ray himself. He'd called him incompetent. Lazy. Too old to know what he was doing. His anger was white hot and he let fly with burst after burst of vitriol. Ray figured he owed him a few minutes of abuse, but he left when Conrad threatened him with a malpractice suit. "I'm sure he'll be out to visit you tomorrow."

"In other words, he was pretty upset."

Ray nodded. "Your dad said he'd talk to your mother. And

he'll speak with your brother Henry, too, as well as your sister in Fargo."

"What about Barrett? Somebody's got to tell him." He seemed to grow agitated.

Barrett Sweeny was Bobby's best friend.

"I'm sure your father will give him a call."

"I need to talk to him. Call Barrett and tell him to come out here right away. Okay? Right away."

"I will," said Ray. "Is there anything else I can do?"

He shook his head. "No more appeals, right?"

"We took it to the highest court available to us. As I explained before, since there are no constitutional issues—"

Bobby cut him off. "God, I could use a cigarette." He got up with all the energy of an old man and walked to the bars, grasping them with both hands, then leaning his forehead against the cold metal.

"Are you going to be okay?" asked Ray. "Would you like to talk to someone? The chaplain? A family minister?"

Again the young man shook his head. "Just Barrett."

"I'm truly sorry, Bobby. I'd hoped for a better outcome."

"I knew this might happen, but . . . it's hard to let go of hope." With his hands still gripping the bars, he continued, "Did you ever dream that you were flying, Ray? High up in the sky, looking down on trees and fields. I did. All the time. And not just when I was asleep. It was like . . . like I was linked to this incredible power, the root of *all* power. But it frightened me. It still does. I think it's about time I take off my wings and learn to walk."

Ray wasn't sure what he was talking about, but he knew Bobby wasn't asking for his thoughts on the matter. Ray also didn't buy all the psychological claptrap that passed for criminal science these days, but perhaps Bobby was the exception that proved the rule: a truly thoughtful, seemingly gentle young man who was, in reality, a cold-blooded murderer. Ray sat and watched the young man's back. He'd never apologized to a client before, but for some reason, he had the urge to apologize to Bobby now.

When the young man finally turned around, Ray could see tears in his eyes.

"Thanks for coming, Mr. Lawless. I appreciate your time, but I'd like to be alone now."

One Week Later

It was Friday night at the Lyme House. The usual gang rush of customers had arrived and the kitchen was a madhouse, as hot and sticky as a summer afternoon in August. Waiters were shouting, their voices rising with impatience. "Table of six. Table of eight. Ordering! How long for the Yorkshire?" Two-foot-high flames leapt from sauté pans. The grill was piled high with chops, steaks, fish filets, and tonight's special: Copper River salmon. Jane had spent the evening expediting the relentless crush of orders. Her normal expediter had to take over the sauté station because her evening sous chef was in the hospital with a herniated disk.

Such was the life of a restaurateur. By ten, the worst of it was over. On the way to the downstairs pub, Jane checked the reservation book. The dining room was full up tomorrow night too. Business was good. She wished she could take credit for the recent run, but the truth was, she'd missed a great deal of work in the past few months. She'd been assaulted in her home in late October, sending her to the hospital in a coma. In many ways, she was still recovering.

On a recent Christmas visit to Connecticut, she'd finally put it all together: She wasn't going quietly crazy, as she'd thought, but instead she was suffering from posttraumatic stress. She'd resisted the label at first. She hated anything that smacked of victim status. But when she returned to Minneapolis after Christmas week, she'd seen a counselor who had confirmed the diagnosis. That had been six weeks ago. Even though her problems hadn't disappeared, the therapist had helped her regain some of her equilibrium. It would take time, but Jane was hopeful that she would recover completely.

Trotting down the stairs to the pub, Jane stood behind the bar and checked the liquor stock, clipboard in hand. As she bent over to pick up a swizzle stick off the floor, one of the waiters approached and handed her an envelope.

"What's this?" she asked, straightening up and taking it from him.

"Somebody left it on the reception desk. It's got your name on it, so Arlene told me to bring it down."

Arlene was the assistant manager. "Thanks, Jerry." She pushed it under the clip. "Hey, will you tell Arlene to get someone in the bathrooms right away? We've had a heavy night. I assume they need some touch-up."

"Right, chief," he said, smiling. "Anything else?"

"You should probably get yourself a clean vest." She pointed to a stain on the brown tweed. A clean waitstaff and a clean restaurant were of paramount importance. Jane wouldn't eat in a restaurant that looked dirty. If the management couldn't keep the waiters looking good—or the windows, the carpet, or the bathrooms, which were all relatively easy—how could they run a sanitary kitchen, which was enormously difficult?

After finishing up behind the bar, Jane pulled herself a pint of ale, then headed down the back hall to her office. The door was standing open, which wasn't the way she'd left it. Flipping on the light next to her computer, she looked around. Nothing seemed out of place, although there was a faint smell of unfamiliar perfume in the air. Had one of her customers wandered in by mistake? Her father, a defense attorney in St. Paul, encouraged her to lock her office when she wasn't using it. She did—sometimes—but most of the time she didn't see the need. Her dad saw ghouls and goblins around every corner. It was one of the hazards of his profession.

Jane set the clipboard and the pint on the desk. Relaxing into her leather chair, she pulled out her bottom desk drawer, leaned back, then propped her feet up on it and closed her eyes. She was exhausted. Her day had started at seven with a visit to the Uptown Y. By eight she was at the restaurant, talking to Chiswick Cottage Brewery, a microbrewer in Canada, about starting a line of Lyme House beers. It was her newest obsession—not that she was obsessive. She wanted to develop a truly English-style draft beer. American lagers were refreshing, but served icy cold, they were often pretty tasteless and undemanding. The reason English beer was served at 52 degrees—not warm, but cool—was because at that temperature, the flavor of the beer came through.

Beer had a long history in the British Isles. Since Jane's mother had been English, and Jane had lived in England until she was nine—and then again for several years in her early teens—English food and drink had always interested her. Contrary to public opinion, English chefs had brought much to the world of international cuisine. In the case of beer, pub patrons had been enjoying unrefrigerated beer since the days of Chaucer's Canterbury pilgrims. Jane was hoping to design a series of monthly specials, beers only available at the Lyme Public House. She had a treacly Christmas Ale in mind, something spiced with licorice and cinnamon. A few other strong, warming, wintry ales would be good. Beer went especially well with pub food—curries, roasts, stews, bangers and mash, hearty peasant breads served with English and local cheeses. Summer beers would be lighter, more fragrant and quenching, but also more complex than an American lager.

Taking a sip of ale, Jane pushed the bottom drawer shut with her foot, then raked a hand through her hair. She was still getting used to the short look, as her father called it. She'd cut her long chestnut hair short right before she'd left for Connecticut. She didn't feel like the same old Jane inside, so she decided it would be a good time to alter the outside as well. She'd worn her hair long for so many years that cutting it felt like cutting off a vital part of her body. But at forty-two, she needed a change. Some of the more recent changes in her life—like the continued weakness in her left leg due to the head injury—hadn't been positive. She'd also lost a lot of weight. Too much, her father said, although her occasional girlfriend, Patricia Kastner, wasn't complaining.

Before Jane started on some paperwork, she decided to take off her white chef's coat and gray checked slacks and change back into her jeans and sweater. She should probably shower first. When she'd built the Lyme House, back in the eighties, she'd had the architect design her office so that it was a small home away from home, complete with bathroom and shower, small closet, and a couch and small fireplace. In the early days, when she was trying to get her restaurant off the ground, she often worked so late that she'd end up spending the night. Before her Christmas trip to Connecticut, she'd slept many nights on her office couch. It was just easier than going home to an empty house.

As she was about to go clean up, her private line rang. Hooking the receiver between her shoulder and her ear, she said, "This is Jane."

The voice on the other end was just short of stentorian. "Do *you* think I'm self-absorbed?"

Jane shook her head and laughed. It was Cordelia, her oldest and dearest friend.

Cordelia Thorn was a local celebrity—the creative director at the Allen Grimby Repertory Theater—otherwise known as the AGRP. The entire world had become an acronym.

"Evening, Cordelia. Where are you?" Jane could hear a buzz of conversation in the background.

"I'm at the Maxfield having a drink with some friends. At least, I thought they were friends. Now I'm beginning to wonder."

"Somebody called you self-absorbed?"

"Me! The original earth mother! If a sparrow falls, I weep."

Cordelia was—to be diplomatic—operatic in her approach to life.

"Well?"

"Well what?"

"Settle the argument. Tell these Freudian wannabes I am *not* self-absorbed."

The envelope under the clipboard finally caught Jane's attention. She sliced through the top with a letter opener, removed a folded page and flattened it against her desk. At the top someone had written *Number One.*

"Jane? Are you there?"

"I'm here. Say, Cordelia—"

"Don't change the subject. Am I, or am I *not*, self-absorbed?"

"You know about tarot cards, don't you? You have people do readings for you, right?"

"In my self-absorbed way, the answer is yes. I'm interested in *all* aspects of myself. Why?"

"Someone just sent me a copy of a tarot card." She turned the envelope over. Her name was printed in bold red ink on the front.

"Just *one* card?"

"It's a color copy."

"Which card?"

"Justice. Except, it's upside down. Under it someone's written 'Justice (Reversed).' "

Cordelia's voice grew more intimate. "Creepy."

"Why do you say that?"

"The card—what does it look like?"

"There's a blond woman in red robes—she almost looks like a queen or an empress—sitting on a throne between two pillars. In one hand she's holding a sword, in the other a balance, like you see on courthouses."

"Themis."

"Excuse me?

"That's her Greek name. Her Roman name is Justitia. It sounds like the Universal Waite tarot. There are lots of different decks."

"What's it mean?"

"Well, like it says, Justice. But not in the legal sense. More in the pure metaphysical sense. Except, since it's reversed, it means the opposite. Injustice."

"Why would someone send it to me?"

"There's no return address?

"None."

"Served any bad shellfish lately?"

"Very funny."

Cordelia paused, her hand muffling the receiver. When she came back on the line, she was laughing. "One of my ex-friends is insisting that I'm ignoring them. Another indication of my perennial self-absorbtion. Why don't you stop by the theater tomorrow afternoon and we'll discuss the tarot thing in more detail. Who knows, by then you may have more to talk about."

"What's that supposed to mean?"

"Maybe another card will drop from the sky."

3

Raymond Lawless leaned back in his chair and stretched his arms high over his head. For the past couple of hours, he'd been composing the closing argument for a rape case that would go to the jury next week. Right now, he needed a break. A cup of coffee. A short walk. Anything to relax his brain cells for a few minutes.

Ray's law practice was located in a renovated 1890s rowhouse across the street from the St. Paul Cathedral—a prime location. A similar brownstone, one where F. Scott Fitzgerald had lived back in the 1920s, was just a short distance away. Ray liked the historic feel of downtown St. Paul. He thought it had a far richer character—and much more class—than downtown Minneapolis, though he wasn't snobbish. He crossed the river whenever necessary to try his cases.

It was Saturday morning. Sun flooded his office through a circular window in back of his desk. Normally he didn't work on Saturdays anymore, but his wife, Marilyn, was in New Orleans taking care of her sick father, so Ray was on his own for the next few weeks. Ray and Marilyn had been married for less than a year, though they'd lived together for over eleven.

His first wife, Helen, the mother of his daughter, Jane, and his son, Peter, had died shortly after Jane's thirteenth birthday. From the moment they first met, Ray knew he was in love with Helen and would ask her to marry him. His relationship with Marilyn was somewhat different. Oh, he cared about her, no doubt about that. But it was a love based more on shared companionship than passion. So many of his friends and contemporaries were divorced these days, out trying to impress the world with the accoutrements of the good life. Cars. Houses. Boats. And if not trophy wives, then young trophy women were on their arms. But Ray knew the score. These were deeply lonely men. A lot could be said for companionship, especially at his age and stage of life.

That was the working theory. In practice, Ray couldn't help but feel that something was missing from his life. He hadn't noticed it so much when he'd been working his usual seventy-hour weeks, but in the last year he'd begun to slow down. That's when he started to become aware of the restlessness. He hated himself for it.

Ray looked up from his desk when he heard a soft knock on the door. "Come in," he called.

Elizabeth Piper, his new partner, poked her head inside the door. "What are you doing here? Shouldn't you be home watching a football game?"

"Football season is over, Elizabeth."

"Basketball then. Or hockey. I'm allergic to all games with balls or pucks. My first husband used to commandeer the living room and the kitchen every Sunday afternoon. I was banished to the malls."

"*Banished to the Malls: The Autobiography of Elizabeth Piper.* Are you here to commiserate?"

"Hell no. I got rid of Mr. Sportsman years ago." She held up a sack. "Interested in taking a break?"

He grinned. "I rarely turn down food."

As she made herself comfortable on the couch, Ray poured them each a mug of coffee from the pot he always kept brewing on a small table in the corner of the room. "What have you got there?"

"Blueberry muffins."

"My favorite."

Elizabeth was in her late fifties, a slim, attractive woman with long blond hair she usually kept pinned up during office hours. Today, her hair was down around her shoulders, looking soft and golden in the morning light. She had a spunky, natural quality that impressed both juries and judges. It had impressed Ray too. Today she was dressed informally: khaki slacks and scoop-necked cashmere sweater.

Ray realized he was staring at her when she glanced down at her clothing and said, "Is something wrong?"

"No, no," he said smiling, handing her one of the mugs. He took a chair across from her.

Elizabeth still wore her diamond wedding ring, though her second husband had died many years ago. As far as Ray knew, she lived alone and didn't date—at least she'd never mentioned anyone special. Not that he had any particular interest in her personal life. She did have a daughter that she talked about occasionally, but she lived in California, so Ray had never met her.

"How's everything going on the Skopelund appeal?"

"Slow," said Elizabeth, breaking off a piece of her muffin. "I should have the brief done by the end of the month, barring complications, of course."

Ray took a deep breath and let it out slowly.

"Something wrong?"

"Oh, I don't know." He wasn't sure he wanted to get into it. "Do you ever just get weary of it all? Of all the wrangling?"

"I never used to. I love what I do. It's a free-for-all and I like winning."

"But?"

"Sure. Sometimes. Especially when I lose, like the Alto case. I still think that kid's innocent."

Ray's assessment of Bobby's innocence was far less certain, but he let it pass. "Maybe what I'm feeling is payback for all the pieces of shit I helped put back on the streets."

"It's all part of the deal. You're a big boy, Ray. You know that. So what's really bothering you?"

They rarely spoke of personal matters, though in the past few weeks, they'd been approaching it. It was a growing friendship, Ray assumed. For some reason, the idea depressed him.

"My wife's out of town."

"And you miss her."

"I suppose that's it."

"Maybe I should take you out to dinner tonight. Get your mind off your troubles."

The thought instantly lightened his mood. "Dinner?"

"Sure. Why not? You have to eat. I have to eat. We might as well do it together."

"You're positive you're up for spending time with an old grump like me?"

She flicked her eyes to his, then looked back down at her muffin. "That's hardly the way I'd describe you."

Ray turned at the sound of another knock on the door. This time it was his daughter, Jane.

"Hey, honey," he said, getting up to greet her. He gave her a hug, then nodded to Elizabeth. "We were just having some coffee. Why don't you join us?"

Jane's smile looked a little frozen around the edges.

"It's pretty cold out there today," said Ray, pouring her a cup without asking. He knew she needed something hot to warm her up.

Taking the mug, Jane wrapped her fingers around it gratefully and took a sip. "Thanks. I'm sorry if I'm interrupting—"

"Not at all," said Ray. He was always glad to see his daughter. She was so busy with her own life, he never felt they got together enough. "What brings you by?"

"I was on my way to see Cordelia at the theater. When I drove past the brownstone, I noticed your car out front, so I thought I'd come up and say hi."

"I think that's my cue to get back to work," said Elizabeth, rising from the couch.

Ray was torn. "Look, if you meant that about dinner—"

"Consider it done. I'll make reservations for us at seven. How does W. A. Frost and Company sound?"

"Too bad it's not a nicer night. We could walk. Cathedral Hill isn't far. And it's so beautiful in the spring."

"Spring is another month away," said Elizabeth, on her way out the door. "Good to see you, Jane."

Ray stood looking after her. When he turned to face his daughter, he had to change gears quickly, but he was an old hand at that. Seeing Jane standing by the coffee pot, nibbling a muffin, her bearing so serious and erect, he couldn't help but smile. She was the spitting image of his first wife, Helen. "You look so much like your mother," he said, slipping an arm around her shoulders and walking her over to his desk. "Especially now, with your hair short." He kissed her again, then sat down in his chair.

Before Jane took a seat, she touched a sheet of paper lying under a paperweight on his desk. "Where did you get this?"

He glanced at it, then shrugged. "It came in the mail today. Looks like a copy of a tarot card."

She picked it up. "It says *Number Two* at the top."

He nodded. "I get crazy correspondence all the time. I don't know why I didn't just throw it away."

"You have no idea who sent it or why?"

"None. Here." He reached his hand to take it from her. "Just give it to me and I'll toss it."

"Can I have it?" she asked, turning it over to look at the back.

It seemed an odd request. Ray had a sense that she wanted to talk to him about it, but he didn't feel like discussing his crackpot mail just now, especially when he hadn't seen her in several weeks. He changed the subject. "How's Peter doing?"

"As good as can be expected under the circumstances," said

Jane. She relaxed into a chair and crossed her legs.

Peter's marriage had hit a rocky patch. Just before Christmas, he and his wife, Sigrid, had separated. Ray and Marilyn had been away at the time so they didn't find out about it until they returned home. Peter hadn't confided many details about the split, other than to say that he and Sigrid had reached an impasse. He desperately wanted to have a child—and she didn't. A middle ground didn't seem to exist. One of them had to give or the marriage was over.

Ray understood Peter's reticence to talk about it. His son wasn't the kind of man to take failure in stride. He still hoped matters could be worked out. But the truth was, both of his kids were stubborn to a fault.

"Is he still staying at your house?"

"I'm glad to have him," said Jane. "Now that Bean's gone, living there alone kind of bothers me."

"I'm so sorry you lost the little guy. How old was he?"

"Fifteen."

"I miss him, too, sweetheart. He was such a funny little dog."

Jane's gaze traveled to the window, then back to her coffee mug. "That counselor I saw in January thought I should move. Sell the house and find another, one that would be free of the memories of the attack."

"Are you seriously thinking about that?" It was the first he'd heard of it.

"I'm not sure. I mean, it was the house Christine and I bought together. My memories of her will never die, but sometimes I think selling it would feel like severing the one tangible link I still have to her."

"Did you explain all that to the counselor?"

Jane took a sip of coffee, then held the warm mug against her cheek. "We talked about Christine a little. She knew we were together for ten years and that Chris died of cancer. She also thought I mixed up my feelings about her loss with Mom's death. I don't know. Maybe I do."

"I'm glad you saw a professional, even if it was only a few times," said Ray, pushing his coffee mug away. "It helps to talk to someone other than a friend or family member. By the way, honey, Marilyn's out of town."

"Is it her father?"

"He's taken a turn for the worse. She may be away for quite some time. What say we get together for dinner one night soon?"

"I'd love to. I'll check my schedule at the restaurant and get back to you." She hesitated. "Say, Dad? Actually, one of the reasons I stopped this morning was to talk about your first wedding anniversary. It's coming up soon. Peter and I would like to throw you and Marilyn a party, invite all your friends. Make a real celebration of it. What do you say?"

Before Ray could answer, Elizabeth burst into the room, her coat tossed over her shoulders and her car keys in her hand. "I just got a call from Harlan Kreiger at Stillwater State Prison. Bobby Alto was knifed in a fight this morning."

"Is he all right?"

"He's dead. A guard found him."

"Oh, God. Have they contacted his family?"

"I guess there was a mad scramble to figure out what had happened. Harlan said they haven't called anybody yet. He thought we might want to take care of it."

"We can't give his family news like that over the phone."

"I know. I'll drive over to his brother's place. You take his father. They can inform the rest of the family."

"Okay." After his last run-in with Conrad Alto, Ray would have preferred to talk to Henry, but he didn't argue the point.

"They've taken Bobby's body to the morgue. After the autopsy, he'll be released. Harlan said there was a team from a local TV station out at the prison this morning to film some reading program for convicts. They got wind of what happened and started asking questions. I think Harlan's afraid someone will break the story on the news before the family gets word."

"That can't happen."

“It can, depending on which station was there.”

Ray shot out of his chair. “Sorry, Jane, but I’ve got to run. I’ll talk to you later, okay?”

“Sure,” she said, looking a little dazed at all the commotion around her.

Ray grabbed his coat and followed Elizabeth out the door.

After leaving her father's law office, Jane drove to the theater. She found Cordelia standing at the edge of the main stage, hands on her hips, studying the set. On such a cold February day, the yellow angora sweater she wore made her look like a sunflower.

The set was new. Thanks to Cordelia and the comps she so liberally supplied, Jane kept current on all the plays at the Allen Grimby. She loved the theater. Way back in high school, it had been an interest she and Cordelia had both shared, one of the reasons they became friends.

The walls of the new set were a deep blue, the doors a fire-house red, and the floors a glossy black. The furniture was Oriental. Long, tinted mirrors had been randomly placed throughout the set, creating a space that seemed both ghostly and oddly raucous.

"It's . . . unsettling," said Jane, moving slowly down the center aisle. "What's it for?"

Cordelia turned around, motioning her up the side stairs. "*Tao House*. The new play I'm directing by Hugo Weller. We're previewing it tonight."

"What's the play about?"

"I told you already, don't you remember? Tao House was Carlotta and Eugene O'Neill's home and refuge when he was writing his last plays."

"Oh, right. I remember now." Jane didn't really. Her concentration lately hadn't been the greatest.

"O'Neill was interested in Eastern thought, as am I," said Cordelia, walking over to a long, low couch. "And Carlotta was fascinated by Oriental art. Hence, the stage design." She swept her hand to the set as if she'd hammered the nails herself. "They were a private couple, but not entirely reclusive. The play takes place during a visit from two old friends, another long-time married couple. It's very dark, very textured. Weller chose the Grimby for the play's maiden voyage. And he wanted me to direct."

Jane could see not only pleasure but pride in Cordelia's expression. "Feel pretty smug about that, do you?"

"Yes, in my self-absorbed way, I do." She sauntered up to one of the mirrors. Standing in front of it, she drew the tips of her fingers through her long auburn hair, ruffling it slightly. She gazed at herself a moment longer, then said, "They say we have the face God gave us until the age of forty. After that, we have the face we make for ourselves. Not bad," she said, running her little finger across her perfectly curved eyebrow.

Cordelia was a large woman. Six feet tall. Large voice. Large opinions. Large personality. She hit the scales at well over two hundred pounds. Through the years, Jane had heard people refer to her as a "freakin' battleship," an "earthmother with delusions of grandeur," and a "ball-busting bitch." Others saw her—more kindly—as Rubenesque. Everyone could agree, however, that she was a knockout. Creamy olive skin. Exotic brown eyes. And curves that wouldn't quit. Sure, she was a little . . . forceful at times. Even obnoxious. But Jane took it all in stride. In a world of change, Cordelia remained a constant.

Turning from the mirror, Cordelia said, "So, let's get down to business. Did you bring the copy of the tarot card with you?"

Jane tapped the pocket of her leather jacket. "Right here. And you were right."

"Ah." Cordelia rubbed her hands together eagerly. "A second card?"

"Arrived at my father's office this morning. It says 'number two' at the top, so it's obviously a progression. I was thinking about it on the way over here. Somebody's probably just playing games. Dad said he gets a lot of crazy mail, so he's used to it."

"But you're not. What's the new card?"

"The Tower."

Cordelia flinched. "Come on," she said, exiting stage left.

They took the freight elevator up to the third floor.

Once they were alone in Cordelia's newly redecorated third-floor office, Cordelia nodded to a half dozen books piled on the floor next to her chair. "I brought these with me this morning. I thought they might help. Now, show me the papers."

Jane handed them over. Looking at Cordelia's extra-high, extra-large desk, she couldn't help but laugh. The old one had been replaced by a modern brushed-nickel and gold extravaganza. It looked more like a throne than a flat surface on which to work. As soon as she sat down in one of the new chintz-covered chairs, she realized that she was a good six inches lower than Cordelia. Cheap tricks. Cordelia didn't want to converse, she wanted to *preside*.

After examining the pages in minute detail, knuckles resting on the desktop, Cordelia reflected for a few seconds, then sat down. "My guess is, this is a spread, or the beginnings of one."

"What's a spread?"

"It's a pattern in which the position of each card carries a special meaning. There are lot's of them."

Jane was impressed.

"I am a mystic, Janey. This is right up my alley."

"How do we tell which spread it is?"

"Beats me."

"But you said—"

"It's complicated, Janey. It's not like a fortune cookie."

Jane was completely out of her depth. She had no interest in the tarot, and no knowledge of how it worked. "Do you do your own tarot readings?"

"Heavens, no. I have a reader. She's very tuned in to me."

"That's nice."

"You needn't take that tone. There are lots of highly educated people who swear by the tarot." She crossed her arms defiantly. "You're too practical, Jane. You need more magic in your soul."

"I'll work on it."

"I've done a few tarot readings for friends. But I'd never read for myself. In my opinion, that would be like a doctor treating herself."

Jane nodded. Anything she said right now would only be annoying. "So, just between you and me, give it your best shot. What do you think the two cards mean?"

Cordelia set the pages side by side. She leaned back in her chair, pressed her fingers against her temples and closed her eyes. After a long moment, she rocked forward, bending low over the desk and glancing sideways at the pages. Next, she flattened her hands on the paper and stared straight ahead.

Jane was growing tired of the theatrics when Cordelia finally said: "Your father received the second one, huh?"

"This morning."

"I get nothing. No vibrations."

"The pages vibrate?"

Cordelia gave her an impatient look. "Let's take them individually." Picking up one of the books, she flipped through to the back. "Okay, here's what it says about Justice. First, it's a very powerful card, and it comes at the center of the Fool's Journey." As an aside, she added, "Some people see the tarot as the journey of an everyman—or everywoman—called the Fool. If the shoe fits—" She flashed Jane a grin. "The theme of the card is justice. Reversed, the card means injustice."

"You already told me that."

"So sue me."

"Look, I fired a waiter last week. Was that an injustice? I don't think so, but I'll bet he does. And I lost my temper with one of our fruit vendors yesterday afternoon. If I don't get the freshest, best produce available, I can't maintain quality. I will *not* be ripped off. I made it crystal clear what he could do with those boxes of garbage. Was that injustice?"

"Calm down."

"It just pisses me off. We've worked with these people for ten years. *Ten* years."

"Okay. But I doubt a fruit vendor sent the pages. What about more personal stuff?"

"Like what?"

"New girlfriends?" Cordelia wiggled her eyebrows expectantly.

"Stop fishing. I'm still dating Patricia Kastner."

Cordelia's eager expression deflated. "Okay, then. Maybe it's her. She sent them."

"Don't be ridiculous. Why would she do that?"

"Because she's a psycho. *Duh*."

"There's nothing there, Cordelia. Drop it. As far as the rest of my personal life, it's all pretty boring. I work. I eat. I sleep. And I'm being a good Samaritan. Peter's staying at my house until he and Sigrid can figure out what to do with their marriage."

"Maybe Sigrid thinks you're facilitating their breakup."

"She knows how sorry I am about everything—and how much I hope they can work it out. Besides, Sigrid is extremely direct. If she had an issue with me, she'd come talk to me, face to face. She wouldn't send a copy of some silly card." Jane could see she'd said the wrong thing. She was handling this badly. "Look, I'm not saying the *tarot* is silly. I'm just saying it's a poor way to communicate. I mean . . . not a poor way for the cosmos to communicate, but—"

Cordelia held up her hand. "It's hard to remove your foot from your mouth while you're still talking."

"Yes. Good point."

"Which brings me back to *my* original point. I think you should look long and hard at La Kastner."

Cordelia detested Patricia on general principles. For starters, she was way too young for Jane. Too materialistic. Too Machiavellian. Too shallow. Cordelia didn't see any inconsistencies in her evaluation, and Jane didn't have the energy to point them out. "Patricia is off-limits."

"Since when?"

"Since now. Why do I feel like I'm the penitent and you're the Grand Inquisitor?" Rising from her chair, Jane walked behind Cordelia's throne and pulled the Minneapolis and St. Paul yellow pages out of her bookcase.

"What are you doing?" asked Cordelia, looking wary.

She returned to her chair, placed them on the seat, then sat on top of them.

"Cute," muttered Cordelia.

"Let's get back to the tarot cards, okay? And don't forget, my father's part of this too. What's the Tower mean?"

Adjusting her heavy turquoise-and-silver squash-blossom necklace, Cordelia flipped forward a few pages in her book. She read for several seconds, then looked up. "First, you need to understand that the tarot is essentially optimistic."

"I don't need a preface. Just give it to me straight."

"Well, actually . . . the book says that it usually means—" She stopped, cleared her throat, then continued. "—chaos and destruction." Her voice squeaked on the last word.

"Nice," Jane whispered.

"It's just a metaphor."

"For what?"

"For—" She glanced back down at the book. "Well, for . . . utter and complete ruin."

"That's clarifying."

"Janey, don't get upset. You're right. It's undoubtedly a joke someone's playing on you."

"And my father."

"There you go. He's probably the one who messed up."

"Then why did I get the first card?"

"Well—"

Sitting on the phone books was uncomfortable. So was the entire conversation. "I appreciate your help, but I think I better get back to the restaurant. At least there I know what I'm doing."

"Don't obsess about this, Janey."

"I never obsess."

"Right. And if you get another card—"

Jane stood up, leaned over Cordelia's desk, and retrieved the two pages. "I'll take two aspirin and call you in the morning."

5

The desk lamp threw a slice of yellow light against the woman's face as she sat finishing up the paperwork. "I usually have my secretary do all this."

"Of course," said the man sitting across from her. Henry Alto was an emergency-room doctor at Metro South in Minneapolis. "I appreciate you fitting me in on such short notice."

"Consider it a professional courtesy. You took very good care of me last fall. I hope I can do the same for you."

After a roller-blading accident in September, Dr. Suzanne Kirsch had come into the emergency room with a badly injured wrist. Henry had treated her. She was a petite woman in her mid-forties. Brown page boy. Fair skin. Not terribly attractive. What struck Henry about her most was her intensity. She reminded him of a raven. He liked people who were quick and smart, and Suzanne Kirsch was both.

After the wrist had been X-rayed and wrapped, they'd talked briefly about her practice as a psychotherapist specializing in depression, relationship problems, and life direction. It was a conversation that Henry had kept in the back of his mind, thinking that when his brother's case was finally decided, he might want to talk to her. His brother's death had taken him completely by surprise. One of the lawyers who'd worked on Bobby's case had stopped by his house earlier in the afternoon with the news, and ever since, Henry had been walking around in a state of shock. On a whim, he'd called Dr. Kirsch. She wasn't usually in her office on Saturdays, but he'd been lucky. She'd fallen behind on paperwork during the holidays and was still trying to dig out. She agreed to meet him at seven.

Dr. Kirsch scribbled a few more words on the intake form, then sat up straight and looked at him with her sharp, evaluating eyes. "I usually like to start our sessions a little differently, but this is an unusual situation. First, let me offer you my sincerest condolences."

"Thanks," said Henry. He folded his long, thin fingers in his lap.

"I assume you're here because of your brother's death."

"Well, yes . . . and no. Actually, I'd been thinking about calling you for some time."

She nodded, still studying him.

What he liked most about her, other than her obvious intelligence, was her lack of sentimentality. She didn't project an aura of kindness, something he'd seen in other psychologists. He couldn't have stood kindness because he didn't deserve it.

"You have a need, a problem, something that isn't working in your life?"

"That's a fair statement," said Henry.

"All right. Let me begin by saying that, in my opinion, I will need a six-week commitment from you—I call it a 'therapeutic unit.' Anything less than six weeks won't do you much good. You can come once or twice a week, or more, depending on my availability. If you're in crisis, I'll *make* time for you. I like to reevaluate where we are at the end of every six-week period. At that point, you can decide to continue, or stop. Therapy shouldn't go on forever. The goal is to regain your personal momentum, your optimum mental health. I can help you do that if you're willing to work with me."

"That sounds fine," said Henry, adjusting his glasses.

"I may take a few notes during the sessions, but mostly I listen. I want to concentrate fully on what you're saying. I prefer talking face to face, as we are now, but if you'd like to use the couch, that's fine too. Some of my patients find it easier that way, less threatening. You might want to try it at some point. See what works best for you."

"I'm quite comfortable in the chair."

"Good. Now." She wrote his name on the top of a file folder. "Perhaps you'd like to give me a bit of your personal background, just so that I can get some context going for you." She hesitated a moment, then added, "That is, unless you're in extreme distress about your brother's death. If you want to talk about him tonight, we could—"

"No," said Henry, cutting her off. "I'm okay. We'll get to him eventually."

"Then tell me about yourself. Just take your time. Let your thoughts flow. We may do this for two or three sessions, unless you want to discuss something specific right away. That's fine too."

He tipped his head back. He didn't like harsh lights. Hospitals had to be brightly lit, but a therapist's office should be more soothing. That's why, before he sat down, he'd asked her to turn off the overhead light. In the semidarkness, the game of Russian roulette he'd come to play seemed less frightening. "Well, I'm thirty-two. A doctor, specializing in emergency medicine. Never married. No girlfriend at the moment."

"Have you had any long-term relationships?"

"One. But I've found that my hours don't suit a lot of women."

She nodded.

"Well, let's see. Both my parents are living. My father, Conrad Alto, is fifty-seven. He was anointed a musical prodigy when he was a child. He graduated from high school when he was fifteen, which always made me feel like I was a failure. I graduated when I was seventeen."

"That doesn't make you a failure, Henry. It just means you're normal."

"Normal isn't valued very highly in my family. My dad studied classical organ after he graduated high school, first here in town, and later in Europe. He has music degrees from both Oberlin and Yale. For a good part of my life, he performed at various venues around the country, which meant he wasn't around much. I suppose I missed him, but I didn't really give it much thought. When he was home he was home, when he was gone—" Henry shrugged. "My parents separated eighteen years ago. They never divorced because Dad thought it was wrong."

"Was it a religious decision?"

"Yes. He was raised Catholic, but he's more eclectic in his religious beliefs now. Actually, he's the musical director at Grace Episcopal Cathedral in downtown St. Paul. He took the position right after the separation, mostly so that he could stay in town, not travel so much. Both my brother, Bobby, and I lived with my mother after the split. My sister was already grown and out of the house by then, so she didn't figure into the living-arrangement wars."

"Wars?"

"Well, skirmishes. Bobby felt protective of my mother, so he wanted to stay with her. I wanted to live with my dad. We switched off for a while, but eventually, Bobby and I both stayed with mom. It was just easier."

"Tell me a little about your mother."

"Well, she was a music professor for most of her life. She graduated from Eastman School of Music with a masters in organ. She taught at the University of Minnesota. She also gave private organ and harpsichord lessons from a studio in Uptown. She and my dad met before he went to Europe. Actually, she was his teacher for a couple of years."

"She must be older than your dad."

"Yes. Fifteen years older. They had a child together before they were married. That was my sister, Leslie. Leslie and her husband and two kids live in Fargo. She's the principal of a grade school. Her husband owns a flooring store."

"How's your relationship with her?"

"Not close, but friendly. We don't have much in common—except the Bermuda Triangle that is our family."

Dr. Kirsch looked at him hard.

He smiled. "That was a joke. I guess it wasn't very funny. Actually, I admire my parents a great deal, but for different reasons. They're polar opposites."

"How old is your sister?" She seemed to be stuck on the subject. It didn't surprise Henry.

"Forty-one." He watched the doctor silently do the math.

"That means . . . your father was sixteen when his daughter was born?"

"That's right."

"Your mother and father slept together when he was fifteen?"

"And she was thirty." Henry enjoyed the startled look on Suzanne Kirsch's face. He placed it somewhere between shock and revulsion. "They had a two-year affair, ending with the birth of my sister. That's when Dad took off for Europe. As you might imagine, his parents loathed my mother. They thought she was the devil incarnate. They weren't wealthy, but they scraped together every bit of money they could to send him as far away from her as possible. Dad lived in Europe for three years before coming back to the states. After he graduated from Yale, he worked for a couple of years on the east coast. But he eventually returned to Minneapolis and convinced my mother to marry him, so in the end, their sacrifice was for nothing. But Dad was always grateful to them. After he made his first CD, he bought them a new house. He tried to be a good son. They're dead now."

"Were you close to them?"

"They refused to set foot in our house because of Mom, so whenever Bobby and I saw them, it was at their place. It always felt kind of stiff and stilted. I think they disapproved of my brother and me because we weren't being raised Catholic. So, no, we weren't close."

Dr. Kirsch nodded, jotting down a few notes. "Go on."

"Well, a couple years after Mom and Dad got married, I came along. My brother, Bobby, was two years younger than me, the baby of the family."

"And how would you describe your relationship with your brother?"

"We fought a lot when we were younger, but he was"—he shrugged helplessly—"my brother." On the last word, his voice cracked, which made him angry.

Dr. Kirsch gave him a minute to recover before saying, "Perhaps this might be a good time to ask why you're here tonight. Why did you seek out a therapist?"

"I want to talk about Diogenes of Sinope, Doctor. The man who went around ancient Greece with a lantern looking for an honest man."

"You'll need to explain that."

"I'm a liar. Is that clear enough?"

It took her a moment to digest the statement. "Are you speaking of a specific lie? Or are you saying you lie all the time?"

"Both. It's an addiction. I want you to help me stop."

She sat forward, resting her arms on her desk. She didn't have his range yet and it clearly bothered her. "Perhaps it would help you to tell me about the specific lie first."

He shifted in his chair. "Well, when the police questioned me about my brother, they asked if I knew anything about the murders, the ones they thought he'd committed. I told them I didn't."

"Are you saying you *did* know something?"

He nodded. "I thought Bobby's lawyer would get him off so, in the end, what I knew wouldn't matter."

"Henry, how could you—" She stopped herself before she completed the sentence. She'd been so stunned by his revelation that she'd momentarily stepped out of her role as therapist. "I'm sorry. I didn't mean—"

"No, I do feel guilty. Terrible guilt," he said, glancing over at a bookcase. He didn't want to look her in the eye.

Hesitantly, Dr. Kirsch continued, "Would it help you to tell me what you know?"

"We're going to have to work up to that a little more slowly."

"Of course," she said. She was trying to be careful, but her face had lost its detachment. "The thing is, Henry, you have to understand that the therapeutic process is based on trust. If you don't tell me the truth, I can't help you."

"I know that."

"You *must* tell me the truth, Henry."

"I will. I promise."

But of course, they both knew he could be lying.

Sunday was another madhouse at the restaurant. By ten, Jane was in the weeds on every front. One of the prep cooks cut himself and had to be taken to the hospital to get stitches, so Jane pitched in, doing some general hunting and fetching, loading the reach-ins, caramelizing onions, portioning filet mignons and filleting salmon. She had twelve unanswered phone messages, one from a food writer at the *Star Tribune*, another from a man who owned an organic pig farm, the one that supplied them with all their pork products, and another some new restaurateur in town—probably looking to steal her executive chef. After the dining room opened at ten, she split her time between expediting orders and chatting with the guests in the dining room, making sure everyone was happy with their food and well served.

Returning to her downstairs office for a midafternoon break, she found one of the waiters standing outside her door. "Can I help you?" she asked, walking swiftly toward him. As he turned to face her, she could see that he was the new hire, the replacement for the guy she'd fired last week. He was Hispanic—tall, dark haired and dark skinned. He was also handsome. His body language suggested he knew it.

"Is this the linen room?" he asked, smiling at her with his amazingly white teeth.

He acted confused, but Jane had a feeling it was just that—an act. "No, it's my office." She nodded to the sign on the door.

"Oh, right. Sorry."

"We haven't met yet. I'm Jane Lawless."

The smile brightened. "Joe Vasquez."

"Didn't someone give you a tour of the building when you were hired?"

He tapped a finger to his forehead. "Bad memory."

"The linen room is around the corner." She pointed.

"Thanks." He hesitated, looked back at her for a second, then turned and walked away.

Jane made a mental note to keep an eye on Joe Vasquez. When she entered her office, she found the light blinking on her answering machine. She kicked off her clogs, punched the button, then sat down to listen.

"Janey, hi. It's Peter. Sorry to bother you at work, but I wanted to let you know that I won't be staying at your house tonight. Maybe for the next couple of nights. I talked to Sigrid this afternoon. We both felt like we should spend more time together." He gave a rueful laugh. "This is so insane. I mean, we both miss each other. If we could just figure out a compromise, maybe . . . just maybe we could save this marriage. I'll be staying at the apartment, just in case you need to reach me. Talk to you later, sis. Wish me luck. Bye."

Jane did wish him luck, all the luck in the world, though she had no idea how two people compromised about having a baby. If Sigrid was dead set against it, and Peter was desperate to have one, where was the middle ground? Jane thought back to how happy they'd been for the first few years. Amazing that they could skirt such an important subject for so long. But then, relationships were always messy, full of quirks and quicksand. Given enough time and love, maybe they could put it back together.

Plumping a pillow, Jane stretched out on the couch to take a nap. Her doctor had recommended lots of exercise, proper nutrition, and a return to work, but peppered with frequent periods of rest and relaxation. The *frequent* part was a problem, but after the day she'd put in, she was definitely tired.

As she closed her eyes, the image of her little dog, Bean, floated up from her subconscious. She missed him so much, missed the way he nestled in her lap, giving her nose a tiny lick—just one. He had been old and in pain, and she'd known he wouldn't last much longer. She'd been holding him a lot lately, especially in the evenings when she'd curl up in front of the fire with a book. He'd even begun to sleep with her, something he rarely did. He'd known his time was coming, and he wanted to be close.

When she got up one morning several weeks ago and found him by the back door, she knew he was gone. She'd cradled him in her arms like a baby, whispering his name, stroking his fur. She sat on the floor for a long time. She just couldn't let him go. The counselor she'd seen to help her with her posttraumatic stress had commented that Jane seemed to have particular trouble with loss. When it occurred, she needed to talk about it, not bury it deep inside. But for Jane, who'd always been a private person, someone who took pride in not wearing her heart on her sleeve, the advice rankled. She would deal with Bean's death in her own way and in her own time. Just because she didn't fall apart in front of everyone didn't mean she didn't feel the pain.

As long as Jane kept busy, she didn't think about Bean—or any of the other problems currently occupying her mind. Work had always been a way to shut the world out, a way to keep on an even keel. As tired as she was, she had the urge to get up and go back upstairs to the kitchen, lose herself once again in the comprehensible chaos of her restaurant. Instead, she did what her therapist suggested. She stayed where she was and finally drifted off.

It was nearly ten before Jane returned to her office that evening. The dinner meal had been hectic, but Jane loved the intensity of her work, the long hours, and especially the beauty of the prod uct. Instead of feeling tired, she felt revved, ready for more. After showering and changing her clothes, she sat down behind her desk. All day, she'd been making a mental list of changes she wanted to make. She decided that this was as good a time as any to write it all down.

First and foremost, she wanted to hire a new, full-time reservationist, one who really knew how to screen. They'd been overbooking dinners for months, and still there were nights when tables went empty. Second, she wanted to check into parking lot security. She'd never needed it before, but lately there had been some incidents that worried her. A fight. A broken windshield. Security would be far less expensive than a lawsuit. Finally, she was sick to death of dealing with the assistant pastry chef. The man was massively arrogant and at the same time, lazy and sloppy. As soon as she found someone with less attitude and more imagination, she'd fire the guy.

Swiveling around to the bookcase behind her desk, she grabbed a copy of the Minneapolis yellow pages. That's when she noticed it. It was a paper sack, crisscrossed with strapping tape, about the size of a large sandwich bag. It had been pushed behind a row of paperbacks, forcing them out. Curious to see what was in it, she lifted the bag over to her desk, then opened her top drawer to get a scissors, clipping off the edge of the wrapper. Inside she found a yellowish-white powder.

"What the hell?" she said, poking it with her finger. It didn't take a rocket scientist to conclude that it was some sort of drug. Maybe cocaine. Maybe something else. But why had someone hidden it there—in her office?

She reached for the phone and punched in her father's home number. If anyone would know what to do, he would. She waited through five long rings, but instead of his deep voice on the other end, his voice mail picked up. She tried his office next, but again, he was nowhere to be found.

For the moment, all she could think to do was get rid of it. If she didn't, if someone had hidden it in her office—or worse, planted it—she could be in deep trouble.

After taping the package back up—and brushing the residue off her desktop—she stuffed it in her gym bag, then grabbed her coat and switched off the light in her office. When she left this time, she made sure the door was locked.

Once outside, she glanced around, trying not to look suspicious. The lot was full of cars, people coming and going, but nobody seemed to be paying any attention to her. So far, so good. It had occurred to her that she could flush the contents of the bag down one of the toilets, but that frightened her. What if a residue remained? What the hell did she know about flushing drugs? She could stay and analyze the situation, come up with a well-considered conclusion about the best way to handle it, or she could leave, take the sack and dump it somewhere safe. Leaving seemed the better—and smarter—part of valor.

Her boots crunched loudly on the packed snow as she walked to the far end of the lot, where her Trooper was parked. Tension made her body feel stiff. She set the bag in the backseat, then pulled Bean's old car blanket over it. It seemed a desecration.

She looked over her shoulder again. In the cold night air, her breath swirled around her face. Sliding into the driver's seat, she started the engine. She hadn't done anything wrong and yet she felt like a criminal. Maybe she should have stayed and called the police. But would they have believed her? Her father had friends in the MPD, but because of his profession, he had far more enemies. Telling the truth might get her into a world of trouble.

Instead of returning to her house, Jane drove north. She knew it was silly, but she wanted to make sure no one was following her. She took side streets all the way to Loring Park, then returned by way of Lyndale and King's Highway to the parking lot in front of the Lake Harriet bandstand. When she finally felt confident she was alone, she drove home, but passed her house without going inside. She continued on down the street to Patricia Kastner's house. She parked her Trooper in the drive, grabbed the gym bag from the backseat, then waded through the deep snow on the side of the house to the front steps.

After pressing the bell, she blew on her hands to keep them warm. Her pulse was racing. Not the perfect time to come calling.

Patricia appeared almost instantly, dressed in a slinky black silk bathrobe, her short, spiky hair recently bleached a stark white. She smiled broadly. "Jane Lawless, as I live and breathe." The accent was Southern. Patricia wasn't. "Great timing. I was just about to go to bed. You can join me." She grabbed Jane's hand playfully and drew her inside. "Hey, what's up?" she said, gripping Jane's hand even more tightly. "You're shaking."

Setting the gym bag down, Jane leaned back against the closed door, thankful for its solidity. "I need to use your phone." She wanted to call her father again. She should probably just bite the bullet and buy a cell phone, but the truth was, she hated the idea of always being available.

"You look like you're being chased by a pack of wolves."

"I am."

She followed Patricia into the sunken living room. Logs were crackling away in the fireplace and soft jazz was coming from the stereo. Normality. It felt wonderful. Jane sat down on the couch, found the cordless phone under a magazine and punched in her father's number, watching Patricia disappear into the kitchen.

Once again, she had to wait on the line until her dad's voice mail picked up. Where could he be? Marilyn was in New Orleans, so they weren't out painting the town red. Not that they ever painted much of anything red. That's when she remembered the dinner date he'd made with his new partner, Elizabeth Piper. But that was for last night. Could they be having dinner again tonight?

This time, she left a message. "Hey, Dad. It's me. When you get back, will you call me right away? It's urgent. *Really* urgent.

I need to talk to you tonight. As soon as you get in." She left Patricia's number and suggested he try it first. Surely he'd have to be home soon. He liked to think he was a party animal, but in truth, he never stayed out past eleven. Glancing at her watch, she saw that it was going on midnight.

Patricia had returned to the living room, setting a tray on the coffee table. Before she joined Jane on the couch, she poured them each a couple of fingers of Dalwhinnie, a single malt scotch they both liked, then added a bit of Evian water to Jane's drink.

Gratefully, Jane accepted the glass, taking several bracing swallows. Her heart was still pounding like a jackhammer.

"Hey, slow down," said Patricia, rubbing her hand soothingly across Jane's back. "Tell me what happened?"

Jane leaned forward, elbows resting on her knees, holding the glass against her forehead. "You'll never believe it."

"In case you haven't noticed, I'm not easily shocked."

Jane attempted a smile, but her face felt like granite. "Okay. Try this on for size. Would you believe I'm a drug dealer?"

Patricia's hand stopped midrub.

Jane turned to view her reaction. Instead of shock, Patricia seemed mildly intrigued.

"You do cocaine?" she asked, keeping her voice neutral.

"No," said Jane. "I don't. But look at this." She took another sip of her scotch, then got up to retrieve the gym bag. Returning to the couch, she removed the tape from the side of the package.

Patricia licked her finger, then touched it to the powder. After tasting it, she made a face. "That's not cocaine."

"What is it?"

"If I'm not mistaken, and I'm usually not, its crank. Crystal meth. Jesus, Jane, where did you get your hands on that?"

"I found it in my office about an hour ago. Someone must have hidden it in there, or planted it. I'm assuming this . . . crystal meth is illegal."

"Oh, yeah. It's illegal."

"And expensive."

"Depends. Street prices vary, but it's usually cheaper than coke."

Jane felt like throwing up. "How come you know so much about street drugs?"

"Because I'm not a freakin' Puritan—with alcoholic tendencies—like you."

"Hey!"

"Oh, stop glowering. I'm just saying that you drink more than you should sometimes. So do I. Everybody uses, Lawless, when you come right down to it. Cigarettes. Caffeine. Booze. Cocaine. Grass. There are even some herbs that can give you a pretty decent high. And they're all dangerous. Some just happen to be illegal."

Jane had heard the argument before. She understood the logic, but she didn't buy the idea that all drugs could be lumped together.

"Come on," said Patricia. "Let's stop calling each other names."

The scotch had helped Jane's nerves a little, but not enough. Finishing her drink in one neat gulp, she got up and walked over to the narrow windows flanking the front door. Before she peeked through one of the curtains she called, "Turn the light off in the living room, will you?"

"You think someone followed you?"

"I drove around for a while. I didn't see anyone."

Patricia switched off the lamp. "Paranoia becomes you."

"Thanks."

The only illumination in the room now came from the fireplace.

"What's it look like out there?" asked Patricia. "Lots of police cars? Maybe a swat team or two?"

Jane ignored the sarcasm. She couldn't see a soul. "I just wish I knew what the hell was going on." She turned around. "Why would someone leave that in my office?"

"Good question. Let's work on the answer." Patricia poured them each another inch of scotch.

"Do you think we should get rid of it? The package, I mean?"

Patricia shrugged. "I suppose. Bring it into the kitchen. Bring the drinks too."

"What are you going to do?"

"Pour it down the sink."

"But what about the residue?"

"What residue?"

"Won't there be traces left behind?"

"I doubt it."

Jane couldn't believe Patricia was taking this all so casually. She grabbed the glasses and followed her. "The police could knock on the door any minute."

"Jane, you're overreacting. You think Cordelia's a drama queen? Just look in the mirror sometime. And calm the fuck down."

Easier said than done.

"Do you know what methamphetamine is made of?" asked Patricia.

"No. Do you?"

"Not exactly, but it's all pretty common stuff. People make it in their basements. But the process is highly volatile. That's why so many meth labs blow up."

"That's comforting."

After pouring the drug down the sink, Patricia let the hot water run for a few minutes. They both leaned against the counter watching the water flow.

"I feel like some pathetic junkie," said Jane. "Sneaking around. Burying my dope."

"You are *so* uncool sometimes, Lawless."

"What's that supposed mean?"

Patricia gave her a heavy-lidded look. "Just chill, okay? See? All gone." She nodded to the sink.

Jane wished it could be taken care of that easily.

"Now, all you've got to do is find out who planted that stuff in your office—and why."

"You really think someone planted it? To get me in trouble?"

"I don't know why else it would be there."

They carried their glasses back into the living room and sat down on the pillows in front of the fire. As Patricia tossed the empty sack into the flames, Jane stretched out. She was finally starting to relax. She talked about the tarot cards. She wasn't sure if there was a connection, but she thought it was possible.

Patricia listened without comment, though she obviously found the entire situation bizarre.

When Jane was finally finished, she placed the empty glass on her stomach and said, "So what do you think?"

"You know what, Lawless? Those cards remind me of a Charlie Chan movie. Kind of cheesy, and at the same time, kind of cool."

"I'm glad you approve."

"This is just a guess, you understand, but I think someone's got it in for you—your dad too. This guy may not be your enemy at all. I mean, your dad must piss off some pretty nasty characters in his line of work."

"True." She waited while Patricia poured her another drink. "You know, here I am, ranting on about my problems—"

"Which pale in comparison to *mine*."

Jane looked over and smiled. "I haven't even asked you how you are."

"Don't I look fine?"

"You always look fine." She turned on her side, closer to Patricia, running her fingers along the edge of Patricia's face. "I care about you, you know that?"

"How cautious you are, Lawless."

"Cautious?"

"Careful never to say anything you can't take back."

"Meaning?"

"Is *love* a four-letter word?"

Jane flipped on her back again. "Look, you're the one who said we should keep it light. When I got home from Connecticut after Christmas, you said—"

Patricia pressed a finger to Jane's lips. "Do you always do what you're told?" Before Jane could answer, she added, "No, you're right. I'm not the kind of woman who could ever settle down. I tried it once and it didn't work. Limiting myself to just one person would feel like prison."

Taking another sip of her drink, Jane said, "Are you sure that's how you feel?"

"Positive."

"Then, next question. Are you trying to get me drunk?"

"Is it working?"

"You assume that if I drink enough, I won't leave."

"Drinking and driving don't mix."

"Except, I live just down the block."

"But why go out into the cold, cold night when you've got a warm bed waiting for you right upstairs?"

Jane rolled on her side again. "Everywhere I look, I'm the victim of a plot."

"It's awful, isn't it?" Patricia began to unbutton Jane's shirt.

"I wonder if my father's going to call me back tonight."

"That's what answering machines are for."

"But . . . I really should try to figure out what to do. I could be in trouble, Patricia."

"You're going to be in deeper trouble if you don't shut up."

We don't seem to be talking," called Peter Lawless. He was standing in the kitchen of his apartment, finishing up the dinner dishes. Sigrid was in the bedroom, cleaning out a closet. "Siggy? Are you there?"

"I can't hear you," came a muffled voice.

He switched on the dishwasher, then picked up his can of diet Sprite and ambled into the bedroom. Sigrid was standing by the bed, looking at a heap of clothes she'd just dumped there. She blew a lock of blond hair away from her forehead.

"We didn't say more than twenty words to each other at dinner."

She glanced over at him. "Were you counting?"

He nodded.

"So what do we do?"

"Let's go out," said Peter.

"Where?"

"I don't know. Just someplace other than here. I think this apartment depresses us. We've had too many fights in this room."

Sigrid looked down at her jeans and sweatshirt. "I'm a mess."

"You're never a mess," said Peter, smiling at her. Sigrid had the fresh good looks of the proverbial girl next door—although one who'd been around the block more than once. She was a lot shorter than Peter, "a shrimp," as she always put it, a fair-haired Swede with a soft, round figure. He was tall and thin, his hair the same rich chestnut as his sister's. The beard he'd worn since college had recently mutated into a goatee. He wasn't sure he liked it, but since Sigrid did, he was willing to give the new look a shot.

Sigrid was the light to Peter's dark. She didn't exactly have a sunny disposition, though she wasn't prone to brooding, the way Peter was. She was ambitious, pragmatic, and always approached life flat on. If she'd ever owned a pair of rose-colored glasses, she'd thrown them away years ago. Jane had introduced them when Sigrid was a senior at the University of Minnesota. Peter had been in his late twenties at the time, working as a photographer/cameraman at WTWN-TV in Minneapolis. Sigrid was twenty-two. The spark from that first meeting had quickly turned to flame. Before meeting Sigrid, Peter had played the field, never staying with one woman more than a couple of years. He'd begun to think of himself as a confirmed bachelor, but Sigrid had changed all that.

"Come on," said Peter. "I'm not dressed for the Ritz either."

She checked her watch. "What about the pub at your sister's restaurant? They have that live Celtic music on Sunday nights. We might be able to catch the tail end of it."

He stepped over to the bed and drew her into his arms. "God, I've missed you," he said, kissing her softly.

She relaxed against him. "Sometimes I think it's all over between us, that we've got to face it and get on with our lives. But then I think, maybe I should just give in. We should have a baby. At least one of us would be happy." She was silent a moment, holding him tight. "It's not just my career, Peter. That's totally cold, to think I'd put my career before everything else."

"I know," he said. "I understand."

"No, you don't." She was suddenly angry and pushed him away. "Don't keep saying that. You *don't* understand."

"Then help me."

She sat down on the bed, looking defeated.

"Come on, Siggy. Let's get out of here. No more talk about a baby tonight. Let's just try to have some fun."

"I'm not sure we know how anymore."

He held out his hand. "Let's give it a try."

The Celtic band was just finishing the last set when Peter and Sigrid entered the Lyme House Pub. The roar in the main room wasn't exactly conducive to a quiet conversation, so they found a table by the fire in the back room. They each ordered a beer and a plate of pub fries. Peter liked his with malt vinegar, while Sigrid was a fan of that great American sauce, ketchup.

They sat and listened to the band until the final song was over. Peter loved Irish music, Celtic music, even bagpipes and drums. He didn't remember his early years in England as well as his sister—he'd been so much younger—but he had taken away with him a fondness for all things British. Tonight's band consisted of a harp, a hammered dulcimer, a flute, a Highland drum, and a fiddle. He'd toyed with the idea of taking up the dulcimer himself when he was in college, but learned quickly that when it came to stringed instruments, he was all thumbs.

And that's what he felt like tonight. When it came to talking to his wife these days, he was all thumbs. They both seemed to have lost their facility for lightness, for joking around, for simply having a good time. The issues facing them were so teeth-grindingly serious, it was hard to put them in a box and forget they existed—even for a few hours.

"I wonder if your sister is still here," said Sigrid, sipping her beer and looking around.

Peter shook his head. "I doubt it."

"Do you want to go see? You could invite her to come have a beer with us."

Even though it would undoubtedly ease the tension between them, he resisted the idea. He'd spent so many weeks without his wife that he wanted her all to himself tonight. Even if he couldn't figure out what to say. "Let's just make it the two of us, okay?"

"Sure. Whatever."

Peter looked down into his beer. There were reasons Sigrid didn't want to have children—reasons that went far beyond her devotion to her career as a family counselor. Her parents had divorced when she was thirteen. Because her mother had to return to work to help support the family, and her father lived out of town, much of the care of her younger siblings—a four-month-old sister, a five-year-old sister, a seven-year-old brother, a nine-year-old brother—fell to Sigrid. Not only was she responsible for getting them up in the morning, getting them fed and off to school or day care, but she took care of them most evenings as well. She cooked most of the meals, did all of the laundry, and settled the arguments. Her mother worked an erratic schedule, and was probably suffering from untreated depression. She provided little help and even less emotional support.

Sigrid was devoted to her family, but by the time she'd graduated from high school, she'd done enough child care to last a lifetime. Her mother had remarried by then, so she was free to attend college. Sigrid had worked hard to get top-notch grades. Thankfully, the scholarship she'd been banking on came through. But instead of entering the university right away, she took a year off. She wanted to "find herself." The phrase always made her laugh. It was such a seventies thing to say, and yet there was some truth in it.

Sigrid had spent most of that year in New York, working as a waitress. She wanted to assert her independence, try her hand at living alone. When she returned to the U of M, she dug in and never looked back. Initially, political science had interested her. She liked running things, seeing her ideas take shape, and for a while she toyed with the idea of a getting a law degree as a stepping stone to a career in politics. But by her senior year, she was taking more and more psychology classes. Her growing interest in human behavior led her in an entirely new direction.

The year after Peter and Sigrid met, she entered graduate school. The year they were married, she took her first full-time job. Peter was proud of what she'd accomplished. Early last fall, she'd begun talking about going back to school again, getting her doctorate in counseling psychology. She was interested in the program at Loyola, and was beginning to wonder out loud if commuting back and forth from Minneapolis to Chicago would be too much of a drag. If she did the program full-time, she could graduate in three years, with a fourth-year internship. If she went part-time, it could be a seven-year program. It finally dawned on Peter that having a baby, starting a family, had no place in her plans. That's when the arguments had started.

At first, Sigrid said she needed more time to think about it. Having a baby was a big decision. She wasn't sure this was the best time, especially if she did start graduate school in the spring. Why was he in such a rush? Had he *really* considered how a child would change their lives? The more they talked, the more he could see that her resistance didn't just stem from bad timing.

Before Thanksgiving, he sat her down one night and explained that he had no reservations. He wanted a child. He knew she would be a good mother, and he felt he would make a good father. If she was set on graduate school, then fine, they would work it out somehow.

Sigrid listened. She was polite, but cool. When he was done, she told him that she loved him, loved their life together, but that she didn't want a child—that she never would.

So there it was. The line had been drawn. From that point on, their marriage had started to come apart. Before Christmas, Peter left. He moved temporarily into his sister's house. It was a terrible time for both of them. He knew that if he gave in, he'd probably hate himself in the end—or worse. He'd end up hating Sigrid. And if she gave in, it was the same scenario. And yet they loved each other. That was never in doubt. It was an impossible situation.

When Peter finally looked up from his beer, he saw that Sigrid was studying him. She had a way of seeming so remote sometimes. He wondered what she was thinking. Probably the same thing he was, although her face betrayed nothing. Peter had always been aware of a fundamental coldness in the center of his wife. He'd ignored it at first, thinking it was curious but peripheral. But now, he couldn't help but wonder if it had some bearing on their current troubles. Except, how did he talk about it without making her feel like he was attacking her?

"How's your job going?" he asked finally, leaning into the table, bridging his fingers over his glass. He was nervous, and hoped she couldn't tell. He also knew the question was lame, not the kind of conversation two people who were supposed to be soul mates had, but he was starting to feel desperate. He needed to connect with her on some level. Any level. *How's the car running? Did you catch the Vikings game last Sunday? Seen any good movies lately?* When he'd walked through the door tonight, all he wanted to do was to take her to bed, show her how much he loved her, though he had the sense not to act on that urge. Being together, intimately, would have helped him, though he knew she probably wouldn't feel the same way. He still hoped they might end up in bed later tonight, though his hopes were fading fast.

"My job's fine, Peter." A smile crept around the corners of her mouth.

"What's so funny?"

"Hell if I know."

"This is so hard," said Peter.

Sigrid sighed. "I spend all week counseling people, and here I sit with the person I love most in the world and I'm totally tongue-tied."

He couldn't stand it any longer. If someone had to give, well, maybe it should be him. Screwing up his courage, he said, "Siggy, listen to me. I've been thinking." He was lying. He hadn't been thinking of changing his mind at all—not until this very second. "If I have to choose between you and a child I don't even know—I choose you."

She just stared at him. After a long moment, she said, "Are you sure?"

"I love you. I can't imagine my life without you in it."

Her eyes glistened with tears. Reaching for his hand, she said, "Oh, Peter. You don't know how much I've wanted to hear you say that."

"I've been such a fool. I don't want to waste any more time. Can you forgive me for being so pigheaded?"

"Let's go. Take me home."

Eagerly, Peter tossed some cash on the table, then followed her out. As they passed through the main room, he noticed two men seated at one end of the long mahogany bar. He recognized them from a story he'd shot recently about undercover cops—drug cops. These guys didn't pal around together just for the hell of it, which meant they had to be working. And if that was the case, what were they doing here?

He hesitated in the doorway, spotting a bulge under the younger guy's leather jacket. Jesus, they were armed. Maybe they were just getting out of the cold for a few minutes, but the sight of them sitting in his sister's restaurant made him uneasy.

Sigrid tugged at his hand. They were both impatient to be together again after so many months apart. Whatever these guys were doing, it couldn't hurt to wait until tomorrow to tell his sister.

Peter wrapped his scarf around his neck while Sigrid buttoned up her jacket, then, arm in arm, they hurried out into the cold February night.

On Monday, Sigrid didn't have to be to work until three in the afternoon, and Peter had the day off, so they stayed in bed until the growling in their stomachs became too loud to ignore. After the night they'd shared, Peter felt wonderfully content. While Sigrid showered, he puttered in the kitchen making breakfast. It felt like ages since he'd been this relaxed, this focused. He'd thought about calling Jane to tell her about the cops he'd seen at her restaurant last night, but he was so filled with his own happiness that it no longer touched him with any great urgency.

The fruit salad had been assembled, the eggs were whipped and all set to scramble, and the pancake batter was ready. Sigrid was taking her old sweet time in the bathroom as usual, but that was all right with Peter. He was back home where he belonged.

Drifting into the living room, he found a stack of unopened mail sitting on top of the TV. He made himself comfortable on the couch and started to flip through it. There were a few bills, the usual junk mail, but one letter caught his attention. His name and address had been typed on the outside of the envelope, but there was no return address. That always made him suspicious. Ripping it open, he drew out a single sheet of paper. It wasn't a letter, as he'd expected, but a copy of what appeared to be a tarot card. He recognized it because he used to play with his grandmother's deck when he was a kid. Not that he knew what the card meant, or why it had been sent to him. It was the Nine of Swords. The picture was depressing. It was the figure of a man sitting on a bed, hands covering his face in what looked like a posture of deep despair. Behind him, hanging on a black wall, were nine large swords, all lined up. At the top of the sheet of paper, someone had written the number three in red ink.

"I'm famished," said Sigrid, breezing into the room. She was towel-drying her hair. "Should we eat here or go out?"

"I've got breakfast ready," said Peter, folding the page back up and stuffing it into his pocket. "Eggs, pancakes and fruit."

"What a guy," said Sigrid, leaning over and giving him a kiss. "Maybe I can think of something to do for you after breakfast."

"I'll help you think," said Peter, watching her turn and stroll into the kitchen.

Once he'd finished frying up the eggs and pancakes, and they were seated at the breakfast table, Peter poured coffee. "God, but this feels fabulous."

Sigrid's mouth was already full of scrambled eggs. She was wearing his flannel bathrobe, the tie pulled halfheartedly around her middle. Underneath, she was naked. Peter wished now that he hadn't dressed. Not that Sigrid wouldn't enjoy undressing him later.

One of the things Peter liked best about his wife was her sexual energy. It exactly matched his own. She made no bones about her exploits in college, which only served to make her more appealing to him—more sophisticated.

"What are you doing today?" asked Sigrid, taking a sip of coffee.

"I thought I'd run over to my sister's house and get my things, bring them back here."

"That won't take long."

"No, I suppose not. I also thought I might swing by the restaurant, talk to Jane for a few minutes."

"Tell her the good news."

He smiled. "She'll be very happy for us." Peter also knew she'd question his sudden reversal on the baby issue. He'd have to defend his decision.

As Sigrid got up to get them more eggs, the phone rang. She picked up the cordless on the counter and said hello. "Hey, Dana, what's up?" She leaned against the sink for a moment, listening, then drifted out of the room.

Peter wondered who Dana was. He'd never heard her mention the name before. Setting down his fork, he bent his head and listened. Sigrid had lowered her voice, but he could still hear her. She was laughing.

"No, I can't," she said playfully. "What?" She paused. "Did anyone ever tell you you're a total jerk?" She paused again. "Yeah, okay. See you this afternoon."

When she returned to the kitchen, Peter was finishing his pancakes. "Who was that?"

"Dana."

"Dana who?"

"You know. Dana Barlow? One of the other family therapists at CNC."

"Man or woman?"

"Man. You met him at that picnic last summer. And he goes to our gym."

Peter had no recollection of ever meeting a Dana Barlow. "You sound like you're pretty good friends."

She shrugged. "Work friends."

"How come he's calling you here?"

"How come you're giving me the third degree?"

"I'm not. I'd just like to know why he's calling my wife."

She stirred some sugar into her coffee. "He wanted to take me to dinner."

Peter's mood instantly soured. "Have you had dinner with him before?"

"Sure. A couple times."

"When?"

"Last week. The week before."

"Just dinner?"

Very carefully, she placed the spoon next to her mug. "If you want to know if I slept with him, the answer is no."

"But you wanted to."

"Peter?"

He was pushing this way too far, pushing her away, but he couldn't stop himself. He thought of their gym. It was a singles bar with exercise equipment. The treadmills, stationary bikes and stair climbers were all lined up in front of floor-to-ceiling mirrors. Behind them were the aerobics classes. It was all arranged for maximum viewing pleasure. Bodies checking out other bodies. Peter spent most of his time in the weight room, but Sigrid liked to show herself off. It drove him crazy, though he knew enough to leave the subject alone. He simply made sure they always went together. Except, for the past few months, that hadn't been possible.

"Are you actually angry at me for going out to dinner with a friend?"

"Yes," said Peter, crumpling his napkin and tossing it at his plate. "I mean, no. Oh, hell, I don't know what I mean." He got up and dumped his dirty dishes in the sink. If he turned around, he knew his face would say it all.

"Where's all this coming from?"

"Honestly, Sigrid, I don't know." He could feel her eyes boring into his back.

She waited a moment, then said, "It's the baby, isn't it? You gave in and now you're sorry."

"I didn't give in, I made a decision."

"All right," she said in her professional voice, the one she used in her therapy sessions. Patient. Detached. Controlled. "But that doesn't mean you're not having second thoughts." When he didn't respond, she added, "*Are* you having second thoughts, Peter? Is that what all this is about?"

He could hear her get up and slide the chair under the table, but she stayed where she was. She didn't move toward him. "Answer my question first," said Peter. "Have you been going out with this guy while I've been gone?"

"We're friends."

He whirled around. "Has he kissed you?"

Her face flushed.

It was all the proof he needed. "What else has he done?"

"Stop it," she demanded. "You're changing the subject."

"The subject is our *marriage*, Sigrid, in case you didn't realize it." He stomped into the living room. "I've been sitting over there in my sister's house for two months, trying to talk myself out of my dream, while you've been dating some asshole behind my back?"

"You're blowing this all out of proportion."

"Am I?"

"Yes. It was all very innocent."

"*You* don't even belong in the same sentence with the word innocent."

She glared at him. "You're a shit sometimes, you know that?"

"I come home to find out you've been dating some pumped-up Neanderthal, and you call *me* a shit?"

"You're uncomfortable with your decision and his call provided you with just the excuse you were looking for to pick a fight with me. It's classic, Peter. Straight out of a textbook."

"Glad to know I'm predictable!"

"I could set my watch by you when you're in a mood like this!"

They were both shouting now.

"Admit it," said Sigrid. "This isn't about Dana, it's about the baby."

"Am I wasting my time in this marriage?" demanded Peter. "Am I?"

"Stop shouting. The neighbors don't want to hear our arguments. The woman next door's probably calling the cops."

"I wouldn't worry about it. She's never home."

"You know everything, don't you. You have godlike qualities."

Peter charged into the bedroom and grabbed his overnight bag. On his way through the living room, he didn't even look at her. "I'm an idiot, a chump. I was willing to give up my dream to make our marriage work and we don't even *have* a marriage."

"Do you ever listen to yourself?" she shouted. "You're jealous of any guy I even smile at. You work yourself up over nothing, you always have. You never feel sure that I love you. That's *your* problem, Peter, not mine. You're always trying to get me to prove my love. You want this baby because of your insecurity about our marriage, not because it's some precious dream. Admit it, Peter. Admit that I'm right."

Coldly, he replied, "We don't have a marriage, Sigrid. We've got me . . . and we've got you and your boyfriends."

"Get out."

"With pleasure." He slammed the door behind him.

The first thing you've got to do is get back over to that restaurant of yours," said Jane's father. "You don't open until four on Mondays, right?"

"Right." Jane was sitting at her kitchen table, gripping a mug of strong black coffee. Her night with Patricia had been typically crazy and fun, but a bad case of nerves had descended on her when she woke this morning. She'd come home around nine to an empty house. No Bean snoozing by the back door. No Peter fumbling through the refrigerator, looking for something to eat. It made her feel sorry for herself and very alone.

Since her father still hadn't called back, she'd phoned him at his office. At last she found him in. She asked him why he hadn't returned her call. He said he'd been out late last night and hadn't checked his messages when he got in. The explanation seemed a little fishy to Jane, especially since Marilyn was out of town. What if she'd called? It wasn't like her dad not to check his voice mail. But Jane was so twisted over the drugs she'd found in her office, she didn't pursue it.

"And don't go alone," continued her father. "Take Cordelia with you. You two have to cover every square inch of that place.

You need to find out if there are any more drugs."

The fact that she hadn't thought of it herself made her mildly sick to her stomach. Where was her brain? She'd been so concerned about getting that package out of her office, she'd never considered that there might be more.

"Call me when you're done," said her dad.

"But why would someone plant drugs in my office?"

"Maybe they figured it was a safe place. They'd stash it and come back and get it later. Are you locking your office door like I told you?"

"Not always."

He sighed the sigh of a father with a recalcitrant daughter. "Worst-case scenario is that someone is using your place."

"Using it for what?"

"As a front, a place to sell drugs."

Jane pinched the bridge of her nose, feeling a headache forming behind her eyes.

"Or, who knows? Maybe someone's trying to get back at you."

"Cordelia said the same thing. But what did I *do*?"

"I don't know, honey. That's what you've got to figure out. Once you've had a chance to look over the restaurant, I'll call Art Turlow. He's a good friend, a sergeant with the Minneapolis drug squad. He'll probably want to come over and interview you. You need to get this all on record with the police, but we have to handle it just right. I wish you hadn't destroyed the evidence."

"I didn't know what else to do!"

"I know, I know. The problem is, it looks suspicious."

"Oh, God." She dropped her head on her hand.

"It's okay, sweetheart. We'll get this all cleared up, one way or the other. Just cross your fingers and hope the restaurant is clean. On the other hand, if you find something, don't touch it. Just leave it where it is. Have Cordelia guard the area while you call me."

"Fine. Thanks, Dad." She felt flattened.

"I'll be in court this afternoon, so call me back ASAP. When

I know what's going on, I'll call Turlow. If you don't find any more drugs, we've bought ourselves some time. But we don't want to wait on this, okay?"

"Okay."

"Hang in there, honey. Call Cordelia right away."

Jane had no idea what Cordelia's schedule was today.

After hanging up, she changed into some clean clothes—a soft pair of gray cords, her favorite rag wool sweater, and a pair of Vasque hiking boots. Since the day was likely to be stressful, at least she'd be comfortable.

Cordelia agreed to meet her at the restaurant shortly after ten. She arrived wearing her bright red cape. Swirling it off like a bullfighter, she tossed it on the couch in Jane's office. Underneath she was dressed all in brown. "I know," she whispered, lowering her sunglasses on her nose. "I usually wear black when we do our crime-caper stuff, but because your restaurant is mostly pine timbers, and it's daytime, I thought this would help me blend into the woodwork." She flashed Jane a knowing look.

"It's not possible for you to blend into the woodwork, Cordelia."

"I know." She sighed. "It's my cross."

They left Jane's office and hurried down the hall to the pub. "And anyway, if you want to blend in, why the bright purple lipstick?"

Cordelia winked. "Spice. It's essential for my personal idiom."

Jane could hear a vacuum cleaner running in the dining room upstairs. Mondays were spent buffing the restaurant, making sure everything was spit-and-polish. She waved to one of her bartenders who was standing on a ladder, wiping down the liquor bottles behind the counter. Another man was swabbing the floor in the front hallway.

Cordelia bent close to Jane's ear and whispered, "Do we split up, or what?"

Good question. To Jane, it felt like an overwhelming task to take the place apart, especially when it was already crawling with people doing normal maintenance. "I guess maybe we should. Remember, if you find something, just leave it. Come tell me right away."

"We should have brought walkie-talkies," whispered Cordelia, eyeing the bartender suspiciously.

"Oh, *that* would be inconspicuous." Glancing at her watch, she said, "You take the upstairs and I'll do the downstairs."

"And I'll be in Scotland afore ye!" Breezing up the steps two at a time, Cordelia was off like the bloodhound she so clearly wasn't.

With less enthusiasm, but no less concern, Jane headed for the wine cellar.

Half an hour later, with nothing to show for her investigative efforts but a mummified centipede and two dead spiders, Jane was about to switch the light off when she noticed a shadow fall across the doorway. Someone was outside the room, just standing there, not moving. She gave it a minute to see what the person would do, but when nothing happened, she stepped quickly into the hallway.

"Ms. Lawless," said Joe Vasquez, the newly hired waiter. "Hi." Today he was dressed in a black T-shirt that showed off all his muscles, and a pair of tight jeans that showed off everything else. He looked down at her and grinned. In his right hand, he held a nail clipper.

"What's going on?" she demanded. "Why are you standing out here?"

He seemed a bit startled by her accusatory tone. "Nothing's goin' on. I just finished scrubbing up the sinks in the kitchen. Arlene issued me a broom and sent me down to sweep the dry-storage room, but I seem to have snagged my nail." He showed it to her. It was bleeding.

All right, she thought. So maybe he wasn't spying on her. It was probably just her nerves. "Wait on the storage room. Do the bar first."

"Sure thing." He stuck his finger in his mouth, but didn't move away. Instead, he continued to stare at her. "You okay, Ms. Lawless? You look kind of strung out."

"I'm fine."

"Just checkin'."

As he walked away, Jane realized he didn't have a broom.

By noon, Jane and Cordelia were both back in Jane's office, deciding what to do next. Much to Jane's relief, neither had found any trace of drugs.

"That new waiter is a real hunk," said Cordelia. She was lying languorously on the couch munching on a ham sandwich, extra pickle, no mustard. "He'd make a great Stanley Kowalski—you know, *A Streetcar Named Desire*?"

"I'm familiar with the play, Cordelia."

"He's earthy. Oozing with sexuality and barely suppressed violence."

"Gee, just the kind of guy I want describing my evening specials."

"He's not Polish, but then, neither was Marlon Brando. I wonder if he's ever tried acting. Most waiters are actor-wannabes, you know." She took another bite of her sandwich.

Jane was too keyed up to think about food or the shortcomings of her waitstaff. She'd phoned her father as soon as they were done, but he'd already left for court. All she could do was ask Norm Toscalia, her father's paralegal, to have him call when he got back. "I just hope we covered everything."

"I don't know where else we could have looked."

"Well, I suppose there are the heating and cooling ducts. The ceiling tiles in the kitchen come down. Maybe—"

Cordelia held up a jewel-encrusted hand. "I don't do building demolition, Janey. Your father's right. Tell the police the truth and you'll be in the clear. If you'd called me last night, instead of high tailing it over to that den of iniquity—"

"Moralistic tones? From you?"

"I don't care if you sleep with the entire undergraduate class of Vassar. I'm just saying that Patricia Kastner has terminally bad judgment. You of all people should know that. Dating her is like drinking a glass of Liquid-Plumr."

"Don't hold your opinions back, Cordelia. I wouldn't want you to stifle yourself."

Cordelia's look was ponderous, heavy, deeply annoyed.

"You don't know Patricia the way I do. Sure, she's a little wild, but she's got a good heart, a good soul. Besides, she's like an emotional vitamin shot. She makes me feel better. And she enjoys my company. Is that so bad?"

"You're not falling for her, are you?"

"I'm not falling for anybody, Cordelia. I'm out of the love business, possibly for good. Patricia and I are friends. That's why I won't sit here and let you badmouth her—any more than I'd let her badmouth you."

Cordelia's eyebrows plunged. "What's she said about me?"

"Nothing. Let's change the subject, okay?"

"As if, *as if*." Cordelia growled, finishing her sandwich in one hefty bite. When she was done and had set her empty plate on the floor, she brushed her fingers off and said, "All right. Let it never be said that Cordelia Thorn cannot *move on*. Get any more tarot cards lately?"

Jane was about to answer when she was interrupted by a knock on the door. "Come in."

It was Arlene, her assistant manager. Instead of her usual wool slacks and tailored blazer, she was dressed down today in a milky tea-colored sweater—complete with shoulder pads—and pleated knit slacks. Tall and slim, her light auburn hair was drawn back into a pony tail, a young style for a woman in her sixties, but with Arlene's attractiveness, she could pull off just about anything. She was the aging Eve Arden to Jane's Mildred Pierce—funny and frank, a great employee.

"Jane, hi." She often chewed gum when customers weren't in the restaurant. "I just took a message for you upstairs. It was from Mary Dresser, your realtor?" Arlene consulted the stenographer's notebook in her hand. "She said she's got you a showing at the Holmes Avenue house at three. She'll meet you there."

"A showing?" said Cordelia, sitting up straight.

"Thanks, Arlene. Tell the chef I should be back before the dinner hour."

After Arlene had left, Cordelia drummed her nails on the arm of the couch. "Pray tell, what are you being *shown*?"

"I'm looking at some houses."

"Why?"

"I'm thinking of moving."

Cordelia was aghast. "From that gorgeous home of yours?"

"Yes."

"Because of . . . what happened to you?"

Jane felt suddenly close to tears. As hard as she tried, her emotions were still all over the place. "Maybe the memories will go away in time, but the truth is, I'm afraid to be alone there, especially at night. When it's dark out, I feel like I'm inside a locked cage. I know it doesn't make any sense."

"Of course it makes sense," said Cordelia gently.

"Sometimes I switch the radio on, or turn up the CD player really loud, but then I wonder what I'm not hearing. It's awful when every sound you don't immediately understand sends you into a panic. Makes me feel like a total chicken."

"You're way too hard on yourself."

A refrain Jane had heard before.

"Remember, you're welcome to stay at my place anytime you want."

"Thanks, Cordelia. You're a wonderful friend, but I can't lean on you—or Patricia, or Peter, or any of my other family or friends—forever. Moving may be the only real solution."

"What's the house on Holmes look like?"

A smile tugged at Jane's mouth. "It's pretty grand from the outside. I'll call you later tonight and give you a rundown. If it seems like a contender, I'll schedule another walk-through and you can come with me, give me your opinion. You can handle that, can't you, Cordelia? Another opinion or two?"

Jane arrived at the house just as her real estate agent was pulling up to the curb in front of her. While they were still outside, the agent explained that the man who owned the place normally wouldn't be home while Jane did the walk-through, but he'd sprained his ankle the day before and asked if it would be all right if he sat on the couch in the sun room and watched TV while she looked around. Jane didn't see any reason to say no. She was just beginning her search. The real estate agent cautioned her to keep her comments about the house to herself until they were all done and out the door. It didn't seem likely that the first house she looked at would be the one she'd eventually buy. Still, the agent didn't want her to show excessive enthusiasm—just in case. They could discuss her questions after the showing.

For a house that seemed so large and well cared for on the outside, the inside was a disaster. The rooms were cramped and dark and the floor plan was nothing but tiny room after tiny room. The kitchen seemed like an afterthought, the counters old and grimy. The basement smelled of mildew and the upstairs bedrooms were full of water damage.

As Jane examined a particularly odd piece of molding around the bathroom ceiling, she asked what the real estate agent would call it.

"I'd call it a dump," the agent whispered.

They grinned at each other and, right then and there, decided to leave. On the way through the living room, the agent thanked the man for his time, and asked him a question about the furnace. While he gave his explanation, Jane turned to look at the TV. He'd been watching Judge Judy. Jane rarely watched afternoon TV, though Peter sometimes did and would tell her about it over a late-night drink. He enjoyed all the arguing. It made Jane want to lock herself in a closet and never come out.

Just as the program ended, a newsman came on with a brief ad for the five o'clock news.

"This is Dan Swanson. Join us at five for coverage of a breaking news story in south Minneapolis. A woman living on the thirty-four-hundred block of Dupont Avenue was found badly beaten in her apartment less than an hour ago. Our reporter, Sandra Lynn Nelson, is at the scene." Behind him was a live shot of the apartment building.

Jane crouched down next to the TV to get a closer look. She couldn't tell for sure, but it looked like the place where Peter and Sigrid lived.

"Sandra, what do we know so far?"

"Well, Dan, as we speak, the victim is being transferred to Metro South." The building was surrounded by flashing lights. "We don't have any names yet, but the police have informed me that the victim is a white woman in her late twenties, and is employed as a family counselor at CNC."

"Oh my God," whispered Jane.

"What is it?" asked the real estate agent, turning to look at her.

The reporter continued: "I talked briefly to a neighbor who told me that she heard a fight between the woman and her husband earlier in the day. Then around two, she heard crashing sounds coming from the same apartment."

Jane closed her eyes. This couldn't be happening.

"Thanks, Sandra," said the anchorman. "Join us at five for this, and the latest on Governor Ventura's new tax proposal."

Jane pushed out of her crouching position. "Sorry, Mary. I've gotta run."

"Sure," said the real estate agent. "Is everything okay?"

"I don't know," said Jane as she rushed out the door.

10

Jane was a good driver. She wasn't a barger-inner or a lead-footed honker, but she was so desperate to get to Peter and Sigrid's apartment that she weaved in and out of traffic, slamming on her breaks, skidding too close to other cars, behaving like the jerks she loathed.

Hennepin Avenue could be total gridlock at this time of day, so she veered off to a side street, all the while keenly aware of a sensation of losing her balance, of being swept into a strong current, one she could no more control than she could understand. First came the drugs at her restaurant, and now this. The world had gone crazy and she was at the center of the maelstrom. She and Peter and Sigrid. Jane had a premonition, a sinking feeling that, after today, their lives would be changed forever.

She roared to a stop a block from the apartment. Up ahead, the police had closed off the street. Scrambling out of the front seat, she rushed through the growing twilight, leaping over mounds of snow and skirting patches of ice, hoping her bad leg wouldn't give out on her. She arrived at the front door, breathless, her heart stuck firmly in her throat. A crowd of gawkers had gathered outside, but she pushed her way through until she found a cop.

"Where's my brother?" she demanded. "I'm Jane Lawless. Is Sigrid all right?"

The man grabbed her by the arm, preventing her from going inside.

"I'm Peter's sister!" she pleaded, struggling to get away. "I need to see him."

The officer dragged her away from the crowd. A couple of stragglers followed, curious about what was going on, but he ordered them to back off. "If you cooperate with me," he barked at Jane, "I'll try to help you." He waited until she stopped struggling, then walked her around the side of the building to the parking lot in the back. Three squad cars had pulled in, lights flashing.

"Okay," he said, turning to face her. "You say Peter Lawless is your brother? Let's see some ID."

Jane fumbled in her back pocket for her wallet. "Here," she said, opening it and pointing at the driver's license. "See? Jane Lawless. Is Sigrid okay? Where's my brother?"

The officer handed her wallet back, then took a moment to size her up. "He's upstairs, but you can't see him. We're bringing him in for questioning."

"Why? You can't think Peter had anything to do with it."

"We don't know anything for sure."

"He loves Sigrid! He'd never hurt her!"

"Okay, okay. Don't blow a gasket." The cop scratched the back of his head, giving her a sidelong glance. "If I was him, I'd be glad to know you were on my side."

"Can I see him when he gets to the courthouse?"

"Maybe later, but not right away."

"What about Sigrid? How bad is she?"

"Bad."

"But she's alive, right?"

"Yeah. For now."

"Was she conscious?"

"Not when I saw her."

"You think . . . are you saying she might not make it?"

"For your brother's sake, let's hope she does."

Jane looked up at the sky. The sun was sinking lower, burning a wintry gold through the tops of the bare trees. "Do you know if Peter's called our dad?"

"He's the lawyer, right?"

She nodded.

"He said he'd meet your brother down at the courthouse."

Jane's gaze rose to Peter and Sigrid's third-floor windows. Every light in the place was on, making the rooms seem cozy and inviting. But it was all wrong. Everything was all wrong.

"You okay?" asked the cop.

She gave a dazed nod. "Thanks," she said finally. She figured there wasn't much else she could ask that he could answer. As she trudged back to the street, she was torn. Should she drive over to the hospital to be with Sigrid, or to the courthouse to be with her brother? She finally decided that the doctors would probably be working on Sigrid for some time. And if her father was headed to the courthouse, maybe he could get her in to see Peter. At least it was worth a try.

The clock on the waiting-room wall said seven-fifteen. Jane had been cooling her heels for over two hours. During that time, she'd drunk five cups of bitter-tasting coffee, which hadn't helped her nerves one bit. She'd called her restaurant and talked to Felix, the evening manager, explaining that she wouldn't be in until later—if at all. She didn't offer details. She called Cordelia and left messages at both her loft and at the theater. She called Patricia, but didn't leave a message. She called the hospital twice to get an update on Sigrid's condition. The first time a nurse said they didn't have any information. The second time the same nurse said Sigrid was listed as critical, and was in surgery. After that,

Jane just sat and stared at the wall. She was about ready to leave to go over to the hospital when a woman stepped into the waiting room and called Jane's name. As they walked down the hallway, the woman's high heels clicking on the marble floors, she explained that Jane's father and brother were waiting for her in one of the interrogation rooms. She asked Jane if she'd like a cup of coffee. Jane would have preferred a stiff drink.

Her dad met her at the door. Peter was seated at the far end of a round table, looking as if he'd been through a war. His blue cotton oxford-cloth shirt was a mass of wrinkles and his eyes were sunken and rimmed in red. He stood up as she came toward him. She pressed the side of her face against his, felt his scratchy beard, held him tight. He was shaking—or she was.

"Why don't you sit down, Jane?" said her father.

She turned to him. She'd never heard his voice sound so grave. "What's going on?" She pulled out a chair, her eyes ricocheting between her dad and Peter.

"The police have arrested your brother on assault charges."

"I didn't do it," insisted Peter. His voice sounded thick, angry. "They can't possibly think I'd hurt my wife. Why don't they let me go? I need to be with her!"

"I've already explained," said Raymond patiently. "You won't be arraigned until tomorrow morning. That's when bail will be set. When it is, we'll pay it and you'll be out of here."

Jane had a strong feeling that her father was holding something back, but she didn't press him on it. Whatever it was, he probably had his reasons. "Are you planning to defend him if there's a trial?" she asked.

Ray shook his head. "We're getting ahead of ourselves, but should it go that far, no, I can't. A father shouldn't represent his son. I've already called Elizabeth Piper. She'll be here in a few minutes. And she'll be the one at the arraignment with you tomorrow, Peter." He looked over at his son. "Do you understand? She's in charge of your case from now on."

"I don't understand a goddamn thing," said Peter, dropping his head in his hands.

"Do you know what happened at the apartment?" said Jane, mostly to her father. Peter had tuned them out.

"Apparently Peter and Sigrid reconciled last night. Peter spent the night at the apartment, but this morning they got into an argument. A pretty loud one. One of the neighbors talked to the police and said she heard some of it. When she was taking her laundry down to the laundry room, she saw Peter leave. That was about eleven. Then later in the afternoon, all the commotion started. The police arrived, sirens blaring, and entered the apartment. Peter was there. His fist was bruised. They put two and two together and assumed he was the one who'd beat her up."

"How did his fist get bruised?"

Ray took off his glasses and placed them on the tabletop. Passing a hand over his eyes, he continued, "He said he was so mad at Sigrid after he left the apartment that he slammed his fist into a wall. Of course, the police have their own theory."

"Wretched timing," muttered Jane. "If Peter hadn't shown up just then, the police might not have arrested him."

"Actually," said her father, "I don't think it was bad timing. Peter said he got a call on his cell phone shortly after two, some guy telling him to get over to his apartment right away. His wife was in trouble. He figured it was a prank call, but he couldn't exactly ignore it. As it happened, he was parked right around the corner, just sitting in his car, screwing up his courage. He'd finally cooled off and wanted to talk to Sigrid. When he got inside the apartment, he found Sigrid on the living room floor. She was barely breathing. He checked her pulse, tried to get her to talk to him, but she was out cold. He was scared to death. Somewhere in there, he says he remembers hearing a noise in the bedroom."

"There's a door to the hallway in that bedroom."

"Exactly. I think that's how the assailant got out. After beating her up, he tried to strangle her, but because Peter arrived so quickly, he had to get out faster than he'd planned. The police received an anonymous tip that something was going down at the apartment. I think our perp made that call. When the police walked in, Peter was kneeling next to Sigrid."

"You think he was set up?"

His eyes narrowed as he turned to look her square in the face. "Just like someone set you up, Jane. The fact that drugs were planted in your office the day before Peter's wife is nearly beaten to death and my son is accused of the crime—" He shook his head. "All I can say is . . . it makes me wonder."

"About what?" asked Jane.

He continued to shake his head.

"If you know something, tell me."

"That's just it, I don't know anything. For sure. It's just a feeling. A gut instinct." He glanced at Peter. Lowering his voice, he added, "People have tried to get back at me before. Lawsuits. Bomb threats. Even death threats. But *I* was always the target, never my children."

Jane suddenly felt lightheaded, as if all the breath in her body had been squeezed out of her. "You think this is happening because someone is angry at *you*?"

He would have continued, but the same woman who'd led Jane down the hall now poked her head into the room. "Mr. Lawless? You've got a phone call at the reception desk."

Ray was on his feet immediately. "Stay with your brother until I get back."

As the door shut behind him, Jane looked over at Peter. He'd put his head down on the table and closed his eyes. Not quite sure how to comfort him, she placed a hand gently on his back and rubbed his shoulders. "It's going to be okay, Peter." He'd always been her little brother. Even as a grown man, that's how she thought of him.

"No it's not. You didn't see Sigrid. God, why won't they let me out of here? I need to be with her."

It wasn't fair. There was no way she could convince him it

was. "When I'm done talking to you and Dad, I'll drive over to the hospital."

"But she needs *me!*" He got up, turning away from her. "Tomorrow may be too late."

"I called the hospital a little while ago. She's holding her own."

He gave himself a minute, then turned back, scraping a hand over his eyes. "Okay, you go. I don't mean to seem ungrateful, it's just—" He rested his knee on the chair. "When you get to her room . . . you've got to ask her a question for me."

Jane wasn't sure Sigrid was even conscious. "Sure, Peter. Whatever you want."

"Ask her why she didn't have her wedding ring on. I know it sounds cold, but when I saw her lying there on the living room carpet, for the first few seconds that's all I could think about. Her wedding ring. She wasn't wearing it." He looked at Jane with desperation in his eyes. "Did *she* take it off? Did . . . whoever hurt her take it off? I have to know. I can't stand not knowing!" Tears streamed down his face. "Tell her I love her. That I'm so sorry. If I hadn't left the way I did, this never would have happened. Do you see that, Janey? Even if I'm not guilty, I'm still responsible."

Before she could respond, Peter pulled a piece of paper out of his pocket. "I need a pen."

She handed him one.

"You've got to call Sigrid's mother right away. Let her know what's happened." He bent over the table and wrote the number down.

"What about her father?"

"He's been living in Japan for the past couple of years. The number's in our phone book at home. You'll have to get it from that . . . or from Sigrid's mother."

Jane assumed the apartment was sealed off. It was a crime scene, which meant the chances of her getting inside were pretty slim.

"You go now. Somebody should be with Sigrid. Try to get an

answer from her, okay—about the ring? And if there's any way you can call me, please . . . please—"

"I will," said Jane. She rose reluctantly from her chair. She hated to leave him. He looked so worn down, so defeated and desperate. "Dad should be back any minute. And Elizabeth Piper's coming."

"I know." He looked at her. "Do you think she's an okay lawyer?"

"Dad thinks so. I trust his judgment."

"Yeah, me too. Don't come to the arraignment in the morning, okay? It's just a formality. I'll call you when it's over. Get out of here now, Janey. I'll be fine."

She wanted to touch him again, but sensed that he was too raw. "See you tomorrow."

"Right," he said faintly, already drifting away from her.

After talking to a doctor, Jane was given the okay to go in and see Sigrid, though she would only be allowed in briefly. Sigrid had just come out of surgery and was now in intensive care. There'd been a lot of internal bleeding and her spleen had ruptured, so it had to be removed. The doctor said, more than once, that it was a miracle she was alive. Along with everything else, she had a severe concussion. Her attacker had attempted to strangle her with his hands, but for whatever reason, hadn't succeeded. The more the doctor said about her condition, the worse it sounded. The next twenty-four hours would be critical.

The intensive care unit wasn't just quiet, it was hushed, like the calm surrounding a violent storm. All the lighting was subdued and so were the staff voices.

When Jane finally entered the room, she saw a nurse seated at a computer terminal. Sigrid was lying motionless in the bed, partially covered by a white sheet, eyes closed, hooked up to various tubes and machines.

Jane's hands shook. She crossed her arms over her chest, then walked closer. Sigrid's skin looked sallow and puffy, like bread dough that had just started to rise. She was breathing normally, which Jane took as a good sign, but the purple-and-black bruises on her face and right arm were horrific. Jane could only imagine what the rest of her body looked like. She was so young, and yet, at this moment, she could have been any age—even an old woman.

Jane stared at her helplessly. Summoning her courage, she said, "Sigrid, it's Jane. You're going to be fine, kiddo. Really." Her voice sounded false, even to her. She figured Sigrid couldn't hear, but on the off chance that she could, she went on. "Peter will come in the morning. He wanted me to tell you how much he loves you. We all love you. I'm so sorry for what happened. But . . . no one can hurt you now. You're safe here. Hold on, Sigrid. Keep fighting."

The image of what had sent Jane to a different hospital mere months ago came rushing back to her with a brilliant, terrible clarity. For a moment, she was back at her house, standing by the front door. She heard the noise in her study and went to check on it. Then came the sensation of pain, of being trapped, of losing control. Jane closed her eyes, she had to get through it, had to stay focused on the here and now, and yet the panic that had nearly exhausted her reserves was still alive and well, lurking just under the surface, pushing against her, threatening to overwhelm her as it had so many times before. When would she finally be free of these panic attacks? Why couldn't she control herself? She'd been so sure she was getting better, but here it was again, the same blackness ready to swallow her whole. Her heart raced. She felt as if she were suffocating. She held her breath and counted, then let the air out slowly. It was a trick she'd learned. Sometimes it worked, staved off the panic, sometimes it didn't. Thankfully, tonight, it seemed to help. She did three more repetitions before she felt the tension between her shoulders ease.

She remembered her counselor's words. She was supposed to stay away from situations that might trigger moments of déjà vu. It was posttraumatic stress. It had a name. It was survivable. But the advice had seemed ridiculous, especially when Jane knew she could sit in a quiet room and suddenly break into a cold sweat. She'd be right back there again, terrified and alone in her house. It hadn't happened as frequently of late, but how could the sight of Sigrid not trigger a memory?

When the nurse touched her shoulder, Jane recoiled and whirled around.

"I'm sorry if I startled you," whispered the nurse.

Jane tried to cover. "I was just . . . I mean, I've been so worried—"

"Of course," said the nurse, smiling faintly. "But I'm afraid you'll have to leave now. I need to examine her."

"Fine," said Jane. "Fine. I'll call later to see how she's doing." Bending close to Sigrid's ear, she whispered, "I'm leaving now, Siggy, but there's a nurse in the room who'll take good care of you. I'll be calling to see how you're doing, and I'll be down again in the morning."

Jane's legs felt like rubber, but she made it to the door, and then down the long corridor to the elevators. One foot in front of the other, she told herself. Keep going. When she finally burst through the sliding front doors into the bitter, windy night, she filled her lungs with great gulps of cold air. She leaned against a railing until she felt more in control. She wanted to be with Peter tomorrow when he saw Sigrid for the first time. In his current state, she knew the reality of her condition would be almost too much for him. He'd need a strong shoulder to lean on and Jane was determined to provide it. But between now and then, all she wanted was oblivion.

11

Henry stood on the sidewalk outside Barrett Sweeny's Minnetonka home, cigarette smoke curling from his nostrils. In his haste to leave the bosom of his family, he hadn't put on a coat, but instead had stepped outside wearing nothing but his thin blue suit.

Today had been his brother's funeral. It had been a cloudy afternoon with light drizzle and a stiff wind blowing off the lake. Henry found it immensely sad that his brother had to be buried on such a day. Ever since he was a child, Bobby had hated dreary weather. Instead of an all-purpose, loving creator accepting his brother's body into the earth with a show of sympathy and respect, it had seemed as if a mortally cold universe was expressing its indifference. In death, Bobby had been snubbed.

After the mourners had sprinkled their handfuls of dirt onto the casket, everyone drove back to Grace Cathedral for a lunch provided by the church. By six, Henry was growing restless. He'd never been very good at small talk. When he saw Barrett leaving, he decided to leave as well. Barrett had issued an invitation to the immediate family to join him at his house for drinks after the church business was over.

When Henry walked into Barrett's living room a short time

later, he found that his mother had already arrived. She'd been so broken up during the ceremony that Henry wasn't sure she'd be in the mood for socializing. But there she was, sitting on the living room couch amidst pillows, Kleenex, and a constantly refilled glass of vodka and lime.

The only member of the family who wasn't inside was Henry's sister, Leslie. The *escapee*, as he thought of her. She couldn't come to the funeral because her youngest son was in the hospital. He'd fallen off the garage roof. To Henry, it sounded like a convenient excuse. Leslie had never really felt like a part of the family. By the time Henry and Bobby were old enough to recognize her presence and want to play with her, she was a teenager, intent on her own devices. And then she was gone to college, never to return. He saw her now every few years. Henry and his sister were always friendly and polite, but neither had the slightest idea who the other was. Sometimes he wondered if that wasn't true of families in general—a veneer of familial affection spread thickly over a chasm of ignorance and incomprehension.

Without Barrett's presence, the funeral would have been unendurable. To end the day at his place seemed fitting, a few stolen moments of relaxation in an otherwise depressing and stressful day. Henry didn't much care for Barrett's house. It was large, modern and obnoxiously ostentatious. But Barrett had grown up poor. What he owned now, he'd worked hard for. Still, Henry preferred his 1920s bungalow in the city. It was far more spartan. Comfortable and yet . . . people-sized. Barrett's house was more of a kingdom fit for a god. And of course, thought Henry, laughing to himself, that was the point.

Barrett had first entered their lives when he was fifteen. Bobby brought him home one winter afternoon and introduced him as his new best buddy. Henry, of course, had seen Barrett around the school. Henry was a junior that year, and Bobby and Barrett were both sophomores. Barrett wasn't exactly popular, although he seemed to command a certain, almost universal, respect. Secretly, Henry was fascinated by him, even before Bobby started bringing him around. The more Henry interacted with him, the more that fascination grew. Barrett exuded a provocative self-confidence that made him seem far older than his years. It was this self-confidence that Henry envied. Barrett wasn't talkative in any usual sense of the word, but he liked to discuss ideas.

Barrett was a serious young man and a good student, as was Henry. There were times when Henry was sure Barrett could see right through him, and that scared him—to feel so opened up, so visible. It also intrigued him. Henry wanted to know what secrets Barrett may have guessed about him, but he was afraid to ask. It was apparent that Barrett thought of himself as a superior life form, and yet he wasn't haughty. If anything, he was unusually kind. Henry had never met anyone like him before. That wasn't to say Barrett was an angel. If anything, his leanings were in the opposite direction. At fifteen, he was already sexually active. Henry saw him quite often with older girls, college girls, which was another thing that made Henry envious.

It didn't take long before Barrett had become the common denominator in Henry's family, the part of the equation everyone shared. To outsiders, it might have appeared strange that Barrett exerted so much influence on them—even Henry's mother and father openly expressed their love for him. On Barrett's side, it was obvious that he preferred Henry's family to his own. It was a marriage, so to speak, made in heaven. Or was it hell?

Henry lifted the cigarette to his lips, inhaled deeply, then exhaled a plume of smoke. Glancing back at the picture window, he could see his ghostly reflection, and behind it, the family gathered in the living room. His father was pouring drinks, passing around a plate of cheese and fruit.

Henry was a bit surprised that his mother and father were being so restrained in each other's presence today. They usually tossed insults like two people batting a tennis ball across a net. Sometimes Henry even found himself keeping score. Whoever issued the first insult became the server. Then, love-fifteen. Fifteen-all. Fifteen-thirty. Fifteen-forty. Thirty-forty. Deuce. Game point.

However it went, it was definitely entertaining. Perhaps the reality of losing a child had derailed some of their normal combativeness. He doubted it would last beyond tonight.

Flicking the cigarette into the snow, Henry reentered the house. The gas fire was going strong in the living room. Fresh from the cold, he felt assaulted by the heat. He wanted to turn around and walk back out the door, drive away in his Camry, but he knew he had to put in a few more minutes before he could make a getaway. He was the last remaining son now, and he felt the pressure of his parent's eyes watching him with a morose, slightly desperate booze-induced concentration, the same concentration that had rocketed him outside in the first place. He took the seat farthest from the fireplace, wishing they would lay off the staring.

At least Barrett and Taylor—Taylor Jensen, Bobby's girlfriend—provided another focus for his parent's attention. Taylor looked worn out from crying. She'd been living with Barrett for almost two years now, just as friends. When Bobby was first arrested, he asked Barrett to take care of her. For the first year, that meant checking up on her at the house where she and Bobby had been living. But when the house payments started to back up, and various utilities began threatening to cut off service, Barrett stepped in and sold the place—all with Bobby's permission. He moved Taylor in with him and that's where she'd been ever since. Henry didn't think it would last too much longer, now that Bobby was gone.

"Henry, come sit over here by me," called his mother, patting the couch. She'd already moved a couple of pillows in anticipation of him joining her.

Henry groaned inwardly, but got up and did as she asked. *Conrad and Shirley, Conrad and Shirley. Sad sad,* he thought to himself. It was his variation on an old theatrical theme. As soon as he was seated, he felt the pressure of his mother's hand against his back. At seventy-one, she was fairly well-preserved. With all the surgical nips and tucks she'd suffered through in her life, she could have passed for a woman in her early sixties, not much older than Henry's father. She was vain, of course, and self-centered, as was Henry and his father. Narcissism. The Alto curse. Only Bobby seemed to have escaped. And now he was dead. Perhaps there was a correlation.

As if reading Henry's mind, Barrett sat forward in his chair. His face was pale, his expression subdued. "The tree does not die, Henry. It waits."

Henry met his eyes.

Conrad crouched next to Barrett's CD collection, looking for something to put on the stereo. After making a selection, he slipped the disk into the CD player, then sat down in a dark corner of the room, picked up his drink and closed his eyes as the opening strains of *St. Matthew's Passion* filled the room with melancholy.

"I can't believe he isn't here," said Taylor. Her voice sounded weak, small. She'd hardly spoken all evening. She was seated on the floor in front of Barrett, her back resting against his chair. She was a sweet-looking woman. Reddish-blond hair and large gray eyes. Barrett rested his hand on her neck, massaging it every now and then. Henry's mother had been watching the hand. So had Henry's father.

Wiping her eyes with a tissue, Shirley said, "I could hardly sit through that service. It was too long, with too much religious music."

Henry watched to see if his father would respond, but he seemed worlds away. He had a look of quiet absorption on his face, a look Henry had seen many times before. If he'd heard his wife's comment, he wasn't interested in a volley right now. His father had, of course, organized the music. He'd selected each piece, directing the choir and the orchestra himself. Music had always been his father's language of choice. It was his solace now.

Music had been his mother's life as well, but as her hands grew more arthritic, she couldn't play without pain. In a strange way, she seemed to blame the music for her impairment. Before she moved to her current house, she'd sold her organ and her harpsichord. She insisted she was done with all that. Music was her husband's all-consuming passion. Her interests lay elsewhere.

"I can't stand churches on general principle," continued Shirley, waving her drink around. "And especially that cathedral. All that pomp and ritual—it's pathetic."

Henry found the open casket curious. Of course he knew it was commonly done. And yet, in a society that tried so hard to deny death, why people wanted to look at a person after he was gone was beyond him. Not that the mortician hadn't done a bang-up job. Henry wasn't the least bit squeamish about dead bodies—as a doctor, he couldn't be. Unless you looked really close, which Henry had, you couldn't see any trace of the cuts from the fight. Even his brother's fingernails were clean—something that they rarely were in life.

Bobby was always at work on some filthy art project. Casting metal. Digging through garbage cans looking for stuff he could use in his "found" sculptures. In his own unambitious way, he was as odd as the rest of them. But he wasn't a murderer. The fact that he was dead was one of life's cosmic jokes. The minister had called Bobby's final hours tragic, and of course they were. It should never have turned out that way.

"Turn down that music," demanded Henry's mother.

Conrad opened his eyes. Without comment, he got up and switched off the CD player. "Are you happy now, Shirley?"

She glared at him.

Henry admired his father's style. When he wasn't around his wife, he might even be called charming. Henry had studied him for years and come to the conclusion that charm in a human being had more to do with simple listening than anything else. His father was a spectacular listener. At the same time, he had the capacity to make people feel as if they were the only ones in the world who mattered.

Henry didn't have much patience when it came to people blathering on and on about themselves, which meant he oozed about the same amount of charm as his stethoscope. A patient was a puzzle, one he needed to solve—and solve quickly. The person behind the illness was secondary. Maybe that meant he was a substandard doctor, but in the emergency room, it gave him the edge.

"I want to take you boys back to Italy," said Conrad, resuming his seat. He glanced at Henry, then at Barrett. "What do you think? Could we arrange our schedules to do it sometime soon?"

Italy, thought Henry, surprised by the invitation. He hadn't expected that his father would ever want to go back.

Henry traced the true beginning of his adult life to that summer, the two months he'd spent in Italy with his father, his brother and Barrett. But going back? He wasn't sure. It seemed wrong, somehow. Foolish. There was no way they could recapture the magic of those last few golden weeks. Even to try seemed a sacrilege. "I don't know, Dad," said Henry. "Do you think we should?"

Barrett sighed. "I've got a lot coming up in the next few months, Con. I doubt I could take the time off."

"You're always thinking about yourself," said Shirley, holding her glass out as Barrett poured her another drink.

"I'm *not* thinking about myself," insisted Conrad, his face turning a deep red. "And I resent the implication. I'm thinking about my son. We found each other in Italy in a way you'll never understand. I want to go back to honor his memory and to truly mourn his loss."

"Bullshit," mumbled Shirley.

Conrad shot out of his chair. "Are you saying I didn't love him? I'd give my *life* for him. Can you say that, Shirley? Can you? If I could get my hands on the man who knifed Bobby, I'd rip his heart out. And as for that lawyer I hired, God help him when I'm finished with him!"

Barrett put his hand on Conrad's arm. "We all feel the same way."

"Time out," called Henry, hoping to stave off an ugly scene.

His parents could do a lot of damage to each other with the amount of liquor they'd both consumed this evening. "Let's turn on the TV, see what's on, okay?"

Since all conversation had essentially died, a little background noise was called for. Henry toyed for a few seconds with the idea of telling everyone that he'd begun seeing a therapist, but because he was the repository of so many juicy family secrets, he didn't think the comment would be greeted with much enthusiasm. On the other hand, it would be fun to watch them all sweat.

Barrett grabbed the remote from an end table and surfed the channels until he found the local news. In the silence of the living room, with everyone already exhausted by the emotion of the day, the TV was a glowing godsend, a flickering eye with a view into other people's tragedies—no response necessary. It was just ten o'clock. The lead story was about a two-alarm fire that had destroyed a supper club in Lino Lakes. Conrad sat down, staring at the footage of flames shooting out of the club's windows. A hand rose absently to his throat.

The next story was about the governor's proposed tax cut.

Henry yawned. He'd stay until the weather report was over and then he'd split. At least he could sleep late in the morning. He didn't have to be at the hospital until three.

Suddenly, Henry's father said, "Turn that up."

The anchor woman was saying, "A young woman fights for her life tonight at Metro South Hospital in Minneapolis." In the background, a picture of the woman appeared on the screen. "Sigrid Lawless, a family counselor at CNC in Anoka, and daughter-in-law of Raymond Lawless, well-known St. Paul defense attorney, was badly beaten this afternoon in her apartment in south Minneapolis. She is currently listed in critical condition. Peter Lawless, a cameraman at WTWN-TV and the woman's estranged husband, was arrested for the assault. In other news—"

Barrett turned the volume down. Nobody spoke for several seconds.

Henry studied his parents. Just the mention of Raymond Lawless's name had the power to send both of them into paroxysms. "I think I should get you home, Mom," he said, rising from the couch. "Come on. I'll drive you. You've had too much to drink."

"Raymond Lawless." His father spit the name.

"Maybe now he'll find out what it feels like," said Shirley, her eyes glassy from too much vodka.

"Barrett, help me get Mom out to my car," said Henry. He tried to yank her to her feet but she wouldn't cooperate.

Barrett switched off the TV set and together they packed Shirley into her coat and wound a scarf around her neck.

On the way out the door, Henry called, "I'll talk to you later, Dad."

Conrad seemed so caught up in his own thoughts, he merely waved.

By the time Jane returned to her house, it was close to midnight. She was shivering so hard that her first thought was to build a fire in the fireplace. She found some dry oak on the back porch, which would burn slow and hot. After bunching up some old newspaper and tossing in a few sticks of kindling, she let it get a good start, then tossed in a log, listening to the bark crackle. She sank down on the couch until she began to thaw out, and only then did she get up and wander into the dining room, kicking off her already unlaced boots and letting them land wherever they wanted, tossing her coat over a chair and dropping her leather gloves on the dining room table. With her scarf still tied around her neck, she removed a bottle of brandy and glass from the kitchen cupboard. When she returned to the living room, the fire was roaring.

She doubted she could sleep. Maybe the brandy would allow her a few hours. It was a law of physics that the faster a wheel was spinning, the longer it took to come to rest. She hadn't eaten anything since breakfast, so she was hungry, but she knew when the food hit her stomach it might not stay down. Instead of food, she just wanted to escape, to disappear, to shut off her thoughts and emotions. She was alone in the house—something she'd carefully managed to avoid for many months. Peter's presence had been a sort of salvation. Now he was the one who needed saving.

When the doorbell rang an hour later, she got up, still holding her brandy glass, and floated to the door. She was feeling no pain now. Maybe she shouldn't drink when she was alone, but it helped.

Cordelia flew into the front foyer like a huge squawking crow. She was all black arms and black legs, herding Jane into the living room with her bulk, cawing at her with her beak open, her tongue wagging, her eyes popping. Jane had a hard time concentrating on what she was saying. She caught a word every now and then. "Phone." Then, "Twenty-first century."

"Slow down," said Jane, dropping back down on the couch.

Before Cordelia tore off her coat, she yanked a package out of the pocket and threw it at Jane.

"What's this?"

"Haven't you heard a word I said?"

"Well, actually—"

"It's a cell phone. I don't care if I have to drag you kicking and screaming into the next millennium, you're going to *use* it. Got it?" She waited for a reaction.

"Got it," repeated Jane, giving her a goofy smile.

"Have you been drinking?"

"Yes, mother."

Cordelia sat down. "How much?"

"Just a little. No lectures."

She glanced at the bottle of brandy. "Listen to me, Jane. I bought *that phone*—and the service—for you this afternoon. No more leaving messages for you all over the freaking universe hoping you'll return my calls. You are plugged in now. Hooked up. *Available*. And see to it that you keep the battery charged."

Jane set her glass down, then took the phone out of the box and looked at it.

"It's very simple," said Cordelia. She quickly explained how it worked. "It's even got a little video game you can play when you're just sitting around doing nothing."

"Gee."

Cordelia glared. "I don't expect gratitude. That would be too much. But I do expect you to keep it with you. *At all times*. Do I make myself clear?"

"Crystal."

"Good. It's all charged up and ready to go."

"What's my new number?"

"It's on the box." She pointed to where she'd written it. "I got you top-of-the-line service, by the way. Nationwide long distance. Lots of minutes per month. No roaming charges. No skimping when Cordelia Thorn is involved."

"Thanks, Cordelia. Really."

"Don't patronize me."

"I'm not. I think it's a great idea."

She narrowed one eye. "Thank God we're not living during the time of the Model A Ford. You'd probably still be riding a horse."

The idea appealed to Jane. "Yes, I probably would."

She shuddered. "I don't *do* nature."

"I know."

Again she glanced at the bottle of brandy. "I thought you'd sworn off alcohol."

"No. I'm just cutting down. But . . . it's been kind of a bad day."

"I don't doubt it. Pass me the bottle."

"Are you sure? You have to drive home."

"No I don't. I'm spending the night. Figured you could use the company."

Jane was embarrassed to tell Cordelia how much better she felt now that she knew she wouldn't be staying in the house alone. Instead of making a fool of herself by gushing, she handed Cordelia the bottle.

"So, give, Janey. How's Sigrid? Where's Peter?"

Jane explained it all. Everything, including her reaction when she saw Sigrid in the hospital.

Cordelia listened intently, occasionally squeezing Jane's hand for support. She seemed most intrigued by Jane's father's comment about someone trying to get back at him by hurting his children. "I wish he'd elaborated."

"I think he would have, but we got interrupted. Actually, I needed to ask him about that cop he was going to call about the drugs planted in my restaurant, but we never had time. And then Peter wanted me to go see Sigrid. I looked around for my dad before I left, but couldn't find him. It's too late now. I'll talk to him tomorrow."

"Good," said Cordelia, taking a swig from the bottle. "And when you're done, you'll call me on your shiny new cell phone and give me the details."

"That's right." Jane thought of all the calls she needed to make tomorrow. "Oh no," she said, suddenly realizing she hadn't called Sigrid's mother. She'd intended to do it as soon as she arrived at the hospital, but with everything on her mind, she'd forgotten. She searched the pockets of her jeans for the piece of paper Peter had given her—the one he'd written the number on. "I screwed up," she said, finally locating it. "I forgot to call Mrs. Munson."

"Oh, Janey. The story was on the ten o'clock news."

"Maybe the police already contacted her."

"Let's hope so."

"I suppose it's too late to call her now." It was going on one-thirty in the morning.

"I think you should try," said Cordelia. She pointed to the cell phone. "Time for its maiden voyage."

It was the last thing Jane wanted to do.

"Look," said Cordelia, getting up and throwing another log on the fire, "you make the call and I'll make us a couple of my famous wee-hours-of-the-morning omelets. You need sustenance, Janey. So do I."

The gnawing in Jane's stomach had been growing worse.

Maybe she should try to eat something. "Okay. Sounds good."

Cordelia was halfway to the kitchen when Jane shouted, "Get back here! You've got to see this!"

"What?" said Cordelia, thundering back into the living room and doing a belly flop over the back of the couch.

"Look." She handed over the piece of paper Peter had given her.

Cordelia unfolded it, stared at it a moment, then scrambled to a sitting position. "*Ohmygawd.* Oh . . . my . . . gawd! Another tarot card."

"There's a number three at the top of the page."

Cordelia's shock turned instantly to wariness. "How did Peter get it?"

"No idea. He needed a piece of scratch paper to write Mrs. Munson's number on, so he pulled it out of his pocket."

"The Nine of Swords. Another cheerful thought."

"What's it mean?"

Cordelia held it closer to the firelight. "I don't remember exactly, but it's definitely not one of the 'your-future-will-be-rosy' cards. Listen, Jane, I think it's time we called in an expert. And for that, there's nobody better than the Amazing Zarda."

"Who's she?"

"My tarot reader. I'll phone her in the morning and make us an appointment."

"What if more cards are on the way?"

"At least she'll give us a head start on the meaning."

Under the circumstances, Jane figured it was a reasonable thing to do. "All I can say is, if somebody wants to tell me something, they can send me a letter."

"But this *has* real concrete meaning."

"I wish I had your confidence."

"I'm not just confident, Janey, I'm certain. After tomorrow, you may not have the name of the person behind all your family's problems, but you'll have a much better idea of why. And *that*," she said, lowering her voice for emphasis, "will lead you to *who*."

Raymond sat in the rear of the courtroom during Peter's initial appearance before a judge. Bail was set at twenty thousand dollars. During the proceedings, the prosecuting attorney explained that, earlier in the morning, she'd spoken with Sigrid Lawless's brother, Todd Munson. Todd was concerned for his sister's safety. He didn't want Peter to have access to her while she was in the hospital—not until everything got sorted out. He petitioned the court for a restraining order against Peter, which the judge granted. Thus, as a provision of Peter's release, he was barred from seeing Sigrid or contacting her in any way.

When Peter heard the ruling, he nearly ejected from his seat. He began gesturing and whispering to Elizabeth, who was sitting next to him. Perhaps Ray should have warned him that this was a possibility, but Peter had seemed so much more positive before the arraignment, saying that at least now he'd be able to see his wife. Raymond couldn't take his hope away from him, especially when he wasn't certain a restraining order would be asked for or granted.

As Peter was led away to be processed out, Elizabeth turned and caught Ray's eye. They met outside the courtroom doors.

"Your son's pretty upset," said Elizabeth, watching Ray's reaction. They both sat down on a wooden bench.

"Of course he's upset. None of this makes any sense."

She covered his hand with her own. "Are you all right?"

"No." Ray wasn't sure how much he should say. If he told her of his suspicions about the Alto family, she'd probably feel partly responsible. After all, she'd argued the appeal for Bobby Alto. "Look, I don't want to upset you, but . . . well, the fact is—" He might as well just say it out loud, get it over with. If she thought he was nuts, she'd tell him so. "I think both my kids have been set up. I told you about what happened to Jane."

"The drugs that were planted in her office."

He nodded. "You recall the day we found out Bobby Alto had died in that prison fight? You drove over to give his brother the news. I went to see his father."

She cocked her head, looking uncertain. "Yes. What's that got to do with this?"

"Conrad Alto threatened me," said Ray. "And it wasn't the first time. I figured I should cut the guy some slack. I mean, his son had just died. I thought he was just blowing off steam. He had a right to his pain and his anger. But now I think it was more than that."

"Threatened you? How?"

"He said if it hadn't been for my unprofessional behavior during the trial, his son would be a free man—or words to that effect. None of this would have happened if it weren't for me. Bobby was innocent and I should have made the jury see it."

"Come on, Ray. You've heard that before. You did everything you could. So did I."

He glanced at her, then looked away. "Alto doesn't see it that way. When we lost the appeal, he threatened a malpractice suit. But after Bobby's murder, he lost it completely. He said that I'd not only ruined his son's life, but now I was responsible for his death. An eye for an eye, he said. He screamed those words at me, Elizabeth. Believe me, he meant it."

"You take his son's life, and he takes yours?"

"I don't know what he's got in mind, but yes, I think he may be after both my children. He's making me pay by hurting them. I don't know it for a fact, but I know it in my gut."

Elizabeth considered it for a moment, tugging absently at one of her pearl earrings. "But . . . he seems like such a quiet, sensitive man. If his son Henry had made the threat, I'd be more inclined to take it seriously. That man is cold to the core. But Conrad—"

"They're all strange." Ray folded his arms. Glancing at Elizabeth out of the corner of his eye, he sensed that she'd drawn away from him, but he didn't know why. "Look, I want you to know how grateful I am that you're taking Peter's case. Once Sigrid is able to talk to the police, tell them what really happened, I'm sure she'll clear everything up. The charges will be dropped."

"I talked to Sigrid's nurse before I drove down to the government center this morning. Sigrid is stable. That's a positive sign."

Ray cupped his hands around the edge of the bench, anchoring himself to the solid wood. "It is. But I called just before the arraignment began and the nurse said that she was in surgery again. Apparently there was some internal bleeding, something they didn't take care of yesterday—or maybe the bleeding started in the night. It wasn't clear to me what happened."

Elizabeth turned to face him. "What's the prognosis?"

"The doctor I talked to yesterday gave her a less than a fifty-fifty chance of surviving. God, if anything happens to her . . . if she doesn't make it—" He bowed his head, unable to finish the sentence.

When he felt Elizabeth's arm slip reassuringly around his back, he looked over at her, realizing how deeply he wanted some physical connection to her. It wasn't sexual, it was merely human. This was one of the worst moments of his life. Marilyn should have been here. She should have been the one to offer comfort, but she was having her own crisis in New Orleans.

"From everything I hear, Sigrid is a strong young woman," said Elizabeth. "Don't count her out."

"Oh, I'm not," said Ray, though the truth was, his usual optimism seemed to be failing him at the moment. "I may have to take a rain check on our dinner tonight."

"Sure. You've got a lot on your plate right now."

"No, it's not that. I've enjoyed our evenings together."

"It's hard when your wife's out of town. You're at loose ends."

He nodded. "I hope you don't think I'm using you."

"Hell, Ray. I'm not a teenager. I know the score. Besides, I've enjoyed your company. Maybe *I'm* using *you*. Did you ever think of that?" She gave a hearty laugh.

Ray cleared his throat. "Tonight, I'm insisting that Peter come stay with me at the house. He can't go back to his apartment."

"I thought he was living at your daughter's place."

"He was. But I think he needs to spend some time with his old man. I know I need to spend some time with him. He can stay in his room upstairs. It will be like old times. Say, that reminds me." He checked his watch. "I told Peter that I'd call Jane when the arraignment was over. Let her know what happened."

"You go ahead," said Elizabeth, rising from the bench. "I'll go down and wait for your son."

As she started to walk away, Ray caught her by the hand. "We'll have dinner again soon."

She smiled. "I'll look forward to it."

"Maybe you, me and Peter can all get together tomorrow night."

"I'd like that," said Elizabeth. She squeezed his hand. "You'll get through this, Ray—with a little help from your friends."

"As long as you're one of them, I count myself and my family in good hands."

Wearing a long blue robe that accentuated the vibrancy of her red wig, the Amazing Zarda met Jane and Cordelia at the front door of her downtown Minneapolis condo. She lived near the river, just a few blocks from Cordelia's loft. She'd just said good-bye to a young woman with porcupine hair who, as Jane and Cordelia trudged up the walk, winked at them knowingly. Jane figured that all sorts of people came to tarot readers. Frankly, she wasn't all that pleased to be among their number.

On the way over from her house, Cordelia was in an upbeat mood. She regaled Jane with her version of "Love Potion Number Nine," in the Amazing Zarda's honor, no doubt.

"Is she a gypsy?" asked Jane.

"Heavens, no. I believe she's Norwegian. Her last name is Sodeberg."

"Zarda Sodeberg?"

"*Evelyn* Sodeberg. Zarda is the name she uses for her business."

The song was a welcome change from the version of "Stormy Weather" Cordelia had been singing—or, more accurately, emoting—while wolfing down the last of Peter's powdered sugar doughnuts. Jane had offered to make her breakfast—a bowl of oatmeal, or a couple scrambled eggs. Real food with vitamins and minerals in it. But Cordelia said—while licking the sugar off her fingers—that the donuts were fine. She washed them down with a Coke. Jane tried not to shudder audibly.

"How much does a reading cost?"

"Fifty bucks."

"Seems kind of steep."

"It's worth every penny, Janey. You'll see."

As they stood in the front hall of the Amazing Zarda's condo, taking off their coats, Cordelia introduced Jane. Zarda's pencil-thin eyebrows raised slightly when she heard the last name. Jane wondered if she'd been listening to the news.

The condo smelled of lily-of-the-valley perfume and stale cigarette smoke. Following Zarda back to the kitchen, Jane saw that most of the furniture was from the fifties—blond wood chairs and tables with tapered legs. Dark, boxy upholstery. Lamps with chartreuse shades. Just as they were about to enter a small breakfast room off the kitchen, a green parrot fluttered out of nowhere and landed on Zarda's shoulder. It flapped for a few seconds, making sure it was properly balanced, then began to nibble at the rhinestone necklace around her neck.

"Mordrid, what did I tell you about my jewels?"

They were hardly jewels, thought Jane. Precious stones didn't come in orange.

"Please, have a seat," said Zarda, sitting down at a round table covered with a black-and-gold silk cloth. On top were several tarot decks, a pen and notepad, and a cell phone. The shades were pulled and the room was suffused with a lurid, sulfur yellow light. Bug lights, thought Jane. At least there weren't any crystal balls.

Zarda had an unusually small mouth, covered in a shade of lipstick that reminded Jane of the methialate her mother used to put on cuts. Her cheeks were heavily rouged, and her eyes were thick with mascara and brushed with purple eye shadow. Not your usual Norwegian. As she placed her hands on the table next to a large tarot deck, Jane could see that she'd tucked a lace handkerchief just inside her sleeve.

"So," said Zarda, giving Jane a thorough looking over. The parrot seemed to be looking her over too, seeing if she had anything on her worth pecking. "Let's get down to business." She switched her gaze to Cordelia. "How's your love life?"

Cordelia gave her a conspiratorial grin. "Complicated, as usual. But we'll save that for later."

"Of course, dear." Returning her attention to Jane, Zarda said, "I understand you're the one who needs my help this morning."

"Show her the pages," said Cordelia.

"Show me the money!" squawked the parrot.

"Mordrid, be quiet." Zarda patted the bird's feet, which caused its wings to flutter and knock her wig slightly askew. Zarda didn't seem to notice.

Jane removed the pages from a file folder she'd brought with her and spread them out on the table. She'd already placed each one in a plastic bag, hoping to preserve them—for what, she wasn't sure.

"Hum," said Zarda, pinching her chin. Her glasses were hanging from a silver chain around her neck. She slipped them on, then pulled the pages closer, arranging them in order. "From what Cordelia told me on the phone, it's my understanding that these were sent to you recently."

Jane shifted in her chair. "I got the first one. My father received the second. And my brother was sent the third."

Zarda continued to study them, her head bent over the table. "It's the Universal Waite tarot. A pretty standard deck. Let's see, I think I've got one of those around here somewhere." She reached behind her to a pile of decks stacked on a low table. Pulling out the one in the center, she said, "I prefer the Arcus Arcanum, or the Russian Tarot of St. Petersburg. But this one is adequate. Now, you say you have no idea who sent these to your family?"

"None," said Jane.

As Zarda leaned back, the parrot began threading strands of her wig through its beak.

"I thought maybe it was a three-card spread," said Cordelia. "But I don't know which one—or what it means."

"Three card spreads are very popular because they represent a unity—a whole. For instance, three-card-spreads are used to understand relationships, like mother-father-child, or mind-body-spirit. Then there are the longer spreads, six, eight, ten, twelve cards, like the turn-of-the-clock spread, the Celtic cross, or the sacred-quest-spread. This is just a guess, you understand, but I think what you've got here is a past-present-future spread. It's very common. Let's proceed on that assumption, see where it leads us."

Jane's inclination was to dismiss it all as mumbo-jumbo, impenetrable and fraudulent, but with everything that had happened to her family in the past couple of days, she couldn't.

Zarda lit up a cigarette. Blowing smoke out of the side of her mouth, she continued, "The first card is Justice. Justice, as the tarot defines it, is all about our ability to understand the past, which in turn depends on our ability to see the truth about ourselves and about life in general. Justice is another name for truth. It's the living force that holds the universe together. In legal terms, it means a *just* decision. The tarot's symbol of Justice wears no blindfold, meaning that she demands absolute honesty. She looks you square in the eyes. But the card has been reversed on the page. Therefore the meaning is a deep injustice. In this case, something that happened in the past."

"How far in the past?" asked Jane.

Zarda shrugged, causing the parrot to lose its balance. As it flapped away, it carried her wig in its mouth. "Mordrid! Get back here. Damn that bird. I'm having your wings clipped!" She patted her pinned-up gray hair, looked momentarily embarrassed, then stubbed out her cigarette, pushed out of her chair and hurried out of the room.

Cordelia waved the smoke away from her face. "I've been

waiting for that awful creature to do something like that for years."

"Strong bird," said Jane, hearing something crash to the floor in the kitchen. "Do you think she needs our help?"

"What she needs is a baseball bat and a good aim."

A few seconds later, Zarda returned. Her wig was back on her head but her mascara had smeared. She looked like a circus clown with a large teardrop on her cheek.

Zarda lit another cigarette. "Sorry about that. Now, where were we?" She glanced at the pages. "Yes, Justice. You asked how far in the past the injustice occurred. It could have been anytime, but my guess is it was in the past year or two. Most likely, something happened recently to set this person off—the one who sent you the cards."

"And the second card represents the present?" said Cordelia.

Zarda tapped ash onto a saucer. "The Tower. Yes, that's your family's here-and-now. It's a pretty dark card, but like the Devil, it has many meanings. Obviously, it talks of disaster. Maybe a friend has turned against you, your work has collapsed, or some kind of violence swirls around you. One of the mysteries of life is that bad luck seems to come in clumps. But sometimes we create our own disasters by neglect or lack of diligence. You have to give that some thought, Ms. Lawless. Of course, other tarot readers might look at this card differently, emphasize certain aspects while deemphasizing others, but to me the meaning has always been clear. The Tower is about violent emotions—emotions that can cripple a person. That could mean you or someone in your family. But in the end, the force of the rage raining down from the tower blows the dam away, releasing the energy locked up inside, so it isn't totally negative."

"Yikes," said Cordelia, looking horrified.

Zarda tapped more ash onto the saucer. "Sorry. I can't wrap these cards in candy floss. Any questions so far?" she asked, looking at Jane.

She shook her head. She'd already determined that this wasn't a normal reading. These cards were a message. They'd been selected and arranged to create a specific impression. No mystical prescience or fortune-telling paradigm was involved. Cordelia might assign great weight to Zarda's interpretation, but Jane saw the situation for what it was. These pages were a threat, pure and simple. A mind game. They had no power to foretell, only to frighten. That was the whole point.

"Okay, let's move on," said Zarda. "The last card, the Nine of Swords, represents your future." She stuck the cigarette in the side of her mouth, and thought for a minute. "Boy, this is some spread."

"Tell me about it," whispered Cordelia, looking positively grim. She patted Jane's hand.

"This is one of the harshest cards in the deck. The image is one of deep sorrow, of terrible mental pain. Sometimes the nine refers not to us, but to someone we love. If we were looking at the Toth deck, for instance, we'd see an animal lying dead behind the swords. A dead dog. Perhaps a future dead dog?"

"That's it," said Jane, pushing back from the table and standing up.

"I'm sorry if I upset you, Ms. Lawless." Zarda looked pointedly at Cordelia, then back at Jane. "Truly, I am. But I simply relay the meaning. You shouldn't ignore what the cards say. The tarot has great power."

"This isn't a reading, it's abuse. I realize you're not responsible, but I refuse to sit here and subject myself to it. Come on, Cordelia. We're done." Jane picked up the pages and slipped them back in the file folder, tossed a ten and two twenties on the table and headed for the door.

15

After saying goodbye to Cordelia and promising to keep her new cell phone at the ready, Jane entered her house feeling pummeled and raw. On the way home in the car, she'd made an effort to explain her reasons for leaving so abruptly. Cordelia was under the impression that Jane had been scared to death, that she couldn't stand to be in the same room with those terrifying tarot cards. But the truth was, Jane was furious.

"Okay, so Zarda was just doing her usual schtick," said Jane, "but it felt like she was laying the doom and gloom on with a trowel. Besides, it wasn't a *real* reading. Somebody chose those cards. The cosmos wasn't trying to send me a message, a human being was."

Cordelia agreed, though Jane could tell she still felt the cards carried a certain power, no matter how Jane tried to rationalize it. For now, that was as close as their thinking was going to get.

But now that Jane was home, the first order of business was to put on the teakettle. She needed something warm and soothing in her stomach. As the water was heating up, she went into her study to check her messages. She had two.

The first was from Patricia Kastner:

"Lawless, it's me. How *are* you? Boy what a mess, huh? Is your brother in jail? Saw it all on the news last night. How's his wife doing? I'll be at the office all day, but if you want to come by the house later to talk—or whatever—I'll be around. Hey, why don't I fix you a late dinner? I'll hit the grocery store on the way home, just in case. I think you need a little TLC. I'm good at TLC, in case you've forgotten. Actually, I'm, ah . . . I'm kind of worried about you. Call me, okay? Bye."

The second message was from Sigrid's brother:

"Jane, hi. This is Todd Munson." He always spoke slowly, as if he were talking to a small child. "I wasn't able to make it to your brother's arraignment this morning. I wanted to go, but I had other commitments. I hope you understand about the restraining order. I'm just trying to protect my sister. I don't know what really happened, but I figure the police will get to the bottom of it. Please understand, Jane, I like Peter. He doesn't seem like the kind of guy who'd snap and do something like that . . . but . . . I can't take any chances where my sister's concerned. I know you left a message on Mom's machine last night. She's out of town. Actually, she's in Israel right now with a church group. It's kind of a special deal. I may call her to come home early. Depends on how Sigrid is doing. She was okay this morning, but . . . well, you probably already know about the second operation." He coughed a couple of times, then cleared his throat. "I just wanted to . . . check in. I know your family must be going through hell right now too. I will say I was pretty angry last night. I guess I still am. I don't want to think your brother is involved, but if he is—" He didn't finish the sentence. Instead, he began again. "I stayed with Sigrid from one until four this morning. I'll try to get down again today by noon. I've talked to my sister Jill in Philadelphia. She may fly home. Carrie and Kyle are both living at my Mom's house right now. You may run into them at the hospital. I guess all we can do is pray that Sigrid will be okay. Tell Peter I'm sorry, but I had to do what I did."

The restraining order was a total surprise to Jane. Her brother must have been crushed. She needed to get in touch with him, and with her dad, right away. She also needed to call the hospital. She hadn't heard anything about a second surgery. It was going on eleven. The last time she'd talked to a nurse was just before eight. She wished now that she'd gone to the arraignment—or to the hospital. Anywhere but that awful tarot reader's place. As she picked up the phone to call her dad's office, the front doorbell chimed. Jane rushed out of the room to answer it.

For years, ringing doorbells in her home were always followed by barking dogs and wagging tails. Gulliver, her first dog, had died a year ago. And now Bean. Jane understood that grief came in waves, in sudden bursts of intensity. Finding an old chew toy. Remembering the feel of Bean's paws as he scratched at her knees, asking to be picked up and hugged. There were times when she wanted to stop the flow of detail, the photographs in her mind, but other times, like this, she wanted nothing more than to hold on to them. Hold them close and never let them go.

Reaching the front door, she found that her father was standing outside. "I'm so glad you came by," she said, giving him a hug. As she helped him off with his coat, the teakettle in the kitchen started to shriek. "I was just about to make tea."

Her father smiled. "I can hear that. Reminds me of your mother." He followed her through the dining room into the kitchen. "I've been thinking about her a lot lately. She enjoyed a good cup of coffee every now and then. She'd make half a pot in the mornings because she knew I liked it. But whenever there was a problem, something important she needed to think over, she always made tea. Earl Grey."

Jane lifted a teapot down from the cupboard. She felt warmed by the comparison. "Tell me what happened in court. Is Peter out of jail?"

"I took him back to his apartment so he could get his car. I don't know where he's at right now. Probably drove over to the the station to talk to his boss, tell him he won't be in for a few days."

"Todd Munson called," said Jane, scooping tea leaves from a tin. "He mentioned something about a restraining order?"

Her father sighed audibly. "Yes, the judge granted it."

"Does that mean Peter can't see Sigrid?"

"He can't have any contact with her whatsoever."

"For how long?"

"Until I can figure out a way to get it lifted, or until Sigrid wakes up and clears him of the charges." His face suddenly flushed.

Her father was on blood-pressure medication, but the stress of Peter and Sigrid's problems—and her own—were taking a visible toll. "Dad, you've got to take it easy, okay? Let Elizabeth handle his legal issues."

He loosened his tie. "That's the plan."

"How's Peter taking it?"

"How do you think?"

She poured boiling water over the tea leaves, then set the pot on the kitchen table along with two mugs.

"I stopped by the hospital before I drove over here. Sigrid was in surgery again this morning. She was bleeding internally, but I think they've stopped it now."

"I just heard," said Jane. "How is she?"

"She looks like death. I've lost count how many units of blood they've given her." He removed his glasses and rubbed his eyes. "Oh, Janey . . . what are we going to do?"

"We'll get through it. We have to."

"Look, sweetheart . . . I came by because we need to talk."

"Sure. Anything you want, just name it." She rummaged in one of the drawers, looking for a tea strainer.

His smile was sad, but grateful. "You and Peter are the best part of my life, honey. But I'm afraid what's happening to our family is all my fault."

He'd made almost the same comment yesterday. "You think one of your clients is unhappy with the job you did?"

"I know it for a fact."

"Who?"

"You remember the Midnight Man?"

"Sure. That was big news. You represented him."

"The man's father, Conrad Alto, threatened me. I get threats all the time, Jane, so I've become pretty adept at figuring out which ones have potential and which don't. Conrad Alto meant business. An eye for an eye. He believes I should have gotten his son off—that if my defense hadn't been halfhearted, Bobby would be a free man today. He holds me *personally* responsible for his son's death. I ruin his family, he ruins mine. A simple equation. I can't prove it, but I think he's behind the drugs planted in your office as well as Sigrid's attack. It's all too slick, too coincidental not to be connected."

"A normal man doesn't attempt that kind of revenge."

"Yeah, well . . . maybe he's not normal."

"What do we do?"

"What can we do?" asked her father. "I have no proof that Alto's behind it, so I've got nothing to take to the police. We just have to pray like hell that Sigrid makes it. Maybe she can ID the guy who sent her to the hospital."

"This is so screwed up," said Jane, sinking into a chair. "What about that police officer, the cop with the drug squad? Should I call him?"

"That's another reason I'm here. Turlow wants to meet with you at your restaurant this afternoon. One o'clock. That all right?"

"Fine with me," said Jane.

"Just explain what happened. Be completely straightforward."

"I will. But tell me more about this Bobby Alto. Was he guilty?"

Her father shrugged. "He maintained he was innocent, but that's pretty standard behavior."

"You don't have a feeling about it one way or the other?"

He hesitated a moment. "I think he was probably guilty."

"Could I read the trial transcript?"

"Why?"

"Why not?"

Ray laughed out loud. "You should have been an investigator, Jane, not a restaurateur."

"No thanks. My profession suits me just fine. But I'd like to get a feel for what happened at trial. If somebody's got a vendetta against me and my family, I'd like to have some idea of what we did wrong. Besides, if I'm actively pursuing something, I won't feel so helpless."

Jane had spent a good part of her childhood sitting at the dinner table listening to her father talk about his court cases. She'd never really considered it before, but maybe that's why she'd always been so drawn to crime solving. It felt natural to her to take apart a crime, look at it from every angle. Gather the evidence. Investigate the players. Form a theory, and then try to prove it—or disprove it. She'd seen her father do it hundreds of times.

Her dad nodded to the teapot. "Pour. And I'll give you the salient points." He waited for her to fill his mug, then leaned back in his chair and began.

"You probably followed the trial in the papers, so you already know some of the details, but here are the highlights. Bobby Alto was accused of murdering two women by drugging them and then setting fire to their houses. One of the murders happened in 'ninety-eight, the other in 'ninety-nine. There were other murders, other torched houses, but these were the two homicides on which the prosecution based its case against him."

"How far back did the murders go?" asked Jane.

"As far as we can tell, back to 'ninety-six. There were five murders in all—meaning, five murders we know about.

"The prosecution's theory was this: Bobby would single out a woman, most likely by meeting her in a bar. He would ask questions about where the woman lived and who she lived with. The age didn't seem to matter. Of the last two victims, one was twenty-nine, the other forty-two. He was looking for women who lived alone in their own home. This is speculation, you understand, but the prosecution figured that when he found someone who fit his criteria, he would watch her until he knew her routine. Then he'd ask her out. He couldn't have dated the women very long because no family or friends of the victims ever met him, or, for that matter, ever heard much about him. That was clearly established.

"Eventually, he would invite himself over to the woman's house. At some point during the evening, he would slip what's called a 'roofie' into their drink. It's often called the date-rape drug."

"I've heard of it," said Jane.

"He'd wait until his victim passed out, then he'd dump her in her bed, strip her clothes off, place this weird pendant around her neck and light the bedroom on fire. He used no excellerants, except for maybe some crumpled-up newspapers. He was also very careful about where he put his hands. Or, maybe after she passed out, he cleaned up. No fingerprints ever linked him to the scene."

"And he didn't sleep with the woman?"

Ray shook his head. "The papers really played up the sex angle, but in fact, intercourse wasn't involved."

"So it wasn't sexual at all."

"Not in any normal sense of the word, but yes, I believe there was a sexual component. Nobody ever agreed on what it was, although there were some fairly wild theories floating around. Nothing that could be proved. Early on, I asked Bobby if he wanted to take a lie-detector test—a private test, one that I'd set up. I told him it wasn't admissible in court, but if he passed, we might approach the DA with it, offer to let the police perform one of their own. At first, he said no. He didn't like tests. That's why he'd dropped out of college. But a couple of months later, he gave me the go-ahead, so I set it up."

"Did he pass?" asked Jane, warming her hands around the mug.

"No."

"So he was guilty, then."

Her father sipped his tea. "It's not that simple. The evasion my operator caught had nothing to do with the murders."

"I don't understand."

"This may sound strange, but he evaded questions regarding his mother. At the time I didn't get it. I still don't, and Bobby refused to explain it. You see, when the operator starts out, he asks simple, concrete questions. What's your name? Where were you born? Do you have a brother? Do you like string beans? He tries to put the subject at ease. Then the questions get more specific, but still easily answered. Does your mother have blue eyes? What year did your parents separate? What's your father's occupation? Your mother's? Every question he answered about his mother showed evasion, so the operator zeroed in on it. It was a disaster."

"So he was keeping some kind of secret about her? You think she was the Midnight Man?"

"She's a seventy-one-year-old matron with almost crippling arthritis who lives in Edina, so no, I don't think that. But whatever he was keeping from us, it must have been significant."

"So, maybe Bobby was innocent after all?"

"Maybe. But I couldn't turn those results over to the prosecution, nor could I allow him to take their polygraph. As a defense lawyer, I've found that it's always best to start from the premise that my client is guilty. Most criminal defendants are, and all criminal attorneys, judges, and prosecutors understand that."

"Doesn't sound like innocent until proven guilty."

"It's not. In reality, the American criminal justice system doesn't work the way it's advertised. It's corrupt. You've heard me talk about it before. If I didn't know it when I started out, I learned it real fast. Our justice system is unfair. It discriminates against minority groups, the poor, the uneducated. But the fact is, it's not grossly inaccurate. The people who populate our prisons, in the main, aren't innocent. They've committed the crimes for which they were convicted. The job of a defense lawyer is—within the law—to prevent the 'whole truth' from coming out, particularly if that 'truthful evidence' was improperly obtained. That was the foundation of our appeal."

"Refresh my memory," said Jane. "I recall something about the police stopping Bobby for drunk driving—searching his car, which led to the search of his house." She grabbed a pen and a piece of scratch paper from one of the kitchen drawers and started jotting down notes.

"The police maintained that Bobby was driving erratically. The night he was stopped, he was already the prime suspect in the murder of Amber Larson. The chain of events happened like this: After Amber Larson's death, Bill Younger, the primary on the case, went looking for handmade jewelry stores, and that led him to Bobby's art gallery in St. Paul. Younger felt that the pendant found at the crime scenes looked very similar to some of Bobby's jewelry. A lot of the jewelry was religious, in one sense or another."

"What did the pendant found on the victims look like?"

"It was a bird breaking out of an egg. Very odd. On the back was the number three-sixty-five."

Jane shook her head. It had no meaning to her.

"The night Bobby was stopped, he and his girlfriend, Taylor Jensen, and another friend were driving back to Bobby's house after dinner. Bobby was completely sober, but he had several ounces of marijuana in the glove compartment."

"Which the police found."

"It was pure luck, because Bobby *hadn't* been driving erratically. Both Taylor and the friend swore that under oath. They'd been driving down University Avenue, traveling within the speed limit, when they were pulled over. Bobby took a blood test and it came back negative, further proof that the police lied about why they'd stopped him. The fact was, the police had been tailing Bobby. Finding the marijuana was just the break they'd been looking for. It allowed them to search the car. That's when they found the long blond hair in the trunk. Once forensics ran tests on it, it was matched to the last victim, Amber Larson. From the fruit of that tainted tree, the police were able to get a warrant to search Bobby's house."

"And that's when they found the sack."

Her father nodded. "It was a red velvet pouch containing a couple of the pendants, all identical to the ones found on the victims. In a pretrial motion, I asked to have that evidence—and the hair found in Bobby's car—thrown out. These were the linchpins of the prosecution's case. Without them, they didn't have one. They'd been improperly obtained, so by all rights, they should have been inadmissible. We maintained strongly that Bobby's rights were violated. The judge assigned to the case was a man I've appeared before dozens of times. He's generally fair, but he's also autocratic, humorless, and occasionally lazy. He's also known as a prosecutor's judge—meaning, if any favoritism is shown, it goes to the DA."

"Obviously, he didn't grant the motion."

"No, he didn't. I made dozens of motions during the trial, all necessary to preserve the pretrial and trial errors for appellate review. Unfortunately, in the end, the state supreme court turned our appeal down."

"What other evidence did the prosecution have?" asked Jane, tapping her pen against the notepad.

"They presented an eyewitness. His name was Kaplan, an elderly man who said he saw a car idling just down the street from Amber Larson's house. He said there was a man inside watching it burn. When the police first talked to him, he couldn't identify the man. But by the time the trial came along, he pointed to Bobby and insisted he was the one. I made mincemeat of his testimony on cross. It was night. He wasn't wearing his glasses. The man in the car was wearing a cap pulled down low over his eyes. And a dark four-door sedan? Come on. No make? No license plate? How many millions of dark sedans are out there? Kaplan was a pathetic witness, and he was poorly prepared."

"Did Bobby have an alibi for either of the murders?"

"None. For the 'ninety-eight murder, he had no idea where he was or what he was doing. He wasn't the kind of guy who kept a daily calendar or a diary. As for the 'ninety-nine murder of Amber Larson, he said he'd been in his basement working on a project. A friend of his did come forward early on and say he'd been with Bobby from six o'clock until midnight on the night of Larson's murder. The guy's name was Barrett Sweeny. Actually, he was the friend in the car the night the police stopped Bobby. Sweeny is quite close to the entire Alto family. But when the police came up with a witness who said she'd talked to Sweeny in a downtown St. Paul bar around nine, Barrett finally admitted he'd lied. There went our alibi. At least we didn't take it to trial and have the prosecution bury us with it. You know, this Sweeny was a good actor because he really had me believing he'd been with Bobby that night. Turns out he had been with him, but it was the night before. He knew how to lie and make it sound plausible. That's a real skill."

"One you've obviously analyzed."

"It's best to take a real event and alter it to fit your needs. That way, you've got lots of detail to make your story sound credible. Bottom line: You alter the truth as little as possible. That's the key. You superimpose the lie over something that *is* true."

"Tell me about Bobby's art gallery."

"Well, it was a little hole in the wall on University Avenue close to the capitol. You couldn't really call it a gallery. Mostly, Bobby sold his jewelry. From what I could tell, his family bought the lion's share of it. Beyond that, I think his father was slipping him money on the side so he could pay his bills. Bobby was the family failure. His brother is an emergency-room doctor. His sister is the principle of a high school in Fargo. His father is a renowned musician, now the music director of Grace Episcopal Cathedral in St. Paul. And his mother was a professor of music. Bobby's claim to fame was the gallery and his art, neither of which were money-makers.

"He wasn't a crackerjack retailer, either. His gallery hours were erratic, partly because he worked a few nights a week as a janitor, and partly because he was a night person in general. He slept late in the mornings and stayed up all night, mostly working on his projects. The first time I met him, his hair was long and his clothes were filthy. He apologized for the way he looked. Bobby was always polite. When the police arrested him for the murders, he was in his basement, working on one of his sculptures. We cleaned him up for the trial, but he never seemed comfortable in a suit. He struck me as a sweet kid. Kind of lost. Very shy. But looks mean nothing. He *could* have murdered those women. Underneath, he could have been a cold-blooded killer. At the very least, someone in that family was."

Jane's head snapped up. "Why do you say that?"

"Instinct, as well as opportunity. That blond hair in Bobby's car got there somehow. If it didn't come from Bobby's clothes, then it did from someone else's. Bobby was a loner. He was only close to a few people. First, his family. Second, his girlfriend. And third, this Barrett Sweeny. See, court cases are all about assigning blame. Somebody dies. Somebody has to pay. The prosecution offers Bobby. We offer an alternate theory."

"Barrett?"

"He would have been my choice, but Bobby wouldn't allow it. As a defense lawyer, I have to decide early on what *my* theory of the case will be. The simpler I keep it, the better the result." Ray picked up his mug and took a sip, then held it while he continued.

"The hair found in the trunk and the platinum pendants were the crux of the case against Bobby. Let's take the pendants first. Bobby made them. There was never any doubt about that. He admitted it."

"Did they have some special meaning?"

"He wouldn't say. I pressed him about it for months, but he insisted it was private. Personal. I knew the prosecution would bury us in court with that answer."

"When did he make them?"

"Shortly after he quit the U in the spring of 'ninety-five. At the time, he'd spoken with his father about wanting to make jewelry for a living, maybe open a shop somewhere, but he needed a financial backer, someone to float him a loan. So his father lent him the money, and he started making rings, necklaces, pins, earrings—whatever struck his fancy. He and his girlfriend bought this ramshackle old house over in Frogtown so that he'd have space to work at home. He said that the pendants were the first pieces he made."

"How many did he make in all?"

"Again, he wouldn't say. But since the platinum was worth a fair amount of money, he didn't want them just lying around. So he hid them under the floorboard in his bedroom."

"He didn't try to sell them?"

"Never."

"That's odd. Did anyone else know about the hiding place?"

"His girlfriend knew. So did his brother, his father, and his friend, Barrett. Kind of limits the field."

"You think one of them took the pendants? One of them is the Midnight Man?"

"That's exactly what I think. Again, they had opportunity and access. They were in and out of Bobby's house and car all the time. I needed to create reasonable doubt about Bobby's guilt. I wanted to build the case against Sweeny. The fact that he jumped in so fast and offered Bobby an alibi made me suspicious. He could have been trying to give *himself* an alibi. See, the houses were always torched right around midnight, hence the name the newspapers gave him. Sweeny was seen at nine. He had no alibi after he left the bar. He said he drove back to his house and went to bed, but who knows what he really did? He drives a dark green Lexus, four-door, so that fits—if we're to believe what Mr. Kaplan saw. When I questioned Sweeny about his whereabouts the night of the 'ninety-eight murder, he seemed vague. He finally came up with the name of a woman he'd been with, but I'll bet anything it was another lie. I had an odd feeling about the guy from the very beginning. Everyone in the family seemed to worship him—including Bobby."

"You make it sound sick."

"That's how it felt."

"So if you couldn't pin the murders on Sweeny, that left you with Henry."

"He would have been a harder sell. A doctor, known for his work with local charities. A pillar of the community. The numbers didn't add up the way they would have with Sweeny."

"What does this Sweeny do for a living?"

"He's a real estate agent. He made a ton of money in the nineties. But Bobby stonewalled me for so long that eventually we ran out of time. I had to go with the unknown-person theory. No name to pin the murders on. No face. It's far more successful to have a face to point at—a person, a physical presence that may help you out by looking furtive, even guilty. The point of the defense in a murder trial is to pound the alternate theory home—again and again, taking every opportunity to create reasonable doubt. I could have done it with Barrett Sweeny."

Jane suddenly recalled something she'd read in the *Star Tribune*. "Didn't Bobby Alto burn down a garage when he was a kid?"

Ray ran a hand through his shaggy silver hair. "Yes, we covered all that at the trial. Actually, it was all his brother's fault. I put Henry on the witness stand as a character witness to clear it up. He told the story of two bored young kids playing with matches. It happens. Henry was the one who took them from his father's study. He was the one who started flipping them at the side of a neighbor's garage. Bobby was a couple of years younger and just went along for the ride. When he mistakenly flipped a lighted match into an open bag of dry leaves near the side door, Henry was already halfway down the alley. Bobby was terrified. He shouted for Henry to come back and help him put the fire out, but it was too late. It had already spread too far. The garage was old, the wood dry. So they ran. It came out later that Bobby had started the fire, but it could just as easily have been Henry. They were both guilty, as far as I was concerned, but Bobby was the one who got punished, and the one who got his name in the papers."

Jane was about to pour them each more tea when her cell phone rang.

"What's that?" asked Ray, cocking his head at the sound.

Jane unclipped the gift from her belt. "A present from Cordelia."

"Well, happy days. It's about time. You've got to give me the number before I leave."

Jane was a bit annoyed that her father was so overjoyed. Did everyone in the universe think she was an old poop just because she didn't have a cell phone? "Hello, Cordelia," said Jane, her voice betraying her lack of enthusiasm.

"Just checking."

"Figured."

"You know, Janey, you can limit the calls you get by only giving the number to certain people. Vastly important people, like myself."

"I realize that."

"You're pissed."

"No, as I said last night, I'm really very grateful. I'm just having a little trouble with everyone's glee."

"Who else is gleeful?"

"My father."

"Is he with you right now?"

"You got it."

"Did you tell him about the tarot cards?"

"No."

"Are you going to?"

"I suppose so."

"Remember to keep your cell phone charged."

"As per your instructions. I have them all written down."

"Gotta run. Catch you later, Janey."

Jane clicked off the call and hooked the phone back over her belt. “Dad, remember that tarot card you received in the mail a few days ago?”

“The what?”

“It was on your desk last weekend, the morning I came over to see you at your office.”

“Oh, that. What about it?”

“Well, actually, I received one too. So did Peter. Cordelia insisted I take them to a tarot reader to find out what they really mean.”

“Janey, I don’t believe in that kind of—”

“I know. I don’t either. But just listen. The three cards were Justice reversed, the Tower, and the Nine of Swords. It was a message. A threat. I think they were sent to us by the same person who planted the drugs in my office and beat up Sigrid.”

“Conrad Alto?”

“It’s possible. The meanings all had to do with fire and lightening, death and destruction, pain and desolation—all because of an injustice.”

“Bobby Alto’s death.”

“Seems to fit.”

Ray shook his head. “This gets more bizarre by the minute.”

Jane tried to pour him more tea, but he held his hand over the mug.

“I’m sorry, honey, but I’ve got a lunch meeting in St. Paul.” As he rose from his chair, he said, “I’ll have Norm messenger over a copy of the trial transcript. Are you sure you want to read it *all*?”

“Positive,” said Jane. “Have him send it to the restaurant.” She wrote down her new cell phone number and handed it over.

Back in the front hall, Ray slipped on his coat. “You’ll have a little light reading before bed for the next few years.”

“I’ll get through it faster than that. We’ve got to figure out a way to nail this Conrad Alto for what he’s doing.”

Raymond held her at arm’s length, then kissed her forehead. “Be careful, Janey. Don’t do anything without consulting me first." As he opened the door, a gust of cold wind blew into the room.

"What a day," said her father, pulling out his heavy leather gloves. "I hear it's supposed to snow. It's almost March. You'd think we'd be done with this nasty weather soon." He looked up at the churning sky.

They stepped outside.

"Oh, by the way, Peter will be stopping by later to pick up some of his clothes. He's staying with me for a while."

"He is?" said Jane. She'd been counting on him returning to the house.

"I thought it would be good if the two of us spent some time together. You understand."

"Sure." She forced a smile. "No problem."

"Something wrong, honey?"

"Of course not. You better get going or you'll be late."

As he hurried to his car, Janc stood in the doorway, shivering.

Before returning to the restaurant, Jane drove over to Metro South to check on Sigrid. She was hoping to spend a few minutes alone with her, especially since Peter wouldn't be able to come. Sigrid might not be conscious, but Jane needed to pass Peter's message on to her again, hoping against hope that she could hear.

After taking the elevator up to the ICU, Jane headed for the nursing station. She was told by one of the duty nurses that Sigrid was still unconscious and in critical condition. If anything, her status had worsened slightly since last night. She'd been in surgery part of the morning and had lost a lot of blood. Everything that could be done for her was being done. Jane had the sense that the nurse was tacitly telling her to prepare herself for the worst. Even in Jane's darkest moments, she'd never really believed Sigrid would *die*. The nurse's words hit her hard. She had to sit down.

Finding a patient waiting room, Jane poured herself a cup of coffee, then pulled a chair over by the windows so she could look out at the tops of the bare trees. Everything was happening too fast. She had to slow it down. She was terrified by the idea of losing Sigrid, but she also feared for the impact it would have on her brother, both emotionally as well as what it might mean for his future. If Sigrid died, he could be sent to prison for murder. Jane tried to resist admitting the image of those damn tarot cards into her thoughts, but there they were, taunting her with their prediction of doom and gloom.

Even though Jane needed time to process what was happing, she couldn't sit still. She hurried back down the hall to Sigrid's room. Before going inside, she glanced through the window and saw that the Munson family—Todd and his younger siblings—were gathered around the bed, holding hands and praying. They looked so serious and intent, Jane couldn't interrupt them. This was a family moment, and she didn't belong.

Feeling defeated, she walked slowly back to the elevator, rode down to the first floor and left the building.

It was nearly one by the time Jane unlocked her office at the restaurant. As she shrugged out of her coat, she heard a knock on the door.

Arlene sailed in with a fistful of messages. "You're office was locked before," she said, looking a little put out.

Jane hung up her coat. "I want you to get someone to change the sign on my door. Instead of 'Office' I want it to say 'Private.' Maybe Barnaby could do it. He's pretty handy with a screw gun." Barnaby was one of the bartenders.

Arlene wrote it down on her ever-present stenographer's pad. "Here are your messages. Oh, and that real estate agent of yours stopped by. She left the address of another house she wants you to look at. I wrote it down." She flipped through the notes. "She said the house was a one-and-a-half-story bungalow in Tangletown, but there was some sort of addition that made it extra nice." She handed Jane the message slips, and the address of the house.

Jane sat down behind her desk. "Thanks."

"I, ah—" Arlene pushed her glasses back up on her nose. "I was wondering how your brother was doing. I heard about what happened. Everyone here has. We're all so sorry, hon. Was he . . . arrested?"

"He's out on bail," said Jane, feeling her stomach tighten.

"This must be so awful for you and your family."

"Miss Lawless?" A man stood in the open doorway. He was wearing a sheepskin jacket and jeans. Blond hair. Stocky. Nice looking. Jane assumed this was Art Turlow.

Arlene backed up to get a better look at him. She had a predatory reaction to handsome men. She could have been his mother, but she still looked him over with hungry eyes. Arlene often talked about her bad luck with men. She was twice divorced, or "manless" as she most often put it. But she was so flip about it, her world-weariness tinged with such wry humor, that Jane found herself laughing along with her. Men were trouble. But they were also irresistible—the Arlene Andrews Basic Philosophy of Life. What was a poor girl to do?

"Come in," said Jane. She stood up to shake his hand, then motioned him to a chair. "We'll talk more later, Arlene. Thanks. Would you close the door on your way out?"

"Sure, hon." She peered over her bifocals at Turlow one last time, sighed audibly, then left.

Turlow introduced himself and unbuttoned his jacket. "You've got a nice restaurant here." He couldn't seem to get comfortable in the small chair. Either his jacket was too bulky, or he was.

Jane had been brought up to say "please" and "thank you," but after the morning she'd put in, social niceties seemed like way too much work. She wanted to get to the point quickly and see where it led. "I assume my father filled you in on what happened."

Turlow nodded. "But I'd like to hear it from you."

Jane briefly explained what had transpired on Sunday night. She'd been working upstairs most of the day, either in the kitchen or the dining room. When she returned to her office around ten, she found the package of crystal meth stuffed behind some books in her bookcase. She figured if she left any important details out, he'd ask for them.

"How did you know it was crystal meth?" asked the detective, finally giving in and taking off his jacket.

Jane didn't want to bring Patricia Kastner's name into the conversation, so she lied. From her standpoint, she didn't have a choice. "I wasn't sure what it was, but when I got home, I logged on to the Internet, found a Web site that described different drugs. It fit the description for crystal meth."

"So . . . you're saying you're not positive it *was* crystal meth?"

"All I know for sure is, it didn't belong in my office. It looked like turbinado sugar, if you know what that is. But it wasn't. I guess I just panicked—jumped to the conclusion that it was some kind of illegal drug. My first instinct was to get rid of it."

"You've never used the drug yourself?"

"Of course not."

Turlow scanned the room with his high-beam blue eyes. "What did you do with it after you took it home?"

"I poured it down the kitchen sink. Then I burned the bag in the fireplace."

"In other words, you eliminated the evidence."

"I was scared."

He looked at her skeptically. "But if you were innocent, why didn't you call the police right away?"

Jane held her ground, keeping her eyes firmly on his. "I would imagine you can guess what it's like to be the daughter of a high-profile defense attorney. My father has a number of enemies in the MPD, some of whom would love to nail his daughter with a drug charge."

He shifted in his chair. "All right, I'll grant you that. Your father does have his share of enemies. But I'm still confused. Why are you coming forward now? You got rid of the package. Nobody caught you with it, so I'd think you'd be home free."

"I don't think it's that simple."

"Why not?"

She hesitated.

"Look, for all I know, you could have made the whole thing up."

"Excuse me?" She wasn't sure she'd heard him correctly. "Made it up?"

He shrugged.

"Why *on earth* would I do that?"

"You tell me."

She was momentarily taken aback. She felt as if something important had just whizzed past her, but she had no idea what it was. "I'm telling you the truth. I have no reason to lie."

"So you say."

Now she was thoroughly confused. "All right, *why* would I make up a story like that?"

"I can think of reasons."

"Like what?"

Again he shrugged. "It's not my job to provide you with a motive."

"Look, whoever planted those drugs might do it again. That's why it's not as simple as it might appear. For all I know, there could already be other drugs stashed on the premises. I couldn't keep quiet about it. Next time, I might not be so lucky."

Turlow scrutinized her face, as if trying to confirm something. "Okay," he said, still studying her. "Give me your permission and I'll get a team in here. We'll do a full search. If there are other drugs, we'll find them."

"Fine," said Jane. "Let's do it."

He seemed surprised.

"The dining room shuts down between lunch and dinner. People are usually out by three-thirty. Can you do it in an hour and a half?"

"We can try. But better still, we could do it tonight, after the restaurant closes."

"Okay. Good idea."

"Then we'll see you at one-thirty. A.M., Ms. Lawless."

Jane spent a good part of the afternoon trying to track Peter down. She finally gave up in frustration and called her father. Wherever Peter was, he apparently didn't want to talk to either of them. Her dad hadn't heard from him either, and from the tone of his voice, Jane could tell he was getting worried.

"Call me if he contacts you," said Ray.

"I will, I promise. And I'll call you in the morning and let you know how the search of the restaurant went."

There was silence on the other end of the line. "Maybe I should be there."

"Why? You're exhausted. I can handle it."

"Call me if you need me. If you've got *any* questions. And . . . if they find something . . . don't say a word until you've contacted me."

During the afternoon, Jane left messages for both Cordelia and Patricia, updating their voice mails on what was happening. Jane asked Patricia for a rain check on dinner. She simply thought it unwise to stray from the restaurant tonight, even for a little while.

All evening, Jane felt alternately anxious and fatalistic. She spent most of her time in the dining room, greeting old customers, welcoming new ones, serving coffee, assisting the wine steward and generally making sure everything was flowing smoothly. By nine she was back in her office doing paperwork. She called the hospital for the third time to find out how Sigrid was doing. There was no change in her condition.

The evening dragged. At one particularly anxious point, she found herself looking at her watch every five minutes. Around eleven, she got up and strolled around the building. Nothing jumped out at her as being anything out of the ordinary. The kitchen was closed down and dark by then, the dining room all prepped for tomorrow. She nursed a cup of coffee in the pub while she read an article in *Gourmet* on eggplants. She loved eggplant in just about any form. Under other circumstances, the recipes in the magazine would have kept her occupied for hours.

But tonight, even a new take on Polpette di Melanzane couldn't take her mind off Art Turlow and the crew that would arrive shortly.

By one-fifteen, she was back in her office, looking for something to help her stay awake. She'd consumed more coffee than was compatible with human life, so that was out. She wasn't hungry. A book would put her to sleep within seconds. Her father had called and left her a message that Peter had finally shown up at his house, but he'd gone up to bed right away, so there was no point in calling until tomorrow morning because he would probably be asleep.

That's when Jane's cell phone rang. She pulled it off her belt and checked to see who it was before clicking it on. "Cordelia, hi."

"Thought I'd stop by."

"Now?"

"Why not?" Cordelia was a night person. By this time in the morning, she was just getting started.

"Okay. Sure. If you're not too tired, that is. I could use the company. Where are you now?"

Jane looked up as the door swung open. Cordelia loomed large under the bright hall light. She was holding her cell phone to her ear, grinning. "I'm right here, dearheart."

"You called me from *the hall*?"

"So?"

"Why?"

"Because I can. Don't you just *love* technology?" She flounced into the room and tossed her cape over a chair.

Jane mentally used the word *flounced* because that's what Cordelia always did when she wore clothes with sequins. Tonight, she was wearing a grape jelly–colored off-the-shoulder evening dress with matching spike heels. She looked seven feet high—perhaps three feet wide. In other words, she was her usual *presence*. Instead of a small evening purse, she carried a canvas sack.

"Quite a dress."

"I've never been to a drug bust before. How should I know what to wear?"

"You dressed up in *that* just to come over here?"

"Heavens, no. I was at a cast party earlier. With Genevieve."

"Who's Genevieve?"

Cordelia gave Jane a bit of significant eye flutter. "She's a trucker. I met her at a party two weeks ago. This is our second date."

"True love, huh?"

"This may be *the one*, Janey. I think I've found my soul mate."

"What does she . . . truck?"

"Mainly building supplies. I never knew drywall and ceiling trusses could be so fascinating." She stalked up to the desk, placed her hands firmly on the desktop, then leaned across close to Jane and whispered, "Where's the fuzz?"

"Not here yet."

"Ah." She gave a conspiratorial wink. "That cute new waiter is making time with one of your bartenders."

"Which waiter?"

"What's his name? Vasquez?"

"I didn't know he was still here. The dining room closed hours ago." If he wanted to hang around and spend his hard-earned cash in the pub, that was fine with her. "Which bartender?"

"Melissa. The itsy-bitsy blonde with the buck teeth." Cordelia draped herself over a chair, crossing her legs and bouncing her foot.

Jane nodded to the sack. "What have you got in there?"

"Goodies. I figure, just because a drug bust is in progress, we can still enjoy ourselves." She pulled out two cans of cream soda and two cans of black cherry soda and set them on the desk. Next came a sack of bright orange cheese curls. A sack of potato chips—BBQ flavored. A canister of Italian Amaretto cookies. A deck of cards. And a cribbage board. "I brought Boggle too, just in case you're in a Boggle mood. And," she added, whipping out the last item, a paperback copy of Shakespeare's *Henry V*, "I thought I'd give you my rendition of Henry the Fifth's famous speech before the battle of Agincourt. Seemed apropos. You know"—her voice dropped to a dark Larry Olivier level—" '*If we are mark'd to die, we are enow/To do our country loss; and if to live/The fewer men, the greater share of honor*,' and so on and so forth." She flipped her hand idly in the air.

They both turned as Turlow entered the room. Cordelia had forgotten to close the door.

Jane stood and introduced Cordelia, who eyed the cop with obvious distaste. A little too obvious for Jane's anxious stomach. She glanced up at the clock. It was one-thirty on the dot. Cordelia had the knack for making time fly.

"I though we'd start upstairs," said Turlow. "I've already sent my men up there. I need you to stay out of the way. We'll do your office last, and then we'll talk."

Jane heard a dog bark.

"We've got a dog with us," said the detective, stating the obvious.

"A doggie drug sniffer," said Cordelia, raising a skeptical eyebrow. "I've read about those. In my opinion, you can't trust a canine to sniff out much of anything other than the usual. A kibble lost in the couch cushions. A dead bat in the basement."

Turlow glanced at her briefly, then turned and left.

"Rude man," muttered Cordelia.

Two hours later, the pop cans were empty. So was the bag of cheese curls. Cordelia was standing on the couch, finishing Henry V's speech to his men:

> *"This story shall the good man teach his son;*
> *And Crispin Crispian shall ne'er go by,*
> *From this day to the ending of the world,*
> *But we in it shall be remembered—*
> *We few, we happy few, we band of brothers;*
> *For he to-day that sheds his blood with me*
> *Shall be my brother; be he ne'er so vile,*

This day shall gentle his condition;
And gentlemen in England, now, a-bed,
Shall think themselves accurs'd they were not here,
And hold their manhoods cheap whiles any speaks
That fought with us upon Saint Crispin's day."

Her voice had risen to a triumphant shout, her right fist in the air, her left hand clutching the front of her dress—revealing even more of her remarkable cleavage.

Jane noticed Turlow standing outside in the hall listening. She wondered if he was too frightened—or deeply moved—to come in.

"We need you to leave your office now, Ms. Lawless, so we can check it out," he said when Cordelia had finally finished.

Cordelia turned to glare at him. " *'Once more unto the breach, dear friends, once more!'* "

"Cordelia," said Jane gently. She got up and walked over to the couch. She could tell Cordelia still thought of herself as Henry the Fifth, leading an army, ready to do battle to save England. "Let's go."

" *'Not yet, my cousin: we would be resolved/Before we hear him, of some things of weight/That task our thoughts, concerning us and France.'* "

"Cordelia?"

"What?"

"Get down."

"Okay."

Thankfully, she'd taken off her shoes. Otherwise, Jane's couch would look like a pin cushion.

As Cordelia stalked out the door in her bare feet, Jane asked, "Did you find anything?"

"No," said Turlow. "The place is clean. So far." He glanced into the room.

"We'll be in the bar."

"I don't trust him," whispered Cordelia, padding down the hall next to Jane.

"You don't trust anyone when you're in one of your moods. He's just doing his job. Don't mouth off to him, got it? I need his good will."

"Cordelia Thorn does not *mouth off*. She states her opinion with elegance and grace."

"Right."

By the time Jane had rearranged some of the liqueur bottles and polished the mahogany bar for the third time, Turlow joined them. They sat down at a table as his crew exited building.

"Anything?" asked Jane.

He shook his head. "The place is clean."

Jane felt the tension she'd been holding inside herself all day finally release. "God, I'm so relieved."

"I'm sure you are."

Once again, Jane felt there was a subtext to his comments, but for the life of her, she couldn't figure out what it was. Maybe he just didn't buy her story, but it seemed like more than that. On the other hand, she didn't want to challenge him over it, just in case she was wrong. She had to proceed with caution. "What do I do now?" she asked. "You may not believe me, but someone did plant those drugs in my office."

"Do you have any idea who that person might be?"

She decided to take a chance. "My dad lost an appeal recently. He believes that the father of the man who went to prison is trying to get back at him by attacking his children. You're aware that my brother, Peter, was arrested last night for assaulting his wife?"

"You're saying it was a setup?"

"I can't prove it, but yes, it was. And I think the SOB who set my brother up is also responsible for planting that sack of drugs in my office."

Turlow scratched his chin, digesting her words. "Care to share a name with me?"

Jane hesitated, but finally said, "Conrad Alto. The father of Bobby Alto."

"The Midnight Man?"

"Bobby Alto was knifed in a prison fight. He died. After it happened, I think his dad went tilt. He threatened my father."

"From what I've heard, your father's no stranger to empty threats."

"This one wasn't empty."

He traced a scratch in the tabletop with his finger. "It could be a convenient excuse."

"Why do you insist on thinking that I'm trying to manipulate you? I'm telling you the truth."

Turlow sat back in his chair and studied her. "You know, just between us chickens, crystal meth isn't exactly the kind of drug I'd associate with a place like this. It's more of a down-and-dirty street drug. People who get hooked on speed end up living like wild animals."

"Your point is?" asked Cordelia.

He glanced at her, then back at Jane. "I thought we might find evidence of crack cocaine—or even more likely, Ecstasy. That's a clubby, upscale drug. More and more of it is finding its way into the Twin Cities. My guess is it's going to rival the crack epidemic we saw in the late eighties."

"What's it look like?" asked Jane.

"Oh, sometimes it's a pink pill," said Cordelia. "Sometimes white or green."

Turlow turned to stare at her.

"I've seen it, okay? I don't use it."

He continued to stare.

Getting huffy, Cordelia replied, "So I smoke a little grass every now and then. Tell me someone who doesn't?"

"Me," Turlow said.

"Well, give the man a cigar," she muttered under her breath.

Jane kicked her under the table.

"Ouch!"

"Look," said Jane, "I don't want this stuff—or any illegal drug—in my restaurant. If Conrad Alto or someone he hires tries to plant more of it, I want him arrested. Tell me what I can do to help you and I will."

"Are you really serious?"

"Am I failing to communicate? Yes, I'm serious."

"Then let me put a couple undercover cops in here."

"You mean. . . . I should hire them?"

"You don't have to pay them, but yes. Put one in your kitchen. Let another one tend bar."

"If you don't mind my saying so," said Cordelia, tapping her fingers on the arm of her chair, "you're going to a lot of trouble to help my friend. Maybe I'm just naturally suspicious, but I can't help wondering why."

"Just doing my job, ma'am." Turlow smiled.

"I suppose we could use another prep cook," said Jane, thinking it over. She didn't much like the idea of cops spying on her staff, but if it prevented Alto from planting more drugs, it was worth it. She looked over at Turlow. "Can you find me someone who can actually peel a carrot? Pour a mixed drink?"

"I think I can handle it."

"Then it's settled," said Jane, feeling even more relieved. With the police on the scene, her problems at the restaurant were covered. If anything, she felt more free now to help her brother. She stood up and shook Turlow's hand. "Thanks."

"Thank *you*, Ms. Lawless. Expect my men tomorrow."

17

After Turlow had gone and Cordelia had said her good nights—issuing her now-standard orders for Jane to keep her new cell phone powered up and at the ready—Jane locked up the restaurant, making sure the alarm system was set, and left in her car. She didn't feel like returning to an empty house and she was too keyed up to sleep. She been cooped up inside the restaurant all day and needed some fresh air to clear the cobwebs out of her head. It wouldn't be light for another couple of hours.

Jane drove around Lake Harriet for a while, then turned up a deserted side street, enjoying the quiet, the sense that all the world was asleep except for her. Most of the houses were dark, covered with a fresh coating of snow that gleamed like diamonds in the moonlight. She stopped her car by the bandstand and rolled down the window, drinking in the night air like drafts of cool water. She hummed a few bars of Bob Dylan's "Girl from the North Country," realizing she'd always thought of that girl as herself.

Sometimes Jane felt that every good thing that had ever happened to her had happened in winter. She'd met Christine, her first love, in December, and Julia, her last love, in November.

Christine had died just a month shy of their tenth anniversary. And Julia was in South Africa now. She missed them both. It was unlikely that Julia would ever come back into her life, and yet Jane still thought about her, still wished things had worked out differently. Julia hadn't written since that last letter in December. Maybe Jane should drop her a note just to say hi. What could it hurt?

Her mood had lightened considerably since the afternoon. She assumed that the calm she was feeling now was borne partially of exhaustion, but she was grateful for any small favor the cosmos chose to hand out. She was alive, and where there was life there was hope. Which made her think of Sigrid.

Around quarter of five, Jane pulled her Trooper into the parking lot at Metro South. This might be her best chance to spend a few minutes alone with her sister-in-law.

Approaching the information booth on the first floor, Jane learned that Sigrid had been transferred out of ICU to a private room on the fifth floor. When she stepped off the elevator, she went looking for a nurse. She finally found a young woman sitting at a small desk behind the nursing station. "I was hoping to talk to Sigrid Lawless's nurse."

"That would be me," said the woman, taking off her glasses.

"I'm Jane Lawless, Sigrid's sister-in-law."

"You're up early."

"How's she doing this morning?"

"She's stabilized. Her vital signs are stronger and her temperature is down. The doctor upgraded her status from critical to serious around midnight, which is all good news. But she's very weak."

"Is she conscious?"

"Yes, but she's somewhat confused. She didn't know where she was or why she was here. That's not unusual, so you shouldn't be unduly alarmed."

"Did you tell her what happened?"

"The doctor told her she'd had an accident. He left it at that. She was too groggy to pursue it."

"Is anyone with her right now?"

"Her brother was here for a while, but he left around one. If you want to go in and see her, that's fine, but keep your visit short, okay? And if she's asleep, don't wake her."

"Right," said Jane. "Thanks."

As she approached the hospital room, she saw a doctor standing outside the door reading a chart. She assumed it was Sigrid's chart. "Excuse me," she said, stopping as he turned around to face her. He was tall and reed thin, with closely spaced, intense blue eyes and a fringe of light brown hair covering a high forehead. "Are you one of Sigrid's doctors?" He was wearing a long white coat over blue scrubs, so it seemed like a reasonable guess. Checking his name tag, she saw that it said DR. HENRY ALTO.

"Oh, God," she said out loud, taking a few steps back. As soon as she'd said it, she wished she hadn't. She tried to cover. "Is Sigrid all right?" she asked, feigning breathlessness.

He looked down at her as if her words had brought him back from someplace far away. "She's doing better. She regained consciousness, which is a good sign." He exuded an air of brittle intelligence, but he did seem genuinely concerned that she might hyperventilate. "Are you all right?"

"Fine," said Jane. "Just worried." She remembered now what her father had told her—that Bobby's brother was an emergency-room doctor at Metro South.

"If you have other questions, I suggest you consult Dr. Maybury, her primary physician. He would know much more than I do. Now if you'll excuse me—" He closed the chart abruptly and walked off down the hall.

Jane watched him walk away, wondering if she should have demanded to know what he was doing outside Sigrid's door. Was it simple curiosity? Was he checking up on her for his father? Henry Alto might be Conrad Alto's son, but that didn't mean he was in on his father's vendetta. His interest in Sigrid could be innocent enough. He must have heard that she'd been admitted—it had made all the papers. He knew the Lawless name. Then again, Henry Alto was one of the men her father had suspected of being a serial killer. Jane felt deeply uncomfortable knowing that he could wander the halls of the hospital completely unmonitored. But how could she prevent it? He hadn't done anything wrong. And her father's theory was just that—a theory.

When she finally pushed through the door and entered Sigrid's room, she found her lying quietly in the bed, still hooked up to IVs and several nasty-looking machines.

The light in the room was dim. Even so, Sigrid was frightening to look at. Human, to be sure, but so terribly ravaged. Her face and arms seemed far more swollen and bruised than they had on the night she was admitted. The TV was on, the volume low. Jane switched it off. She gazed down at her sister-in-law, tears filling her eyes. She was glad that Peter couldn't be here to see what had happened to his wife.

Swallowing hard, Jane felt a wave of nausea wash over her. She smoothed the sheet over Sigrid's legs, trying to center herself, to push the feeling away. It was so hard to just stand around and wait. She needed something to do, some way to feel useful. But there was nothing to be done.

Sigrid stirred. Her eyes fluttered open. She looked straight ahead, her gaze unfocused.

Jane could tell that she didn't know anyone else was in the room.

Sigrid moved her legs, then looked to the side. "Jane," she said weakly.

"I'm here, Siggy." She wanted to take hold of Sigrid's hand, or touch her arm. She needed to physically connect, but every spot on her body was so bruised and battered, it was impossible.

"Where's . . . Peter?" asked Sigrid. Every word she spoke clearly hurt.

"He can't be here right now," said Jane gently. "But he wanted me to tell you how much he loves you."

She closed her eyes.

"You're going to be okay, Siggy. The worst is over." She wanted to say something positive.

"What . . . happened . . . to me?" asked Sigrid.

"You don't remember anything?"

Swallowing with some difficulty, she said, "No."

Not good news for Peter. But it was early. She would probably regain her memory as she got stronger. "You had an accident, Siggy." Jane decided to go with the same line as the doctor.

"What kind of accident?"

"Well—" Before Jane could answer, Sigrid closed her eyes. For the next few minutes, she seemed to doze.

Jane stood by the bed, her arms resting on the metal rail. Exhaustion was starting to drag her down. Her body felt deeply heavy. She didn't want to leave without saying goodbye, but she didn't want to wake Sigrid, either. She was just about to tiptoe back out to the waiting room to get some coffee when Sigrid opened her eyes.

"Please, Jane . . . stay . . . with me," she said weakly. "Please."

The ache in her voice was heartbreaking. "Of course," said Jane. "I'll be right here, for as long as you need me."

"I'm scared," she whispered, her sunken eyes closing again.

Jane traced her fingers along the less bruised portion of Sigrid's cheek. "I know you are, Siggy. But you're going to get better now." She pulled a chair up to the bed and sat down, resting her hand next to Sigrid's so that she could feel her presence.

"Thank you," whispered Sigrid.

"Go to sleep. I'll be here when you wake up."

Jane sat in the chair until her own eyes grew so heavy that she, too, drifted off.

18

My brother's funeral was on Saturday," said Henry. For today's session, he was trying out his therapist's couch. He didn't like it. For one thing, lying down made him feel less in control. For another, he couldn't see her face. Dr. Kirsch sat to the side and behind him slightly, away from his view, as if she were trying to hide her reactions.

"Was the day hard for you?" asked the doctor.

"Yes," said Henry, "but I didn't cry."

"Is that important to you? Not to cry in public?"

"I suppose it is. I just felt kind of empty inside."

"Henry, I was hoping that today you would tell me a little more about your family. I'd like to take you deeper into your relationships, your past."

"Jesus, if we're going to start with my friggin' childhood, this could take forever."

"No, I'm not saying that."

He could sense her leaning closer to him.

"I'd just like to know what you think is important about your life. All you have to do is start somewhere—anywhere."

"Stream of consciousness."

"Yes, exactly."

He considered it for a moment, lacing his fingers over his stomach. "Okay. Let me tell you a story." He paused for a moment, then continued, "When I was a senior in high school, I made a stupid mistake. To look at me now you might think I'm a pretty confident guy, but when I was younger, I was the classic geek. Skinny. Bookish. Glasses. I think I always knew I wanted to be a doctor, but my grades weren't the best—especially in math. I was a whiz at science, English and the rest, but math just never made sense. Fifty percent of my grade in geometry first semester of my senior year rested on the midterm. I won't bore you with details. Lets just say I was able to get my hands on a copy of the the test. I memorized all the answers and aced the exam. Everything was going great until I found out that someone knew what I'd done."

"May I ask who that was?"

"Another student. His name was Derrick Warner. Warner was a sly, weasily kind of guy. I'd never had much to do with him, but he let me know the day after the test that he knew what I'd done."

"Did he tell the teacher?"

"Hell, no. This kid wanted power. I'd never met anybody like him before. I found out later that he'd done it to other guys—got dirt on them and then made them be his slave."

"Slave?"

"First it was little things. He needed ten bucks. I'd give it to him. Or he'd need a ride somewhere, so I'd borrow my mom's car and drive him. One afternoon he started admiring my watch. It was clear he wanted it, so I gave it to him. When I'd get out of school, sometimes he'd be waiting for me. He'd walk me partway home, all the while talking about how awful my life would be if my secret got out. Every scenario was worse than the last. I don't know why I listened to him, but I couldn't stop myself. I was relieved when Christmas vacation finally arrived and I didn't have to see him for two whole weeks. But one night, on the way to the ice rink by my house, he popped out from behind a tree—started talking as if he was picking up a conversation right in the middle. He told me that he had a Christmas present all picked out for his mom, but he didn't have the bucks to buy it. I thought he was going to hit me up for more cash, but instead, he told me he wanted me to steal it from this particular store by his house. It was a set of six German-made steak knives. I couldn't believe how expensive they were. I told him no, that I wouldn't do it. He said he'd give me a day to think about it. If I still refused, he'd have to call my teacher and tell him what I'd done."

"Did he have proof?"

"Oh, you bet he did. I didn't sleep all night. I couldn't believe the mess I was in. I was horrified by what my parents would think of me, especially my dad. In a matter of weeks, Warner had turned me into a nervous wreck. So out of fear and frustration, I did it. I took the knives off the shelf, stuffed them under my coat, and got the hell out of the store. Thank god I wasn't caught. I didn't realize until I handed Warner the knives that now he had even more on me. He became my tormenter. It went on like that for months, until one day, Barrett Sweeny, this friend of my brother's, sat down beside me at lunch. He told me that he'd dreamed about me the night before. I thought, well, big deal. I wasn't in the mood to talk. But he went on. He said that in the dream, he'd rescued me. Wasn't that interesting? Did I need rescuing? I laughed, said I didn't know what he was talking about.

"After school, he waited for me. We walked home together. He said he'd noticed how anxious I'd been lately. Even my brother Bobby had mentioned it. Bobby was Barrett's good buddy. Anyway, he said he'd like to help. He wanted me to open up and tell him what was going on, to trust him, but I couldn't. I was too afraid of what Warner would do. That's when Barrett guessed that it was Warner who had something on me. He said he didn't know him well, but that he seemed like a useless sort of person. He said I should get rid of him. If I couldn't find any other way, that I should kill him. But no matter what I did, I should definitely stop being afraid of him. People like Warner were cowards at heart. Barrett said he liked me, liked talking to me, that I was an intelligent guy, just like Bobby. Most of the other guys he knew were brainless and boring. He said he could help—that he would prove Warner was a coward. I asked him how. He told me to relax. That he'd take care of it."

"Let's back up a minute. Barrett told you that you should . . . kill someone?"

"You have to understand it in context. It was a casual remark. He wasn't actually saying I should do it."

The therapist was silent.

"I begged him to leave it alone. He said not to worry. A few days went by. Then a few more. By the following Monday, I realized I hadn't seen Warner in over a week. I started to get worried that Barrett had screwed everything up. I went looking for Warner and found him bent over the drinking fountain outside the gym. When he turned around and saw me, he took off like he'd seen a ghost. I didn't even get a chance to talk to him. Not that I needed to. His face told me everything."

"Is it important for me to know what Barrett did to him?"

Henry shrugged. "I never found out. I asked him if he'd threatened Warner. He said that threats were Warner's way of doing things. He'd simply talked to him, made him understand that making my life miserable wasn't a good way to spend his time."

"That's all?"

"They went swimming together. That's all I know."

Again, Dr. Kirsch was silent.

"Frankly, I was less interested in what he'd done than in the fact that I was free of Warner forever. From that day on, I was in awe of Barrett. To me, he was a magician. An enchanter."

"Are you still friends with this man?"

"Close friends."

"Can you describe to me what sort of man he is now? As an adult?"

"Believe it or not, he's a very spiritual person, believes that religion is the essence of all the beauty in the world. In college, he majored in philosophy. He thought about teaching, but shortly after he graduated, he got into real estate. He's been selling it ever since."

"Would you describe him as an honest businessman?"

"For the most part. I know he's hidden some of his assets in dummy companies, mainly because taxes were eating him alive. For instance, he loves sailing. He's got this incredibly beautiful forty-foot sailboat that he keeps moored up on Lake Superior. Ever been to the Castle Danger marina?"

"No, Henry, I haven't."

"The boat is owned by a dummy company that's supposed to give lake tours in the summer. Northland Yacht Tours. But it's Barrett's boat. He uses it whenever he wants. I don't really think of it as dishonesty. Then again, I know nothing about tax laws."

"During our last conversation, I sensed that religion is an important issue with you. Would you agree with that?"

"I suppose. In a way. Now, if you were talking to my mother instead of me, you'd find out that she's the family heathen. She's not an atheist, exactly, but she calls Christianity a moral rummage sale. If you shop long enough, you can find anything you want. Dad wanted to baptize my sister, but Mom wouldn't hear of it. If you recall, my father was only sixteen when she was born. My mother was thirty-one. They weren't married. From what my father told me, my mother just laughed at him. He had no power, no standing with the child. His name wasn't even on the birth certificate. My father may have been a budding musical genius, but he'd gotten in way over his head with my mother—kind of a dumb kid, in my opinion. Or maybe he was rebelling against parental authority. I asked him about it once, but he doesn't like to talk about that time in his life. He adored my mother back then, but I think it eventually struck him that having a kid might alter his life plans."

"Did your grandparents take any responsibility for the child their son had fathered?"

"None. They wanted no part of it. They never believed that Dad was really the father."

"Did your mother wait for your father to come back and marry her?"

He laughed. "Hardly. I don't know why she married him. Boredom, maybe. He certainly wasn't her type. They had nothing in common except music."

"And your sister."

"Right. My sister. The way it worked was this: My father loved my mother and she treated him like dirt. It's a delicate dance, but it worked for them for years. Actually, I suppose that's my paradigm for a love relationship. Must be why I'm so screwed up, why I can't seem to find the right girl."

"Are you telling me the truth, Henry? Remember your promise."

"As much as I know it."

"All right. Go on."

Henry wasn't sure what to say next. He decided that since she'd brought it up, he might as well stay with the religious theme. "When I was growing up, my father didn't seem all that interested in religion, but after the separation, he changed—had a sort of spiritual awakening."

"Would it be helpful to me to know why your parents separated?"

"Do you want the standard line or the truth?"

"The truth, Henry."

"Well, they separated when my father learned that my sister Leslie wasn't really his daughter."

Dr. Kirsch remained quiet for a few seconds. "Had your mother known all along?"

"Actually, no. You see, Leslie's always been kind of sickly. She needed a blood transfusion in the mid eighties, so we all had our blood typed. Turns out Dad couldn't have fathered her." Henry wished he could see the look on the doctor's face.

"So your mother never knew for sure if he was the father or not?"

"Right. He wasn't the only person she was sleeping with when Leslie was conceived, but she said she had a gut feeling Dad was the father, so she went with it."

"I see."

"Yeah, kind of sucks, doesn't it? Dad told me once that he was afraid he'd lost his soul during their marriage. The only way to get it back was through suffering. Losing Leslie woke him up."

"But he didn't lose her—not really."

"It changed things between them. Leslie got all hot and bothered about wanting to find her real dad, and that hurt him a lot. He started going to church again right around that time, started dragging my brother and me along when we stayed at his place on weekends. I suppose, of the two, my father is the better human being, but my mother is more subtle. I've always been drawn to subtlety."

"Henry, you talk about religion in relation to other people in your life, but not in relation to yourself. I ask because, if you are a religious man, religion has a great deal to say about lying. Since that's your stated reason for coming to me—to help you change your pattern of lying—I wonder what impact your moral training's had on you."

"Moral training." He thought about the words. "Well, I suppose I'm a hybrid—part heathen, part pious. Dad says that if you've got a soul, you should take care of it."

"Is that why you're so bothered by your lying? Because of your immortal soul?"

Again, he turned around to look at her. "Do you think I have one, doctor? A soul? I'd really like your opinion."

"I'm not a priest, Henry, I'm a therapist."

"And never the twain shall meet."

"I wouldn't go that far. Lying can be a moral issue as well as a psychological one. If you lied to the police about your brother—"

Henry held up his hand. "We'll get there, doctor. Don't push."

"I'm sorry. I wasn't trying to push you." But she rattled her notebook. She was getting impatient.

He had to take his time, lay the proper foundation. There were things she had to understand before he answered her question. "Let's move on." He cleared his throat. "What else do I think is important about my life? Well, the summer after I graduated from high school—I was eighteen, my brother sixteen—my father convinced my mother to let him take us—and our friend, Barrett—to Europe for two months. Dad had some business in Paris, but mainly, he wanted to give us a tour of his favorite religious relics. He said it was for our moral edification."

"Religious *relics?*"

Henry could feel himself warming to the subject. "Sure. Pieces of the saints. Amputated limbs, severed hands, skulls, mummies with rawhide skin, enshrined corpses all tarted up with vestments and cowls and wimples. Dead little girls wearing satin dresses. They're all over Europe, and I mean *all* over. We toured Italy mostly, because that's what Dad knew best. He rented this apartment in Venice and we took day trips. Later we moved down to a hotel in Florence. At first I thought it was totally stupid and boring. I was still a kid and I wanted to be out having fun. But after a while, I kind of got into it. Then I *really* got into it. So did Bobby and Barrett. We bought guidebooks and pored over them, trying to find all the really obscure places to go.

"Religion in Italy is like a circus side-show. Tacky and glitzy and ghoulish. Take this one place—the Basilica of St. Anthony. Outside the church there were these street hawkers selling souvenirs out of the backs of vans. Kmart for the spiritual tourist. They'd put St. Anthony inside plastic paperweights holding a baby Jesus, on laminated bookmarks, tape measures, key chains, ballpoint pens—stuff for your bathroom, school supplies, it was endless. There was even a pink plaster St. Anthony that could predict rain by turning blue. My mother would have died laughing. All of this was juxtaposed with the real thing—these magnificent, creepy medieval churches. St. Anthony's tongue was enshrined at a basilica in Padua. People stood in long lines just to look at it. My dad brought roses to every reliquary we visited. I was just blown away. Totally awestruck."

"A lot of Christians don't believe in that sort of thing."

"Sure, I know that, but I was mesmerized. It *was* bizarre, even disgusting, but it was also seductive, miraculous, and deeply moving. In the evenings, Dad would read to us from the lives of the saints. All of them punished themselves in terrible, masochistic ways. They would meditate on the agony of the cross, contemplating Christ's wounds, every last detail of the crucifixion—not just for a few minutes, but for hours at a time. For lifetimes. They wanted the same agony in their own lives so they could purify themselves as Christ had, so they could be worthy. They tortured themselves with flagels, or wore clothes that had sharp iron studs sewn into them. They had visions. They bled or sometimes their hands glowed. They begged to die to their senses, denying themselves food, water, shelter. These men and women were epic in every sense of the word. Today, we might consider them insane, but the Catholic church venerates them. The people I saw that summer worshiped them."

"Do you think about these saints a lot?"

"Not much anymore. But that summer I did."

"Would you say that the trip to Europe affected you quite profoundly?"

"It affected all of us. When we got home, we all realized were bound together by a new understanding of what it was to be human."

"Can you define that understanding for me?"

"Words are so inadequate. It's like the writer Hermann Hesse says. We can try to understand each other, but each man is able to interpret himself to himself alone."

"I'd still like you to try."

Henry closed his eyes. "Well, it had to do with rules, with boundaries. With freedom—and most importantly, with pain.

That trip made me realize that, more than ever, I wanted to be a doctor. I wanted to help people who were *in* pain find a way out, if only temporarily. That's what those saints wanted more than anything. A way out of their own personal pain."

Dr. Kirsch didn't ask another question right away. Henry could hear her writing something down. Finally she said, "Have you experienced a lot of pain in your life, Henry?"

The question was like being pelted with a wet sock. "Look, doctor—" He swung his feet off the couch and sat up. "I'm not sure this is working. I don't think you get it."

"Remember, Henry, you committed yourself to six weeks."

She was shaming him, and that pissed him off. It also made him remember why he'd come. "What else do you want to know?" he asked coldly.

"Go ahead and lie back down."

He grunted his dissatisfaction, but did as she asked.

"Tell me a little more about your brother."

"You mean the Teflon kid? It's funny, but Bobby got away with murder. Oops." Henry raised a hand. "Slip of the tongue. But really, it was like I had a bull's-eye painted on my back, but my brother was totally invisible. Oh, he got in trouble, sometimes big trouble, but it never seemed to stick. Mom never held a grudge when it came to Bobby, the way she did with me and my father. She thought the sun rose and set on him. People were drawn to him, even though he was quiet. Barrett said he had charisma. I thought Barrett had charisma. Nobody thought I had much of anything, except poor posture. Mom liked Barrett because he flirted with her. She loved to flirt. She had lots of affairs while they were married."

"You knew about them?"

"Sure. The men came to the house. My father only had one affair. He probably would have hidden it from us, but my brother and I walked in on them."

"That must have been terrible for you."

"Actually, it was kind of funny. Bobby and I knew the other

party. We'd already suspected something was going on."

"Again, do you think it might be helpful if I knew who that person was?"

"It was Barrett." He waited until he could sense her shock, then continued, "He and Dad had been going at it like rabbits for almost the entire two months we were in Europe. Pretty torrid stuff."

"Would you say your father and Barrett are gay?"

Henry shrugged. "I think they both mostly like women, but . . . Barrett likes to experiment. And my dad . . . well, he's always been drawn to beauty. My mother was extraordinarily beautiful when she was a young woman. And that summer, Barrett looked like a young Greek god."

Again, the doctor was silent for a few seconds.

"I know what you're thinking," said Henry. "You figure that since my father was attracted to Barrett, that he and my mother couldn't have had a satisfying sexual relationship. That's why she had so many affairs. But the fact was, their sex life was what kept them together. Don't ask me to explain it. Whenever Dad was home, their bedroom was off limits. They had huge fights and then they'd end up in bed. Anger got them off. It was their aphrodisiac."

"Was there ever any physical violence?"

"Never. They used words, not fists."

"That isn't the norm, Henry. Most people don't behave like that. You know that, don't you?"

"It worked for them for eighteen years."

"Yes, but—"

"You of all people should know that *normal* as a psychological construct has very little meaning. Are you normal, doctor? Am I? Human beings are a vastly intriguing mystery. Psychology isn't a science, it's just another religion, another way of looking at the world. It's a mixture of fact and fiction."

"If you believe that, then why are you here?"

"Because I don't look to science as a savior, any more than I look to Jesus. I need to make a confession, doctor, and I prefer to do it with you."

"A confession about your brother?"

"Yes."

"But I can't give you absolution, Henry, if that's what you're looking for."

He fingered the chain at his neck. "I don't need absolution. Someone else does." He considered pulling the chain out and showing her the pendant dangling from it, but it was too early. Perhaps during their next session he would tell her a different story, the tale of what had really happened on that long-ago trip to Italy.

19

On Wednesday morning, Peter woke before sunrise with an immense hangover. He'd tied one on last night at a bar on Hennepin Avenue, but was regretting it now. The room he'd slept in was as familiar to him as his own skin, but his body didn't fit inside it any longer. The proportions were all wrong. He'd become the giant in the fairy story, instead of the little boy who wanted to climb the beanstalk. His father hadn't even changed the wallpaper—fifteen freakin' years and he hadn't even changed the freakin' wallpaper.

Peter realized that his dad had wanted to spend last evening with him, playing checkers probably, drinking cocoa—or something equally sentimental. It was an attempt to recapture a time long past and it wouldn't work. This wasn't Peter's home any longer, it was just another prison cell. His dad wanted to keep an eye on him, that was painfully obvious, and that's why Peter hadn't come back until late. He couldn't face his dad's concern or his scrutiny. He'd even begun to wonder if his dad really believed him when he said he'd had nothing to do with what happened to Sigrid. It was probably just his own insecurity talking.

He should be with Sigrid right this minute, not pretending to be seventeen again, like his father seemed to want.

Around six A.M., Peter dragged himself out of bed to the phone on the desk by the window—the window that overlooked the garage. His father's Mercedes was in the drive, covered by a light dusting of snow. Peter watched the sky grow lighter as he tried to shake the cotton from his head. He called Metro South to check on Sigrid. The big news was that she'd regained consciousness. She was extremely weak, and confused about where she was, but Peter was elated. It was only a matter of time now until the police would learn the real story of what had happened. Once Peter was released from the restraining order, he would stay by Sigrid's side until she was out of danger. That was his prayer, his hope, his need.

The nurse on duty also said that Sigrid's sister-in-law had been with her for the past few hours. Peter was deeply grateful to find that Jane was at the hospital. He'd call her later in the day to thank her, and to get a firsthand report. Sometimes Jane took her big sister role a little too seriously, but he forgave her for that. He trusted her like he trusted no one else in his life. He wished he could go back to her house right now and stay there until things got sorted out. Peter loved his dad, and respected him enormously, but that was the crux of the problem. His father's successful life only reminded Peter that his own was in shambles. The comparisons were too obvious and too brutal. Jane had made her share of mistakes, so around her, he didn't feel like he was in the presence of such damning perfection.

After hanging up, he crawled back into bed and spent the next few hours trying to sleep off his headache. He eventually gave up. Scooping up his clothes off the floor, he dressed quickly and then sat back down at the desk and began to plan the day ahead. He'd spent yesterday afternoon scanning microfilm at the library, ferreting out every article he could find on the trial of Bobby Alto. His father had explained his new theory about the motivation behind Sigrid's attack, and it made sense to Peter. But Peter's take on it was slightly different.

His father felt that Conrad Alto was out for vengeance because Ray had been unable to keep Bobby out of prison. It seemed plausible. But Peter reasoned that it was unlikely there were *two* deranged members in the same family. He agreed with his dad that one of them was undoubtedly the Midnight Man, but if Bobby had been the guilty party, the craziness would have ended with his death. It hadn't. In Peter's opinion, simple vengeance wasn't enough to explain the brutality of what had happened to Sigrid. Someone wanted her to suffer and then die. Peter had arrived too quickly and the attacker had fled out the back door. With Bobby out of the picture, that left his brother, his father, and his best friend, Barrett Sweeny, as possible suspects. One of them had put Sigrid in the hospital and had placed Peter squarely in the line of police fire.

It was clear from the reports in the newspapers that the Midnight Man planned his actions carefully. He choreographed his movements with the precision of a dancer. He was smart, but he was putting himself in a more vulnerable position now because he wasn't picking his targets at random anymore. Peter felt that fact alone might be enough to bring him down. There were two people Peter needed to talk to today. That is, if his father ever left the house.

Checking the time, he saw that it was going on ten. His father's car was still in the drive. Awfully late for such a busy attorney to be getting to the office. When Peter caught a whiff of the frying bacon, he smelled a rat—or a ploy. His father was trying to lure him downstairs. Peter was caught. His dad wasn't about to leave until they'd had a chance to talk. His attempt to hide in his room until his dad left wasn't going to work.

When Peter finally sauntered into the kitchen, trying to look as casual as possible, he saw that the table was set for two. The orange juice had been poured, the coffee made, and the bread was in the toaster ready to toast. His father was standing at the stove wearing the red-and-black barbecue apron Jane had given him for his last birthday, the one that said, I MAY NOT KNOW HOW TO COOK, BUT I CAN INCINERATE WITH THE BEST OF THEM.

"Hey, there, sleepyhead," said Ray, turning to smile at his son. "I figured the only way to get you out of bed was to feed you."

Peter was a sucker for bacon. His father knew it.

"This looks wonderful," said Peter. He sat down at the table, his head still pounding like a jackhammer.

"How did you sleep?"

"Not very well." Next to the juice, Peter noticed that his father had placed a bottle of aspirin. He quickly downed a couple of tablets while his dad's back was turned.

"I've got a meeting at eleven," said Ray, arranging the food on the plates. "I thought I'd stop down and see Sigrid this afternoon. I would imagine the police will want to talk to her right away."

"You'll call me after you've talked to her, right? I'll make sure I've got my cell with me."

"Absolutely." Ray set the plates on the table, then poured them each a cup of coffee. "Are you meeting with Elizabeth this afternoon? She's in court this morning."

"No. I see her tomorrow."

Ray pulled out a chair and sat down. "We should know more then. Hopefully, if Sigrid can tell the police what really happened, the charges against you will be dropped. We'll get the restraining order lifted and you can go see her. By the way, I've got my investigators working the case, checking out anything and everything they can find on Conrad Alto."

"They need to check out the entire family."

Ray's eyes rose to Peter's. Taking a sip of coffee, he said, "What are you going to do today?"

"I need to see Jane."

"Good. That's good. She's had a rough couple of days too. Late last night, the police swept her restaurant for drugs."

"Did they find any?"

"Thank God the place was clean. I talked to her a short while ago and she's doing okay, but she's pretty worried about you."

Peter felt guilty now for not calling her yesterday, but he'd been too preoccupied, and then too drunk.

"Got anything else on the agenda for today?" asked his father.

"Why do you need to know what I'm doing every minute?" His voice was sharp, sharper than he'd intended.

"I'm concerned, Peter. That's all."

"I know," he said, staring gloomily at the bacon on his plate. "It's just . . . I'm not used to people keeping tabs on me. I'm an adult, Dad. Besides," he added, trying to look a little more cheerful, "I don't have any firm plans. I'll probably sleep some more. I'm pretty tired." He lied because he didn't feel like getting into it. If he told his father what he was really planning, he'd probably be bombarded with a whole raft of instructions, or reasons not to do what he wanted.

"Let's have dinner together tonight," said Ray. He'd barely touched his food, and now he was looking at his watch, making sounds like he had to leave.

"Sure," said Peter, feeling trapped.

"I'll make reservations. What do you feel like? Italian? Thai? Seafood?"

"How about I meet you at the Maxfield at seven?"

Ray smiled. "It's a date. Now that Sigrid's conscious, maybe we'll have something to celebrate."

A couple of hours later, Peter and Bill Younger, the arson cop who'd broken the case against Bobby Alto, sat in a booth at a café across from the Metrodome.

"Your phone call got my attention," said Younger. He was a big guy, a good thirty pounds overweight, salt-and-pepper crew cut, probably in his late fifties. "Let's cut to the chase. What's your bottom line?"

"I don't think Bobby Alto was the Midnight Man."

He grunted. "I've heard that before." He bit into his roast beef sandwich and chewed slowly. "Seems to me your father tried to make that point at the trial. The jury didn't buy it."

"But look at what's happened to my family." Peter had already explained about Sigrid, and about his sister. "Somebody's after us."

"If what you're telling me is true, hell, it could be anyone. Your father doesn't win all his cases, you know. And even when he does, he makes his share of enemies."

"Enemies who would resort to murder? My wife could have died. She's still barely holding on."

"Lots of crazy people in the world, kid."

"Okay, I grant you that. But why is it happening now? Bobby Alto was knifed less than a week ago. The day after he was killed drugs get planted in my sister's office. The day after that my wife is attacked and nearly killed and I'm dragged off to jail. It's too much of a coincidence not to mean something."

Younger took another bite of his sandwich.

"Look, would you agree that the Midnight Man was deranged?"

"Sure. He was a classic sociopath. No guilt or remorse, but able to tell right from wrong. One of our forensic psychologists called him a sexual psychopath. Even though he didn't sleep with the victims, she felt there was a sexual element to the murders. Possibly even an element of ritual or torture. The Midnight Man was what we call an *organized offender*. Above-average intelligence. Socially competent. He was precise and controlled in the way he went about the crimes. Probably had inconsistent childhood discipline. It all fits Bobby Alto."

"Okay, so we're on the same page there. The guy is crazy."

Younger picked up a fork and tucked into his cole slaw. "*Was* crazy. He's dead."

"Maybe," said Peter. He pulled his coffee cup closer in front of him.

"But *you* honestly think he's still alive."

"I do."

"And he's the one after your family."

"Yes."

"Why?"

"Because my father didn't get Bobby off. It made him angry. I've read all the reports in the papers. If Bobby wasn't the Midnight Man, it had to be someone close to him."

"Okay," said Younger, wiping his mouth with a napkin, "here's a question for you. If the motive behind your wife's attack is vengeance against your father, why isn't this guy going after the other people in the equation? I should be a target. So should the prosecutor. What about the supreme court judges who ruled against Bobby's appeal?"

"I don't know the answer to that."

"Kind of a big hole in your theory."

"But consider this. My dad thinks Bobby's father, Conrad Alto, is behind it all. Dad defends his son but doesn't get the guy off. Bobby dies in prison. Conrad Alto threatens my father."

"Did that happen? Did he threaten him?"

"Yes, after the appeal was rejected and again after Bobby died."

"Threaten him how?"

"He said, 'An eye for an eye.' "

"That's original."

"He blames my dad for what happened to his child, and so he decides to get back at him by hurting *his* children."

"In other words, Ray Lawless now thinks Conrad Alto is the Midnight Man."

"Well, not exactly." Peter stirred more cream into his coffee. "He thinks Conrad Alto is out for revenge."

"So he admits that Bobby *was* guilty."

"He's . . . never been sure about that. I'm the one who thinks Bobby was innocent. Like I told you on the phone, it doesn't seem plausible to me that there would be two psychopaths in the same family."

Younger's laugh was more of a wheeze.

"You think it's funny?"

"It's a house of cards, kid. When you place one unsubstantiated assumption on top of another unsubstantiated assumption, all you get is hot air. I deal in facts. In evidence. You've given me nothing but opinion."

"Okay, then follow us."

"Pardon me?"

"Put a tail on me, on my dad and my sister. This guy isn't done with us, I know it. He's out there figuring the angles, deciding what to do next."

"Even if that's true, I don't have the authority. Besides, the Alto case is closed."

"But it *isn't*. Don't you get it? The same guy who killed those women, who burned down all those houses, is after us now. *We're* the targets. Follow us and you get your man."

Younger thought about it for a few seconds. Tossing his napkin over his empty plate, he said, "You bring me some honest-to-god proof that the Midnight Man is still alive and I'll back you all the way. But in lieu of that, I can't help. Sorry."

"Then we're sitting ducks."

"Look, somebody hurt your wife. That's a tough break. If you didn't do it, then we'll figure out who did. Your sister had another bad break. She should call her precinct and report what happened. It seems unlikely to me, but if Bobby's father is behind it, or someone else in Bobby's family, then maybe he's done enough damage and he'll stop."

"What if he doesn't? What if I'm right and the Midnight Man is still alive and after my family?"

"Then—" He shrugged. "I guess I'd say my prayers."

20

After a night of virtually no sleep, Jane felt a little goofy, as if there were two of her and both of them were leaning sideways. But she was buoyed by the fact that Sigrid was now awake. She'd stayed at the hospital until Sigrid's brother, Todd, had arrived. He was polite, as always, but his usual warmth was missing. It seemed pretty obvious to her that he wanted her to leave, so after kissing Sigrid goodbye and whispering that she'd be back, she took off.

Back at the restaurant, Jane summoned all her stealth. She managed to pass the double doors to the pub without falling down or being seen. So far, so good. She hurried down the back hall to her office, locked the door behind her, then took her desk phone off the hook, turned off her cell phone—Cordelia would just have to sputter and fume—and curled up on the couch with a pillow and a blanket. All she wanted was a few hours of peace.

She woke to the sound of rattling. Sitting bolt upright, she watched the knob on her office door being twisted back and forth. The sound was soft at first, but grew louder as an unseen hand yanked and shook the handle. In her fuzzy, semiawake state, she wasn't sure whether to be alarmed or annoyed. The lock was a deadbolt and the door was solid wood, so it was unlikely anyone could get in without causing major damage and a hell of a lot of noise. Feeling confident that she was safe, she waited to see what would happen.

The rattling finally stopped, but started again a few seconds later. Jane got up and crept over to the door. Whoever was on the other side was either a moron or knew more about locks than she did. It was unlikely anybody on her staff even realized she was here, so why was someone trying to get into her office? The answer seemed both obvious and ominous.

Jane wished now that she'd had a peephole installed so she could see outside. The events of the last few days would make anyone paranoid, even someone as rock solid and stable as she was these days. Taking a chance, she slipped the bolt back. She heard a shout, then a whooshing sound coupled with footsteps pounding away. When she finally drew back the door, she found that Joe Vasquez was halfway down the hall making for the stairway.

Slowly, quietly, she followed. When she came to the base of the stairs, she looked up and saw that the service door to the loading dock was open. She rushed up the steps two at a time, figuring he'd leapt the fence and was gone for good. At the same time, she was mentally calculating what she'd say to Turlow. The bad guy had finally shown his hand. Here's his name, go find him. Oh, and I won't need your guys to permanently stake out my restaurant anymore.

Stepping outside, Jane was surprised to find Vasquez still standing at the edge of the dock, looking off toward the lake. He was dressed in his waiter's uniform—black slacks, white shirt, tie and tweed vest—so he'd probably been working the lunch shift in the dining room.

When he turned to come back inside, he saw Jane blocking the doorway. "Hey, boss. I didn't know you were around."

"Why were you trying to get into my office?"

"Me? No, you've got it all wrong. I was coming down the stairs from the main dining room when I saw this guy standing by your door, messing with the lock. I shouted for him to stop, but he took off up the stairs. I chased after him, but he got away." He seemed genuinely frustrated—either that, or he was a good actor.

"This . . . *guy*," said Jane, scrutinizing his face. "I never saw him. All I saw was you."

"You must have been in your office."

"Good guess."

"Well, he was there, all right. Late teens. Bad case of acne. Black coat and ripped jeans. By the time you opened your door, he was probably up the stairs."

"Faster than a speeding bullet."

"Yeah." He flashed his pearly whites at her. "You should be glad I'm around. Who knows what that dude was up to?" He blew on his hands, rubbing them together. "I'm freezing to death out here. What do you say we go back in?"

Jane didn't know what to believe. She hadn't seen this phantom for herself, but he could be telling the truth. On the other hand, from the very first, something about Joe Vasquez had bothered her. He seemed too accommodating. Too chipper. And way the hell too omnipresent. "Thanks," she said on the way back down the stairs.

"No problem, boss. I'm here to help."

When she got to the bottom, she glanced up and saw him looking down at her, hands resting casually on his hips, a broad smile on his face.

The sight of him made her shiver.

Back in her office, she folded up the blanket and stowed it and the pillow in her closet. Then she sat down behind her desk to take stock of the day—what was left of it. It was going on one-thirty. She switched her cell phone back on and was immediately assaulted with a call.

"Hi, Cordelia." She didn't even have to check the caller I.D.

"What happened to the phone? I've been trying to reach you for hours!"

"I bet you didn't even get up until noon."

"Well, minutes then. When I didn't get an answer, I panicked!"

"I turned the phone off so I could get some sleep. After you left, I spent the rest of the night at the hospital with Sigrid and didn't get back here until ten."

"You mean, you never went to bed? How decadent."

"It doesn't feel decadent. If feels like someone stuffed my head with sawdust. Sigrid's awake."

"Oh, Janey, I'm so glad to hear it! Really, that's wonderful news. Have the police talked to her yet? Did she tell them what really happened?"

"She opened her eyes while I was there, but only for a few seconds. And she seemed pretty confused, which isn't unusual. It's going to take some time for her to pull it all together."

"Not too much time, I hope. For Peter's sake."

"Where are you?"

"In my car. On my way to the theater. Have you heard from the cops today?"

"I took my office phone off the hook too. Maybe Turlow left me a message." She picked up a pencil and tapped it against the side of her computer. "You know, Cordelia, the more I think about it, the less sense all this makes."

"Define 'all this.' "

"Somebody plants drugs in my office. I get rid of the evidence, so the police only have my word that it happened."

"Right."

"Don't you think the fact that they send out drug-sniffing hounds and a whole raft of burly-looking men to search the place is an overreaction? Not to mention asking to plant informants on my staff."

"Well, when you put it like that—"

"It's a waste of manpower. Unless they know something I don't."

"Like what?"

"If I knew, Cordelia, I wouldn't be in the dark, now would I?"

"You needn't take that tone with me. I'm not the enemy."

"I'm just tired. And hungry."

"Listen, Janey, you're the one who asked them for help. They're just following your lead."

"Yes, but it feels like I asked them for a hand and they called in the National Guard."

"Yeah, I see your point."

"I'd like to tell Turlow I've changed my mind about letting his people work here."

"But you won't."

"No. I won't. I can't."

"Because someone did plant those drugs, and might do it again, thereby placing you in a world of trouble."

"Yes." She sighed. For the past few years, her business had been making a good profit. But if she lost the restaurant, she'd lose everything. "Look, Cordelia, something weird just happened." She went on to explain that someone had tried to get into her office while she was asleep on the couch. Cordelia went into her usual hysterics, ranting incoherently about bulletproof vests and full body armor, but she stopped, thankfully, when she reached the theater. She had an important meeting and had to go.

Jane promised to phone her later with updates. When she checked her messages, she found that, sure enough, Turlow had called.

"Ms. Lawless, this is Art Turlow. I'm sending over two people this afternoon. Your new bartender's name is Scott Amsdahl. Your new prep cook is Sunny Zhang. They've both been briefed, and they've both worked restaurants before so they know the drill. I'd prefer you schedule Amsdahl in the evenings—particularly weekends. If you've got any questions, give me a call. I'll be in touch." He left his number.

Jane's second message was from Peter. "Janey, hi. It's me. I stopped by the restaurant, but nobody knew where you were, so I thought I'd leave you a message. I was tied up all morning. Actually, I talked to the cop who broke the case against Bobby Alto. His name is Bill Younger. Can't say I got anywhere with him, although I did explain what had happened to Sigrid—and to you and me—and how I thought it all tied together. I told him Alto's father had threatened Dad, and . . . well, I gave him my take on what's happening, not that he bought it. See, I think Bobby was innocent, that the Midnight Man, whoever he is, is still out there and he's after us now because he holds us responsible for Bobby's death. But I've got no proof. Younger said if I could get him evidence that the Midnight Man was still alive and kicking, he'd help me. Fat chance of that. Anyway, I'm calling you from your house. I thought you might be home, but since you're not, I may take a nap. Dad's house feels pretty claustrophobic. Didn't sleep very well last night. But I'm fine, sis. Really. I'll be even better when Sigrid tells the police what happened and I can go be with her. Thanks so much for spending the morning with her, Janey. That meant a lot to me. Dad's stopping down to see her this afternoon. I'm having dinner with him tonight, so one of us will call you with a report. Talk to you soon. Bye."

The last message was from Patricia. "Hey, Lawless. Just called to remind you about tonight. I'll have a light supper ready and waiting. Imagine you'll be by late, as usual. I'll be home after eight. Don't blow me off just because you have another crisis, okay? Bring it along and we'll work on it together—like we did the other night. Or better yet, just come to relax. Maybe I'll crank up the hot tub and open a bottle of that Pinot from Sancerre you like so much. Later, babe."

It sounded like heaven to Jane, that is, if she could stay awake long enough to enjoy it.

As her thoughts wandered over various related and unrelated topics in a jumbled, exhausted, stream-of-consciousness sort of reverie, Arlene's face appeared in the open doorway.

"Joe told me you were here," she said, turning and snapping

her fingers. "This was delivered for you about an hour ago. I thought you might want it right away."

One of the bartenders pushed a dolly containing several heavy-looking boxes into the room.

"It's from Lawless & Associates. Your father, I assume."

"It must be the trial transcripts," she said, thinking out loud.

The bartender dumped the boxes against the wall next to the door, then wheeled the dolly out of the room.

"Thanks, Tony," she shouted after him.

"No problem," he called from the hallway.

"How's your sister-in-law doing?" asked Arlene, folding her slim frame into the chair on the other side of Jane's desk.

"Better."

"Thank God."

"Yeah. Say, Arlene, since you're here, I should tell you that I've hired two new people. Names are Amsdahl and Zhang. They'll be stopping by later today. Amsdahl is a bartender. I'd like him scheduled nights and weekends. And Zhang's a prep cook. Will you see to it that they both get an orientation? Make sure all their forms are filled out. Oh, and have them scheduled as soon as possible."

"Will do," said Arlene, jotting it down on her steno pad.

"How's lunch going up there?"

"Busy. So's the pub. It's been a good day."

"Arlene—" Jane hesitated. "You've had a better chance to observe Joe Vasquez in action than I have. How's he doing?"

Mulling the question over, she stuck her pencil behind her ear. "He's competent, I guess. He says his tips are good. He shows up on time and keeps his uniforms neat. Seems to get along with everybody. He makes friends easily and fast, which is always a plus."

"What do you think of him personally?"

She shrugged. "With his looks, he's got to be a heartbreaker."

"No, I mean . . . personally as it relates to his job."

"Well, he strikes me as a little too eager sometimes, but that's probably just a matter of style. By the way, I think he's hustling one of the bartenders—Melissa. The blonde? And don't tell Melissa, but I think he's also hustling Ellen."

Ellen Greenberg was one of the line cooks.

"Just another horny guy with a pretty face," said Arlene, adopting her standard can't-live-with-'em, can't-live-without-'em tone.

Jane smiled. "I'll be up to work the dinner crowd. Until then, I'll be here in my office."

"Gotcha." She glanced back at the boxes. "If that's all reading material, I'd say you need a little peace and quiet." As she stood, she added, "You might get a couple of hours—if you're lucky. I'll try to run interference for you. You know, if you don't mind my saying so, you look tired, Jane. Aren't you supposed to be getting extra rest? You're still recovering from that head injury."

"I've got a lot going on right now."

"I realize that. But Felix and I will cover for you if you need to go home and rest. We've had lots of practice, what with you being gone so much before Christmas."

"I know. You guys did a great job. But I'm feeling better. Work is good for me."

"You know best. But take it easy, kid. You only get one go 'round in this life."

After she was gone, Jane shut the door and opened the top box. She hadn't realized that reading the transcripts would be quite this daunting. Placing the boxes next to each other, she took a few minutes to examine the contents of each, selecting the dossiers her father's investigators had done on each individual connected to the case. None of them were terribly long, so she thought it would be a good place to start. But before she sat down to read, she phoned up to the kitchen and asked for one of the waiters to bring her a bowl of mulligatawny soup and a basket of bread and butter, a pot of black coffee, and whatever chocolate dessert was on the menu. She needed fuel to keep her eyes open and her mind operating, even if it wasn't at full capacity.

By three, Jane was lying on the couch, reading through the fifth dossier. She'd already covered Conrad and Shirley Alto's life, as well as Henry and Bobby's. She knew some of the details from what she'd read in the papers, but a lot of what she'd read had been inaccurate—or had only given a part of the story. Instead of making notes, she highlighted portions with a yellow marker.

The fifth report was on a family friend. Barrett Sweeny. The attached picture showed a young man with a tanned face, dark hair that curled at his neck, and shining eyes. Jane knew what her aunt Beryl would say about a face like that. He was too handsome for his own good. Jane had no idea of his sexual orientation, but she wondered for a moment whether his beauty was the type that would appeal more to women or to men. He was an above-average student. B.A. from the U of M. Currently a real estate broker. During his junior year, he'd changed his college major from forestry to philosophy.

For the past six years, Barrett Sweeny had been employed by Lakeland Realty and from all reports, he'd made himself a killing in one of the best housing markets in the last sixty years. His hobby and his passion was sailing. He'd come from a poor family—his father had owned a convenience store before he retired and sold it to a Hmong family. Now, thanks to Barrett, they were living in a beautiful home on Deer Lake in northern Minnesota. It had always been their dream to get out of the city, and their only son had made it possible. Barrett's mother had encouraged his friendship with Bobby Alto, and later with the entire family, stating that they were people of "high quality, good influences on her son."

Jane had just about reached the end of the dossier when several facts jumped out at her. It seemed that, in his early twenties, Barrett had been part of a local crew that was affiliated with the National Wildfire Coalition. For three years running he'd traveled to Oregon and California to fight wildfires. By all reports, he'd done an excellent job, even been awarded two commendations. According to an interview with Barrett, he considered himself a man seeking both "high adventure and a way to help my fellow man."

Fascinating, thought Jane, taking off her reading glasses and letting the pages drop to her lap. It all sounded so noble. Barrett was a generous son, a hard worker, and a man given to charitable acts. Still—and she knew this was a dark thought—she wondered if a man who liked to put fires out might not also like to start them.

21

Late Wednesday afternoon, Raymond pulled his Mercedes into a parking space on the second floor of the Metro South ramp. He sat for a moment in the car just enjoying the quiet. For the first time all day, nobody was talking to him, nobody was demanding an explanation, a justification, or an answer he didn't have. The last few weeks had been hectic, but even before that, he'd begun thinking of retirement. What the hell did he need all this aggravation for? He had plenty of money. He was still young. Why not quit while he was ahead? Besides, money was a whore. What he valued now was time.

Ray used to love his job, but that had ended years ago. The people he defended now seemed far more blatant in their corruption than they used to. Or maybe it was just him. He was sick to death of dealing with the dregs of society dressed up in Armani suits, even if he still saw his job as an important one.

Ray hated to admit it, but Conrad Alto was right. He wasn't putting the effort into his cases he used to. Or worse, maybe he had lost his edge. But if he left the practice of law, who would he be? Playing golf had never seemed like a compelling end to an active life. He couldn't help but believe that as soon as matters got straightened out with his daughter, his son, and his daughter-in-law, some of the old energy would return. But would that be good enough? Good enough for Ray Lawless?

Ray had always handled the stress of his profession well. It was the personal matters that confused him into a state of inertia. For the past few days, he'd been walking around mumbling to himself, making mental notes about what he had to do next, who he had to call, how he should handle this or that. And none of it had one thing to do with any of his current cases.

He'd talked to his wife, Marilyn, shortly after lunch. Her father was still holding on, but the cancer was eating him alive. He wouldn't last much longer. And that frightened Ray to his very core. Marilyn's father had worked hard all his life, retired late. Three years to the day after his retirement party, he'd been diagnosed with lung cancer. He'd fought it like a trouper, but in the end, it would get him. He would be dead before he had the chance to enjoy the fruits of his labor. Ray was terrified that the same thing would happen to him. That's why he'd always been so careful about what he ate and drank, careful to make sure he got proper exercise, sleep, vitamins. He drank his orange juice every morning, stayed away from coffee, and only drank wine—and not very much of that. He got yearly physicals and kept his weight down. Maybe that was his problem. He was so damn careful about his daily existence that he'd stopped living.

Marilyn had sounded discouraged on the phone, which was only natural, but at the same time she'd been unusually short with him. He figured he'd done something to upset her, and that she was attempting in her usual oblique way to let him know. He missed her, but what he'd discovered in the past few days was that what he really missed was the old Marilyn, the one who liked to have a good time, who laughed at his silly jokes, occasionally drank an unnecessary cocktail, and didn't mind eating red meat two nights in a row. She'd changed into the same cautious, half-alive creature he had. They were both frightened of life, terrified by potential loss. Marilyn looked at him now with such wounded, searching eyes. She didn't understand what was happening to her any better than he did. He hated to disappoint her, and yet that's just what he'd done when he talked to her today. With every breath he took he was not only failing her, he was losing her.

It was so much easier with Elizabeth. Not only was he attracted to her, not only did he enjoy all the super-charged electricity in the air when they got together, but there was also—blissfully—none of the baggage. She occasionally drank a bit more than was good for her. She loved to laugh, to stay up late. And she ate filet mignon with reckless abandon. He asked her how she'd escaped the creeping cautiousness of age, and she'd just shrugged. Life was too short not to live it, she'd said. It was like she was speaking a foreign language—one he desperately wanted to learn, but one he felt certain he never could.

Ray realized the situation with Elizabeth was a tired, pathetic old cliché. He was an older guy, having trouble with his marriage, and so, like a salivating dog, he trotted after the first pretty face that came along and showed him a little interest. And yet, Elizabeth was far more than a pretty face. She was a deeply fascinating woman with a unique perspective on life—one he envied—as well as a complex past of her own. She had children and grandchildren, all of whom she worried about more than was good for her. In her own way, she needed something to distract her from her everyday concerns, just as he did. The desire to be in the company of a woman who thought he was not only intelligent and accomplished, but sexy and fun, was a hugely attractive proposition. When Marilyn finally returned from New Orleans, the dinners with Elizabeth would end. They had to. Ray loved his wife, or at least he used to. The two of them needed to work on their problems, not turn their backs on each other as they'd been doing for months. But with so many other problems in his personal life right now, his marriage would have to wait.

Ray had made reservations for his dinner tonight with Peter. He wished it could simply be a pleasant occasion, a time to shoot the breeze and get caught up on each other's lives, but he and

Peter needed to talk—really talk. His son still hadn't explained, in anything approaching specific terms, what he and Sigrid had been arguing about the morning of her attack. It might not have any bearing on what had happened later, but if it ever did go to trial, the fact that people in the neighboring apartments had heard an argument didn't bode well.

Once inside the hospital, Ray took the east elevators up to the fifth floor. Before entering Sigrid's room, he tracked down her nurse and introduced himself. He needed to know if the police had been by to question her.

The nurse told him that she'd just come on duty, but that she'd heard that two officers had stopped up around eleven. They hadn't stayed long. Sigrid was still too weak to answer more than a few questions. The nurse had no idea what had been said, but cautioned Ray not to tax Sigrid. Ray promised he wouldn't, then hurried off down the hall.

When he entered the room, the sight that met his eyes sickened him. Sigrid was lying in the bed, hooked up to all sorts of monitors and IVs. Her face was swollen and bruised almost beyond recognition. What kind of a monster could do that to another human being?

Standing next to the bed, he watched her for a few minutes while she slept. The doctors had no doubt given her something to ease the pain, and yet now that she was conscious, nothing could ease the mental agony of knowing what had happened to her, to her body, to her life. He remembered what Jane had gone through after her ordeal. Sigrid's recovery would be every bit as difficult. More so, perhaps, because of her forced estrangement from Peter. So far, Ray hadn't been able to come up with a way around the restraining order. He was still hoping legal machinations wouldn't be necessary.

After a few minutes, Sigrid stirred and opened her eyes.

Ray thought he detected a hint of a smile. "Hi, sweetheart. How're you doing?"

"How do I look?" she whispered. It was more of a rasp, but at least she hadn't lost her knack for sarcasm.

"You look wonderful to me."

"Put on your glasses, Ray." She tried to clear her throat.

"Peter sends his love."

She closed her eyes, then opened them and looked away. "The police came. They think Peter did this to me. That's why he can't be here."

"That's right, sweetheart. That's why we're all hoping you can tell the police what really happened—so Peter can come visit you. Every time I talk to him, that's all he talks about—that he wants to be with you."

Sigrid was growing restless. She tried to move her arms, then her legs.

"What's wrong?" Ray asked. "Can I help you?"

"Raise the top of the bed. The controls are on the side."

He found the lever and pushed until she nodded for him to stop. "Better?" he asked.

She still seemed uncomfortable.

"Do you want me to get the nurse?"

"I don't know what I want." She seemed confused.

"Sigrid?"

She looked up at him.

"Do you remember who did this to you?"

"No," she rasped. "It's all blank."

"What's the last thing you remember?"

She grimaced as she reached for her water cup. "Peter leaving, telling me our marriage was over."

Ray just stared at her. "God, I didn't know. He didn't tell me."

"Help me with this."

Ray held the cup steady while she took a sip from the straw. The small amount of moving she'd done had exhausted her.

After a few seconds she said, "Ray?"

"What, honey?"

"Where are my earrings? They're tiny diamond studs." She brushed a hand over her ear. "I always wear them."

"Someone probably took off all your jewelry when you came to the hospital."

"Will you find them and take them home? God, I feel like shit."

Ray looked around as the nurse entered.

"Look there, she's awake." The woman's voice was chipper. "I've got to take your vitals, Sigrid." Glancing at Ray, she said, "You don't have to leave." She placed a thermometer in Sigrid's mouth, then watched a the digital readout on her belt.

Ray figured blood pressure would be next. But instead, the nurse felt Sigrid's forehead. "You've got a temperature, honey. I don't much like that."

"How high is it?" asked Ray.

"Hundred and three. Her last reading was normal." Bending closer to Sigrid, she said, "I'm going to call your doctor. He's in the hospital so he'll be up soon. How do you feel?"

"Kind of funny."

"Light-headed?"

She nodded.

"Does it hurt anywhere in particular?"

"I hurt all over, but my chest is the worst."

"Are you cold?"

"I'm hot."

"Okay." She placed the call button in Sigrid's hand. "If you need me, just call. I'll be right back." She turned and rushed out of the room.

Ray didn't much care for this turn of events. Sigrid had closed her eyes again, so he bent his head next to her ear and whispered, "I'm here, sweetheart."

"Good," she said weakly.

"Is there anything you want me to tell Peter?"

He waited for almost a minute. When she didn't respond, he

figured she'd fallen asleep. Finally, she roused herself and said, "Tell him I said hi."

Not exactly what he'd been hoping for. "I will, honey."

Ray wasn't sure what to do next. He didn't want to leave until he knew what her doctor had to say, but he felt too agitated to sit down. He decided to do what Sigrid had asked—search for her jewelry. It didn't seem terribly important in the scheme of things, but if that's what she wanted, at least he'd have some good news to give her when she woke up.

The first place he looked was the tall nightstand next to the bed. He opened the top drawer, but found that, except for a pen, it was empty. All the drawers underneath were equally bare. That left the closet. When he drew back the door, he found a bunch of empty hangers on a rod. On a shelf near the bottom, someone had tossed a white plastic sack. He picked it up and walked over to the window. At the bottom of the sack, he found a clear plastic bag. Sure enough, inside was her watch and her earrings. But there was something else as well. He held the bag closer to the light of the window.

"Oh my God," he whispered. His body tensed. Next to the watch was a small platinum pendant, one he'd seen before. It was the Midnight Man's calling card. The message was unmistakable.

Ray slipped the plastic bag into his pocket. He couldn't use his cell phone in the hospital, so had to find a pay phone. But before he could leave, the doctor entered the room, followed by the nurse. Ray waited in the corner while the doctor checked Sigrid over. Her temperature was taken again, and her blood pressure. The doctor listened to her chest with his stethoscope. Ray recognized the look on his face. He was a competent man, and he was doing what he was good at, but he was uneasy.

"I'm ordering X rays, stat," he said. Glancing over at Ray, he said, "I'm sorry, but you'll have to leave."

"Of course. But can you tell me what's going on?"

The doctor motioned him out into the hall. "I'm afraid she

may have developed pneumonia." He held the door open as Sigrid was wheeled out.

"But you can treat that, right?"

"We can, but in her current condition it's not what I was hoping for."

"But she'll be okay. She's past the worst of it."

"Are you her father?"

"Father-in-law. Ray Lawless."

"Don Feingold. I'm Dr. Maybury's partner."

They shook hands.

"Let me be frank with you, Mr. Lawless. I'd like to tell you that your daughter-in-law will be fine, but the fact is, she's a very sick young woman. I think there's reason to be hopeful, but only time will tell."

"I thought . . . I mean, the fact that she was awake . . . I thought she was getting better."

"It's a good sign, but the pneumonia is a definitely a complication she didn't need."

Ray nodded gravely.

"Now, if you'll excuse me, I've got to order those tests. You can call the nursing station later for the results. Or you can call my office."

After he was gone, Ray retrieved Bill Younger's card from inside the back flap of his billfold. When a nurse walked by, he asked her where he could find a phone. She directed him down the hall to the patient's waiting room.

Ray took a seat by the phone and tapped in Younger's number. "Answer it," he whispered to himself.

After five rings, a voice said, "Younger."

"Bill, it's Ray Lawless."

"It never rains but it pours. I talked to your son earlier today."

"Peter?"

"You got any other sons?"

"What about?"

"His problems with his wife. And his theory about the Midnight Man homicides."

"Look, Bill, I'm at Metro South right now. I was visiting my daughter-in-law. I assume you know what happened."

"I know what your son told me."

"My son told you the truth."

"So he says."

"Listen, you've got to get down here on the double."

"Why?"

"My daughter-in-law wanted me to look for her earrings, so I did. Someone must have taken off all her jewelry when she was admitted and put it into this clear plastic bag. I found it in a bag in her closet."

"So?"

"I also found one of those pendants, exactly like the ones the Midnight Man left around his victims' necks."

"Shit, Lawless. What are you trying to pull?"

"The guy's not dead, Bill. Isn't it obvious?"

"Not to me. Was your son's wife burned in a fire? Was it a late-night murder attempt?"

"No, but—"

"If she'd been wearing one of those pendants the officer in charge would have found it."

"Look, I can't explain it, but I'm telling you he's still alive. He left his calling card to prove it. For chrissake, Bill, get down here and look at it for yourself. I want you to reopen the investigation."

"You better not be messing with me, Lawless."

"I'm not. I swear it. Just get down here, okay? I'll be waiting for you outside room fifty-one-twenty."

Peter left Jane's house shortly after sunset. He had one stop to make before meeting his dad at the Maxfield, and he didn't want to be late. He'd called Grace Cathedral in St. Paul earlier in the day and asked when Conrad Alto would be there. The woman on the other end said that he'd scheduled a practice for both the choir and the brass ensemble for five-thirty. It usually lasted about an hour. He was combining the two for this weekend's Evensong. The woman said it was a lovely service—six P.M., on Sunday evening, and that it was free and open to the public. She encouraged Peter to attend.

Peter didn't necessarily want to talk to Conrad Alto up close and personal, but he did want to get a good look at the man his father thought was responsible for the vendetta against his family.

Grace Cathedral was located on Kellogg Avenue, along the river in downtown St. Paul, just a few blocks east of the restaurant. Before he'd left his sister's house, Peter had put on a suit. He knew he'd feel out of place in the restaurant if he didn't. It might also serve to make him more invisible in church as well. Peter had been a Lutheran for most of his life, but because his mother had been English and the family had lived in England for a while as he was growing up, his early years had been spent in Anglican churches, and later at this very cathedral in St. Paul. Before her death, his mother had brought Peter and Jane here often.

As a child, Peter was fascinated by the massive brownstone architecture. His mother laughingly called it Minnesota Gothic. If he remembered correctly, in back of the altar were twelve high slender windows that allowed morning light to fall directly on a wooden pulpit, one that reminded him of an ornately carved water goblet.

Entering the arched front doors, Peter was immediately struck by the lovely choral music coming from the sanctuary. He stepped to the back of the nave and looked inside. A tall, thin, sandy-haired man in a light brown sport coat and a tan turtleneck was directing the cathedral choir. His hand movements were fluid and graceful, keeping time to the beat of the music. Peter assumed that this was Conrad Alto.

The church was arranged just as he remembered it. Altar at the front, then the chancel where the choir sat—two sections of pews facing each other across a narrow walkway. The congregation sat in the nave. Peter walked down the side aisle and took a seat along the wall, close to the front. Thankfully, he wasn't the only one who'd come to listen. Fifteen or twenty other people dotted the pews, some sitting with their eyes closed, some gazing peacefully at the stained-glass windows. Heavy wrought-iron chandeliers hung from thick chains high above their heads. The amber glass washed the darkened sanctuary in a reverent, golden light. Behind the choir, between the pews and the altar rail, Peter now noticed a row of men and women standing silently, each holding a horn. This must be the brass ensemble the woman on the phone had spoken about.

The choir sang for another few minutes before Conrad stopped them.

"Okay, that's good for tonight. Next Monday, at our normal practice time, I want to continue our work on *St. Matthew's Pas-*

sion. We don't have all that much time left before the first Easter Eucharist. Canon Alder should be with us that night, as well as Maureen Larson and the Trinity chamber orchestra. We'll set up downstairs as usual." His voice was moderately high, and sounded pleasantly cultured, with no trace of Minnesota thud. As he talked, he rocked back and forth on the balls of his feet.

"Remember to bring your copies of *Canticle* with you on Sunday night. Oh, and one more thing. The rededication of the tower bells will be two weeks from tonight. This will be the first time the new automatic controls for our Westminster chimes will be heard by the public. We intend to use this system to strike the hour in downtown St. Paul, as well as ring the Angeles, so mark it down on your calendar." He bowed slightly. "I bid you all a good evening."

As everyone filed out, Conrad stopped a couple of the older men and talked with them briefly. He helped a woman in a wheelchair negotiate the narrow aisle between the choir stalls, then walked down each pew and picked up leftover bits of paper. Once he was done with his duties, he looked over and smiled at a young dark-haired man sitting in the front pew. Unbuttoning his jacket, he sat down next to him. For the next few minutes, they talked quietly. Peter couldn't catch any of their words, but Conrad's mood grew increasingly serious.

When Peter finally looked around behind him, he saw that, with the exception of Conrad and his friend, he was the only person left in the sanctuary. He was about to get up make a quick exit when Conrad and the man rose and started down the aisle. Peter kept his eyes glued to a gilded cross in the center of the altar as they moved past. Getting up immediately, he followed them at a respectful distance, but close enough to overhear their conversation.

Conrad said, "I'm not angry, Barrett. Please don't misunderstand."

The younger man replied, "I know what I promised you, but I can't do it anymore. Taylor is a mess, and she's dragging me down with her. I mean, it's spooky. Sometimes she says she sees Bobby standing at the foot of her bed in the middle of the night. She says he looks so sad. He's told her in some telepathic sort of way that he can't leave this earthly plane until the truth finally comes out. Someone did him a great injustice and he can't rest until he's vindicated."

"You've done all you can," said Conrad, his voice full of sympathy. "Let her stay with us now. Between Shirley and Henry and me, we'll bear the burden. Where is she tonight?"

"I'm not sure. She left four or five messages on my service today, but I haven't answered any of her calls."

Peter ducked into the coat room just outside the sanctuary door, but continued to listen.

"I tried to be good to her during the trial," continued Barrett. "I tried to take her mind off what was happening to Bobby. But I feel smothered by her need for me. I think we should cut her loose, Con. Before she does something really off-the-wall."

"But you can't just throw her out. We've got to handle this carefully. Decide what's best."

"For Taylor."

"And for us."

Peter knew enough about the trial to know that Barrett Sweeny was Bobby Alto's best friend, and that Taylor Jensen had been Bobby's girlfriend.

Conrad stood with his hand on the stairway rail leading up to the balcony as Barrett slipped into his leather jacket.

"I don't suppose you've got time for a drink," said Conrad. "I think we need to discuss this a bit more."

"Sorry," said Barrett. "I'm showing a house out in Plymouth tonight. But maybe we can all get together soon."

"I spoke briefly with my travel agent yesterday about the Italy trip. It's off-season right now, so there wouldn't be as many tourists. I feel like I need to be with you and Henry. It's the only way I can properly mourn Bobby's death."

"I told you, Con, I can't commit to that right now."

"Just think about it," said Conrad, rubbing his back. "In the last few years, we've . . . well, we've gotten off track."

"It hasn't been the same without Bobby."

Conrad's face darkened.

"You're thinking about Lawless."

"It frightens me how much I hate that man. None of this would have happened if he'd just done his job."

"I agree. But, still . . . don't do anything you'll regret."

"What I intend to do to him, I'll never regret. You're the one who taught me about the world of light and the world of darkness. We are who we are. It's not possible for us to apologize."

"It's always difficult to be born." Flipping the collar of his coat up around his neck, he added, "Whatever you decide, I'm with you one hundred percent."

Peter stood near the coat room door. As far as he was concerned, he'd just witnessed another threat against his father—and this time, he'd heard it himself.

"Look, Con," continued Barrett, lowering his voice. "We should perform the ritual again. Even without Bobby, I think it's time."

"I'll talk to Henry. He may not want to do it without his brother."

Barrett nodded. "All we can do is ask."

As Conrad stepped away from the stairs, he noticed Peter standing in the coat room. Since Peter wasn't wearing a coat, it was obvious that he'd been eavesdropping.

"Can I help you?" asked Conrad, moving toward him.

"No thanks," said Peter. "I was just looking around. My first time here." He smiled.

"I see. Well, I'm Conrad Alto, the organist and choirmaster at the church." He extended his hand.

Peter couldn't exactly ignore it. Conrad waited for him to introduce himself. He supposed he could just be rude and leave, but he wasn't in the mood to roll over and play dead. "Peter Lawless," said Peter, shaking his hand.

"Lawless?" repeated Conrad, his expression turning to stone.

"I'm Raymond Lawless's son."

"May I ask what you're doing here?"

"I wanted to get a good look at the guy who's after me and my family."

"Excuse me?" said Conrad.

"You just threatened my father."

"I don't know what you're talking about." His voice was annoyingly calm. "And I don't think I care to know." He turned to walk Barrett to the door.

Peter grabbed him by his arm and spun him around.

"Hey, buddy," said Barrett, cutting between them. "Pick on somebody your own size." With quick, staccato movements he shoved Peter backward, again and again, finally slamming him against the heavy sanctuary door. Peter hit his head hard. He felt momentarily dazed.

"Stop it," demanded Conrad. "This is a church. We can't behave like common street thugs in here."

"Sorry," said Barrett, though his tone let Peter know he wasn't sorry at all. He was just getting started. "You want to take it outside, pal?"

"Absolutely not," said Conrad. "I'm sure Mr. Lawless will leave quietly now. Isn't that right, Mr. Lawless?"

Peter straightened his rumpled lapels, then brushed off the front of his suit coat. On his way out the door, he called over his shoulder, "It's not over."

He hadn't used the name Hyde in years, not since the trial started, but he would use it again tonight.

Adjacent to Hyde's bedroom was a large walk-in closet, windowless, six feet square. He always kept the door locked. Inside the inner sanctum was his most precious possession: a small piece of coarse cloth stained with the blood of St. Gaspare. He'd placed it in a gilded reliquary and hung it on the wall above a row of simple white tapers. He lit them now, then closed the door and stripped down to his waist. His naked flesh pebbled in the chilly air, reminding him of the first time he'd entered the church called Santa Maria in Trivio.

It had been a warm late summer afternoon. He was in Rome, out searching for relics, when he turned a corner and found himself facing the Trevi Fountain. As he stood admiring it, a young man from one of the kiosks sauntered over and tried to sell him some piece of junk. Hyde told him that he wasn't interested. He was looking for sacred relics. The man said he knew of a nun who might sell him one, if the price was right. As they were discussing this, a man who'd been standing quietly next to the fountain suddenly called, "It's a scam." He spoke in broken English. "Go visit Santa Maria in Trivio instead, where the remains of St. Gaspare rest." He offered directions.

An hour later, Hyde had just about given up when he finally found the church. The narrow, unadorned entrance looked so ordinary, so utterly common, that at first he'd thought it was a laundry.

The church itself was tiny and dark, merely a gilded slit in a wall. The altar had two electric candles resting on it, both of them unlit. Scaffolding against the far wall suggested some repairs were underway, though he couldn't tell what had been done. After a little searching, he found the remains of St. Gaspare hidden under a life-size bronze sculpture that showed the saint dressed in his clerical vestments, freshly dead. Hyde was disappointed not to be able to see the real thing, a preserved body or even just the head, but he knelt anyway to say a prayer. As he was about to get up, an elderly priest entered the church from another narrow door in the side wall. They nodded to each other.

As if they were actors on a stage and were moving through their marks, Hyde sat down on one of the benches. The old man came and sat down next to him.

"Are you American?" asked the priest.

Hyde smiled. Something always gave him away. He never knew exactly what it was. "Yes, father," he said. "I came to see St. Gaspare."

"Ah. Yes, of course." His English, though heavily accented, was excellent. He stared at Hyde, scrutinized his face so hard that it made Hyde uncomfortable. "You are devout," he pronounced finally.

"In my own way."

The priest reached over to touch Hyde's hand, but drew back, wincing, as if he'd been burned. He looked suddenly afraid.

"What's wrong?"

Passing a hand over his eyes, he said, "I sense something dark in you, my son. Something . . . hidden. You are in pain?"

"Not that I know of."

"You cannot deceive me. There is a reason you came here. You must ask God's forgiveness and remember what our Lord said to the harlot. *Go and sin no more*. Your immortal soul is in great danger."

Hyde didn't remember now how he'd responded, but he did remember that he'd changed the subject awfully fast. "Tell me about Santa Maria in Trivio," he asked, looking back at the bronze.

Reluctantly, the priest complied. "The church itself dates back to the sixth century. It was built by a penitent who fought the Ostrogoths. In the sixteenth century, it was rebuilt by a student of Michelangelo. Even so, we are obscure. It is both a blessing and a curse. Later the church was given to Gaspare for the brotherhood."

"What brotherhood? Who was St. Gaspare?"

"A man of great torment," replied the priest, looking deeply, sadly, into Hyde's eyes. "Much like you. He loathed his strong will and his evil inclinations. At fourteen he received his first tonsure. Eight years later he became a priest and threw himself into his work as a missionary in Rome's slums. Later he formed an evangelical brotherhood called the Archconfraternity of the Most Precious Blood."

The name delighted Hyde, and he must have shown it because the priest looked at him curiously.

"Gaspare and his men staged public floggings, extravaganzas to lure people to the church. Everyone would come out of their lairs to watch the brothers flagellate themselves. The sound of whips striking flesh echoed across piazzas all over Rome. The townspeople would come out to dip bits of cloth in the holy blood, which they then revered as relics."

Hyde shook his head. "To a modern ears, it sounds like a medieval form of psychosis."

The priest seemed confused. "It was a penance. Do you not understand?"

"Pain makes God forgive you?"

"Not just the pain, my son, but the attitude of contrition. You must have both. I once saw an ancient book written by an Italian cardinal praising this discipline. To whip yourself with a flagel, to prostrate yourself before the Lord is not sickness, it is a great piety, a great glory."

Hyde looked up at a painting of Gaspare. He stood amidst the clouds, a crucifix tucked into his cummerbund. Off to the side a pink-gowned angel stood calmly by, offering him a golden chalice overflowing with blood.

"You've come to Gaspare because he can help you," continued the priest. Forgetting his earlier fear, he touched Hyde's hand. "*Santa Maria*," he mumbled, closing his eyes. "*Non posso, non debo, non voglio*."

"What?"

"I rebuke the devil in Gaspare's own words. It is what he said to Napoleon Bonaparte when the great general asked him to renounce his faith. He said, 'I cannot, I should not, I will not.' "

"Why do you say that to me?" Hyde was growing impatient with the old man.

"You truly do not understand?" asked the priest. "Wait. I will be back." He departed through the same small doorway from which he'd entered. A moment later, he returned. Standing close to the altar this time, he said, "I have something for you. You must take it and go."

"What is it?" asked Hyde, his impatience turning to curiosity.

The priest opened his hand. In it was a folded piece of tissue paper. Inside the paper was a rust-colored cloth. "It is my most precious possession. This is from the vestment of Gaspare himself. It is his holy blood, my son. Keep it with you. Cherish it. Ask Gaspare to help you find a way out of your darkness."

"I can't take something like that from you. It's too . . . valuable."

"You must." He forced it into Hyde's hand.

From that day to this, Hyde *had* cherished the relic. He wasn't sure it had any more value than a lock of Elvis Presley's hair, but in a strange way, deep in some archaic part of his brain, he believed in its power.

Kneeling before the altar in his closet now, he bowed his head. "Forgive me father, for I am about to sin." He knew that this wasn't exactly the right order, but it was the best he could do under the circumstances. He *was* sorry, mostly for himself, but for Bobby too. He was deeply, deeply sorry, and surely that meant something. The sorrow came first, then the pain. At least that was correct.

Reaching over to a small table, Hyde picked up the flail. It was a fake Roman scourge he'd bought at an S/M shop in downtown Minneapolis, six flat braided strands ending in Turk's-head knots. After he was finished, after his body was covered with an acrid sweat and his cheeks were streaming with salty, stinging tears, he would shower, treat the cuts on his back as best he could, and then dress.

By eleven he was out the door. When bright midnight finally arrived, when the fire started, his soul would shine immaculate.

24

Jane needed caffeine to stay awake—long enough to enjoy the supper Patricia was preparing. Falling asleep in the hot tub wouldn't be cool. Grabbing the biggest, baddest, meanest cup of coffee from the oldest dregs she could find, she returned to her office after the dinner rush and slumped into her desk chair. A message was blinking on her answering machine.

"Hi, honey. It's me." It was Jane's father. "I'm at the hospital. I've just got a few seconds, but I had to call. I've got important news. Believe it or not, I found one of the Midnight Man's pendants in a sack in Sigrid's closet—along with her watch and earrings. I called Bill Younger right away. He came down to the hospital and we talked. I laid it all out on the table—told him about my suspicions. He insists that if Sigrid had been wearing the pendant when she was attacked, the police would have discovered it. He's got a point. But anyone could have planted it in her room *after the fact*. It would only have taken a few seconds. And however it got there, the meaning's pretty obvious. I think Conrad Alto is behind it. Either he planted the pendant—or had someone else plant it—to prove that Bobby was innocent, or the system screwed up big-time and Conrad is, himself, the Midnight

Man. Sigrid was his latest victim." He paused, then continued: "Younger finally agreed to push to reopen the investigation. That's the good news. The bad news is, Sigrid may have pneumonia. Her temp is one-oh-three. Her doctor ordered tests, so I assume we'll know more in a few hours. I'm having dinner with Peter tonight. I'll call you later."

Jane had a lot to think over, so she grabbed her coat and locked her office door. If she'd stayed and tried to work, the depression she'd been fighting all day would have engulfed her.

Standing at last on the empty deck outside the main dining room, she tucked her hands into her pockets to keep them warm. A spray of fine white powder tumbled off the roof and drifted across her face. In the distance, tiny specks of light surrounded the frozen lake. Everything was so peaceful here, such an ordinary winter evening. It seemed impossible to believe that such menace existed in the world. And yet it did. Tears filled her eyes. Sigrid had to be all right—she just had to.

Crossing the parking lot, Jane climbed into her Trooper. It was too early to drive over to Patricia's house, so to burn up some time, she decided to check out the newest house her real estate agent wanted her to look at.

Ten minutes later, she pulled up in front of a small, Craftsman-style bungalow on Pillsbury Avenue in the Tangletown area of south Minneapolis. The real estate agent had been right. This house was half the size of her current home. Jane stood for a few minutes on the front sidewalk, studying the place. The house itself looked sturdy and well cared for, and there was a second-floor deck off the side that Jane thought was a nice feature. The front yard was small, but the backyard appeared to be large and fenced, perfect for a dog—not that she had to think about that anymore. An immense elm on the east side of the building and a smaller tree next to a back fence shaded the backyard, making gardening prospects iffy at best.

Pushing through the side gate, she saw that there was a three-season porch built on the back, and a new two-story addition off the north side. Wood smoke puffed from a vent attached to the north wall. The owners clearly loved the place. She wondered why they were selling.

As she unlatched the gate by the garage, she thought she saw a tiny flicker of movement near one of the neighbor's garbage cans. Whatever it was, it was close to the the ground. Curious, she stood still. Her first thought was that it was a squirrel, but it was too late at night for squirrels to be out. When she stepped a few paces closer, she heard a low, frightened growl, clearly canine. A second later, a black head poked out cautiously.

"Hey there, buddy," said Jane. She crouched down and smiled. "What are you doing there?"

The dog watched her for a few seconds, then moved around the can and stood in the alley, closer, but still keeping its distance.

"You're a beauty," she said. Even in the moonlight, she could tell that he—or she—was a Lab. Or, at least, part Lab. The dog seemed to have a distinctive white marking on its chest, which suggested it wasn't a purebred.

"You out for a stroll?" she asked, holding out her hand.

The dog sniffed the air, but didn't move.

She could be mistaken, but she had the sense that he was lost. "Let me get a look at your collar," she said gently, waiting until he came a little closer. She didn't want to spook him before she got a chance to see where he lived. When he was finally within reach, she scratched him under the chin, then on top of his head, moving her hand slowly down the length of his fur to his tail. He wasn't as burly and houndlike as some Labs she'd seen. "You're a friendly guy, you're just a little scared." She could see now that he was a male—neutered, which suggested that somebody loved him. She wished the alley light was a little closer. He had two tags jingling on his collar. One looked like a rabies tag and said *1998* in large type. Not a good sign. The other had something stamped on it, but it was so tiny, the only word she could make out was *Cedar*. If he lived on Cedar Avenue, he *was* a long way from home.

"Are you lost?" she asked as he sat down in the melting snow. He looked her square in the eyes, then lifted a paw. "You're a smart boy. We need to figure out what to do with you."

Just then, a car pulled into the alley. The bright headlights startled the dog and he bolted away. "Hey," called Jane, standing up and chasing after him. "Come back here!"

By the time she rounded the end of the next garage, he'd disappeared. Jane's injured leg was much stronger now, but trying to follow him on foot over snow and ice was suicide. All she needed was to fall again, to hurt her leg and spend the next few weeks limping around with that damned cane.

Rushing back to her car, she started the engine, but didn't turn on the lights. For the next twenty minutes, she drove through side streets and alleys, looking in vain for the dog. She stopped and got out a few times, shouting for him to come, but it was like searching for a needle in a haystack. She didn't even know his name.

Feeling thwarted, Jane finally gave up and drove over to Patricia's house. The dog had a good coat of fur on him, so he would probably be okay outside in the cold. The temperature tonight was in the high thirties—by Minnesota standards, almost balmy. She'd look for him again tomorrow, though by then, he could be miles away. Dogs led such perilous lives. If she could, she'd clean out every pound and humane society in the state, take all the dogs home and love them the way they deserved. Jane connected with dogs—sometimes better than she connected with people.

Patricia's house was brightly lit when Jane pulled up a few minutes later. Inside, a fire was blazing in the fireplace. Instead of the usual jazz, an old Elvis Presley tune was playing on the stereo: "One Night With You."

"Your musical tastes have evolved," said Jane, taking off her coat and her wet boots.

"I like to mix it up. I don't like ruts."

Truer words were never spoken. If there was one overriding

reason why Jane would never have a long-term relationship with Patricia, it was just that—in a nutshell. It had nothing to do with Patricia's youth, or her recklessness in business or personal affairs, but it had everything to do with her essential restlessness.

Jane didn't feel it was a condemnation, just an observation, one she needed to bear in mind. Cordelia was all wrong in her assessment of Patricia. She's wasn't Minnesota's answer to a valley girl. She was an intelligent woman who had a fascinating, possibly even brilliant future ahead of her—if she could keep a lid on her impatience and her penchant for ignoring the law. But Patricia would never be content living a status quo existence, settling down to a routine. She liked variety—in everything. She valued change because she thought anything "old" was inherently suspect. She was drawn to what was new, quick, cutting edge, and occasionally dangerous.

In an effort to impress, to prove how much they had in common, Patricia always maintained that she liked to cook. But that truth was, her cupboards contained two things: the bare necessities and exotica. Most of the food she served, she bought already prepared.

And that's why it worried Jane when Patricia started making sounds about wanting a permanent relationship. *Permanent* had no precise meaning to Patricia. Jane was the flavor of the month—or the year—and that was just fine with her. She couldn't handle a heavy entanglement right now, so she and Patricia were well matched. Where Patricia wanted variety and experimentation, Jane wanted comfort and stability. They were at two vastly different places in their lives. Maybe Jane should take a page from Patricia's book and never look for true love again. The fact was, in the past few months, she'd lost her appetite for strangers.

"So tell me how Sigrid's doing," said Patricia as she headed into the kitchen.

Jane followed. "She may have pneumonia."

"God, I'm sorry. Peter still hasn't been able to see her?"

"No."

"What about the tarot cards?"

Jane popped a macadamia nut into her mouth. Patricia had set a bowl of them on the kitchen table. "I haven't received any more. I think I'll show the ones I have to the police. I just found out they may be reopening the Midnight Man investigation. I realize those pages aren't exactly evidence, at least of anything other than psychological warfare against me and my family, so I'm not sure if they'll check them out or not."

"For fingerprints?"

She nodded. "Except none of us were terribly careful with the pages when we first got them."

"They might still be able to lift a print and prove who sent them."

"Yes, but then what?"

"You still think it was someone in the Alto family?"

"That would be my guess, but sending copies of tarot cards through the mail is hardly a federal offense." She stepped up behind Patricia, who was arranging kiwi preserves over a wedge of Brie, and put her arms around her waist. "I'm helping," she said, nuzzling Patricia's hair.

They moved clumsily over to the refrigerator together and Patricia removed a package of Champagne grapes and a bottle of wine. "This is an awkward way to cook, but I could get used to it."

Jane smiled and kissed her neck. "Good."

Turning around, Patricia said, "Are you hungry?"

"Famished. In every way."

They left the food sitting on the counter and returned to the living room, undressing in front of the fire. Jane threw some pillows on the floor, arranging them with her foot, and then the two of them lay down, their bodies gliding together like raw silk.

"I missed you last night," said Patricia.

"I missed you too," said Jane, her fingers trailing slowly down Patricia's back.

"Maybe we should get married."

Jane laughed. "Maybe we should learn to fly."
"I'll take that as a 'no.' "
"Shhh."

The next morning, as they were finishing their toast and coffee in the kitchen, Jane's cell phone rang.

Peter's voice said hurriedly, "Turn on the TV."

"What?" said Jane.

"Channel seven. Turn it on! Quick."

Jane jumped up and ran into the study where Patricia kept a small TV. After switching it on, she said, "What am I supposed to see?"

"The news. Just watch it."

Jane sat down on the couch while Patricia stood in the doorway.

The anchor woman was in the middle of her story. "—the officer was found in his backyard, dead of stab wounds. Firefighters were able to put the fire out, but the house was badly damaged. So far, there are no suspects in the homicide."

"Who died?" asked Jane, still holding the phone.

"Bill Younger," said Peter. "The cop who developed the case against Bobby Alto. He called Dad last night while we were having dinner, said he'd talked to his superior and they were going to reopen the case. Now this."

"The woman on the news said the police didn't have any suspects."

"Like hell they don't. They know the Midnight Man murdered him, they're just not letting it out yet. And I think there's other stuff they're holding back about how he died."

"Why do you say that?"

"Because Dad called one of his friends in the MPD this morning. He wouldn't say anything over the phone, but Dad got that impression. He's going to meet with him later. Don't you understand what this means, Janey? We're not the only targets. As of last night, the Midnight Man is back—he showed his true hand.

That could mean he's after the prosecutor, other cops, the judge, or even the supreme court justices. The police are sitting on a powder keg."

Good for us, thought Jane. She felt guilty even thinking it, but it was true. "We're not alone in this anymore."

"Damn right. Cops get nasty when other cops get killed. They'll get to the bottom of it now, and soon."

Henry scanned the hospital cafeteria until he spotted his mother. She was sitting at a table along the back wall, finishing her breakfast. Her new black dye job made her skin look unusually sallow. He wondered if it was time for another liver-function test.

He approached the table. "I don't appreciate being summoned when I'm working. I'm not a car mechanic, Mother. I can't just toss a dirty rag over my shoulder and leave the shop whenever I feel like it." He loomed over her, hoping his height and youth would intimidate her. It was a vain hope. His mother was never intimidated.

"Sit down, Henry."

He sat. "Your hair looks like it was part of last year's Halloween costume."

"My, aren't we in a cheerful mood."

"What are you doing here?"

"Don't be cruel, Henry. No one ever loves a son like his mother. You won't have me around forever, you know. I'm not getting any younger."

She would not only be around forever, thought Henry, but she would hang around the neck of his family like a rotting albatross.

"Why don't you go get yourself a cup of coffee?"

"I don't have time," said Henry.

"All right. If you want to be pouty, that's up to you."

With just a few words, she'd reduced him to a seven-year-old child. "Just get to the point, okay?"

Leaning close to him, she lowered her voice. "Did you hear what happened between Taylor and Barrett?"

"He kicked her out," said Henry. "Did you come here to tell me *that*?"

"She showed up on my doorstep last night."

"Mine too. I'd just gotten home from work and I couldn't handle her nervous breakdown. I told her to go see Dad."

"Which she did, but he wasn't there. I was, apparently, her last resort. Do you know how that makes me feel, Henry? To be her *last resort*?"

"No, but I'm sure you're going to tell me."

"Not that I want her staying at my house indefinitely."

He snorted. "I'll say."

"But what could I do? She was so pathetic. I think she really cared about Barrett. I can't believe he acted so coldly."

"Mother, get rid of her. She's a big girl. She can figure out her own life. Besides, she might find out about you. You wouldn't want that."

"She won't. And if she does, she'll keep her mouth shut, just like the rest of you. I told her she was staying with you tonight, and that tomorrow, you would take her over to Conrad's. We need to help her get back on her feet."

"Mother, she's an adult, not a child. She can go find herself a hotel room."

"She's too frightened to be alone at night. I've never noticed it before, but that girl is terribly high-strung. Ever since Bobby died, she says he's been appearing to her, not in dreams, but in visions. She says he's haunting her, that he's trying to tell her something about his death."

Henry just stared at her.

His mother's voice grew even softer. "Do you believe in spirits, Henry?"

"No."

"I do," she whispered. "I always thought Bobby was innocent, but what does a mother know? *Squat*, that's what. The world is full of mothers wringing their hands over their guilty-as-sin sons. None of us are innocent, Henry. *None of us*."

"I know, Mother. You've told me that a million times."

"But Bobby—" She took a sip of coffee. "It's simply impossible. He didn't do any of the things the police said he did. He was too gentle, too sweet. *You* could take a lesson from his book, dear."

He glared at her.

"Your father and I haven't agreed on much in the last thirty years, but we do agree on Bobby's innocence. He never should have gone to jail. Your father blames Raymond Lawless for that, and I agree. That man was sleepwalking through the trial. There's such a thing as bad karma in this world, Henry, and that man's karma can't help but affect his entire family. It's all there in the tarot."

"Not the tarot again." He groaned.

"Don't knock it. It's been my guide since I was a girl. For one thing, it doesn't damn me to hell everlasting because I break some archaic commandment. What on earth I'd want with my neighbor's ox is beyond me anyway. And it doesn't promise me a heaven that doesn't exist. Have you ever thought about how *boring* heaven would be? Streets of gold? Mansions everywhere? Angels playing harps. Everyone lovey-dovey all the time. I'd lose my bloody mind. Just think about this one thing: Where would we be without a little junk, Henry? There won't be any garage sales in heaven."

"Calm down, Mother."

"Don't tell me what to do."

"I'm not. I'm just—"

"You're patronizing me, like your father."

"Mother, I've got to get back to work. I have patients waiting for me."

"The tarot is about our lives in the here and now. Not about pie in the sky."

"I'm leaving, Mother."

"I did a reading for Taylor last night. That and a couple of stiff shots of vodka finally calmed her down."

"Since we're back to Taylor, she can't stay at my house."

"I wonder if Barrett would float her a small loan? It's the least he could do. I suppose I could handle it, but I hesitate to get involved that way. You understand. Not that I'm opposed to getting involved when it comes to my son. That's why I sent the tarot cards."

"What tarot cards? What are you talking about?"

"I needed to warn them." She finished her coffee, then set the cup down as if the conversation was over and she was dismissing him.

"Warn who?"

"*Whom*," she said, correcting him. She tapped a napkin against her mouth, careful not to smear her lipstick. "Why, the Lawless family, Henry. First I sent a copy of the card Justice—only I reversed it—to Raymond's daughter, then the Tower went to Raymond, and the Nine of Swords to his son. I saw to it personally that they got the message."

He couldn't believe his ears. She was so fucking *dense*.

"It's all very simple. Raymond participated—or more precisely, *caused*—an injustice, so he and his family will pay the price. It's karmic tit for tat."

Henry had a vision of himself reaching over and grabbing his mother's throat. He squeezed and squeezed, but she wouldn't stop talking. Her neck cracked and fell sideways, her eyes rolled back in her head, her body grew limp, but her mouth kept moving. "Do you realize what you've done?"

"Of course I do, Henry dear. I allowed the cosmos to use me as an oracle."

"Did you ever think about fingerprints? Your prints are probably all over those pages."

"Your point is?"

"If Lawless hands them over to the police—"

"Why would he do that?"

"Because he might perceive them as a threat. Don't you get it? And thanks to your business 'activities,' your prints are on file. At the very least, you could be hauled in for questioning—and you know you don't want that."

"Nonsense." She patted his hand. "I believe I did just what Bobby wanted me to do. We all have to do our part, Henry. Otherwise, according to Taylor, his spirit will be imprisoned on earth forever."

He gritted his teeth. "I'm leaving, Mother."

"Fine, dear. Expect Taylor tonight around seven. And don't snarl at her. Her condition is delicate."

26

Before Jane returned to the restaurant on Thursday morning, she drove back to Tangletown, the neighborhood where she'd discovered the stray dog the night before. As she sped down Lyndale, she called the hospital on her cell phone to get an update on Sigrid's condition. The nurse told her that Sigrid's temperature was down and that she was resting a bit more comfortably. Finally, some good news.

For the next hour, Jane searched the side streets and alleys, looking for the Lab. Lots of dogs barked at her from behind fences, but none of them were the smallish Lab she'd found hiding behind a trash can. She hated to think what his fate might be if someone didn't take him in, or try to get him back to his owner. She thought of the few times Gulliver and Bean had escaped from her backyard. Without the kindness and concern of strangers, their lives might have ended very differently.

She didn't want to give up, but the clock was ticking away. She had so much she needed to do. But the only way she could make herself stop the search was by making an agreement with herself to come back later and look a while longer. It was probably futile, but she couldn't give up.

Jane's plan for the day was to check in with Arlene, then take a stack of trial transcripts home and read. If all went as planned, she'd be back at work by four for the dinner meal. She'd spent so many weeks away from the restaurant while she was recovering from her head injury that she felt guilty—like she needed to make up for lost time.

As she unlocked her office, she heard a muffled crash, followed by a male voice swearing. Glancing down the hall, she saw that the dry-storage room door stood open. She hurried toward the noise. She found Joe Vasquez standing next to one of the storage racks, brushing flour off his slacks.

She couldn't help but laugh. He was always so flawlessly turned out, so careful about his clothing, that she found his current predicament amusing. "Drop something?" she asked, leaning against the door.

He looked up at her, obviously in a foul mood. "It's not funny." He brushed for a moment more, then straightened up. "Carl asked me to get him a sack of flour. How the hell was I supposed to know the wrapper was torn?"

"Better get it cleaned up."

"What about my clothes? I can't wait on tables looking like this."

"Do you have an extra pair of pants with you?"

"I'll have to run home."

"Then make it quick."

When she got back to her office, she found her dad sitting on the couch, waiting for her.

"Hi, honey." He stood up. "Sorry to stop by so unexpectedly, but I was hoping to catch you in. I just need a couple of minutes."

He'd been the harbinger of such bad news lately that she could feel the tension in the room rise as she sat down next to him. She offered to call up to the kitchen and have lunch sent down, but he said he couldn't stay.

"So what's up?" she asked. Judging by the dour look on his face, it wasn't good news.

"I understand Peter called you earlier, told you about what happened to Bill Younger."

"He said the police were keeping the details quiet, but that you might be able to get some additional information from a buddy of yours in the MPD. Is that why you're here? Do you know more?"

Ray took off his glasses and pinched the bridge of his nose. "I'm afraid so," he said solemnly. "But before I fill you in, you have to promise me something. This information can't get out. You've got to keep it under your hat, okay?"

"Sure."

"Bill has a cabin in rural Scott County. He occasionally spends the night there—that's where he was last night. The nearest house is miles away. Bear in mind, Bill's been a cop for over twenty years. He's not stupid and he's not careless. He knows how to handle himself in a tricky situation. But somehow, the visitor he had last night got him out on the front porch. He murdered him there with a knife—must have been thirty stab wounds. Whoever killed him was in a powerful rage."

Jane fought hard not to visualize the scene, not to crawl into it with the poor cop and feel his terror.

"There's more," said Ray. "The killer started a fire in the bedroom, just under the window. He used charcoal lighter, which is out of character, not part of the Midnight Man's usual MO. Contrary to popular opinion, however, serial murderers do change their methods when the need arises."

"The police are sure it was the Midnight Man?"

He nodded. "At first, they wondered if it was a copycat murder, but they changed their minds."

"Why?"

"Bill's killer dragged him into the backyard and propped him up in the snow. We know that because there was a blood trail from the front porch to the backyard. Even though Bill was already dead, it was almost like his murderer wanted him to watch his house burn down."

"Any footprints?"

"Most of the snow melted from the heat, but maybe the police can retrieve something. One of Bill's neighbors drove past around twelve-thirty and saw the house burning. He's the one who called nine-one-one."

"I don't suppose he saw anyone."

"Afraid not. Whoever murdered Bill was long gone by then."

"But . . . I don't understand. There are similarities to the way the Midnight Man did his killings, but without the pendant—"

Her father took hold of her hand. "They found one, Janey."

"Peter didn't say anything about that."

"That's because the police are sitting on it. They don't want to set off a full-scale panic in the criminal-justice community. If what they suspect is true, a psycho just declared open season on everyone associated with Bobby's trial. That includes a lot of people."

"Where did they find the pendant?"

"Before the Midnight Man left the scene, he stuffed it inside Bill's mouth, then glued both his mouth and his eyes shut. I imagine it was meant as a message."

"How . . . ghastly," said Jane, turning her face away.

"Are you okay, honey? This is all pretty brutal stuff."

"It just . . . kind of takes your breath away."

"If it's any consolation, the guy's already gone after us. Until he's caught, I'd say his focus will be elsewhere. He's angry now—acting from emotion. That could trip him up. Homicide cops are good at what they do, Jane. We just need to be patient and let them do their job." He paused. "Listen, honey, if you get a chance, talk to your brother today. He was suspended from his job this morning—until his legal problems get resolved. It hit him pretty hard."

"I can't believe they'd do that. Especially now. Peter will be cleared soon, right?"

"Yes, but his boss doesn't know that. It'll get straightened out, but it may take some time. Bureaucracies move incredibly slowly." As he got up, he leaned over and kissed her on the forehead. "I'm sorry to drop all this on you and then run, but I'm due back in court at one-thirty."

She walked him to the door.

"Be careful, Jane."

"You too. None of us are immortal."

The oddest look came over his face.

"Did I say something wrong?" she asked, puzzled by his response.

His smile was stiff. "I'll talk to you later."

27

As soon as Jane walked in the front door of her house, she could hear the television blaring. The sound of canned laughter poured out of the bedroom where Peter had been staying since Christmas. In the months since he'd left Sigrid, Jane had become familiar with his more adult habits. Except for a few talk shows, he rarely watched TV. The fact that he was watching it now, channel surfing the late-morning programs, suggested he was at loose ends, unable to concentrate on anything else.

Jane climbed the stairs and started down the hall, but stopped before she reached the doorway. She needed a moment to formulate her thoughts, figure out her approach. She was glad Peter had come back to her place, glad that he felt comfortable and safe in her home. But he had to be upset. She wanted to reassure him without resorting to empty platitudes.

The canned laughter stopped.

"Jane, is that you?"

Adjusting her expression, she stepped into the room. "Hey, bro." He was lying on the bed looking rumpled and morose, a can of Mountain Dew resting on his chest.

"Have you talked to Dad?" he asked.

"He stopped by the restaurant."

"He told you about how Younger died?"

She nodded.

"Pretty grim, huh?"

"Yeah. Pretty grim."

"Did he tell you about my job?"

"I'm really sorry, Peter." She sat down on the edge of the bed.

His gaze returned to the TV set. "I'm just a walking disaster. I'm not allowed to see my wife because the police think I beat her up. My boss agrees, and so my career's in the toilet. And even if I could see Sigrid, who's to say she'd want to see me?"

"Of course she wants to see you."

"Don't be so sure." He fixed his gloomy gaze on the can of soda.

"She loves you, Peter. And you love her."

"I used to think so."

"Even when you were in counseling, that was never an issue."

"It is now." He pushed a fringe of hair away from his eyes.

"I don't understand. Did something happen I don't know about?"

His expression turned suddenly fierce. "Before Sigrid ended up in the hospital, I found out she was seeing someone else."

Jane was stunned. She didn't know what to say.

"That's what the fight was about that morning, the one the neighbors heard. I mean, here I'd been agonizing over our problems for months and all the time she was playing footsie with some asshole at work. His name is Dana."

"Are you sure about this?"

"Of course I'm sure. He called her up and asked her for a date right while I was sitting at the kitchen table. She didn't deny she'd been seeing him." He looked away. "We'd reconciled the night before the attack, Janey. Did you know that?"

She shook her head.

"And do you know *why*? Because I gave in. I told Sigrid that I wanted her more than I wanted a child. And then, the next morning, this Dana calls wanting another date. Right there in my own kitchen! Sigrid insisted I was blowing it all out of proportion. It was all my fault—that I was having second thoughts about giving up my dream of having a child and Dana gave me just the excuse I needed."

"Was that . . . true?" asked Jane.

Peter rubbed his eyes. "God, Janey, I don't even know anymore. She said I was insecure about our marriage, that's why I kept pushing her to have a child. She said I constantly demanded proof that she loved me. But that's not why I want a child, Jane. It's not."

"I believe you."

"I've always wanted a family. But, then I got to thinking, maybe Sigrid is right. Maybe I am . . . insecure. I know I'm jealous of every guy she looks at. But damn it all, she flirts! It drives me nuts."

"Did you talk about this in your counseling sessions?"

"Some, but we were so protective of each other, neither wanted to say anything that would hurt the other person's feelings, though, of course, we did. She made me feel like some fundamentalist patriarch, demanding that she bear me children."

Jane was savvy enough to know that both her brother and Sigrid had legitimate points of contention. Even the best relationships were a delicate balance. She did believe that Sigrid and Peter loved each other. Except, in the final analysis, love rarely conquered all.

"I just feel like there's something she's not telling me," said Peter. "I know she likes kids. I see her watching them when we go the park, or out to dinner. Sometimes—" He paused. "You're going to think I'm making this up."

"Tell me," said Jane.

"Well, there have been times when I've caught Sigrid looking at children with this incredible longing in her eyes. If she doesn't want a child of her own, what's all that about?"

Jane didn't have an answer. "This is a conversation you need to have with her."

"Don't you think I know that?" he snapped.

She felt his desolation, and her heart ached for him. "Just keep holding on, Peter. Maybe Dad can get the restraining order lifted."

"Dad," repeated Peter with an indignant grunt. "That's another problem. To add insult to my current injury, he insists on treating me like I'm still a teenager. He wants to know where I am every minute of the day, what I'm doing."

"I'll talk to him."

"No, don't. It'll just make things worse." He finished his Mountain Dew, crushing the aluminum can in his fist. "Look at me, Janey. I'm reduced to watching the shit they put on daytime TV. Boy, if that doesn't say it all, I don't know what does." He flipped to another channel, but left the sound on mute.

"You want to come downstairs and have some lunch?"

"I want to vegetate right here. It's all I'm good for."

"Peter—"

He shot her a cautionary look. "No big sister lectures, okay?"

"Okay," she said reluctantly. "But I'm here for you."

"And I'm grateful. I just need to be alone."

She understood. They were a lot alike. To process the world around them, they both required solitude—Jane perhaps more than Peter. But Peter had been pounded so hard in the last few days, she wasn't sure how much more he could take. There was a dullness about his eyes that disturbed her.

Rising from the bed, she said, "If you need me, I'll be downstairs reading."

"Fine. Whatever." He switched the sound back on, then back off again. "Oh, I just remembered. You had a call from Patricia Kastner right before you got home. She asked me to tell you that she had a business crisis. She was in her car headed for the airport."

"Where's she off to?"

"San Francisco, I think. She said she'd call you, but she might not be back until sometime next week."

"Okay," said Jane. Her gaze drifted out the window.

"Something wrong?"

"No, I'm just a little disappointed. We'd made some plans for later tonight."

"You two getting pretty hot and heavy?"

"Not really. We're friends. We like each other's company."

"No major relationship in the offing?"

She shrugged. "What can I say? In my old age, I guess I've turned over a new leaf. Sex without commitment. A true adult relationship."

"Not exactly your usual style, but what the hell? Whatever works." He turned the sound back up.

It all sounded so simple. *Whatever worked*. But what if it didn't work? As far as Jane could see, an "adult" relationship was every bit as problematic and unpredictable as love and commitment. In the beginning, she'd worried that she might be using Patricia. Jane had been so lonely after Julia left. She was hungry to be with another person, to be held, touched. But Patricia's constant protestations about the need for variety in her life—of never wanting to settle for just one person—made Jane rest easier. If anything, they were using each other—or enjoying each other for as long as it was good. No strings. Caring and passion—and fun. Except now, Patricia was making comments that had begun to worry Jane—talking about love. In her own way, Jane did love Patricia, but it wasn't the kind of love she would want to build a relationship on.

For the next few hours, Jane sat at the dining room table, reading, taking notes, and eating a sandwich. Every time she looked up from a police report or the trial transcript, she thought of the dog that was outside in the cold, lost and alone. She struggled to put him out of her mind, but it was a losing battle. By three, her eyelids were growing heavy. She needed to stretch her legs, so she walked quietly back upstairs to check on Peter. She found him sitting at the foot of the bed, staring intently at the TV screen.

"What are you watching?" she asked, curious what had captured his attention so completely.

"*Some Like It Hot*."

"Oh, sure. That's a great movie. Tony Curtis. Jack Lemmon."

"Yeah," he said, so absorbed that he barely registered her presence. His eyes had lost their vagueness. Instead, they almost glittered.

She watched him a moment more, glad to see him in a better mood, then returned downstairs. On her way through the front hall, the doorbell chimed. Squinting through the peephole, Jane saw that Cordelia was standing outside, cradling a large sack of what looked like groceries.

"I come bearing gifts," announced Cordelia, sweeping into the room, her red cape fluttering around her.

"What sort of gifts?"

"This!" She held up the sack, then headed for the kitchen.

Jane followed.

"You remember my old girlfriend, Andromeda?"

"The one who sold exercise equipment?"

"Well, now she's selling health food on the Internet."

"Figures."

"Don't be snide." She looked around. "Where's your blender?"

Jane lifted it down from one of the cupboards.

"This will fix you right up. It's the fountain of youth, Janey! Andromeda swears by it."

"I wasn't aware that I needed to be 'fixed.'"

"It will give you tons of energy. Boost your immune system. Balance your electrolytes. Detoxify your liver—or was it your bladder? Build strong abs and pecs and metatarsals. Oxygenate your glands. Sweeten your breath. Organize your acids and alkaloids into the right slots in your . . . pancreas. It also removes the phlegm from your nose. Improves your bile ducts. Protects you against freedom-loving radicals. And it has absolutely no psyllium in it."

"What's psyllium?"

"How the hell should I know? But it's bad for you. Andromeda knows all about this stuff. Oh, and if you've got gout, this is a total cure-all."

"I don't have gout."

Cordelia bugged out her eyes. "But you could. Someday. You never know."

"What's in it?"

"Well, a little of this, a little of that." She began unloading bottle after bottle onto the counter.

"Do you have a recipe?"

She tapped her head. "Mind like a steel trap. Never forget a thing. Andromeda gave me the full spiel before I left. Oh, and speaking of memory, this helps that too." The last item Cordelia lifted out was a quart of soy milk.

"You hate health food, Cordelia."

"This isn't fern food, it's . . . it's . . . pure power packed in a glass!"

"Another one of Andromeda's observations?"

"Exactly. Now," she said, rubbing her hands together. "We're both in for a rare treat. Andromeda said this tastes like nectar of the gods." She poured the soy milk into the blender.

"What's in the little bottles?"

"This one's bee pollen. And this is protein powder." She held each up as she went along, reading off the labels as she added them to the brew.

For an instant, Jane had an image of Cordelia presiding over a boiling cauldron in a dark, medieval forest, adding her ground bat wings and mouse whiskers, stirring and stirring as the dark mists of winter swirled around her Medusa hair.

"What's in that capsule?" asked Jane.

"Spirulina."

"What's that?"

"It's green."

The explanation probably made total sense to Cordelia.

The last item she added was a glop of buckwheat honey. "Ready for a taste of pure mother earth? Everything in here is totally natural."

"So's plutonium."

"You are *such* a cynic." She filled two glasses to the brim, then picked hers up, waiting for Jane to do the same.

How bad could it be? thought Jane. She clinked her glass to Cordelia's, then both took sips of the viscous, slightly greenish-brown liquid. "Say, it's not bad," Jane said, pleasantly surprised. "It's good for you, right?"

Cordelia's face looked like a watch that had stopped ticking.

"What do you think? Good, huh?" Jane drank it down.

Cordelia didn't move.

"You liked it, right?"

She rushed to the sink, emptying the contents of her mouth into the drain.

"I'll take that as a no."

Wiping her mouth with the back of her hand, Cordelia slowly turned around. "A person might as well drink sewer water!"

Jane studied her empty glass. "Yes, it does have a rather earthy finish. A few grassy notes, with an unattractive vitamin insouciance. Certainly more racy and, shall we say, *gripping* than plain soy milk. But it could grow on you."

"Like a carbuncle."

"May I point out that I knew you wouldn't like it?"

"Don't be smug. Where are your breath mints?" She began rummaging through Jane's drawers.

"Did you really think it would taste like a chocolate malt?"

Cordelia raised her hands to her hips. "Andromeda said *nectar of the gods*. With that description, I hoped for something more than *pond scum*." She was about to sweep everything into the garbage when Jane stopped her.

"Leave it. I might make myself another one later."

"You've *got* to be kidding."

"If it's supposed to be good for you, I wouldn't mind drinking it every now and then. Besides, I have to watch out for an attack of gout, right?"

"I am *so* not into this," said Cordelia, stomping out of the room. Her parting shot was: "That sack of horrors cost me over two hundred dollars!"

"I guess you can't be poor and healthy these days," said Jane.

Peter stepped onto the ancient freight elevator along with half a dozen other people on their way up. He didn't have a key, but nobody challenged him to produce one, so he just acted as if he belonged in the building. He rode to the fourth floor, where Cordelia's loft was located. He'd been going back and forth all afternoon, deciding if he had the guts to go through with his crazy idea. When he found out from his sister that Cordelia had the night off and was planning to spend a quiet evening at home, he knew it was now or never.

Cordelia had lived at Linden Lofts in the city's warehouse district for the past six months. Peter had been invited to her loft-warming party, so he knew the lay of the land. To say that Cordelia was fond of big was an understatement. She also believed in beautiful, brilliant, extravagant clutter. She'd worked on the place a lot since that party, at least according to Jane. Peter was about to find out for himself.

Cordelia had a touch of kleptomaniac in her, and tended to pilfer parts of the theater sets—she called it "borrowing." She used them to create themes. He'd been at her old place during her russian peasant period (*The Cherry Orchard*), her Palace of Theseus period (*A Midsummer's Night's Dream*) and her Dunsenane Castle period (*Macbeth*).

Standing outside her door now, he waited to have an emotion. Any emotion. He needed a clue, a light in the darkness to tell him what to do next. Was he about to make a total fool of himself? Get himself in worse trouble? Had he lost his mind?

He knocked on the door. From inside, he could hear the deep thump and the high whine of a Joan Jett CD. When the door finally drew back, Cordelia stood before him dressed in a silver lamé robe. She was so bright and big, Peter had the urge to put on his sunglasses. He often wanted to tell her that she reminded him of Jupiter or Mars, some massive and dazzling planetary mass, but he couldn't figure out a way to say it nicely. She probably already thought of herself as the sun, with all the lesser planets spinning around her, so to be reduced to mere planetary status would be insulting.

Cordelia's long auburn hair hung loose around her shoulders. And she was holding a martini glass.

"Am I interrupting you?" he asked tentatively. Cordelia might be three inches taller than he was, and outweigh him by a good hundred pounds, but he still found her incredibly glamorous—large in every way. In a different age, one that celebrated the voluptuous figure, she would have been an icon.

"Come in," shouted Cordelia over the pounding base and guitar riffs. "I just got off the phone. My sister called from Connecticut." She rolled her eyes.

"How's she doing?" Peter shouted back.

"As always, she remains the light of my life." She turned the music down.

Peter caught the sarcasm. After last Christmas, Cordelia had returned to Minnesota announcing to everyone who would listen that her sister would be the death of her. Cordelia hadn't spoken to Octavia in many years—not until Octavia's recent marriage. Now that she was pregnant, her husband deceased, she called Cordelia several times a day—according to Jane.

"Her phone calls leave me in a state of total mental collapse," said Cordelia, walking over to a low, flat, Egyptian-looking table that doubled as her bar. "I often have a vodka martini and listen to some soothing music to mellow out." She held up the bottle of vodka. "Want one?"

"No thanks. How's her pregnancy going?"

"About as well as can be expected, since she is gestating the spawn of the devil."

"I thought you liked her husband."

"That whole thing last Christmas was pretty hinky, if you ask me."

Peter glanced up at the ceiling. Cordelia had hired a friend of hers to paint a mural—sort of a modern take on an old classic: the hand of God touching the white gloved hand of Minnie Mouse. All the Renaissance flourishes were there in the God part. Gold leaf. Beautiful partial nude male. The artist had even captured some of the subtle, parched quality of an ancient fresco. The Minnie Mouse part was flat, bright and bold, straight out of a Walt Disney cartoon. It made an interesting statement, although Peter wasn't sure what it was.

"Have a seat," said Cordelia, nodding to one of three couches. The loft was entirely open, a good eighty feet long, forty feet wide. One entire wall was made up of the large, many-paned windows that were once used in old warehouses and factories to save on lighting expenses. Downtown Minneapolis glittered in the distance.

Peter lowered himself onto a particularly paunchy-looking leather couch. As he did, he felt the cushions deflate, like a balloon losing air. He was now about a foot off the floor.

"I'm glad you came," said Cordelia, taking a small sip of her drink.

"You are?"

"You're in pain, dear boy. You came to Auntie Cordelia to help, always a wise decision. Perhaps I should do a reading for you. I have my tarot deck right here." She stepped over to a low cabinet and began rummaging through the top drawer.

"Actually, you *can* help," said Peter. "But I had something else in mind."

She twisted around to look at him. "Something else?" Draping herself over a love seat, she gave him a piercing look. "I am intrigued. But first things first. Tell me how Sigrid is feeling."

"Better. I talked to a nurse a little while ago. She said Sigrid had been up twice today. She sat in a chair for a while, even went for a short walk."

"Heavens. With what she's been through? Sounds like torture."

"No, it's important that they get her up and moving."

"My heart aches for you, Peter."

"Thanks."

"It must be terrible, not being able to see her."

"It is."

"You are a brave stoic with a kind and gentle soul, just like your sister. But sometimes it's not good to keep it all bottled up inside. You need to talk, Peter, to let it all hang loose as they used to say. Tell Cordelia *all*."

The earnest, sappy look on her face made him want to laugh, but he knew she was sincere. And he needed her help. "Uh, well, here's the thing." He cleared his throat. "Have you ever seen the movie *Some Like It Hot*?"

She blinked. "Is this a trick question?"

"No, no. See, I was watching it this afternoon. In the movie, Jack Lemmon and Tony Curtis dress up like women."

In her most droll voice, she replied, "Drag is not a new concept for me, Peter."

"I realize that. That's why I came. I want you to help me do it—what they did. That way I can get in to see Sigrid and nobody will be any the wiser. It's possible, right? If anybody knows how to do it, you would."

She was already studying him critically. "You'd have to shave off your goatee."

"I know. Sigrid's never even seen me clean shaven. At first I thought maybe just using a wig and a pipe—or something like that—would be enough, but it's too dangerous. With everything that happened yesterday, they'd be on the lookout for a strange man. But not a strange woman. Can you do it, Cordelia? Tonight?"

"Now?"

"Sure. Then, if you wouldn't mind, maybe we could go to the hospital together. You could do the talking. That way I wouldn't call attention to myself because of my voice."

"You realize, this . . . transformation will take some time."

"I've got all the time in the world."

She cocked her head, her eyes traveling the length of his body. "The clothes could be a problem. But . . . I'm sure I've got some old thing around here you could wear."

"Will you do it? Will you help me?"

She studied him a moment more, then got up. "Wait here," she said, gliding up the stairs to her bedroom loft. She returned a few seconds later carrying a towel, a bathrobe, and a razor. "Take a shower, then give yourself a close shave. And don't leave any little hairs in the bathroom sink."

"Yes, ma'am."

"Now then, when you're done, holler. We'll sit you down in front of my lighted mirror and see what we can do. You have a certain Angie Harmon thing going on. It could work."

"You think so?" Peter struggled off the couch. "Thanks, Cordelia. You're a doll." He threw his arms around her.

"Thank me later, after we've gotten in and out of the hospital without being arrested. Cordelia Thorn does not *do* jail time."

"You won't have to. We'll pull this off, I know we will."

She eyed him skeptically, then pointed to the stairs. "Go."

Jane spent the evening at the restaurant, but the fate of that stray dog weighed so heavily on her mind that she left after the dinner rush to do some more searching. Cordelia often said Jane obsessed over things. Maybe she was right. Jane just couldn't let go of the idea that the dog was lost and alone. She'd traveled far afield earlier in the day looking for him, but tonight she planned to concentrate on the neighborhood where she'd first found him. Perhaps he had some connection to that area—or even that block.

Parking her Trooper near the house where she'd first seen the dog, Jane retrieved Bean's old leash from the glove compartment, slipped out of the front seat and locked the door. It was a foggy night, temperatures in the low forties. The snow had been melting all day, which made the evening air damp and especially piercing. She walked toward the end of the block, then turned east.

As she entered the alley, it occurred to her that she might be putting herself at risk by wandering around alone in the dark. Especially now. But she couldn't help herself. She had to find that dog. She promised herself that she'd be careful.

She moved slowly, carefully past each garage. She'd considered bringing along a flashlight, but figured that the light might scare the dog off, much as that car's headlights had the other night.

As she passed under the first of two tall alley lights, she caught a tiny movement out of the corner of her eye. She stopped and squinted into the darkness, stepping up to the gate that enclosed the yard where the movement had come from. All appeared to be quiet, so she moved on.

She arrived at last at the spot where she'd first seen the dog. She spent extra time here. But once again, her efforts were fruitless and she eventually continued on.

An hour later, after canvassing the entire neighborhood, she turned once again down the now familiar alley. She would walk it once more, give it one last look, then return to her car and admit defeat.

Jane had planned on spending the night with Patricia, but because she'd been called out of town, that left her with only one other choice: the couch at the restaurant. Without Peter's presence, she had no intention of staying at her house. Perhaps she was beginning to come to terms with what she thought of as her cowardice—or maybe she was just growing weary of beating herself up. If she *was* suffering from posttraumatic stress, then she had to cut herself some slack, do what gave her the most peace of mind. The couch in her office was comfortable. Until she worked out her living arrangements, it was a fine alternative.

Stopping for a moment, Jane kicked some matted leaves away from the alley's sewer grate. When she looked up, to her astonishment, she saw the dog. He was about ten feet away, directly under the alley light. He was just standing there, watching her. She was totally disarmed by the sight of his wagging tail. He could have been an apparition, a dream, but he was real.

"Hi, there, buddy." She was desperate to catch him this time. "Good to see you again." She crouched down. "Come here, boy."

The dog seemed hesitant.

"Are you cold, fella? I'll bet you are. I've been looking for you. You're a hard guy to track down."

She let him take his time. The wagging tail just meant he was excited. He'd take a few steps, then stop. Then a few more. "Are you a good boy? A friendly boy?"

When he finally reached her, he sniffed her hand. She allowed him to examine her clothes and her boots, then she scratched him under his chin for a few seconds, trying to win his confidence. She wanted to get the leash on him as soon as possible, but she didn't want to scare him away. She had the sense that he was a highly intelligent animal—assessing her as much as she was assessing him. And he was frightened.

After nearly a minute, he butted his head against her chest, allowing her to stroke the full length of his fur.

"You need a bath, buddy," she said, feeling his backbone, his ribs. She wondered how long he'd been homeless—and how much weight he'd lost. Carefully, she removed the leash from her pocket. He wanted to sniff it, so she let him. When he was done, she clipped it on his collar and stood up. "Let's go home." She said the words without thinking, but she realized as soon as she said them that that's exactly what she meant. She would take him to her house. He needed more care than she could give him at the restaurant.

All the way to the car, he trotted along beside her as if he'd known her all his life.

"I think we're going to be good friends," she said, looking down at him and smiling.

As soon as they got home, she knelt down in the front foyer and checked his tags in the light. His name was—enigmatically—M. Mouse. Mickey? That seemed the most likely candidate, though she couldn't imagine calling a dog Mickey Mouse. Maybe it was Morris Mouse. Or Manfred Mouse. For now, she would just call him Mouse. It was an odd name for a dog, but he seemed to light up when she said it, so it was obviously familiar to him.

"Okay, Mouse. It says here you live on 3912 Cedar Avenue." Underneath the address was a phone number. "Somebody's probably heartbroken that you're lost. Let's give your owner a call, okay?"

Mouse checked out the living room while Jane sat down on the couch and made the call. As she punched in the numbers, she watched him examine the rug by the fireplace, the spot where Bean and Gulliver had snuggled together for so many years, keeping their old bones warm in the winter. Bean had curled up there all alone after Gulliver was gone. For Jane, the sight always tugged at her heart.

Nosing around behind a chair, Mouse found one of Bean's old chew toys—one that Jane had missed when she'd cleaned the house after his death. Bringing it over to the couch, Mouse dropped it on the rug, then sat down and began to rip it apart. He was a much bigger animal than either of her little terriers, and the flimsy rubber didn't stand a chance against his far more powerful teeth.

The phone rang several times before the line was answered. An abrupt male voice said, "Leave a message." That was it. No hello or goodbye. Next came the beep. Jane spoke clearly into the mouthpiece. "Hi. My name is Jane. I think I may have your dog. You can call me at—" She gave him her cell phone number. "Please call me as soon as possible. Thanks. Bye."

"So," said Jane, leaning back, "I guess it's just you and me tonight." That was fine with her. She watched him rip apart the rubber toy. "I'm sure I've got a tennis ball around here. Something more suitable. But first, you're probably hungry. Let's check out what I've got in the kitchen." She rose from the couch.

Mouse stood up immediately, looking wary.

"Do you know the word 'food'?" He didn't respond. "How about 'treat'?"

He cocked his head, then barked.

"Okay, let's have some treats."

She found an old bag of kibble in the back of one of the bottom cupboards. Even before she could get it in the bowl, Mouse was leaping around the kitchen, acting silly and excited. For the first time, she had the distinct impression that he was a young animal. She set the dish on the floor. It would have taken Bean all day to eat that much food, but Mouse finished it off in a less than a minute. She filled the bowl back up. While he was eating, she filled another bowl with water.

When he was done with the second bowl of food, she glanced at the directions on the back of the package. "It says here you're supposed to have five cups a day if you're forty pounds or over. I think that's about right for you. Except, I only gave you three cups. I know you're probably still hungry, but I don't want to give you too much unfamiliar food right away."

He chugged the water.

She sat down on the floor with him. His mouth still dripping, he sat down too, putting his paw in her lap. "I assume you're house-trained."

He licked her hand, tasted it all the way up to her elbow, then sneezed.

"Are you allergic to me?"

He pawed her leg, wanting to play.

"You need a bath, Mouse. You stink."

His tail thumped against the floor.

"Do you like being a smelly dog?"

His tail thumped louder.

"I see." She knew he was must be tired, but she needed to see what commands he understood, so she put him through his paces. He responded to the word "sit." He seemed to come when she called him. He didn't know "lie down" or "stay," but he did shake on command. He also seemed to understand the words "treat" and "outside." Every now and then he would cock his head at other words, or at questions, but he cocked his head a lot so it didn't necessarily mean anything. And now that he was out of the cold with some food in his stomach, he seemed even friendlier. For the night at least, they were going to be housemates. Tomorrow, his owner would probably return her call.

She let him outside, watching him from the kitchen window. He did his job near the fence, then drifted around the yard, sniffing this and that until she called him to come back in.

She was filling his water dish for the third time when the phone rang. She picked it up in the kitchen. "Hello?"

"Is Jane Lawless there?"

"Speaking." She recognized the voice.

"This is Sergeant Art Turlow."

"I was hoping I'd hear from you."

His voice betrayed the strain he was under. "I lost one of my best friends last night. It's been a bad day."

"You mean Bill Younger?"

"Yeah. The entire force is scrambling to find his killer. Actually, we're rethinking some of our conclusions about the Midnight Man homicides."

"My brother's innocent. The restraining order you've slapped against him has been devastating."

He didn't respond directly. Instead, he said, "If Sigrid Lawless *was* one of the Midnight Man's victims, then it's the only situation we know of where he didn't actually succeed. Maybe this is the mistake we've been looking for."

"You're checking out Bobby Alto's family, right? His brother, Henry, works at Metro South."

"I work the drug squad, so I don't have all the details. But trust me, Ms. Lawless. We're all over it. Last I heard, Jamar Green—he's taken over the case—had issued an order to post a guard on your sister-in-law's hospital door."

"Good," said Jane, feeling an immense sense of relief. "When?"

"Tonight."

"What about those copies of the tarot cards I gave you? Have you tested them for fingerprints?"

It was his turn to hesitate. "I don't have any information on that just yet."

For the first time, she wasn't sure she believed him.

"As far as your restaurant goes, we've got our men in place. If anything is going down, we're there."

"You might want to check out one of my waiters. Joe Vasquez."

"Vasquez? Any particular reason?"

"Let's just say it's a feeling I have."

"Okay. I'll put it on my list. You've got my number, right? In case you need to get in touch with me?"

"I do," said Jane.

He was silent for a moment. Finally he said, "Look, Ms. Lawless, I came on kind of strong the other day. I want you to know that . . . that I'm sorry for what's happened to you and your family. Your father's in a dirty profession. On a personal level, I like the guy, but there can be repercussions. Same for anyone in law enforcement. The problem is, somebody's got to do it. Somebody's got to make the system work."

"I know," said Jane.

"I'll be in touch."

After she'd hung up, she stood for a few seconds leaning against the counter. She would have spent more time reviewing the conversation, but Mouse had nosed open one of the lower cupboards and was in the process of rooting through the trash can.

"Hey there, buddy." She grabbed his collar and pulled him back. "I'm sure you've been eating out of garbage cans for a while, but it's not the way we do things around here." She slapped a piece of duct tape across the doors to prevent him from getting in again, then scratched the top of his head. "What am I going to do with you?"

He sat down, looking up at her expectantly.

The next order of business was a bath. He followed her upstairs. After running some warm water in the tub, she lifted him in. He didn't like it much, but he finally calmed down enough to let her scrub him—twice. She was aghast at the amount of dirt in his fur. She was thoroughly drenched herself when she was done. She toweled him dry, then tried to use the hair dryer on him, but he wouldn't stand for it. He padded into the bedroom and waited while she stripped off her wet clothes and put on a robe.

Once they'd returned to the downstairs, Jane built a fire in the fireplace. She dug out Bean's old brush, poured herself a brandy, then sat down on the floor. She combed through his fur as he sat next to the fire to dry. She was amazed at his mellow temperament. After two terriers, he seemed like another species entirely. He didn't bark at every little sound. She kept the fire roaring until she couldn't feel any more dampness in his coat. By then, she was on her fourth brandy and was feeling no pain.

She'd been keeping up a running patter with him. She liked talking to him, and he seemed to respond by actually listening—most of the time.

"Do you like this house?" she asked, sweeping the hand holding the brandy glass around the living room.

Mouse was resting with his head in her lap. By now, it was close to midnight.

"I'm not really afraid to stay here." She looked down into his eyes, knowing that he saw the statement for what it was—a lie. "Okay, so I am afraid to stay here by myself. I guess I'm here tonight because of you. If you stuck around, maybe . . . maybe it would help me. Maybe I wouldn't have to sell the place and move somewhere else. But that won't happen. You've already got someone who loves you."

She stroked his fur.

"Sometimes I stay at a friend's house. Her name is Patricia. I think you'd like her, Mouse." She took a sip. "I . . . I don't actually *love* her, but I sleep with her, which I enjoy a lot. I guess I feel guilty about it sometimes. That's because I'm a dinosaur. Nobody feels guilt for that sort of thing anymore. I'm stuck in another century. I still think I should love the person I make love to."

She gazed down into his gentle brown eyes. "I've loved only two women in my life, Mouse. Christine was my partner for almost ten years. I lost her to cancer. And then there was Julia. What do I tell you about her? She was amazing. Beautiful. Smart. But she lied to me—over and over again. How can you build a relationship on lies?"

Mouse scratched his ear.

"Yeah. You see my problem. So that leaves Patricia. When I was with Christine, and later Julia, I always felt like I was, well, home. Do you understand what I'm saying? They felt like *home* to me." She held the brandy glass up to the firelight. "But with Patricia, it's different. I've been trying to puzzle it out for months and I think I finally figured it out. Do you know how I feel when I'm with her, Mouse? Do you?"

He lifted his head to look at her.

"Lost. I feel . . . lost, Mouse."

The grandfather clock in the living room struck midnight, chiming twelve times. Mouse turned his head, but didn't bark.

"Good boy," she said, her fingers playing with the fur on his back.

Suddenly, he jumped up and bolted around the side of the couch, heading for the back of the house.

Jane scrambled to her feet, following him into the kitchen.

"Mouse, calm down." She found him standing about three feet from the back door, barking and snarling, acting like he wanted to kill the doorknob.

She was mystified by his intensity. "It's okay, buddy. You're not familiar with the house. It's old. It makes lots of creeks and groans, especially at night."

Mouse kept on barking.

She put her hand on his back to reassure him, then moved to the door, peeking through the blinds to look outside. Nothing seemed out of the ordinary. "See, it's nothing," she said. "Peaceful and calm. Just like it should be in the middle of the night."

When she turned around, Mouse was on his way back into the living room. "Hey, what's up?" she called. The room was spinning. She wanted to lie down.

Mouse was standing at the front window. His barking had stopped, but he was growling now. Jane moved around him and parted the curtains. A car was driving slowly past the house. "It's just a car," she said, crouching down next to him. He finally seemed to relax. "I'm exhausted. How about you?"

She turned off the lamp in the living room, but left a night-light on in the kitchen. Slowly, she and Mouse dragged up the stairs to her bedroom.

"Where are you going to sleep?" she asked, looking around for a suitable place. "Bean usually slept downstairs." She found an old quilt in her closet. "Just for tonight, how about this?" She placed it next to the bed, fluffing it to make sure it was soft enough. Then she dropped on the bed. She didn't bother to open it up, she just covered herself with a couple of blankets.

Switching off the light, she said, "I seem to need a few drinks when I stay here alone." She could hear Mouse get up. "I'm not sure why I need to explain myself to you. I guess I want you to think well of me. You're going to find out soon enough, so I might as well tell you up front. I try hard, but I'm not always a paragon of virtue."

She could sense that he had moved to the bottom of the bed.

"But I'm glad we had this little talk. Now you know what to expect." Her eyes were already closed. She knew she was making no sense, that she was babbling. She felt something touch her feet, then ooze up next to her legs.

"Mouse? What are you doing?"

Before she realized it, he was lying next to her under the blankets, his head tucked next to her shoulder. When she turned toward him, he sighed. "Just this once. Just for tonight," she mumbled as she drifted off.

29

The elevator doors opened and Cordelia and Peter stepped off.

"This way, *Claire*," said Cordelia, a little too loudly for Peter's frayed nerves. She steamed down the hall toward the nursing station, with Peter wobbling behind in his two-inch heels. He tried to keep in mind all of Cordelia's instructions. Keep your legs together, even when you're walking. Don't shuffle. Hips forward, shoulders back. Glide, don't galumph. Hold the purse with finesse, not gripped like a football. Look pleasant. Don't glower. Keep your mouth shut unless absolutely necessary.

They'd decided on the name "Claire" in the car on the way over. Peter felt ridiculous in the tasteful navy dress with subdued gray trim that Cordelia had pulled from her closet with all the flourish of a saleslady at a bridal shop producing the perfect wedding dress. He'd lobbied for slacks and a blazer, but Cordelia insisted that, because he already looked a little too butch, they had to emphasize his female qualities. The brassier was padded with socks. A scarf covered his Adam's apple. The hair on his legs had been shaved so that he could wear nylons—Cordelia's monster nylons. Even though they were stretchy to accommodate different sizes, they were still too big and had begun to bunch around his ankles. He'd tried to tug them back up while they were in the elevator, but Cordelia elbowed him in the ribs, telling him to cut it out, to stand up straight and suck in his stomach. Peter was particularly annoyed by the nylon situation because Cordelia had assured him that his legs were his best feature.

The worst part of the transformation was his head. Cordelia had surrounded it with a short brown wig, one that made him look like a frumpy maiden aunt. To offset the dumpy image, she'd thinned his heavy eyebrows, making him look permanently startled. She'd also worked hard on his makeup. She'd used a plum blush with bits of glitter in it, a plum lipstick that tasted like bubble gum, and turquoise eye shadow. She said it lent his new persona an air of mystery. The mystery, to Peter's way of thinking, seemed apparent. He was a maiden aunt by day, a hooker by night. He'd nicked his chin while shaving, so Cordelia had turned it into a large beauty mark, only it looked more like the kind of mole you'd see on a wicked witch. To recap: a maiden aunt who was part witch, part hooker. He wasn't a pretty sight.

When he finally reached the nursing station, he stopped next to Cordelia and tried to look demure.

"I know it's late," said Cordelia, slipping an arm around his shoulder. "But we've been traveling for two whole days. We *have* to see our dear niece tonight. We can't wait a moment longer. Isn't that right, Claire?"

Peter nodded. Thinking the nod wasn't enough, he said, "Yes." Unfortunately, the word came out sounding entirely too breathy, too Marilyn Monroe. The nurse looked at him skeptically.

"We're from . . . Alaska," said Cordelia. It was apparently the only explanation the nurse was going to get. "We were told that Sigrid was feeling better this evening," she continued, trying to sound pleasant. "As you can tell from my sister's voice, we're both extremely tired, so we wouldn't stay long."

The nurse stared at them. "You two are . . . sisters?"

"Certainly," said Cordelia. Leaning across the counter, she lowered her voice. "We have different fathers. It's amazing, isn't it, what's out there in the general gene pool?" She tipped her head knowingly to Peter.

It took a few seconds, but the nurse finally gave in and said okay. "I was in the room just a few minutes ago, so I know she's still up. But don't stay long."

"We won't," said Cordelia, flashing the woman a sunny smile.

Peter reached the room first and pushed his way through the door. "Oh my God," he gasped, witnessing the bruises on Sigrid's face and arms for the first time. He rushed to her side.

Sigrid appeared to be sleeping. She looked so pale, almost to the point of translucence. As he stood over her, mascara tears falling helplessly down his cheeks, he felt an overwhelming sense of tenderness. A moment later she opened her eyes and looked up at him.

"I'm so sorry," he whispered, touching her shoulder.

She recoiled. "Do I know you?"

"Of course you do. It's Peter."

"Peter who?" She reached for the call button.

"Peter your *husband*."

She looked up at him, clearly confused.

Cordelia sailed through the door. "The marines have landed. Break out the chocolate bars."

At the sight of her, Sigrid looked even more confused. "What's going on?"

"It's me, honey. Really, it's Peter. Cordelia lent me these clothes and the wig."

"I'm dreaming," said Sigrid, looking dazed.

"No you're not." Cordelia stood on the other side of the bed, beaming with pride. "I did a spectacular job of disguising him, don't you think? Nobody would ever figure this frumpy female is in reality Peter Lawless, boy wonder. Except, I realize now I should have used waterproof mascara." Frowning, she added, "God, you look awful, Siggy. How are you feeling?"

Sigrid reached up and touched Peter's face.

"I shaved off my mustache and goatee, sweetheart," he said,

folding his hand around hers. “I had to come. I couldn’t stand not seeing you. I know I’m breaking the law—”

“That restraining order—” She swallowed to clear her throat. “—it was a mistake.” The reality of the situation was finally starting to sink in. “I told my brother to fix it—to cancel it. But he’s so angry. He needs someone to blame.”

“I understand,” said Peter, kissing her forehead.

She tried to sit up in bed.

“Don’t, Siggy. Just stay where you are and let me look at you.”

Turning to Cordelia, Sigrid said, “It’s nice to see you, but could you give Peter and me a few minutes alone?”

Cordelia huffed a little, but an idea lit up her face. “I’ll be the lookout. Just in case.”

“Do that,” said Sigrid. She returned her gaze to Peter.

When they were alone, Peter leaned over and gave Sigrid a real kiss, as gentle as he could make it. He was starved to see her, to touch her and hear her voice. “Say something,” he said, looking at her longingly.

“What’s that thing on your chin?”

Not what he’d expected. “I cut myself shaving. Cordelia turned it into a beauty mark.”

“*That’s* a beauty mark?” This time, she smiled. “As a woman, you’re not exactly a knockout.”

“You didn’t see my legs. Cordelia tells me I’ve got great legs.”

She poked one of his breasts.

“Socks,” he said.

“Right.”

“Do you feel any better, Siggy?”

“I did, but that was before you walked in.”

“You’re joking, right?”

She grinned. “Yes, Peter, I’m joking.”

He cupped both his hands around hers. “I’m so sorry for the fight we had. You’re right. I was being a jealous jerk. And . . . maybe I *was* having second thoughts about my decision about a baby. I’ve given it a lot of thought in the past few days. I want you, Siggy. *You*, not some silly notion of an idealized family. I want you safe, and happy, and us living together again." He could see tears in her eyes. "You want that too, don't you?"

She looked away.

"Siggy?" His heart nearly stopped when she didn't respond. He felt guilty for putting any pressure on her. Maybe he wanted too much, just like always, but he had to know how she felt.

Looking back at him finally, she said, "I've been doing some thinking too. I haven't been honest with you, Peter. I was ashamed. Afraid. We need to talk, but not tonight."

"Sure, of course. But . . . can't you at least say you still love me?"

"I never stopped loving you," she said, her eyes softening. "But you'll have to decide if you still love me—after you hear my story."

She was scaring him. She looked so grave. "Nothing could change how I feel about you." He paused. "This story, is it about . . . what happened to you when you were attacked?"

"No. I can't remember any of that. I wish I could, for your sake."

"Maybe it's for the best. The last thing you need is to lie here and think about that afternoon."

"But you don't know what it's like, having your memory erased. It's there, somewhere, and I dig for it, but it's just blank. It's as if I'd gone suddenly deaf. I hate it."

"You're getting better, Siggy. Every day. You'll be out of here before you know it." He held a plastic glass while she sipped water from a straw. "But . . . there's one thing I do have to know. Your wedding ring. You're not wearing it. Did you take it off because you were angry with me?"

She held up her hand. "I don't know," she said. "I guess I must have taken it off. I don't remember doing it. The nurse said I wasn't wearing a wedding ring when I was brought into the emergency room."

Outside in the hall, Peter could hear Cordelia talking loudly.

A moment later, she burst into the room followed by a police officer.

Peter stiffened as he turned to face them.

"Time to go," said Cordelia, her expression both rigid and cheerful, her eyes opened much too wide. "Sigrid, it was great seeing you as always. Claire?" She thrust her thumb over her shoulder. "Visiting hours are over."

The cop gave Peter the once-over, his gaze lingering on the drooping nylons. Shifting his attention to Sigrid, he introduced himself as Officer Maki and explained that he'd been assigned to stand guard at her door for the rest of the night. Someone else would be assigned tomorrow. He made it sound as if it was nothing out of the ordinary, but they all knew what it meant.

"You think I'm in danger?" asked Sigrid.

"It's just a precaution, ma'am."

The last thing Peter wanted was to leave.

"Couldn't we have just a few more minutes?" said Peter in his breathy Marilyn voice.

The cop did a double-take.

"This is . . . my Aunt Claire," said Sigrid, trying to explain.

"We're from Alaska," added Cordelia, apropos of nothing. "Come on, Claire. We can come back tomorrow."

Peter knew there wouldn't be a tomorrow—unless his father could get the restraining order dropped. He turned and gave Sigrid a kiss on her cheek, whispering "I love you" in her ear. As he crossed to Cordelia, he could see the officer staring at the black thing on his chin.

"It's a beauty mark," he breathed seductively. It was his last opportunity to give the cop the finger, and he took it.

The cop lifted an eyebrow.

"Ta," called Cordelia, waving her fingers and yanking Peter out the door.

30

Jane spent the next few days talking to people who'd known the victims of the Midnight Man's first homicides. The presence of the pendant at Bill Younger's murder scene had somehow been leaked to the press, so the Midnight Man was once again on everyone's mind. Jane found that people associated with the crimes wanted to talk, especially when they learned that Jane and her family had been victimized as well.

The charges against Peter were finally dropped, as was the restraining order. He'd asked for and received a longer leave of absence from his job so that he could be with his wife while she recovered. Peter moved back into the apartment, telling Jane that Sigrid had alluded to a secret she'd been keeping for years, one that had something to do with her not wanting to have a child. He didn't want to push her, but every day he felt as if he were simply waiting for the other shoe to drop, for a revelation that would end their marriage once and for all. At the same time, he told Jane they were growing closer than they'd ever been. He helped her go for short walks. Brought her tea. Combed her hair. Held her hand. He'd come to the Lyme House twice for a late dinner, but both times he'd eaten virtually nothing. Jane's concern for him and for Sigrid hadn't diminished with the end of Peter's legal problems. She didn't know how to help them, except to be there when they needed her.

Nothing drug-related had happened at the restaurant since the new bartender and prep cook had been installed. Jane hoped she'd seen the end of the Midnight Man's attack on her business. But she felt uneasy, as if he could pop out of the woodwork at any moment. The tarot cards still bothered her too, though she felt she saw them for what they were: psychological manipulation. Mystical terror wasn't the Midnight Man's usual MO, but lately he seemed to be experimenting. If the police could only lift a fingerprint from the Xeroxed pages, they might have their man. Until he was caught, he posed a threat to her, to her family and to the entire criminal justice community.

Jane still hadn't heard from Mouse's owner. She'd left additional messages, but so far no one had returned her calls. With each passing day her hope grew that no one would.

Mouse had settled into her routine without a hitch. After being with him for only one day, she realized she'd fallen hopelessly in love. He nosed her awake in the mornings, ready and eager to start the day, and slept with his back pressed against her at night. He was by far the gentlest dog she'd ever known, and yet he had a fiercely protective nature. The more familiar he became with the sounds in the house, the more watchful he was. Jane admired the courage with which he charged at situations he didn't understand—the refrigerator compressor going off and on, wind blowing the branches of a pine tree against the side of the house, mail coming through the mail slot. He followed her around wherever she went, and when she was busy, he would lie contentedly on the floor and snooze. He seemed equally at ease in her office at the restaurant and in the backseat of her car.

On Saturday morning, Patricia had called her from the Plaza Suites in San Francisco, saying that she hoped to be home in a few days, although there was a chance she might have to fly to Hong Kong—all part of her job at Kastner Gardens. She told

Jane that she couldn't wait until she finally got *her* pet project, the Winter Garden Senior Residence, up and running and could quit working for her parents for good. Before she said goodbye, she told Jane that she missed her. She hesitated slightly on the word "miss," giving Jane the impression that she wanted to use the word "love," but had changed her mind at the last minute. As a way of covering, she went on to describe in graphic detail a few of the specific things she missed most. They made a date to get together when Patricia got back.

The rest of the weekend was spent tracking down parents, siblings, boyfriends, girlfriends and work associates of the Midnight Man's victims. Jane was certain there was one important element that linked all the homicides—something other than the pendant. The police hadn't found the link because they'd spent their primary efforts digging up information on the last two murders. By then, they had a theory that centered on Bobby Alto, a theory they needed to prove in order to make an arrest. Jane understood the motivation—searching for facts to prove a theory—and yet it was no way to get to the truth.

Keeping her three suspects in mind—Henry Alto, Barrett Sweeny, and Conrad Alto—she developed a series of questions based on their police profiles. There were five known victims. Jane had spoken to the father of the third victim, Lora Pine, murdered in 1997, as well as to her ex-husband. The ex maintained that Lora would never have dated a man like Bobby Alto. For one thing, he didn't make enough money, and for another, he had no status or claim to fame. The ex didn't qualify either. That's why they were divorced. He sounded bitter, although he was sad that Lora was gone. Jane also learned that Lora Pine had worked in downtown St. Paul, not far from Grace Cathedral, but that she wasn't particularly religious and rarely attended church. She hated water sports with a passion, didn't know how to swim, and had never spent time in a hospital—Metro South or any other. That just about covered the range of Jane's prepared questions.

The second victim, Cindy Hiltzak, worked for a mortgage company in St. Louis Park. Her mother said she knew a lot of realtors, so thought it was possible she'd met Barrett Sweeny, although she had no proof. Cindy dated occasionally, sometimes went clubbing at night, but most of her spare time was devoted to her dog, Mazie, and a youth group she'd organized at her synagogue. Like Lora Pine, she'd never been in the hospital. She did sail occasionally in the summer with friends, but her mother never remembered her talking about anyone named Barrett. Jane also spoke to a friend of Cindy's who said she'd liked to date older men. Cindy was thirty-nine when she died.

Jane had asked every question she could think of, but in the end, nothing had clicked. By the end of the weekend, she could tell her methods weren't going to produce the immediate results she'd hoped for. Still, she persisted. She instinctively felt that an investigation of the first two victims, Paula Trier and Cindy Hiltzak, might bear the most fruit. The police had spent little time with those cases because their deaths initially were ruled accidental. By the time they tied them to the Midnight Man, the cases were cold.

On Monday afternoon, Jane and Mouse drove to Prior Lake to talk to the mother of the Paula Trier, the Midnight Man's first homicide. Sandra Hoagstrom lived in a small brick apartment building on a quiet street. Since the day was balmy by late February standards, the temperature in the high forties, Jane left Mouse in the car, telling him she'd be back shortly. He gave her nose a lick, then watched from the backseat as she hurried off.

There was no security at the front entrance, so Jane climbed the two flights of stairs and knocked on number 308. The hallway smelled of gingerbread. When Mrs. Hoagstrom answered the door, she was wearing a freshly ironed house dress, a frilly apron and a subdued smile. She was a small woman, most likely in her mid sixties. She led Jane through the living room to the kitchen, where they sat at the kitchen table waiting for the coffee to brew.

A pan of gingerbread was cooling on an wire rack. Jane's nose had once again proved infallible.

The warm afternoon sun hit the kitchen blinds above the sink, turning them golden. It was a pleasant enough apartment. Big rooms. Lots of light. Jane saw a number of framed family photographs on the walls. She assumed the young woman with the bright, cheerful face was Paula Trier, Sandra Hoagstrom's daughter. Initially Sandy, as she insisted on being called, wanted to know more details about what had happened to Jane and her family. Misery did indeed love company. Only after the coffee was poured and she felt more at ease did she open up about Paula's death.

"Paula and her twin brother, Paul," Sandy began, folding her hands in her lap, "started a carpentry and painting company several years after Paul finished his time in the navy. Paul managed the crew and Paula managed the office. From nineteen eighty-nine to nineteen ninety-six, they put all their time and energy into the business. I loved the fact that they were working together. It just seemed right to me. And they were actually starting to make money too. Paula had been living in an apartment in Minneapolis for several years, but had closed on a new house two months before her death." She took out a tissue from her apron pocket and just held it in her hand.

"After the fire . . . my son blamed himself. He'd been after her for years to quit smoking. If he'd only succeeded, she would never have died. I told him it wasn't his fault, but he was devastated. Later, after we learned what really happened, Paul completely fell apart. He couldn't work for months. He and his sister had always been so close. She'd been dating an electrician for several years, but a few months before she moved into the new house, they'd broken up. Paul had never liked the man, and told the police that he should be their number-one suspect. But when he learned that the man had been at a Twins game the night of the fire, and later at a bar with dozens of people for witnesses,

Paul had to back off and admit he was wrong. He still carries a grudge against the man. I have no idea why."

"You never asked him?"

She shook her head. "He won't talk about Paula anymore. He says it hurts too much. I guess I'm the exact opposite. I can't stop talking about her." She dabbed at her eyes with the tissue.

Jane asked all the rehearsed questions. Did Paula sail? Had she ever been in the emergency room at Metro South? Did she like organ music? Had she ever attended church at Grace Cathedral? Had she ever met a real estate agent named Barrett Sweeny? The answers were all negative. Sandy said Paula listened to country western music sometimes, attended mass once or twice a year, fished regularly in the summers and sometimes water-skied but never went sailing. Her brother did some sailing on the St. Croix, but Paula didn't much care for it. She'd broken her leg falling out of a tree when she was twelve, but other than that, she'd never set foot in a hospital. She didn't even go for regular physicals. And her real estate agent was a second cousin. A woman.

After pouring more coffee, Sandy Hoagstrom offered Jane a piece of gingerbread.

"I wish I could stay," said Jane, glancing at her watch. She couldn't think of any more questions to ask, and if she didn't leave soon, she'd hit rush hour traffic on her way back to the city. "But I need to get back to my restaurant."

"Of course," said Sandy. "I've kept you too long already. You probably don't even like gingerbread."

Jane could sense the older woman tucking in her emotions, pulling everything back inside.

"No, it's not that," said Jane.

"I'm not a very good cook. My husband always said so. But gingerbread is my specialty."

"I'm sure it's delicious." The problem was, Jane had promised Arlene that she'd be back by five. It was Arlene's birthday today and she planned to leave early. Her latest boyfriend had asked her out to dinner. After that, they were off to Orchestra Hall to hear Doc Severenson. Felix wouldn't be arriving until seven. If Jane didn't return by five, that meant there would be no manager on duty for two hours. And *that* was tempting fate.

"You have a business to run. I understand." Sandy looked dejected. "Loss is a terrible thing, Jane. It affects you in waves. My daughter's been gone for nearly six years, but sometimes it feels just like it was yesterday."

"I do understand," said Jane.

"My son lost his best friend when Paula died. Maybe I did too. My husband and I divorced about a year later. It's funny how that works. Our shared grief should have brought us together, but instead, it broke us apart." She glanced up at the clock on the wall. "But you go. It was just nice to be able to talk about Paula for a few minutes."

Jane hesitated. "Maybe . . . maybe I should try a piece of that gingerbread. It is your specialty, after all."

"Really? Would you like some more coffee to go with it?"

"Sure," said Jane, seeing the rush of pleasure on Sandy's face.

"While we're eating, I'll show you the family album. Paula was such a beautiful child."

31

Ray? Have you got a second?"

Raymond looked up from the papers on his desk and saw Elizabeth standing in the doorway. He glanced at his watch, surprised at how late it was. "It's after eight. How come you're still here?"

"I could ask you the same question." She hesitated, then moved into the room and took a chair across from him. "You looked pretty deep in thought. I wasn't sure I should interrupt."

"No," he said, stretching his arms over his head, then clasping his hands behind his neck. "I could use a break."

"What are you working on?" She nodded to the papers.

"Nothing important." He could tell by the look on her face that she wasn't going to be put off that easily. She knew something was up. Everyone in the office did.

"Norman told me that Conrad Alto stopped by around five," said Elizabeth. "What did he want?"

"Just more abuse. He's been calling me, sending me letters, even E-mailing me at least once a day."

"The man's deranged."

"And then some."

"So . . . he came by this afternoon to yell at you?"

Raymond figured he might as well tell her. She had a right to know. "He's suing me for malpractice." By her reaction, he could see that the news didn't come as a surprise.

"I thought he might try something like that."

All day, Ray had been feeling so hopeful and upbeat. For the past few days, Sigrid had been gaining ground. She might even be allowed to go home at the end of the week. Peter seemed happier than he'd been in months. And the police appeared to be on top of the drug problems at Jane's restaurant, so Jane was more hopeful too.

Before a court appearance earlier in the day, Ray had run into a cop named Burt Fallon. Burt worked homicide at the MPD. Confidentially, he informed Ray that the police had put a tail on Barrett Sweeny and Conrad and Henry Alto. That meant Ray—and everyone else in town—could finally breathe a sigh of relief. If one of them tried something now, the police would be all over it. It was just a matter of time before they made an arrest, although Burt said the Midnight Man worked extremely clean. He hadn't left a single clue in Younger's murder. Still, they had a few other leads they were checking out. A couple looked promising.

Whatever they had to do to make it happen, an arrest couldn't come fast enough for Ray.

"What are you going to do?" asked Elizabeth. Her pale blue eyes radiated sympathy.

Ray felt like a starving man in her presence. So many times he'd pictured taking her in his arms, telling her how much he needed her in his life. But he also knew he wouldn't. He wasn't that kind of guy. He might cheat on his wife in his thoughts, but he'd never translate those thoughts into action. Besides, at this moment, he was too ashamed. He'd finally admitted his professional failure to himself and that had opened the mental floodgates. He realized now that everyone must know. "You understand, don't you?"

"Understand what?"

"You went over those trial transcripts with a fine-tooth comb. You could see how badly I screwed up."

"That's not true."

"Of course it is. We've both known it all along, but you were too diplomatic to say it out loud, and I was too pigheaded to admit it. Conrad Alto's not only got a case against me, he's going to win. I'm washed up, Elizabeth. Finished. After the facts become public knowledge, the only people who will ever hire me again are drug dealers and pimps. I did my time with them long ago. I'm not going back to it."

"Ridiculous. We'll fight it."

He shook his head.

"I've got a good friend who specializes in malpractice law."

"He'd be wasting his time."

"For God's sake, you can't just roll over and play dead. You're too good a lawyer for that."

Running his fingers along the edge of his desk, Ray said, "Look, Elizabeth, I need for you to understand something. I'm not excusing what I did, but there were mitigating circumstances. Something happened to me during that trial and . . . if I don't talk about it, sooner or later, I—" His voice was quavering so badly, he had to stop.

Elizabeth's sympathy turned instantly to concern. "What is it, Ray? You can tell me anything."

"Can I?"

She held his gaze. "Yes. You know how I feel about you." Her eyes softened. "We both know what's been happening between us. I'm not so naive to believe we'll ever have a future together, but you must realize how much I care about you. I'm not a mind reader, but I could tell something's been eating at you. I assumed it was your marriage, that you and Marilyn were having problems."

"We are."

"But it's more than that."

He sighed. "I'm afraid it is." Leaning back in his chair, he continued, "About two weeks after Bobby Alto's trial began back in the fall of nineteen ninety-nine, I had my yearly physical. I felt fine, so I didn't expect problems. My doctor did all the usual stuff, but noticed something odd about my prostate. I don't know if it was from the exam or the PSA levels, but he sent me to have more tests done. Turns out I had something called high-grade prostatic intraepithelial neoplasia."

"In English, please."

"It's a condition without symptoms, at least it is for me. For many men, it's a precursor to prostate cancer. I've always been terrified of cancer, Elizabeth, especially that form."

"But . . . it's curable. I read articles in the papers all the time that say they've made great advances."

"Some of that is hype, some is accurate. But the cure options remain a modern-day Tower of Babel. During the trial, I had several biopsies. My doctor said the condition was something they needed to watch carefully. I can't tell you what that did to me. I felt as if I had a time bomb ticking inside my body and all I could do was wait for it to go off. I had all these thoughts about my mortality, things I'd never thought about before. It was during that time that I married Marilyn. I'm not saying that was the reason I married her. We'd been together a long time. My son had been married for a while and he was so happy I thought that might be the answer for me too. Real stability. A marriage to someone I loved. Formal commitment."

"Did you tell Marilyn about your condition?"

"I wanted to. I meant to. I even broached the subject a couple of times, but . . . it never seemed to be the right time. And, to be perfectly honest, I knew talking about it would only make it more real. I just wanted it to go away. I started having problems sleeping. My doctor gave me something to help, but the medication made me feel groggy in the mornings so I stopped taking it. There's nothing more disorienting than insomnia. I was already working sixteen hours a day on the Midnight Man trial, so when I'd get home at night I'd have a couple of drinks and fall into bed for a couple of hours, but I'd wake up in a cold sweat. I couldn't seem to get a grip on myself. My concentration was shot. In court, my mind wandered. I tried my damnedest to put my personal problems out of my thoughts, but I couldn't. I failed my client, Elizabeth. I *failed* him."

"Stop using that word. You're not a failure." She got up and walked behind the desk, crouching down and taking his hands in hers.

"It's how I feel."

"What about your health, Ray? That's more important than anything else. Have you seen a doctor recently?"

He took a deep breath, then let it out slowly. "I had another biopsy on Monday. I should get the results in a day or two."

"Then we have to stay positive."

"We?"

She smiled. "Yes, *we*."

"Elizabeth—" He wasn't even sure what he wanted to say. "This is all so confusing. My life has been turned upside down and I have no idea where I'll land."

She squeezed his hand. "I'm not asking for anything. Just let me be your friend, okay?"

"I don't deserve you." He felt tears burn his eyes. God, he wasn't going cry in front of her. That would be the last straw. "You should cut your losses. Find another firm to take you on. With your skills, you could write your own ticket anywhere in town."

"Let me make my own decisions, Ray." She stood up. "Now, have you had dinner?"

He shook his head.

"Then I'm taking you out. No arguments."

He looked up at her with gratitude in his eyes.

"A bottle of wine. A good dinner. And a chance to talk—or not to talk, whatever you want. I know just the place. Let me make one phone call and I'll meet you downstairs in ten minutes. Deal?"

He couldn't help but smile. "Thanks, Elizabeth. It's a deal."

32

Henry sat in the back of the choir loft and listened while his father played the last strains of Bizet's "Agnus Dei." As if in a trance, his father's fingers moved over the keys.

Henry knew that it was his father's love of music that had led him back to the church. As a young man, with nothing but secular interests, Conrad had studied the pipe organ in Paris with Laurent Palou, in Leipzig with Ute von Mahlsdorf, and in Oxford with Paul Auster. He'd returned to the United States for further schooling, and when he was twenty-four he'd taken the position of assistant organist at St. Mark's Cathedral in Boston. From there, his fate was sealed. He would forever after be among the ranks of the devout. But a fateful trip to Italy with his two sons and their friend, Barrett, had altered the course of that devotion forever. Henry wondered if the four of them actually constituted a cult. A cult was a community of intoxicants with feasts, sacred rites and mysteries. That fit. Perhaps they were, after all, a cult, now down to three members.

Henry watched his father's fingers linger on the last pristine chord. With his eyes still closed, the old man savored the sweetness of his prayer and only then did he lift his hands and allow the sound to drift away into the high cathedral air. Making several quick adjustments to the stops, he moved on to a tense section of Mozart's *Requiem*. Henry loved to watch his father play. He played like a madman, like a race-car driver thundering down a straightaway. The organ was pure power and he was riding it. He swayed. He was a puppet and the music was the master.

Always, there was a master.

Henry's father had called him earlier in the day to ask for a ride over to a family meeting tonight. His car had unexpectedly conked out as he'd backed out of his driveway in the morning. It had to be towed to a garage and wouldn't be repaired until late tomorrow. His dad had already talked to Barrett, who suggested he borrow one of his cars until it was fixed. Barrett was like that. Generous, sometimes to a fault. But his generous nature hadn't been enough for Taylor. That was the matter they would all have to deal with tonight.

As the last strains of the music swelled into the highest reaches of the sanctuary, Henry got up and walked toward the organ. His father, catching the movement, turned toward him. "Henry. I didn't know you were here. Why didn't you say something?"

"I was enjoying the recital. Were you . . . summoning your courage?"

"You mean about Taylor?" He shook his head. "Maybe Barrett's got some ideas."

They rode in silence to Edina. When they finally arrived at Henry's mother's house, he parked his car in the drive next to Barrett's. Before they got out, he stopped his father by placing a hand on his arm. "We need to talk before we go in."

"About what?"

"Don't play dumb, okay? We both know what's going on."

"I don't know what you're talking about."

"*Barrett.*"

Conrad stiffened. "What about him?"

"The *murders*. I love him—we *all* love him. But this is too much. He's changed, Dad. Sometimes . . . he frightens me."

Narrowing his eyes, Conrad looked over at his son. "Did the police call you in for questioning?"

"This afternoon."

"What did you tell them?"

"If I'd said anything, do you think Barrett would still be walking around a free man?"

"We don't know anything for sure, Henry. Remember that. Nothing concrete."

"Which is the way Barrett wants it."

"I know what you're thinking. I've had the same thoughts. But Barrett had nothing to do with those murders. Neither did Bobby. I have to believe that."

"If you're right, then that leaves you and me. I know I didn't kill those people, so I guess you did."

"Drop it, Henry. I mean it. And if the police call you again, keep your mouth shut about what you *do* know."

Entering the house, they found Barrett and Henry's mother sitting in the living room enjoying a glass of wine together. Barrett appeared to be growing a beard, which Henry didn't much like. In his mind, Barrett should always remain that same clean-shaven youth he'd first met all those years ago—a boy with the eyes of a man.

Dimming the lights, Barrett walked over to the front window and looked through a crack in the blinds.

"Are they out there?" asked Conrad.

Barrett nodded. "I can see two unmarked cars, one at either end of the block."

"The police put a tail on you?" asked Shirley. She didn't seem all that shocked.

Henry grabbed himself a can of Coke from the refrigerator, then returned to the living room and sat down on a bench by the arch. "For your information, Mom, in the last two days, Barrett, Dad and I have all been interrogated by the police."

"I've been hauled in twice," said Barrett, his back to them, still looking outside.

Shirley finished her glass of wine, then got up and poured herself another. Standing in front of the gas fireplace, she said, "Before we start on Taylor, I've got something I want to say." She made sure all eyes were on her, then continued, "I suffered through that goddamn trial knowing my son was innocent. I believed him when he told me he made those pendants, but that he had nothing to do with the crimes. I want my pound of flesh from Ray Lawless just like the rest of you, but now I'm beginning to wonder. Is it possible one of my precious brood really *is* the Midnight Man?"

Henry was about to answer when his father said, "The police need a scapegoat, Shirley. We're it."

"That's all it is? Rotten police work?"

"Are you accusing one of us?" said Barrett, regarding her with nothing more than simple curiosity.

"What if I said *I* did it?" said Henry curtly. There, that stopped them.

Barrett shifted his gaze to Henry. A slight smile tugged at the corners of his mouth. "Don't be a fool."

"You're a notorious liar, Henry," said his mother. "Even if it were true, how do I know I can believe you?"

"You should really work on that, son," said Conrad. "A man's word is his bond."

"Maybe I *am* working on it," said Henry, taking a cigarette packet and a matchbook out of his pocket and lighting up.

Barrett walked over to the chair where Conrad was seated, moved behind it and placed his hands on the older man's shoulders.

It struck Henry as a gesture of anointing. He wasn't sure what it meant.

"We've all got to stay strong and be smart," said Barrett. He spoke softly to emphasize his point. "This too shall pass. The police found one clue and they ran with it. They pinned the murders on Bobby, but in the end it got them nowhere because he was an innocent man. Now they're trying to pin it on us." As he said the last word, he stared straight at Henry.

Shirley downed half her glass of wine. "I may not have lived an exemplary life—"

Conrad laughed. "Running a high-priced call-girl service for the past twenty years hardly qualifies you for sainthood."

"I needed to support myself somehow," said Shirley. "It's how I put myself through college—"

"And how you got your kicks during our marriage."

She smiled. "I never charged for my services while I was employed at the university."

"Really? If you ask me, I paid a pretty high price for what I got."

Shirley glared at him. "To repeat, I may not have lived an exemplary life, but I draw the line at murder. Okay, so maybe the police are wrong, but I've got a strong hunch they're not. If we do have some goddamned deviant in our midst, if one of us knows the facts and is holding that information back out of misplaced loyalty, that man better think long and hard about it, that's all I've got to say."

The room seemed oppressively silent. Henry couldn't seem to rouse himself to utter a single word.

Finally, Barrett sat down next to Shirley, stretching his long legs out in front of him. "Your point's well taken. And I'm sure we'll all think about what you've said. But right now, the subject on the table is Taylor. That's our stated reason for being here tonight." His manner was both chilly and intimate. Like everything else about him, he was a study in contradiction. "I've tried everything. We all have. I don't think we have a choice anymore. She needs professional help."

"What about her parents?" asked Conrad. "Shouldn't we contact them?"

"She left home when she was sixteen," said Barrett. "Her father was an alcoholic. Her mother wasn't much better. I don't think they'd be of any help."

"You're suggesting a psychiatric hospital?" said Henry, looking thoughtfully at the thread of smoke swaying gently in front of his eyes. "About committing her against her will?"

At the sound of footsteps on the stairs, they all turned.

Henry was astonished to see Taylor awake. He'd stopped by around five to give her a sedative. By all rights, she should have been out for the rest of the night. He could tell by the way her body drooped that she was still half asleep—but she'd managed to get herself downstairs right at the wrong time.

Timidly, she entered the room, one drowsy forearm shielding her eyes from the light. "Were you talking about me?" she mumbled. Even in her sedative-induced fog, Henry thought she looked terrified. "I didn't do anything wrong."

"Of course you didn't," said Shirley soothingly. "But even you have to admit, you haven't been yourself lately. We were just talking about how we could help you."

"It's . . . Bobby," said Taylor. Her eyes widened into a childish stare. She pushed her hands through her long, tangled hair. "He won't leave me alone. I can't sleep. He wakes me up."

"Come sit next to me, honey," said Shirley, patting the ottoman.

"You think just because you can't see it, it doesn't exist?"

"I would never say that," said Barrett, fixing her with a smile of great warmth and sweetness. "The world is full of mystery, most of which we don't understand."

Taylor wobbled toward the ottoman, but stopped herself, shaking her head. "I need some air."

"You need to rest," said Barrett, nodding to Henry. "Take her upstairs and give her something to help her sleep."

"I already did," whispered Henry.

"Then give her something *more*."

As Henry rose Taylor moved away from him, backing into the hallway.

"I'm *not* crazy. You're the ones who are crazy! I can prove it."

"I agree with you," said Henry, grinding out his cigarette in an ashtray by the door. "This family has never been normal." She looked like a panther ready to spring. Except, when he took hold of her arms, she crumpled against his chest, weak as a kitten. "Come on. Let me take you upstairs. I'm a doctor. You can trust me." The joke had always worked on her before, but tonight she was too strung out to care.

Once she was back in bed, Henry ran out to his car to get his medical bag. He didn't want to overdose her. He considered a couple of drugs he had with him, but when he returned to her room, he found that she'd fallen asleep. The sedative he'd given her earlier was working, she'd just been fighting it. Closing the door behind him, he returned to the living room. "She's asleep," he said at Barrett's questioning glance. He left it at that.

"So, it's agreed?" said Conrad.

Henry retrieved his Coke from an end table. "I haven't agreed to anything."

"Don't be difficult, Henry," said his mother.

"I'm not being difficult. I actually believe Bobby may be haunting her. No psychiatrist is trained to handle *that*."

"You know what the Egyptians used to say," said Shirley knowingly.

Conrad gave her a disgusted look. "No, Shirley. I don't know what the Egyptians used to say."

She lowered her voice. "To repeat the name of the dead is to make them live again."

"*Yah hear that, Bobby?*" shouted Henry, his eyes thrust upward.

"Shut up," said his father.

"Stop it, all of you," demanded Barrett. "This isn't helping." His expression suddenly changed into something very like tenderness. *Very like* being the operative words.

Henry ignored him. "I'm not *voting* on whether or not to commit Taylor. It shouldn't be handled that way."

"We're her family," pleaded Barrett. "We're all she's got."

"Then God help her," said Henry.

33

Late Tuesday night, Jane was finishing the table setup for the morning meal in the restaurant's main dining room when Cordelia breezed in looking flushed and excited.

"Where have you been?" she demanded, placing a hand over her heart and pausing to catch her breath.

"Right here," said Jane. "All evening."

"Where's your cell phone?"

"On my belt where it always is." When she reached for it, she saw that it was missing. "Ooops. Must have left it downstairs in my office."

Exuding a vast arctic chill, Cordelia crossed her arms over her chest. "I've been trying to reach you for hours."

"Sorry about that."

"I don't know why I gave you that damn thing if you're not going to use it."

"Look, Cordelia, it's the first time I haven't had it with me in days."

"This is an emergency!"

Jane had the sneaking suspicion that Cordelia would have a lot more emergencies now that she was instantly available. Maybe the cell phone would need to have an unexplained technical breakdown sometime in the near future.

"Come on," said Jane, motioning for Cordelia to follow her. "I'm done here, and I think we could use some privacy." They pushed through the swinging kitchen doors and took the back stairway down to her office.

As Jane unlocked her office door, Mouse bounded over the back of the couch. Jane crouched down and gave him a good scratch.

"What's that?" asked Cordelia, clearly taken aback.

"A dog."

"I can *see* that. What's it doing in here?"

"He was lost. I found him the other night, took him home and cleaned him up. He had some tags on him so I called his owner, but so far, I haven't heard back."

Cordelia inched away as Mouse sniffed her shoes. "Nice doggie." She patted his head. "He's kind of . . . big."

"He's larger than my terriers were. But for a Lab, he's small."

"Nice boy." Surreptitiously, she wiped her hand on the side of her cape. "What's his name?"

"Mouse. Or—to be exact—M. Mouse."

"How French. What's the M. stand for?"

Jane shrugged. "Got me."

Cordelia was a cat person through and through, but she generally tolerated dogs well. "Mouse is a terrible name for a dog."

"You'd prefer Spot? Rover?"

"I will ignore your sarcasm, Jane. If the owner doesn't turn up, will you keep him?"

"In a minute," said Jane, hugging him to her. Mouse gave her cheek an affectionate lick.

"He obviously likes you."

"The feeling's mutual." Straightening up, she closed the door. "So, tell me what's up?"

Cordelia flipped off her cape and draped herself across the couch. "You'll never *believe* what I found out today."

Jane sat down next to her. Mouse put his head in her lap to get a few more scratches. "What?"

"Well, last night I got to thinking. You and the police seem to be mired in your 'investigation period,' but there has to be a quicker way to get us the information we want. So, I dug out my Ouija board."

"Oh, Cordelia," groaned Jane.

She held up her hand. "Just wait. Okay, so, I dimmed the lights, surrounded the board with small votive candles, and then draped a silk shawl over my shoulders. Given the opportunity, I always prefer intuition to reason, instinct to plodding cerebration. I haven't become one of the great theatrical geniuses of my generation by relying on slavish, left-brained analysis."

Jane just nodded. When Cordelia got going, she was like a runaway train. You either leapt off the tracks, or you got run over.

"I got right to the point—asked the Ouija board what the Midnight Man's name was. The board spelled out *wrong man*. Well, I already knew that. It's not like the board to simply state the obvious, so I asked another question, politely emphasizing my need to have an actual name—like Henry, Conrad or Barrett."

"And?"

"If a Ouija board could hem and haw, this one did. It finally spelled out the word *vile*. Again, accurate, but not very helpful. Is it Conrad Alto? I asked. The little shuttle didn't move. What about Barrett Sweeny? Still nothing. Suddenly, it was as if someone had picked up my hand and thrust it back at me. The candles even flickered. I felt like I was in an Ann Rice novel."

"Really."

"Yes, *really*. I decided to make the next question a little more general. I said, What can I do to help? This time, the answer came in a flash. *Tarot,* it spelled. That was it, Janey! I was amazed I hadn't thought of it myself. I called the Amazing Zarda right away and made an appointment for this afternoon."

Jane's eyes rose slowly to Cordelia's. "Why, exactly, should I care?"

"Because nobody but the cosmos had control of the cards this time."

She shook her head. "So what did you learn? Is my family going to be devoured by hyenas? Attacked by deer flies? Maybe Zarda should toss in the plagues of Egypt for good measure."

"Jane—"

"How about this? The Five of Cups will dance with the Seven of Swords and give birth to a new kind of blender."

"Are you finished?"

"No."

"Do you want to know what I learned?"

"Not if it came from a bunch of cards."

Cordelia looked down at Mouse, who was trying to ooze his way up on the couch without being noticed. "Look, we did a yes/no reading. You pick out all the major arcana and use just them. Each one has a meaning—either yes, no, or maybe."

Mouse was lying between them now, his head in Cordelia's lap, his rear end in Jane's.

"Why can't it just be yes or no?" asked Jane.

"The cards apparently need a little wiggle room. I can see the disbelief in your eyes, Jane. And it pains me."

"It's not disbelief. It's disgust."

"Well, whatever it is," said Cordelia, her voice just above a whisper, "get this. I asked three questions. Is Conrad Alto the Midnight Man? Is Barrett Sweeny? Is Henry Alto?"

"And?"

"It was inconclusive."

"Figures."

"Except in one case. Conrad Alto's card was the Devil, which means no."

"That makes me feel so much better, Cordelia. Conrad Alto is the Devil, but he's not a murderer."

"Zarda said that the meaning of the card wasn't important in this kind of spread—just the yes or no value. I did some checking when I got back to the theater. Looked up some sites on the Internet. Talked to a couple of friends. The upshot is, I think she's wrong. The larger meaning of the card *is* important." Cordelia retrieved a page of notes from the pocket of her cardigan. "Ready?"

"If I said no, would you stop?"

"Of course not." Cordelia flapped the page out in front of her. "Now. Conrad Alto's card was the Devil. In essence, this has to do with illusion, with being a slave to desires that overpower innate good judgment, with sexual obsession."

"What's that got to do with Conrad Alto? With the Midnight Man?"

"Let me finish. This image of the devil isn't the one we're used to in Christianity. The devil of the tarot is related to the Greek god Pan. He wasn't a god of evil, but of excess, of wild abandon. Remember that Pan's pipes supposedly drove people to a wild sexual frenzy."

Jane assumed she must be missing something. "Are you saying that when people listen to Conrad Alto's organ music, his playing incites orgies? If that's true, it's the best-kept secret in the Twin Cities. Hey, maybe we should attend church at Grace Cathedral next Sunday. See what's really going on."

"I know you're mocking me, Jane, but there's an important meaning in here somewhere. We just have to find it. Now, to continue, Henry Alto's card was the Moon."

"A maybe card?"

"Right. But the moon doesn't give much light. It's hard to see by. One book I read said the moon moves in hidden ways."

"Meaning Henry is a tricky one. Hard to see clearly."

"Bravo, Jane. Now you're getting into it. The moon leads us on a journey of instincts, dreams and primal emotions. Henry *could* be our man. Or, he could simply be a guide, a dim light helping us see just enough to keep going."

"*He's* not leading us anywhere. That has no meaning."

"Sure it does," said Cordelia, although she looked less than certain.

Jane thought it was all a bunch of mystical blather. She wanted to take Mouse and go home, but she couldn't insult Cordelia by just walking out. She had to sit through this recitation, pointless as it was. "And what about Barrett?"

"His card was the Hierophant."

"The what?"

"It's like a high priest."

"Barrett sells *houses*, Cordelia."

"Don't be so literal." She sat up straight, giving her sweater a yank. "This was another 'maybe' card. Could be yes, could be no. It didn't strike me as important at the time, but later I realized the card came up reversed. That gives it a special meaning. See, the Hierophant symbolizes the religious teachings of our culture. You always see him with disciples, which could be significant. The Hierophant suggests orthodoxy, but reversed, it becomes a symbol for those who seek their own path through life rather than following the one that society dictates. And that *could* be Barrett. It could also describe the Midnight Man."

"The Midnight Man is a sociopath. He wouldn't have an inner life because he doesn't have human emotions."

"But he might have an *intellectual* inner life. Sociopaths know the difference between right and wrong, they just don't care. Human *feeling* isn't there. But human intellect is."

"We're boring deeply into twigs, Cordelia. It's all interesting, but it gets us nowhere."

Squaring her shoulders, Cordelia huffed. "Sometimes you are *such* a wet blanket."

As if to punctuate the statement, Jane's cell phone rang.

"Hey, that's where it is," she said, digging it out from between the couch cushions. "I better answer it." Since it was getting late, she wondered what was up. "Hello?"

A male voice on the other end of the line said, "I'd like to speak with Jane Lawless."

"This is Jane."

"Hi. My name is Eddy Dellman. I believe you have my dog."

Jane's heart instantly sank. This was the call she'd hoped would never come.

"He's a black Lab, about fifty pounds. White spot on his chest."

"That's him," said Jane, running her hand gently across Mouse's fur. "I found him on Forty-sixth and Pillsbury."

The man sighed. "I don't believe it. That's where we used to live. I got divorced about a year ago. My wife and daughter moved to Anoka. Mouse and I moved into a duplex on Cedar Avenue. I travel a lot with my job. When I'm gone, the boy downstairs feeds the dog and let's him out. He plays with him too, mostly after school. It's worked out okay until this last trip."

"You must have been gone a long time."

"Two weeks."

Jane looked at Mouse. That was no life for a dog.

"The kid downstairs was really upset. I guess the gate was open and the dog got out. He looked all over for him, but couldn't find him. I was in Europe, so there wasn't much I could do. I didn't even know he was missing until I got home a couple of hours ago. I'm glad somebody found him. He's a good dog."

An understatement.

"I want to thank you for taking him in. I'd be happy to offer you a reward."

"I don't want money," she said, feeling more depressed with each passing second.

"You must be a dog lover."

"I am."

"Yeah, I wish I had more time for the big guy. We bought him for my daughter three Christmases ago. He was a puppy then. Real cute. When I got divorced, my wife moved into a place that doesn't allow dogs. Too bad, really. Mouse misses my little girl a lot. She only comes to stay once a month, and she's into cats now, so Mouse isn't such a big deal anymore."

"I'm sorry to hear that." Jane felt like her brain had switched to auto pilot. She was saying the right words, but they had no meaning.

"But then, I couldn't just give him away. I made a commitment to him when I bought him. I figure, if I eat, he eats. If I don't, neither does he. We're in it together."

"Sure."

"So, your message said you live in Linden Hills. I'm real close to there right now. I'd like to come by and pick him up if it's okay with you."

Something inside Jane seized up. She couldn't respond. All she could do was stare at the dog. Mouse climbed down off the couch. He sat down in front of her, pawing her knee. God, but she loved him. She couldn't stand the thought that he was leaving.

"Ms. Lawless?"

Cordelia put her hand on Jane's arm. *Is something wrong?* she mouthed.

Jane gave the man the address of the restaurant. She added, "You know, if you ever need a baby-sitter for him, I'd be happy to take him for a day, a week—whatever."

"Thanks, but no thanks. I'll make sure he doesn't get out again."

"If you ever decide to sell him—"

"I won't. We're a team. I'd miss him if he wasn't around."

For the five freaking minutes a week you're probably home, thought Jane.

"So, I'll be by in about ten minutes. That okay?"

"Fine."

She clicked off the phone.

Mouse was whining softly. It wasn't fair. He lived with the disappearing man, and now here she was, burdening him with *her* pain.

"I take it that was the dog's owner," said Cordelia.

Jane gave a stiff nod.

"Are you okay?"

"No."

"You wanted to keep him, didn't you?"

"Of course I did."

"I'm sorry, Janey. I really am. Finding him right now was bad timing. I mean, you just lost Bean."

"I'll be okay."

"Sure you will. It's just . . . too bad."

Running her hands up and down Mouse's fur, Jane said, "You're going home, buddy. Isn't that great?"

He just looked up at her.

"You're going home," she said again, this time getting down on her hands and knees and hugging him.

34

It was just after midnight. Jane sat at a table in a dark corner of the pub, nursing a beer. She felt morose, resentful, and incredibly fragile. Going home without Mouse was intolerable. Bedding down in her office, trying to sleep, was impossible.

She refused to cry in front of Ed Dellman, even though she felt like it. She'd wished Mouse a good life, kissed the top of his head and sent him off. On the way out the door, he'd stopped and turned around to look at her. Jane could read it all in his face. He liked Dellman well enough, was happy to see him, but he didn't want to leave her any more than she wanted him to go. He said goodbye in the only way he knew how—with his eyes, his body, his drooping tail. It was painful to see him looking so torn. She tried to give off happy vibes, but it was no use. Her heart twisted as Dellman led him away.

Dellman didn't get it—didn't realize how hard it was for her to see the dog leave. Not that he should. Never one to miss a personal drama, Cordelia had stayed to watch the tragic scene, to hold Jane's hand until the music swelled and the curtain fell. There was nothing anyone could say or do. Mouse was back with his owner and that was the end of it. It would take some time, but Jane would get over it. She always did.

Instead of ordering another beer and wallowing a while longer, she decided to go for a drive. The night was clear and cold, lit by a full moon ringed with a pale haze. She didn't have any destination in mind, but when she turned onto a quiet street just off Fairlawn in Edina, she realized she was only two blocks from Shirley Alto's house. In her subconscious, she must have wanted to take a look at the place. She'd already driven past the homes of the three suspects—Henry, Barrett and Conrad. In Jane's opinion, Shirley was just an innocent bystander. She had nothing to do with the crimes, although, if Henry turned out to be the man, she'd raised a serial killer.

Jane approached the colonial slowly, cautiously, drawn by her curiosity. As she passed directly in front of the house, she noticed that a light was on in a second-story window. She pulled over to the curb and switched off her headlights. A moment later the light inside the house went off and the window was drawn up. A dark form crawled through the opening out to the roof.

Jane cut the motor, watching the figure hoist itself over a balcony railing, then shimmy down between the drainpipe and the chimney, finally finding firm footing on a square, sturdy looking trellis. Once down on the ground, Jane could see that it was definitely a woman, young, with blond hair. When the young woman fell, Jane pushed out of the front seat and darted across the street.

"Are you okay?" she whispered, stopping a few feet away.

"Go away," said a thin voice. The young woman eased into a crouching position, but didn't get up. She was breathing hard.

Jane waited a few seconds, unsure what to do. Finally, she said, "Look, I know this house belongs to Shirley Alto."

Large, fever-bright eyes stared out at her. "You a friend of hers?"

"No. We've never met."

"Then what are you doing here?"

Before Jane could answer, the young woman stood up, swaying so violently that Jane feared she might fall down again.

"Don't tell her I left!"

"I won't tell anyone."

Steadying herself, the young woman looked around.

Jane could tell she was about to bolt. "Why are you leaving like this? In the middle of the night?"

"Keep your voice down, okay?"

"Sure, but—"

"I've got to get out of here before I get caught. They're after me! They want to commit me to a loony bin!"

Jane touched her arm.

The young woman twisted around, as if the touch had been a blow. Her hand trembled as she brushed a lock of hair away from her eyes. Hesitantly she said, "He told me to stand at the window. Leave the lights on and just stand there. Somebody would come to help. But I couldn't wait. I had to get out."

Jane was confused, but tried to sound sympathetic. "Who told you that?"

"My boyfriend. They drugged me. Henry did. He gave me something to make me sleep. He seems so nice sometimes, not like the others, but it's all a game with them. I'm all alone. I've got nobody to help me except Bobby."

"Bobby? Bobby Alto?"

"Yes!"

"But . . . Bobby Alto's dead."

"Not to me he isn't!"

Jane took a chance. "Are you . . . Taylor Jensen?"

She didn't answer, but once again seemed ready to run.

Jane wasn't sure what she was getting herself into, but she couldn't stop herself. If this young woman had been drugged by the Alto family, perhaps she knew something they didn't want anyone else to know about. "Let me help you."

"I want to go to my brother's house. He lives in Duluth. He'll take me in. But I don't have any money." Her voice grew more strident with each word. Jane had to calm her down or they'd both get caught.

"Come with me," said Jane, trying to sound encouraging.

"Are you the one Bobby said would come?"

"Yes." She knew it was what Taylor wanted to hear. She motioned for her to follow.

They spoke little on the way back to Jane's place. Taylor seemed unfocused, perhaps as a result of whatever drug she'd been given. Jane hoped that when the medication wore off, she'd be more lucid, more able to explain what was going on.

Helping Taylor into her house, Jane sat her down on the couch, then quickly built a fire in the fireplace. They were both chilled to the bone. "Have you eaten anything today?" she asked, covering the young woman with a quilt.

"I . . . don't remember. I don't think so."

Jane left her there and went into the kitchen to put on the coffee pot. While it brewed, she made some sandwiches. The green tennis ball lying on the floor in front of the refrigerator, the one Mouse had been playing with earlier in the day, was a mute reminder that he was gone and wasn't coming back. She kicked it into the dining room and tried to put it out of her mind.

Returning to the living room with a tray of sandwiches and two steaming mugs of coffee, Jane set everything down on an end table. "You'll feel better if you eat something."

Taylor moved her head stiffly to the side as Jane sat down. "Who *are* you?"

"My name's Jane Lawless."

"Lawless?" repeated the young woman.

"My father is Raymond Lawless. He represented Bobby at his trial."

Her eyes narrowed.

"Drink some coffee," said Jane, handing her the mug.

Taylor blinked a couple of times, then accepted the cup. She took a sip. "It tastes good. Thanks." Picking up half a sandwich, she nibbled at it absently. "Why would you of all people want to help me? Conrad said your father thought Bobby was guilty. That's why he did such a bad job of defending him."

Jane let the comment pass. She assumed Conrad Alto had said lots of terrible things about her father. "Look, Taylor, I believe Bobby was innocent. He should never have been convicted."

"He *was* innocent," she agreed. "Even the police think that now."

"Whoever the Midnight Man turns out to be, he's been targeting my family. I'm part of this, Taylor. I don't want to be, but I am."

Taylor finished her sandwich before she spoke again. She seemed to be working something out in her mind. "Did you know that I was Bobby's girlfriend?"

"Yes," said Jane.

She set the coffee mug down. "When he was sent to jail, he asked Barrett to take care of me. He trusted Barrett. And . . . he trusted me. But it was such a long trial. And then, after he was convicted and the appeal process began, it started to seem like forever. I was . . . totally lonely." She lowered her head. "And Barrett, he's a very, well, sexual man. Do you understand what I'm saying?"

"I think so," said Jane.

"I was unfaithful to Bobby with my body, but never with my mind." She looked up defiantly. "I loved Bobby. He was a wonderful man. A kind man. He didn't deserve what happened to him."

"I know it must have been hard for you," said Jane.

"When I first met him, I was working on a degree in communications at the university, living with three women in a crummy rundown apartment. I could only take a few classes a quarter because I had to work almost full-time. After we got together, my life changed for the better. Bobby and I moved in together. I only had to work part-time. But after he was arrested, I dropped all my classes because I couldn't concentrate. You don't how terrible it was for me. And now, that family of his, they want to commit me to some mental hospital. Do you know why?"

Jane shook her head.

"Bobby's haunting me! He's been appearing to me, mostly at night. I hear his voice and then, sometimes, I see his form in the corner of the room. It's never very distinct, but I know it's him. He says he still loves me, but that he has to haunt me because he's so angry and I'm the only person who will let him through. He was cheated out of his life."

"By whom?"

"He never says. That's odd, isn't it? But it's someone he loved. He says he can't rest until that person is punished. Not that Bobby will ever find much rest. The other side isn't anything like we think. Bobby says it's cold and it's dark, and full of violence. There is no heaven or hell, no houses or warmth, just space. These groups of beings are at war with each other. He never feels safe. He's being forced to pick a side, even though he doesn't want to. It's all about religion and doctrine and history. He's not interested in any of it, but he says he'll go where his grandparents are because they love him and want him with them. Being with his family is the only good part. He says that if he fights hard for his side, there's a higher plane he can get to where there's no fighting or suffering or religion, at least that's what he's heard, but he doesn't understand it very well yet because he's been so tied up with what's happening back here. He's being allowed to stay close to the earth so he can get revenge. I guess revenge is something the other side understands."

"That's awful," said Jane, feeling a sudden chill.

"I'm not crazy, Jane. I'm not. I don't want him to appear anymore because it frightens me. I don't like what he says."

"You know his family. You must have some thoughts on what's really going on."

She picked up the the mug again and held it with both hands, taking little sips as she thought it over. "It's kind of hard for me to believe that anybody I know could have done the stuff the Midnight Man did. I mean, they're just people. Sometimes they're funny, sometimes they're serious. Barrett likes to eat French fries. Always French fries. Every tie he's got has ketchup stains on it. Henry is part of a bowling league. And he likes to collect rocks. Conrad is crazy about gardening. They all seem pretty ordinary. And yet—" Her voice trailed off.

"What?" said Jane, sensing that she wanted to be coaxed.

In a protective gesture, Taylor pulled her legs up close to her body. "Sometimes, when Bobby and I would make love, I'd notice these marks on his back."

"What kind of marks?"

"Like he'd been whipped."

"Did you ask him about it?"

"I tried, but he said it was personal. He refused to talk about it. But then later, when I was sleeping with Barrett, he had the same marks. Not all the time, but enough so that I noticed it."

"What did Barrett say about the marks?"

"I never asked him. You don't know Barrett. I could always sense when he didn't want to discuss something. He may be an extrovert, but he's also very closed off emotionally with rigid boundaries."

"What do you think was going on?"

"I don't know."

"But you must have some opinion."

Taylor hesitated. After a few seconds, she said, "Well, there was this one time. It was a month or so after Bobby and I first met. We were supposed to have dinner together, but he left me a message saying he couldn't make it. We weren't living together then. His dad hadn't bought him the house yet. I thought maybe he had a date with someone else. I guess I was already feeling kind of possessive, so I drove over to his apartment. I got lucky 'cause he was just coming out the front door. I made sure he didn't see me and then I followed him. He drove out of the city to this secluded, really fancy house on Lake Minnetonka. He parked his car in the drive next to a couple of other cars.

"After he disappeared inside, I went over to the mailbox and saw that the house belonged to Barrett. I'd met Barrett a couple of times, so I knew he was a good friend of Bobby's. It was pitch dark outside, early fall, and all the lights were on inside the house. The curtains were open, so it was pretty easy to see in. From what I could tell, there were four men—Bobby and Barrett, and then two others. Later I realized that the men I didn't know were Bobby's brother, Henry, and Conrad, his father. Anyway, I went back to my car and sat for a while. I was curious to see if any women showed up. About half an hour later, the lights started going off, one by one. I rolled the window down so I could get a better view of the picture window, but just as I did, the curtain was pulled.

"That's when I heard this booming organ music start up. It was really spooky. Reminded me of a horror movie. I knew Bobby's father played the organ because Bobby had played some of his CDs for me, so I wondered if his dad was one of the other guys. I sat in my car for a while longer, but then I started getting antsy, so I climbed out and crept up to the house. Like I said, all the curtains and shades were pulled, but I could see this one window way in the back of that house had a gap in the curtains and there was a dim light coming from inside. I had to stand on a clay pot to see in." She stopped, as if something about the memory upset her.

"What did you see?" asked Jane.

She gazed into the fire with a far-off look in her eyes. "They'd all stripped to their waists and were kneeling in a circle, passing around a cup. It was more of a chalice, really. They looked very solemn, like it was some kind of ritual. The room was lit with candles, nothing else, so the light was flickering. It made their faces look totally strange."

"Did they pass the cup around only once?"

"No, they kept passing it back and forth. It was silver, I think. And there was an alter in the corner with a figure on it. I couldn't make it out. I thought maybe it was something Bobby had cast.

And they were all wearing chains around their necks with a pendant hanging from it."

"Could you see the pendants?"

"I was too far away."

"What happened next?"

"They set the cup down on the floor, and then they held hands. They started to sway to the music. That's when I fell off the pot. They must have heard the noise because a few seconds later, the music stopped. I rushed into the woods just as Barrett came outside to look around. He had a flashlight with him, but thankfully, he never shined it in my direction. As soon as the coast was clear, I was out of there."

"Did you ever talk to Bobby about it?"

She shook her head. "I didn't want him to think I was checking up on him. He felt trapped by so many things, and I never wanted to pressure him."

"To your knowledge, did the four of them ever do it again?"

"I never saw them do it again, but I think they did. Some nights, when Bobby would come home late, he'd be really secretive. He wouldn't tell me where he'd been, and he wouldn't want to touch me, to make love. He'd tell me to go to bed without him. Then he'd sit up until the wee hours, drinking wine and listening to music. Bach, mostly. Sometimes Mozart or Handel. Always religious music. It's funny, he was a religious man, but he never attended church. But he talked a lot about good and evil, about morals and . . . destiny. All the time, destiny. I'm not much for philosophy myself, so I never listened very carefully. I think he actually liked that about me. I didn't agonize over ideas the way he did. He was a very intense guy, but he relaxed with me, and I thought that was good for him."

"I'm sure it was," said Jane. "But getting back to your story, when you saw Bobby with his shirt off after that night, did you notice if he had marks on his back?"

She nodded. "He did. They faded with time and I forgot about it. But then, sometimes, they'd be back."

"When you saw the four of them together, did it ever appear that one or the other was the leader?"

"Oh, Barrett. For sure. I know this sounds kind of strong, but sometimes it seemed like they almost idolized the guy. I thought it was totally weird. I mean, he was so full of himself. But then, after we got together, I saw another side of him. He could be really kind and gentle. I started to think I'd been wrong, that he wasn't just Mr. Arrogant.

"After Bobby was arrested, I went to visit him in jail. He told me to listen to Barrett and do what he said, that Barrett would look out for me until he was released. I believed him. Eventually, I moved in with Barrett. Like I said, it took a while, but we ended up in bed. It was all pretty normal at first, but one night, well, things got kind of strange. Barrett brought out this leather whip and wanted me to beat him with it. He said it was a big turn-on. I did it, just like he asked, but only once. He wanted to use it on me the next night, but I refused. After that, he got real cold. It went on like that for months. I know this sounds terrible, but I missed him. I mean, he'd been my friend for a long time and I just didn't get it.

"Then when Bobby died, Barrett got nicer again. I thought maybe he'd forgiven me for refusing to have that kinky sex. Maybe he felt guilty. Whatever it was, he started taking me out to dinner again. We slept together a few times—vanilla sex, he called it. I knew it was a slam, but I was so alone. He was familiar, and he could be so wonderful sometimes, make you feel like you were the only person in the world. I wanted him to be like he used to be. For a while I thought we might even get married, but eventually I realized it wasn't going to happen. The worst part was, I didn't have a dime. He'd been giving me money because I'd quit my job, but I knew things couldn't go on like that forever. Bobby was gone. And Barrett was never one to let grass grow under his feet when it came to women. I was past history. Used goods. He didn't come out and say it exactly, but I knew he totally wanted me to leave.

"That's when Bobby started haunting me. I lost it, Jane. I admit it. When the clock struck midnight, I'd get all scared and weepy. I thought I was losing my mind. A few times I thought Barrett was scared too. He wanted to know everything Bobby said to me. But then later, he'd just shrug it off. I'd applied for a bunch of jobs, but I couldn't seem to find anything. All the while, I realized Barrett was just biding his time, waiting to get rid of me. When I totally freaked one night, he took me over to Henry's house and dumped me there. Henry was really tired. He'd been working a twelve-hour shift, so he took me to his dad's. I've been bouncing back and forth from house to house ever since. And now I find out they want to commit me. I had to get the hell out."

"Is Bobby still haunting you?"

She shook her head. "The last few days have been quiet. But I'm still so weepy, I cry at the drop of a hat. Henry asked me yesterday if I felt guilty about anything. He said that sometimes guilt did odd things to people. If I did feel guilty, he said it was a waste of time. I should just get on with my life. Bobby would have wanted that."

"Maybe it's good advice," said Jane.

Taylor didn't respond.

After getting up to toss another log on the fire, Jane said, "Why don't you stay here tonight? You don't have anywhere else you'd rather be, right?"

She shrugged. "No."

"In the morning, we'll call the bus depot, find out when the next bus is leaving for Duluth. Then you can call your brother and tell him when you'll be arriving."

Taylor hung her head. "I don't have enough money to buy a ticket."

"I'll take care of it," said Jane. "Don't worry. You've had a rough time. I meant what I said before. I'd like to help."

"But . . . you're totally a stranger."

"Who knows," said Jane, giving the fire a good stoke. "Maybe I really am the person Bobby told you to watch for, the one who would come to help."

"Yeah," said Taylor, tossing the hair out of her eyes. "Cool."

35

I suppose you've heard the news by now," said Henry. He slipped his hand into the pocket of his sport coat, but stopped himself. "Look, I realize you don't want people to smoke in your office, but I'm not sure I can get through our session today without a cigarette."

Dr. Kirsch leaned back in her chair. "Are you tense, Henry?"

"I am."

"Go ahead, then. We'll make an exception." She took an ashtray out of her drawer, placed it on the desk and pushed it toward him.

He tapped a cigarette out of the packet and lit up. Drawing the smoke deep into his lungs, he felt instantly centered. One more draw and the calming effect took hold. Crossing one leg over the other, he said, "You've heard that the police have changed their mind about Bobby. Now they think someone else in my family is the Midnight Man. 'Ooops. Wrong guy. Sorry about that.' "

"You sound bitter."

"You're damn right I am. They ruin that kid's life and now they change their minds? Life isn't a blackboard, doctor. You don't just get to erase your mistakes and start over." He paused to tap the ash off his cigarette. "In the past week, the police have hauled me in twice to question me. Ditto for Barrett and Dad. They've searched our houses, our cars, our workplaces. They've even put a tail on us."

Dr. Kirsch gazed at him intently. "I've been following the case in the news. You know, Henry, when you first came in, you said that you'd lied to the police. My guess is that part of your anger is directed at yourself because you're feeling guilty. Perhaps it's time you told me the truth."

Henry studied her face through the smoke from his cigarette. "I'm a liar," he said without preamble. "I lied to the police. I lied to my mother. I lie all the time. How can you believe anything I say?"

"But you haven't lied to me, have you Henry?"

"No. Everything I've told you, subjective as it was, is the truth. It's just . . . I haven't told you the whole truth. That's just another form of lying."

"Then go on with your story. I want to help you, but I can't unless I know what's really going on."

He shifted in his chair. Studying the tip of his cigarette, he said, "Have you ever read the novel *Demian* by Hermann Hesse?"

She shook her head. "But you mentioned Hesse once before."

Drawing on his cigarette, he continued, "Remember I told you about the trip my dad took Bobby and Barrett and me on? The one to Italy?"

She nodded. "You spent your time searching for the relics of Catholic saints."

"We also spent time reading that book. Barrett called it his bible. He said he never went anywhere without it. We ended up passing it around and eventually found ourselves talking about it. We couldn't *stop* talking about it."

"Why is that, Henry?" She looked at him with eyebrows lifted.

He hated her patient, therapeutic tone. She was so caught up in her role, she couldn't see this moment for what it was. *The hell with her*. "Well, for me," he went on, "it was like looking into a mirror. It was *my* story. I thought I was the only one who'd ever felt like that, but I was wrong. I've always been an outsider. Especially in high school, although I still feel that way even now. The book is a fairy tale, a memoir, a poem. It's about a small group of like-minded souls, guys who hook up because they have a complete lack of desire to conform to the accepted moral codes. In the book, each of the main characters is seeking self-discovery according to the dictates of his own inner nature. There's no pity in the novel, no false compassion. But the most important thing about it was that it introduced us all to Abraxas."

"Who's that?"

"An ancient god. The Gnostics worshiped Abraxas—so did the Egyptians and the Romans. It appealed to the four of us because with Abraxas, you don't have to rationalize away the existence of evil in the world. You can simply accept it as part of the whole. Abraxas is half god, half devil. Apollo and Dionysus all rolled into one. He represents a mystery, an enigma—the marriage of good and evil, love and hate, silence and madness. Three-six-five was his number—that's why Bobby put it on the back of the pendant." He waited a moment, hoping his words would penetrate. "The early Catholics attacked the Gnostic faith, tried to stamp it out, so it went underground. Gnostic thought eventually resurfaced through the writings of Carl Jung. Hesse was a friend of Jung's. I think he even sought therapy from him, so some of these ancient ideas took seed in Hesse's works."

"That's very interesting, Henry. But can you tie it all together for me? Help me understand what it has to do with you and your life right now?"

"I thought that would be obvious. Barrett, Bobby, my dad and me—we became a group of seekers, just like in the book."

The therapist folded her hands on the desk top. "Go on."

"Over time, the four of us developed our own mysteries, our own rituals. Barrett was the leader, the master, but more than anything, we felt as if we were brothers. Those pendants everyone's been talking about, the image on them was from the novel. I still have mine on." Henry reached under his polo shirt and lifted out a leather cord. Attached to it was the now-familiar pendant. "Bobby admitted to the police that he made a bunch of them, but he refused to tell what the image meant. We all respected him for that. It was a deeply private issue of faith. And besides, nobody would have understood. They would have thought he was nuts. He made so many of them because we all thought that someday, we'd run into other people who were just like us. If they joined us, we'd give them one. That's why it had to be beautiful—and valuable." He took a drag from his cigarette. "Bobby also made another decision." Henry could see the eagerness in Dr. Kirsch's expression and it sickened him. "I think he knew who the Midnight Man was, but he kept his mouth shut. Quite frankly, we all did."

"You all knew?"

"Let's say we suspected."

"Did your beliefs prevent you from coming forward?"

"No," said Henry, exhaling smoke.

"Then . . . I don't understand. Why did you allow your brother, an innocent man, to be put in jail for the rest of his life when you could have saved him?"

Leaning forward in his chair, Henry tapped a bit of ash into the ashtray, then sat back again. "Do you really want to know?"

"Yes."

Looking thoughtfully through a thread of smoke, he began, "My father has an obsession with order, doctor. He passed that obsession on to Bobby and me. My mother called him controlling, and I suppose he was. I see that quality in myself all the time. Can you understand, then, how the concept of loss of control could fascinate people like us?

"It started so innocently. We were in Pianella. It was late summer—almost fall. The air was magnificently soft. I remember that somewhere off in the distance, wood was burning. We could smell it in our hotel rooms. None of us could stay inside that night. Have you ever noticed that woodsmoke has the quality of memory in it, doctor? It's primal. We decided to have a moonlit picnic. Dad packed several bottles of wine for us—and a bottle of fine French cognac for him—along with some cheese, olives and bread, and we hopped in his rental car and drove until we found a empty field bordered by a small wood. We walked for a while until we found a suitable spot to spread our blanket. Dad had brought several flashlights, but we didn't need them because the moon was so bright.

"As Bobby was uncorking the first bottle of wine, Barrett opened his backpack and took out a bottle of a fruit drink he'd bought in town. He insisted that we all taste it. He laughed, said there was magic in it. I thought it was pretty good. And Bobby liked it, but Dad thought it was too sweet. After we finished it, we started in on the wine and food. I got drunk pretty fast. I closed my eyes and listened to the rest of them talk, but I wasn't really concentrating. When I finally opened my eyes, everything had changed. The meadow where we were sitting was bathed in this amazing celestial moonlight. I asked what Barrett had put in the fruit drink. He laughed again. 'A potion to loosen us up,' he said. His face was as radiant as an angel's. Something was happening to me, but I didn't know what. The woods shimmered. I felt a presence hovering at the edges of my vision—something light and unearthly, but I couldn't get a good look at it. Whenever I would turn my head, it would flutter away. I was drunk with beauty. I had these odd, almost erotic sensations coursing through my body. At the same time, I had the sense that I was on the cusp of understanding something I'd never understood before. I couldn't have defined it. I still can't, and I've experienced it dozens of times since that first night.

"When I finally looked around, I saw that everyone had stripped down to their waists.

" 'Take off your shirt,' said Barrett.

"I don't know why, but I did it. It seemed totally reasonable.

"Then he said, 'I've always wanted to experience the divine.

That's what those saints were after. Divine ecstasy. I think they knew more about how to get there than we ever realized.' He reached into his backpack and pulled out a leather flog. 'If we follow their example, who knows? Maybe we'll get there too. I think the key is cleansing. We can't invite the divine into our bodies unless we've purged them.'

"Bobby was like a sweet, adoring spaniel around Barrett. He would have done anything for him, so he volunteered. We ran to the wood, tied him to a tree with a rope Barrett had brought with him, then took turns whipping him. We did it until he cried. Then Barrett stood in front of him and whispered something. I didn't hear it. We were all still drinking, but had moved to Dad's cognac by then. When my turn came, I accepted the pain. Everything grew white and empty inside me. There wasn't a sound in all the world except for the sting of the leather hitting my skin. I closed my eyes and prayed for enlightenment. When it was all over, Barrett stepped in front of me, just as he had with Bobby. He put his hands on the sides of my face and kissed me, first on the eyelids, then on the lips. I could smell his sweat, feel my body respond to his touch. Then he leaned even closer and whispered in my ear the last words from the novel, altering them slightly. 'I found the key, Henry. And now, when I bend over the dark mirror to behold my soul, I see you, my brother, my master." His voice was ineffably tender. At that moment, I loved him more than I thought I could ever love anyone.

"After the flogging was finished, we built a bonfire. I don't recall every detail of what happened next, but I know that it was glorious. There was a terrible pressure in the air, and a noise inside my head. I could see us swaying together in front of the fire almost as if I were above us, outside my body. I was always a greedy child, and I was greedy for each new sensation, each revelation.

"When I woke up the next morning to the first rays of sunlight, I was lying in the field about twenty feet from my father. I was naked and bruised and chilled to the bone. I felt like I'd been in a street fight. But I was also fundamentally altered—forever. From that day on, I was bound to those three men in a way that transcended family or blood. They've become part of my destiny. That's why, when Bobby was arrested, I couldn't tell the police what I suspected. What I . . . knew."

Dr. Kirsch was silent.

"Do you see now? Do you understand what I'm telling you?"

"I'm sorry, Henry, but I don't."

He turned his head away.

"You had some sort of religious experience that obviously turned sexual, fueled by drugs and alcohol. If I'm reading between the lines correctly, it's a ritual the four of you have participated in again, perhaps many times. Maybe you do gain something spiritual from the experience, though you must know how bizarre it is."

Henry turned to look at her. "You're wrong."

"I'm no longer speaking as your therapist, Henry, I'm speaking as a human being. If this is what you've been lying to everyone about, I understand why you wouldn't tell the truth. Your problem isn't with lying, Henry, it's with your behavior. I'd like to think you simply followed the wrong man."

"I didn't follow anyone!"

"It sounds like Barrett is the one who led you into these experiences. Is he the one you're all protecting?"

"No."

"I wish you would tell me the truth, Henry. You'll never begin to heal unless you admit what's really happened."

"Look, doctor, whatever I think I know means nothing because I have no proof. Neither do you. And you can't tell the police what I've confided to you because our relationship is therapeutic."

"Is that why you came here? To confess that you knew Barrett was the Midnight Man? Why didn't you go to a priest, Henry? At least he could have given you absolution."

He shot out of his chair. "I haven't confessed a thing. I told you a story. And I don't need absolution from anyone."

"Perhaps I'm wrong, but I wonder if you've been manipulating me from the very beginning. Have you, Henry? I may be a therapist, but I'm also human. You got my interest by tantalizing me with what you might know about the Midnight Man. But now I see more clearly. I think you feel intense guilt because you let your brother die without lifting a finger to help him. You don't want to turn Barrett in because of some misguided loyalty, but you reached a point where you finally needed to tell someone the truth. That's a healthy sign, Henry. We can work with that."

Henry put his hands over his ears to drown out the sound of her voice.

"What we need now is to move a little closer to your pain. I know it's difficult, but I'm just talking about small steps. Stay with me. I think it's possible that you do have proof of Barrett's guilt. Would you say that's a correct statement? Think hard before you answer."

"I don't!" said Henry. "I swear it."

"Think of yourself for a minute. Your own mental health."

"Coming here was a mistake."

"No it wasn't, Henry. Your instincts were sound. But you have to keep going. We're so close now. Think of the truth as your lifeline. Hold on to it."

"The truth will set me free?"

"Yes!"

Henry was sick of talking, sick to death of the sound of his own voice. "I lied, doctor. Everything I said to you was a lie, from beginning to end. I made it all up."

"I don't believe you."

He couldn't help but smile. "But you'll never really know for sure, will you, doctor? You'll never *really* know."

36

Ray stood in the front office, drinking a cup of coffee and talking to his paralegal, Norm Toscalia. Glancing out the window, he noticed a woman in a red Audi pull into a parking spot across the street. As she got out, she consulted a note in her hand, then looked up at the row houses, searching the numbers until she found the one she wanted.

Ray met her at the door. "Morning," he said, opening it for her. "Can I help you?"

"I'm looking for Raymond Lawless." Her tone was businesslike, almost curt. She was a short, middle-aged woman with brown hair and bangs. Raymond thought she looked a little like Imogene Coca, although nobody would recognize that name nowadays.

"You found him," he said smiling. "What can I do for you?"

It was close to noon. He'd been thinking about asking Elizabeth if she wanted to join him for lunch. He hoped this woman wouldn't nix his plans. He knew Elizabeth had appointments all afternoon, so his window of opportunity was tight.

"I'm Dr. Suzanne Kirsch," she said, extending her hand. "I wonder if we could talk privately. I don't have an appointment, but I assure you it's important."

Ray led her up the stairs to his office. He offered her a cup of coffee, but she declined. She seemed determined to get down to business.

Sitting behind his desk, Ray said, "I assume this is a legal matter."

"Yes . . . and no. I'm a psychotherapist, Mr. Lawless. For the past few weeks, I've been working with a patient who knows a great deal about the Midnight Man homicides. You represented Bobby Alto, is that correct?"

"I did," said Ray, leaning forward in his chair.

"You must understand. Ethically, I can't reveal this person's name to you, or tell you what we've discussed. I'm only allowed to break that confidence if I know for a fact that someone's life is in imminent danger."

"I understand," said Ray.

"You also need to understand that my coming here today falls into a gray area. I've been agonizing over this all morning. Coming here wasn't an easy decision to make. You see, I don't know for a fact that a life is in danger. But I do believe I have a piece of important information. It's something I can't take to the police, for obvious reasons. That's why I came to you."

"Please continue." She had his full attention.

"My client has led me to believe that a certain person is the Midnight Man. I can't go into detail. Suffice it to say, I'm convinced that I know the man's true identity. The problem I have is that I have no actual, tangible proof. Neither does my client. In fact, my client refuses to point the finger at this person, though he's done so in every way but actually naming him."

"Who is it?" asked Ray. "If you know who the Midnight Man is, you've got to tell me."

She hesitated. "First, I want you to promise that you won't directly discuss our conversation with the police."

"For God's sake, just give me the name."

She held his eyes. "It's Barrett Sweeny. I assume you know him."

"Yes, of course I know him."

"I understand the police have been interrogating members of the Alto family, as well as Mr. Sweeny. Their houses have been searched, as well as their places of business, but so far, nothing has been found to tie any of them to the murders."

"Exactly right."

She folded her hands in her lap. "I've spent most of the morning going over the notes I made after the sessions with my patient. I think I may have found something—a place the police may not have searched. It may or may not yield anything definitive, but it should be checked. You understand, I can't give the police this information directly, so I'm asking you to do it for me."

"Sure," said Ray, not even trying to hide his eagerness. "I'd be happy to."

"Mr. Sweeny owns a sailboat. A large one. Do you know if the police are aware of that?"

"They know he loves to sail. He never tried to hide it. But I know for a fact they don't know about a sailboat."

"During the winter, he keeps it moored at the Castle Danger marina up near Duluth. It's owned by a dummy company Barrett set up. Northland Yacht Tours. Since he's obviously a suspect, I doubt the police would have any trouble getting a search warrant."

"None at all."

"Then will you inform them about this boat right away? Can you do it without mentioning where you got the information?"

"I'll find a way." He stood up. "You did the right thing, Dr. Kirsch. Don't have any doubts about that."

She stood up and met his gaze. "Thank you. I hope you're right."

"You know a lot more about this than you're able to tell, don't you?"

She nodded. "I've probably said too much already, but let me just add one more thing. My patient is . . . a very troubled man. After his session this morning, he may never return to my office. I pray that's not the case. In my opinion, the entire family needs professional help, but nothing can be done until Barrett Sweeny is arrested and sent to jail. He has a Rasputinlike influence with the men in that family. I wish you luck, Mr. Lawless. Let's hope the police find what they're looking for."

Two hours later, Ray was in his car, heading up 35W, following two squad cars on their way to Duluth. As soon as Dr. Kirsch had left his office, he'd phoned Sgt. Jamar Green, the detective in charge of the Midnight Man investigation, and passed along the tip. In addition to the information, Ray had added a request. He wanted to be present when the boat was searched. He knew the request was a long shot, but he'd known Green for many years. They weren't friends, but because Ray was still so intimately involved in the case, Green said okay—with the proviso that Ray stay off the boat and out of their way.

Ray figured Dr. Kirsch's patient had to be either Henry or Conrad Alto. It didn't really matter which one it was, although Ray would have liked his own suspicions confirmed. Conrad Alto's behavior toward him—his continuing harassment even *after* Ray had been served with a malpractice suit—suggested that he was a deeply disturbed man. Ray no longer took phone calls or opened correspondence from him. Everything was passed on to the lawyer Ray had hired to handle the case.

Rolling down the window to get a little fresh air, Ray looked around at the fields whizzing past. The snow was almost gone now. For early March, it was a glorious afternoon, the kind of day that made a man feel young again. From here on out, Ray intended to live his life—whatever there was left of it—in a very different fashion.

The biopsy results had come back yesterday. He didn't have cancer. Not yet. His condition remained something his doctors needed to watch. Prostate cancer was usually slow-growing, which meant he had time. He was scheduled to have another biopsy in three months. It was terrifying, all this waiting around, but Ray had made a decision. No more passivity. From here on out, he intended to focus on what was good in his life. The parts that weren't working, well, he'd try to repair them. At the top of the list was his marriage. He and Marilyn needed to find a good marriage counselor. Without help, Ray figured they didn't have a chance.

As his thoughts turned to Elizabeth, as they so often did lately when he contemplated his crumbling marriage, his cell phone beeped. Clicking it on, he said, "Lawless."

"Ray, it's me." It was Marilyn.

"Hi, how's everything going in New Orleans? How's your dad?"

"He died this morning."

"Oh lord. Honey, I'm so sorry."

"We knew it was coming. He went into a coma late last night. Mom said he didn't want any heroic measures taken, so we kept him on the morphine, but that was all."

"Were you there?"

"Yes. So was Mom and my brother. My sister and her family are flying in today. Uncle Scott is already here. Others will be arriving tonight."

"When is the funeral?"

"On Saturday afternoon."

"I'll book the next flight."

Silence. "Ray, I've been thinking about that. Actually, I'd rather that you stay home."

"Why?"

"It's . . . well, it would just be easier for me."

"But you need support, Marilyn. A shoulder to lean on. You must be exhausted."

"I am. That's why I called my office a few minutes ago. I asked for an indefinite leave of absence. Mom needs so much help right now. But . . . also, I need some time to think."

"About what?"

"About us, Ray. About . . . what's best."

"Honey, we can't have this conversation over the phone. I need to see you in person."

"I know. But . . . give me a few more weeks. I'll call you, okay? Let you know my plans."

Attempting to swallow the lump in his throat, he said, "Okay."

"Is everything all right with you?"

"Fine."

"And the kids? How's Sigrid doing?"

"Better. She'll be coming home from the hospital in a few days."

"Good. That's good. I better go, Ray. I'm at a pay phone at the hospital. Someone else wants to use it."

"Right."

"I miss you."

"I miss you too."

"Bye." The line clicked.

She didn't say she loved me, thought Ray. *Her father just died and she didn't say she loved me.* He hadn't said it either. It was a huge omission and they both knew it. She must be thinking the same thoughts he was. And like him, it didn't sound as if she'd reached any conclusions. In frustration, Ray banged his fist on the steering wheel. "Damn it to hell! What's wrong with you, Lawless? Look at how you've hurt her!" He should have said he loved her. Even if she hadn't, *he* should have.

Around four, he pulled into the Castle Danger marina and parked his Mercedes in the lot. Several St. Louis County squad cars were there to meet the cops from Minneapolis. After talking to the manager of the marina, Green and his men were escorted down the dock. Ray trailed behind. When they reached slip number 79, they stopped.

The forty-foot boat was covered in blue tarps, but from what Ray could see of it, it was a beauty. Probably cost more than most houses. It was sitting in a wooden cradle, kept out of the water by a series of stilts. The police climbed up a ladder near the rear of the boat, then went to work on the hatch. Since it was a keyed entry, the only way to get into the cabin was to break the lock.

Ray pulled his collar up around his neck. A cold breeze blew off the water, chilling him to the bone. He paced for a while, trying to keep warm, then found a bench and sat down. The sun was starting to set over the water when Green reappeared. In the growing twilight, Ray couldn't make out the expression on his face.

"Get over here, Lawless," called Green. "I've got something you need to see."

Ray stood, working the arthritis out of his knee for a few seconds, then walked back to the boat. Green's dark hands were covered with white latex gloves. He was holding a plastic sack of what looked like jewelry. "I think we got him," he said. He wasn't smiling, but there was a definite note of satisfaction in his voice. "Both of the profiles we had done of the Midnight Man said that he probably took something away from the scene of the crime—something small and personal, like jewelry. Recognize any of this?"

As Green held up the sack, Ray studied the contents. It didn't take but a second for him to make a positive ID. "That's my daughter-in-law's wedding ring."

"You're sure?"

"Absolutely. You can check it for yourself. My son had the words 'Sigrid, my love forever' engraved on the inside of it."

Now the cop smiled.

"Where did you find it?" asked Ray.

"It was taped under a cupboard in the galley." He opened his top coat and removed a cell phone. Hitting a number, he waited. "Knutson? Green. We got him. Pick him up, read him his rights and book him."

As the cop continued to talk, Ray walked to the edge of the dock and looked out across the water. He needed a moment alone to absorb the news. Watching the wind toss the whitecaps around the lake, he thought of all the chaos one man had caused. All the needless pain. In the end, horror like this was always inscrutable. Were monsters born or were they made? It was a question Ray knew he would never be able to answer. But it didn't worry him now because, finally, this horror was over.

A week later, Jane was in her front yard, raking up dried leaves. She always took a couple of days off during the early spring to clean up the yard. She still hadn't made a decision whether or not to sell the house. Patricia was back from Hong Kong, so she'd been spending several nights a week at her place. And there was always the couch in her office at the restaurant. But her house, particularly at night when she was alone, remained a place that haunted and frightened her.

Her aunt Beryl and new husband, Edgar Anderson, would be back from England in less than a month. Beryl, her mother's sister, had come from England for a short stay a few years back and had ended up living with Jane until her marriage to Edgar. They'd been on a honeymoon trip for the past few months, staying at Beryl's cottage on the southwestern coast of England. Beryl had written saying that their intention was to live with Jane half the year, and spend the rest of the time in Lyme Regis. Jane hated to break the news to them that she might be moving. Edgar had plans to start building Beryl's new greenhouse in her backyard. And Beryl would be heartbroken to think she'd be losing the garden she'd worked so hard on for the past few summers. Of course, after they returned home, Jane wouldn't be alone in the house anymore. But that was just a temporary solution.

As she hooked up the hose in the backyard next to the screen porch, her thoughts turned to Mouse. She hoped he was doing okay—that he hadn't gotten out of his owner's yard again. She thought of him every day, just as she did Bean. Cordelia kept encouraging her to adopt another animal—a cat was her suggestion. Cats were cool. They had *attitude*. But Jane was a dog person. And she didn't want just any dog—she wanted Mouse. Except that wasn't possible.

After she'd bagged all the leaves in the front yard and hauled the sacks around to the side of the garage, she took a moment to survey her work. There was still a lot to do. Pruning. Seeding the grass. Fertilizing. Returning to the front to retrieve her rake, she saw that a car had pulled up to the curb.

"Morning," said Art Turlow, getting out of the front seat.

"What's up?" said Jane, feeling suddenly anxious.

Turlow was dressed in plain clothes, as always. Today it was a suit and tie. "I stopped by your restaurant and they said you'd taken the day off. Thought I'd come by and see if you were home."

They both drifted toward the front steps.

"Would you like to come in?"

Turlow shook his head. "I can't stay more than a couple minutes. I'm on my way to a wedding. It's a nephew I hardly know, but my sister says I have to be there."

"And you always do what your sister says?"

He grinned. "Yeah, pretty much. Say, you must be feeling better now that we finally put the Midnight Man behind bars. I understand your father was instrumental in catching him."

"It was a lucky break." Jane knew the story. Her father had told her about Dr. Kirsch's visit to his office. She also knew not to talk to the police about the particulars.

"Yeah," he said, scratching the back of his head. "It's funny how these things work."

"Why do you say that?"

"Well, we gave Sweeny a polygraph test a few days ago. His lawyer said he wanted to do it, that he was begging to. Sweeny insists he's innocent. He says he had nothing to do with any of those murders. Damn if he didn't pass the test with flying colors."

Jane's jaw tightened. "How do you explain it?"

"Me? I can't. Of course, one of our shrinks said that sometimes a true sociopath can beat the test. Sociopaths believe their own lies, so they come across as telling the truth. But it doesn't matter. We know the guy's guilty."

His certainty made her nervous. She could have pointed out that the police had been equally certain about Bobby Alto.

"Anyway, I better get down to business," said Turlow. "I'm actually here this morning because I need to explain something to you. I figured it was about time." He pushed a hand into his pocket, jingling some change. "For the past, oh, six months—this was prior to our first meeting—I'd been getting tips from various sources that said your restaurant was a place we needed to watch."

"We? You mean the drug unit?"

He nodded.

"You thought I was a drug dealer?" She laughed.

Turlow didn't even smile. "We knew something was going on, but we didn't know what. When your father came to me with that story about drugs being planted in your office, well, I had to wonder what was really going on. Then you threw us a curve."

"Look, I know *nothing* about—"

He held up his hand. "I understand that. But it took a while. When you let us search your place, I was still pretty leery. I figured since you were related to Ray Lawless that you were smart. But I realize now that you're also innocent. The downside is, something *is* going on at your restaurant."

"Define 'something.' "

"Drug dealing, Jane. Specifically, we think it's Ecstasy. One of your employees is using your restaurant as a base of operations."

Jane immediately thought of Joe Vasquez. "We hired a waiter a couple months back. His name is Joe—"

"Vasquez. Yes, I know. You mentioned him before."

"You think he could be behind it?"

Turlow shook his head.

"How can you be so sure?"

"He's a cop. We planted him without your knowledge. I'm sorry, but at the time, we didn't have a choice. I just wanted to reassure you that we'll get to the bottom of this. But it may take a while. And . . . when you're dealing with drugs, there's always some danger."

"How did this happen?" It was a question put both to the universe and to him. "Why did someone target my restaurant?"

"I don't have a specific answer for you, but a contributing factor may have been the injury you suffered last fall. You were away from your business for quite some time. And after you returned, you only did so on a part-time basis. You know what they say: When the cat's away, shit happens."

Now Jane was angry. "Do you have any idea who's involved?"

"We do, but the less you know for now, the safer you are. It's a rough business, Jane. Let us handle it, okay? Don't be a vigilante. Don't try to figure out what's going down on your own. If you come across something you think we should know, you've got my number. But remember, these people play rough—and they play for keeps. I assume you figured the drugs you found in your office were tied to the Midnight Man. You may be right. I'm sure you hoped that with Sweeny's arrest, your problems were over. I wish that were the case, Jane, but it's not." He checked his watch. "Look, I'm sorry to drop a bomb on you like this and then take off, but—"

"Your sister will come after you with a shotgun if you don't get to that wedding."

He nodded, smiling ruefully.

"Thanks for stopping by," said Jane. "And for trusting me."

"No problem. Keep your nose clean. I'll be in touch."

After lunch, Jane sat down behind the desk in her study and took out the information she'd compiled over the past few weeks on the Midnight Man. She wanted to read it over again. In the back of the file were the notes she'd taken during her conversations with the family and friends of the victims. All of the people she'd contacted had been interrogated by the police. Most were willing to talk to her at great length about the loved one they'd lost. A few weren't.

Lora Pine's ex-husband had confided that Lora liked guys who made a lot of money, especially older guys—the more gray hair, the better. Father figures, he called them. The ex also said that before Lora died, she'd been dating someone new. Lora's best friend, Beth Ann, had told him that Lora was positively glowing about some new guy, but that Lora didn't want to say much—she didn't want to jinx it. His name was John or Jeff or Jerry—something like that. John-or-Jeff-or-Jerry Hyde. They'd laughed about the last name. Maybe he was a Jekyll-and-Hyde kind of guy. Lora's ex didn't think it was all that funny. He said she always had some new man on the string.

Jane had also been able to clear up one minor mystery. After driving out to Prior Lake to talk to Paula Trier's mother, Jane had received a phone call from Paula's twin brother, Paul. It turned out that Paula *had* been in the emergency room at Metro South about three months before her death. She'd had a miscarriage. The electrician she'd been dating—a man Paul loathed—was the father. The miscarriage had happened while she was at work, so Paul had driven her to the hospital himself. He remembered that they'd talked to a doctor at some length, but it was so long ago that he couldn't describe the man. Jane asked if he'd passed this information on to the police, and Paul said he had. But he didn't want "the situation" to get back to his mother for obvious reasons. Jane promised to keep his confidence.

So that was it. In the final analysis, all her digging had been for nought. Barrett Sweeny was in jail and that should be the end of it.

Then why wasn't it? thought Jane. Why couldn't she just let it go?

38

Peter sat slumped in a chair in his apartment, watching Sigrid doze on the couch. She was too stubborn to stay in bed. She didn't want to miss a thing, she'd told him, which Peter took as a good sign. For the past week, they'd even begun going for short walks together when the weather cooperated. But she was still so very weak.

They'd both been relieved to hear that Barrett Sweeny had been arrested. It seemed fitting, somehow, that the day Sweeny was put in jail, Sigrid and Peter had renewed their wedding vows, toasting with sparkling cider and enjoying a special dinner that Peter had made for the occasion. He'd even presented her with a new wedding ring, one to replace the ring that had been lost. They hadn't found out until a few days later that the original ring had been discovered on Sweeny's sailboat, along with jewelry he'd taken from his other victims. It was a grim reminder to both of them of what could have been if Peter hadn't arrived early that day at their apartment, preventing another tragedy.

Peter and Sigrid were back together now in every way. And yet, Peter knew that Sigrid was keeping something from him. From his point of view, he didn't care if she ever told him what this secret of hers was. But he knew she would. One day, he'd have to hear it.

For good or ill, Sigrid's memory of that awful afternoon still hadn't returned. Her mind might not be able to recall the details of the beating, but Peter sensed that her body could. Sigrid had never been a timid woman, and yet he would catch her hesitating now, as if she was frightened by something she couldn't quite put her finger on. She'd become overly cautious. Before they went to bed each night, she'd insist that he check the doors to make sure they were locked. Or it might be making sure the coffee maker or stove was off. But it was always something.

Her primary doctor had explained to him privately that Sigrid's recovery wasn't just a matter of regaining her physical health. There would be psychological consequences as well. That's why Peter had dedicated himself to making her recovery as comfortable as possible. He tried to fit his mood to hers—to be ready to talk about whatever she wanted, or to be quiet and give her space to relax and heal. She was so happy to be home, and yet she went for long periods without speaking, just staring out the window. That wasn't like her. Sigrid was a person who was always in motion. The change worried him.

As she stirred, Peter sat up.

"What time is it?" she asked, glancing over at him as she raked a hand through her hair.

"It's just after three."

"In the afternoon?"

"Yes. In the afternoon."

"What time do you have to leave for the station?"

"Four. I should probably take a shower before I go."

This would be Peter's first night back at work. He'd managed to convince the powers that be at WTWN that his initial few weeks back should only be part-time. He'd been leaving Sigrid for longer and longer periods during the day, working up to that first six-hour shift. She seemed to be fine with it. Peter was the one who was the basket case.

"How are you feeling?" he asked, watching her lift her legs off the couch and sit up.

She wrapped the quilt around her shoulders. "Fine. A little chilled."

"How about a cup of tea?"

She rubbed the sleep out of her eyes. "Maybe."

"What kind?"

"Peppermint, I guess."

He started to get up.

"Wait."

"Why?" He wanted to sit next to her for a few seconds. Give her a kiss. Touch her hair. Tell her how much he loved her.

"Just stay there, okay?"

"Sigrid?"

"I . . . I made a decision last night. I need to tell you something, but I didn't want to do it until I knew . . . well, that you'd have to leave right afterwards. You'll need some time to think about what I tell you."

"You make it sound so ominous."

"I don't mean to. It isn't really. In a lot of ways, it's an old, old story. It's just . . . I should have told you what happened a long time ago. I don't want you to be angry with me, Peter, but . . . oh, hell, I'm just so ashamed. I hoped I'd never have to tell *anyone*."

"Ashamed of what?" He sat on the edge of his chair. He wanted to go to her, but she obviously preferred to keep some space between them.

Sigrid tipped her head back against the couch cushions and closed her eyes. "I know I've always projected this image of a woman who's got it all together. I don't take shit from anyone. I'm tough and I'm smart and I get what I want. Sigrid the scholar, graduating third in her class. Sigrid the social butterfly, president of her sorority. Sigrid the sexually liberated—never turning down a good time. When you met me, maybe I was all that. But when

I was younger, the summer after my senior year of high school, I was a mess."

"Honey, listen. Why don't we wait until I get home tonight. Then we can—"

She shook her head. "No. I know what I'm doing. Now shut up before I lose my nerve."

He smiled at her. She was sounding more and more like herself every day. "I just meant that you don't want to rush through this."

"Yes, I do. And hey, who the hell are you to tell me what I want?"

"Sorry."

She grinned at him. "That sounded pretty good—like the old Sigrid."

"Pretty damn close."

She was wearing slacks and a V-neck sweater. She'd lost so much weight that everything hung on her.

Clearing her throat, she continued, "You know my family history, how I took care of my brothers and sisters from the time I was twelve until I was seventeen. That and schoolwork were my entire life. By the time my senior year came along, my mother had remarried so I had a little more free time. I even took some college courses that winter to get a jump on my freshman year. I planned to enter the university in the fall."

"But you changed your mind," said Peter. "You needed time to 'find yourself,' so you went to New York City to live on your own for a while." He laughed, assuming she would too. But she didn't. This time her expression remained serious.

"That's the part I need to talk to you about. I did go to New York, but not to find myself. Here comes the cliché. I met a boy my senior year of high school. He was the lead in the school play. Very cool dude. Looks and charm. Devastating smile. I was into shallow back then, Peter, so don't get jealous. Anyway, I thought I was in love. By July, I was pregnant. Mr. Charming accused me of sleeping around, said he didn't believe it was his child and he took no responsibility for it. He was headed for Stanford and he wasn't dragging a girlfriend and a kid along. If it really was his child, I should get rid of it."

"What a bastard."

"Exactly. Unfortunately, that knowledge came a little late to help me. All I knew was, I couldn't abort. I also couldn't tell my mom. She would have been devastated. So I did some checking around and I found this lawyer in New Jersey who said he'd place the baby for me. I could choose the family I thought sounded the best, so I had some say in the matter. The guy finally found a couple in New York that seemed right, so that's where I went. The deal was, they would pay all my living expenses and doctor bills, and when the baby was born, if I signed away all rights to the child, the family would throw in an extra ten thousand to sweeten the pot. I did learn a lot about myself that year, Peter, but not all of it was good. When the time came to deliver her, I went to the hospital. I was in labor for twelve hours—hard labor for five."

"It was a girl?"

"They named her Margaret. Margaret Tanhauer. Daughter of Carrie and Matt Tanhauer. I only saw her briefly before they took her away. She was bald—and incredibly gorgeous. I wanted to hold her, but they wouldn't let me. The family who adopted her kept their part of the bargain. They even bought me a ticket back to the Twin Cities so I could enter the University of Minnesota the following fall. It was handled with privacy and finesse. It could have been much worse."

Peter didn't know what to say. "Sigrid . . . I'm so sorry. I can't even imagine how hard that was for you."

Drawing the quilt across her chest, she continued, "When I got back from New York, I put that part of my life behind me. It was like it never happened. I entered the U and never looked back. I made friends, had a wild time—although, after what happened, I always used protection, and demanded that my boyfriends did too. Except, the thing is, it did happen, Peter.

Secretly, I mourned that child. Her existence colored everything for me. I think about her every day and wonder what kind of life she has."

"How old would she be?"

"Eight."

The light was beginning to dawn, although he didn't understand entirely. "That's why you didn't want to have a child with me?"

Sigrid gazed out the window. "What if she came looking for me one day and what if she found me? And *what if* she found out about our child. How could I tell her that her birth wasn't convenient and the other kid's was?"

"Convenient isn't exactly the word I'd use."

"You know what I mean."

"But it's true. If you'd kept her, you never would have gone to college or grad school. You might have been stuck in some low-paying job you hated, or married some idiot before you were ready. You might have done things to get by that would only have dug you in deeper. You had no father in the picture to help. No skills to speak of, and very little money. What you did was hard, but it was necessary."

"Right."

"You don't sound convinced."

"No, I agree with you. If I'd kept her, I could easily have ruined her life, or she could have ruined mine. I made sure she had the best possible start in life I could give her and then I left. But it wasn't noble. It was mostly *me* I was thinking about."

He rubbed the back of his neck, thinking about it. "So let me get this straight. Because of Margaret, because of a mistake you made when you were what—seventeen?"

She nodded.

"You never want to have another child."

"That was my reasoning. The idea of looking into Margaret's eyes some day and seeing pain and rejection just stopped me cold. At least if I didn't have any other children, she would get a different picture. Maybe she would figure I wasn't the maternal type. That I did her a favor. But if I have children around me—our children—children I love and who love me in return, then what do I say? Gee, sorry about that, Margaret. Bad timing. Hope you had a nice childhood. Sorry I didn't have time to be around."

"But look at it this way, Siggy. Maybe what you do is ask her to forgive the seventeen-year-old girl you once were. Maybe you tell her you did the best you could with what you had."

Sigrid shook her head. "Not enough."

"What are you afraid of? That she won't understand? I think she will."

"It's not good enough!"

"For who? Who are we talking about here, Sigrid?"

"*Me*. It's not good enough for me." Tears rolled down her cheeks. "Margaret did nothing wrong. I did. I didn't have the strength to keep her. I should have, Peter. It was the biggest mistake of my life."

"But I thought you understood why—"

"That's just a bunch of rationalizations."

"No they're not!"

"She's my flesh and blood, Peter. My daughter. She should be with me."

Peter could see that she wasn't interested in a discussion. She'd already made up her mind. She was guilty and she had to be punished. Part of the punishment was never having another child. It was ludicrous, but he knew enough to back off. She couldn't handle an all-out argument right now—she didn't have the internal strength for one. And he didn't want to browbeat her into seeing it his way. Her feelings were valid, even if her solution wasn't.

"You think I'm crazy, don't you? That I was some stupid, sex-crazed teenager who messed up and then was too chicken to assume responsibility for what she'd done. You think I'm selfish and self-centered." She wouldn't look at him.

Peter got up. Against her wishes, he sat down on the couch,

putting his arms around her. "No, sweetheart, that's what *you* think of you. I think you're a wonderful, strong, clear-headed woman who did the best she could with the hand she was dealt."

"And . . . and you think I'm this . . . this emotional cripple because I don't believe I deserve to have another child." She was crying now, choking on her sobs.

"Honey, I love you."

"How *could* you? You have no taste."

If it wasn't so painful, it would be funny. He held her until her sobs turned to hiccups.

"God, but I'm a mess." Scraping a hand across her eyes, Sigrid added, "I think we better table this conversation for now."

"You mean it isn't a closed subject?"

"No," she said, resting her head on his shoulder. "Besides, you don't believe in closed subjects. No one in your family does."

"Hey, now you're attacking my heritage?"

"Go on," she said, pushing him away. "You've got to take a shower. And you don't want to be late for your first night back."

"Maybe I should call the station and tell them I can't come."

"Because your wife has dissolved into a puddle of tears at your feet?"

"Something like that."

She sniffed a couple of times. "I want you to go. I need some time alone. So do you, if I'm not mistaken."

He was hardly going to find time alone at the station, but he knew what she meant. He kissed her on top of her head, then got up and headed into the bathroom.

Fifteen minutes later, he was in the kitchen grabbing a bottle of spring water to bring with him when he heard the phone ring. Sigrid answered it. He walked into the living room as she was talking.

"Who?" She looked up at him and smiled. "No, not really. I was pretty out of it those first few nights." She listened. "Much better, thanks. My memory is still blank. It really bothers me." Again, she looked up at Peter. "Sure, that would be fine. I'll be home all evening." Winking at him, she said, "No, I'm sorry. He'll be at work until eleven. Would another night work better?" More silence. "Right, he can meet you when I come into the clinic. Okay. I'll see you then. Bye." She clicked off the phone.

"Wuz up?" asked Peter, nuzzling her neck.

"That was a doctor. He's part of the neurology practice working on my case. Anyway, he wants to stop by tonight on his way home from work to check on me."

"That's nice. I guess."

"He's getting paid for it, Peter, so it isn't kindness. He said he's got a few questions he'd like to ask me, as well as a couple of simple tests to perform. Won't take long. He wants me to make an appointment to come talk to him at the office ASAP."

Peter gave her one last kiss. "You sure you're going to be okay?"

"Fine. If I need anything, I'll call Susan down the hall."

"Okay. And I'll phone you later. If you get lonely, you can call Jane, or Dad."

"Or my brothers or my sisters. Stop worrying, Peter. I'll be fine."

Still feeling guilty, he retrieved his coat from the front closet, blew her a kiss, and forced himself out the door.

Jane was cleaning out the garage when she got a call on her cell phone. It was a welcome interruption. She was covered head to toe in cobwebs and dust. A leaking can of car oil had fallen off a shelf and stained her favorite U of M sweatshirt. She was a mess—glad that picture phones weren't in common usage yet. Removing her work gloves, she clicked the phone on.

"Janey, hi. It's Peter."

"Great timing, bro."

"Why?"

"Don't ask." She stepped out of the stark light of the garage into the early spring twilight, sitting down on a rusted metal chair she'd already tossed in the garbage.

"Listen, Janey, what are you doing tonight?"

"Taking a bath."

"Other than that."

"Nothing special. I thought I might head over to the restaurant later."

"What about Cordelia?"

"I imagine she's at the theater."

"The reason I ask is, I was hoping you—maybe Cordelia too—

could do me a huge favor. This is my first night back at work. I feel terrible leaving Sigrid alone. She says she'll be fine, that she'll call one of our neighbors if she needs anything, but I'm just uneasy about being gone. My shift is over at eleven, so I wouldn't be that late, but I thought, well, maybe you and Cordelia could pick up a movie and the three of you could watch it together."

"Sounds like fun. I can't answer for Cordelia, but I'll give her a call and see if she's free. What time is it?" In the growing dusk, Jane couldn't see her watch.

"It's ten after six."

"I'll stop right now, clean up, and be over at your place in an hour or less."

"You're a lifesaver, Janey."

Glancing over her shoulder at the mess in the garage, Jane decided that Peter was the lifesaver.

By the time she got to the apartment, Cordelia was already there. Jane could tell Cordelia had arrived by the smell of popcorn wafting from the kitchen and the can of black cherry soda sitting next to an empty chair. She hoped the refrigerator was stocked with other soft drinks—or better yet, beer.

"Hold the butter," called Jane, smiling at Sigrid who was sitting in the recliner rocker near the front window.

"Boring. Boring. *Boring*," called Cordelia from the kitchen's inner sanctum. A moment later, she appeared carrying a huge bowl and three smaller bowls. "Who wants a black cherry soda to go with it?"

Nobody raised a hand.

"Humph. Boring *and* tasteless. What *do* you want then?"

"I'll have a Dr Pepper," said Sigrid. She was wearing a thick wool cardigan, her legs covered by a blanket.

"Fine with me," said Jane.

"What's tonight's flick?" called Cordelia, once again in the kitchen.

"I picked up two," said Jane, stepping over to the VCR. "*The Usual Suspects* and *Chinatown*."

"Either is fine with me," said Sigrid. "You guys didn't need to do this, you know. Peter worries too much."

"We know," said Cordelia, reentering the living room and handing around the Dr Peppers. "But it was either you or that stack of paperwork on my desk."

"Gee. You make me feel so special," said Sigrid.

Jane grabbed a handful of popcorn. It was bathed in butter. Things were getting off to their usual roaring start. "I'll get us some napkins."

"Just lick the butter off your fingers," said Cordelia impatiently, dumping herself on the couch. "It's part of the fun."

In the kitchen, Jane opened a cupboard drawer, still listening to the increasingly rancid banter in the living room. Sigrid had been amenable to watching either movie when Jane announced what they were, but now that Cordelia had weighed in on the side of *Chinatown*, Sigrid was insisting that *The Usual Suspects* was the better film. No doubt about it. They brought out the five-year-olds in each other.

"I'm not interested in form," said Cordelia. "I'm interested in essences. Janey, bring more salt!"

"What's that got to do with anything?" asked Sigrid. "You're so esoteric sometimes you fade to incomprehensibility."

"Do you understand *anything* about the rules of dramatic structure?"

"No, but I know a brilliant movie when I see one."

As Jane returned to the front room, Sigrid said, "But there's no use starting the movie, whatever one we decide on, until the doctor's come and gone."

"What doctor?" asked Cordelia, picking popcorn kernels out of the plunge in her neckline.

"Dr. Hyde. My neurologist."

Jane stopped. "Dr. *Hyde*?" She felt a tiny trickle of dread.

"He called a little while ago. Actually, he examined me at the hospital, but he said it was the first couple of nights so I don't remember him very well. To be honest, I don't remember him at all."

"Why is he coming here?" asked Jane.

"He wants to check on me, see how I'm doing."

"Why not make an appointment at his office?"

"I'm supposed to do that too. But since he lives nearby, he said he'd just stop in for a few minutes. He's concerned about my continuing amnesia. I still can't remember a thing that happened the afternoon I was attacked."

"What time is he coming?"

"Around seven-fifteen." She checked her watch. "Actually, right about now."

Walking over to the window, Jane looked down at the parking lot. Everything looked quiet and dark. "Turn off the lights, Cordelia."

"Let's wait until the guy's come and gone before we start the movie, okay?" she said.

"I'm not talking about the movie. I want all the lights off. Now!" Jane snapped the lamp off next to her. "We've got to get out of here."

"Pardon me?" said Cordelia, between sips of her soda.

"Why?" asked Sigrid.

"I don't have time to explain it. Cordelia, get Sigrid's coat and help her put it on."

Sigrid looked confused.

"Janey, this is silly." Cordelia set the bowl of popcorn down on the coffee table, but didn't get up.

"I don't have time to argue with you. Just do it!" She slipped into her coat and ran around turning off lights. "Move, Cordelia. I'm not kidding. One of the Midnight Man's victims was dating a man named Hyde right before she was murdered."

"Janey, the Midnight Man's in jail," said Cordelia. "If that's what you're thinking."

"No, he's not. He's right outside this building and he's on his way up."

Everyone started scrambling. Sigrid was moving slowly, obviously still in pain.

"Lean on me," said Jane as they turned out the last light. She opened the door a crack and looked out. The hallway was quiet.

Sigrid and Peter's apartment was located at the end of the third-floor hallway, directly next to the stairs. There were two stairways in the long, three-story building—one at either end.

Jane pushed open the fire door and they started down.

"Shhh," said Jane, stopping after only a few steps. She thought she heard a door clang shut beneath them, but when they stopped, the stairwell was silent.

"There are other people living in this building too," whispered Cordelia.

Jane turned to look at her. "Why are you wearing your sunglasses?"

"It's a fashion statement."

"This isn't funny."

"You think I don't know that?" She lowered her glasses, bulging out her eyes.

They continued on. When they reached the first floor, Jane peaked into the lobby. "So far, so good. Cordelia, I want you to help Sigrid out to your car. Drive her over to the Maxfield Plaza in St. Paul and get her a room. If Hyde turns out to be the Midnight Man, he's here for one reason only. When Sigrid gets her memory back, he's a dead man. He couldn't touch her while she was being protected by the police, but now that Sweeny's in jail, he's free to do what he wants."

"Aren't you coming?" asked Sigrid.

"I'm right behind you."

Lowering her sunglasses one last time, Cordelia gave Jane a scrutinizing look.

"Get going."

"Jane?"

"Get out of here!"

As soon as they'd disappeared out the front door, Jane bolted back up the stairs. Hitting the second-floor landing, she took it more slowly, more quietly. She had to get a look at him. Inside her head, a voice kept repeating, *This is dumb! This is totally dumb! This is so freaking dumb!* But she didn't listen to it. After all this time, after everything that had happened, she *had* to know.

Once up on the third floor, she peered through the small window in the fire door. The door to Sigrid's apartment was standing open and a light was on inside. They hadn't left it that way, which could mean only one thing. Hyde had come in, looked around, and finding no one, had left. Unless he was still inside.

Jane waited another minute, hoping he might come out, but her resolve was rapidly fading. The better part of valor was to get the hell out and live to tell the tale. Knowing that she had to be careful, that he could still be in the building, she hurried down the stairs.

On the second-floor landing, she stopped and looked into the hallway. She wasn't sure what to do—how best to get out of the building. She should have left with Cordelia and Sigrid. She *was* totally dumb. Entering the hallway, she walked quickly to the elevator. As she bent to press the button she saw that the elevator doors were about to open. Feeling suddenly panicked, she rushed to the other end of the hall. Pushing through the fire door, she stopped for a moment and looked back. An older woman had stepped off and was standing in front of one of the apartments, searching through her purse for a key.

That's when she felt it, an arm gripping her around her neck, yanking her off balance. She tried to pull away, but the pressure against her throat was making her lightheaded.

Close to her ear, a voice whispered, "Don't make a sound." She felt the tip of something sharp press against the soft flesh under her chin.

"Where's Sigrid?" whispered the voice. He eased the grip around her throat, but didn't let go.

Jane could smell his foul breath, but she couldn't see his face. He stood almost directly behind her. "She's gone."

"Where?"

"I don't know."

The knife pierced her skin.

Jane let out a cry.

"Shut up!" He gripped her harder. "You *do* know. Tell me."

"If I do, you'll kill me."

"No I won't," he whispered. "All I want is Sigrid."

"Why didn't you kill her when you had the chance—at the hospital?" Jane looked around wildly, trying to figure a way out.

"I never thought she'd make it. And then the police put a guard on the door. Tell me where she is!" He held the knife in front of her face, bringing the blade slowly toward her eye.

She twisted her head to the side. "A friend of mine drove her away. I don't know where they went. I just told them to get out of here."

"I don't believe you." He sounded more menacing than angry. "Maybe we should take a little drive ourselves. Would you like that? I know just the place for a quiet conversation." He ran the tip of his knife across her chest.

"Drop the knife and let her go!" ordered a voice from behind them.

The man whirled around, pulling Jane with him. At the top of the third-floor landing stood Cordelia, a gun held firmly in both hands.

"Put the knife down and I won't blow your head off."

"You'll hit your friend," said Hyde. It was the first time he hadn't whispered.

Cordelia took a couple of steps down. "Believe it or not, I dated a cop once. She introduced me to firearms, turned me into a crack shot. Don't mess with me, jackass, or what little brains you've got will decorate the wall behind you."

Once again, he tightened his grip around Jane's neck.

"Drop the knife!" demanded Cordelia.

Jane could see that her hands were shaking. She hoped that Hyde couldn't.

"Do you want to be responsible for killing your friend?" asked Hyde.

Using Jane as a shield, he backed into the first-floor hallway, dragging her to the front door. At the last minute their feet tangled and they both went down. Jane rolled away, shouting, "Shoot him, Cordelia! Shoot!"

Cordelia burst out of the stairwell.

Hyde scrambled to his feet and lunged outside.

"He's getting away!" shouted Jane, seeing for the first time that he was wearing a ski mask. She pushed off the floor. "Come on, Cordelia. We've got to stop him."

"I can't," said Cordelia, dropping the hand holding the gun to her side. She leaned heavily against the wall.

"We can't let him get away!"

"You don't get it. I *can't help*."

"Then toss me the gun."

"You won't get very far with a stage prop."

Jane's eyes opened wide. "A what?"

"You heard me."

Gunfire erupted outside.

"Where's Sigrid?"

"In the backseat of my car under a blanket. I told her to call nine-one-one."

Jane rushed to the door and looked out. Two cops were standing over Hyde. He was lying on his stomach in the center of street, his hands handcuffed behind his back.

Only now did Jane realize that blood had trickled down her neck onto her jacket.

Outside, lights were flashing. A police officer, a sergeant by the stripes on his uniform, stopped her as she rushed into the street.

"Are you all right?" he asked, seeing the blood. He was an older man. Bald. Pot belly.

“That man over there tried to kill me.” She watched as one of the officers pulled off the ski mask.

“Henry,” she whispered, feeling a sense of elation.

“You know him?” asked the bald cop.

“His name is Henry Alto. He’s an emergency-room doctor. You just broke a major case, sergeant. That guy over there is the Midnight Man.”

The cop rested his hand over his gun. “The Midnight Man’s already in jail, miss.”

“Afraid not. But he will be. Momentarily. And if there’s a God, he’ll stay there for the rest of his miserable life.”

One Month Later

It was a beautiful April afternoon. Jane and Cordelia sat on the front steps of Jane's house, waiting for a taxi to arrive. Beryl and Edgar's plane had landed a few minutes ago at Twin Cities International. Jane knew because she'd called the airport to make sure the plane was on time. Her aunt and Edgar were finally back from England.

Jane wanted to pick them up at the airport, but Beryl insisted that she had entirely too much luggage—a result of several trips to Paris and Lucerne. Beryl asked Jane to encourage Cordelia to stop by as soon as they got back. She had a couple of gifts she'd bought especially for her.

Never being one to defer gratification, Cordelia arrived at Jane's house shortly after lunch. "I'm not greedy," she said, adjusting her sunglasses. "I'm just . . . curious. Besides, I have to be here to welcome the happy couple home, don't I?"

"Of course." Jane smiled.

"Wipe that smirk off your face."

"Cordelia, you're like a kid at Christmastime. You love to get presents. Nothing wrong with that. You also love to give them."

"True." She patted the back of her auburn curls. "I am the *soul* of generosity."

Jane looked both ways down the street.

"How's Sigrid?" asked Cordelia, flicking a ladybug off her knee.

"She's talking about going back to work."

"Seems kind of soon."

"Peter thinks so too. But she hates just sitting around."

"No more information on the baby front?"

Jane shook her head. "From what Peter said, I think he's dropped the subject—permanently. Sigrid may not look it, but she's very fragile. She still has no memory of the afternoon she was attacked. I guess it's possible that she may never remember what happened. From my perspective it seems like a lucky break, but she doesn't see it that way."

Cordelia sighed. "All I can say is, at least they finally put the right man in jail."

Jane didn't respond.

"You *do* think they have the right man, don't you?"

"Without a doubt. I'd just like him to admit his guilt, instead of insisting he's being victimized by me and my family. I'm not looking forward to testifying at his trial."

"Me neither. That guy makes my skin crawl. Those dark beady eyes, that raptorlike gaze." She shivered.

"I wish the police had more evidence against him."

"Which is why they need us to testify."

"What he said in the stairwell—it's just our word against his. I've conjured this nightmare scenario, Cordelia, where he gets off."

"Not possible."

"From your mouth to God's ears." She was silent for a moment. "What do you think makes a serial killer?"

"Improper toilet training."

Jane groaned.

"No, really. That's one theory. I read about it in *Time* magazine. The truth is, I'm not sure anybody knows. The life experiences that create a sinner can also create a saint."

Jane thought about it. "That's really quite profound."

"Of course it is. I said it."

"I just wish . . ." Her voice trailed off.

"Wish what?"

"Oh, that I understood the world better."

"Meaning you wish you understood *yourself* better."

"Yes, that's a big part of it."

"You're a hero, dearheart. If you hadn't done those interviews with the families of Henry's victims, you'd never have been able to put it all together at the right moment. You're like a bloodhound. Watery eyes. Cold, wet nose. An occasional flea."

"Let's just say I was lucky."

"And I was lucky I had a box of theater props in my trunk," said Cordelia, elbowing Jane in the ribs.

A car drove past.

Jane looked at her watch. "They should be here any minute."

"I wonder what Beryl got me," mused Cordelia. "The Swiss make beautiful linens. Great watches."

"Maybe she got you your own personal Swiss bank account."

"Do you think?"

A van rumbled up the hill from the lake, turned right and crawled to a stop in front of Jane's house.

"Geez," said Cordelia standing up. "She had to rent a *van* to get all her stuff home? You're going to need a bigger house, Janey."

Jane watched as a man got out of the front seat. For a moment, she didn't recognize him. Then it hit her. "Eddy Dellman," she whispered.

It was Mouse's owner.

"Hi," he called, waving at them. He stood by the back of the van, looking uncomfortable. "I was hoping I'd find you home."

"Did Mouse get out again?" asked Jane, her stomach tightening.

"No. It's nothing like that." He took off his baseball cap and held it in both hands.

"Something wrong?" asked Cordelia.

"Well, yes and no."

"Is it Mouse?" asked Jane.

He nodded.

"What? Tell me. Is he all right?"

"Sure, he's fine. But, well, remember how I said Mouse and I were a team? That if I ate, he ate. If I didn't, he didn't. The thing is, I lost my job."

"I'm sorry to hear that," said Jane, taking a step toward him.

"And I may have to move."

"That's a tough break."

He nodded. After a few seconds, he continued, "Keeping Mouse will be a problem for me because there are so many places that won't rent to a guy if he's got a dog."

"Sure. I understand." Jane waited for the right words to come out of his mouth.

"The thing is, the two of you really hit it off. I was wondering—"

"Yes," said Jane. He didn't even need to finish the sentence. "Yes, I want him. Where is he?"

He nodded to the van. "I brought his leash, his food, and a couple of bones he likes to chew." He unlatched the back door and let the dog out.

Seeing Jane, Mouse let out a squeal and charged straight for her.

She crouched down and let him fill her arms. "Oh, Mouse," she said, scratching his back, burying her head in his fur. "I've missed you so much." He covered her face in kisses.

"Here's the sack with his stuff," said Eddy, handing it to Cordelia.

Cordelia glanced down into the bag and pulled out a dark-colored dog "thingie." "What's this?" she asked, holding it out in front of her as if it might bite.

"It's a pig hoof."

"Charming. It stinks."

"Yeah, Mouse really loves it."

As the dog raced back and forth across the yard, Jane stood up. "Thanks, Eddy. I know this must be hard for you."

"Yeah," he said pulling his cap back on. "Mouse is a good boy. But truth be told, he needs more than I can give." He clapped his hands. Mouse ran over to him. "You be good now. Mind your Ps and Qs." He patted the dog's head.

"I'll take good care of him," said Jane.

"I know you will."

"You can come visit him any time you want."

"Thanks, but I'm headed out of state. There's a job in Ohio that looks promising."

"Then, I wish you well," said Jane.

Mouse ran back to her as Eddy climbed into the front seat of his van and drove off.

"Well," said Cordelia, dropping the pig hoof back in the sack. "I guess you officially have a new pooch. But we've *got* to do something about that name. M. Mouse. The M. must stand for something."

"We should have asked Eddy."

"Too late now." She considered it a moment. "How about Montague? Or Maximilian? No, no. What about *Marcel?*" Her eyes gleamed.

"Mouse will do just fine," said Jane, hugging him close.